SPECIAL MESSAGE TO READERS

THE ULVERSCROFT FOUNDATION
(registered UK charity number 264873)
was established in 1972 to provide funds for
research, diagnosis and treatment of eye diseases.
Examples of major projects funded by
the Ulverscroft Foundation are:-

- The Children's Eye Unit at Moorfields Eye Hospital, London
- The Ulverscroft Children's Eye Unit at Great Ormond Street Hospital for Sick Children
- Funding research into eye diseases and treatment at the Department of Ophthalmology, University of Leicester
- The Ulverscroft Vision Research Group, Institute of Child Health
- Twin operating theatres at the Western Ophthalmic Hospital, London
- The Chair of Ophthalmology at the Royal Australian College of Ophthalmologists

You can help further the work of the Foundation
by making a donation or leaving a legacy.
Every contribution is gratefully received. If you
would like to help support the Foundation or
require further information, please contact:

THE ULVERSCROFT FOUNDATION
The Green, Bradgate Road, Anstey
Leicester LE7 7FU, England
Tel: (0116) 236 4325

website: www.ulverscroft-foundation.org.uk

HOPE COMES TO EMMERDALE

World War II rages on. Rationing, blackouts, evacuees and military training camps have become the norm in the village of Beckindale, but happiness has been found during these hard times. Lily Dingle is getting married, Annie Pearson has returned after volunteering with the Wrens, and there are new neighbours to get to know . . . including a female vet, of all things.

The new inhabitants are about to learn things are never dull here. Exploring the lives of these much-loved families during World War II, including favourites such as the Sugdens and the Dingles, *Hope Comes to Emmerdale* is an upbeat and nostalgic novel about community, friendship and love.

KERRY BELL

HOPE COMES TO EMMERDALE

Complete and Unabridged

MAGNA
Leicester

First published in Great Britain in 2020 by
Trapeze
an imprint of The Orion Publishing Group Ltd
London

First Ulverscroft Edition
published 2020
by arrangement with
The Orion Publishing Group Ltd
An Hachette UK company
London

ISBN 978–0–7505–4820–5

Published by
Ulverscroft Limited
Anstey, Leicestershire
Set by Words & Graphics Ltd.
Anstey, Leicestershire
Printed and bound in Great Britain by
T. J. International Ltd., Padstow, Cornwall

This book is printed on acid-free paper

In memory of Helen Childs, who wrote all the best *Emmerdale* episodes

Prologue

It was, Annie Pearson thought as she got off the bus, weather more fitting for a funeral than a wedding. It was raining in the sort of insistent way that suggested there was no chance of it stopping soon, and even though it was the middle of the morning the sky was still a sullen grey. But even the drips running from her smart uniform cap couldn't dampen her mood. She was happy to be home and she couldn't wait to see her friend Lily Dingle in her wedding dress.

There was no one about. Everyone was indoors, sheltering from the awful weather. The River Emm, which ran around the edge of Beckindale, was high and it was so quiet in the village that as she walked she could hear the water tumbling and rushing its way towards the pond.

It was strange to be back home after weeks away doing her Wrens training. She was grateful that she had managed to get a day off to come to see Lily tie the knot with her sweetheart, Jack Proudfoot. If the wedding had been just a few days later Annie would have been working already. She was going to be doing clerical work, based down on the south coast. She was nervous about getting started but eager to be doing her bit. And she was very glad she could make it to the wedding. Annie smiled as she remembered

1

Lily's lovestruck letter, where she'd written about how her feelings for Jack, the local policeman, were growing almost as fast as her swelling belly. That was another reason for Jack being such a find — Lily was expecting a baby and Jack wasn't the father. But Lily had poured her heart out to Annie in her letter, telling her that Jack had promised to love her child as his own and be a good father to the little one. Annie had been dubious at first, but it seemed Jack was serious and he clearly adored Lily. The wedding was very close to when Lily's baby was due, but Lily had explained they'd had to delay their ceremony a little because the vicar had been called away to work in another parish for a few weeks. It had worked out well in the end because Lily's father, Mick, had recently got married to an artist called Nina Lazenby, who lived in the village, so there weren't two Dingle weddings too close together.

Annie turned the corner towards the church and was pleased to see a hubbub of activity outside. Someone — Annie suspected Lily's new stepmother, Nina — had artfully draped swathes of greenery around the entrance and it looked pretty despite the gloomy day. Jack was waiting by the door, looking white with nerves and wearing his dress uniform. His face lit up as he saw Annie approach.

'You made it,' he said.

'Wouldn't have missed it.'

'Lily will be chuffed to bits to know you're here.'

'I can't wait to see her.'

2

Jack made a face. 'She's really late. I hope she's coming.'

Annie chuckled. 'Oh get away. She's smitten with you. She's just keeping you waiting, is all.' She squeezed Jack's arm. 'I'd best get inside. Good luck.'

Inside the church was dark and it took a second for Annie's eyes to adjust to the dim light. But after squinting a bit she saw her mother, Grace, sitting in a pew near the back. She waved and Annie slid into the seat next to her.

'Made it then.'

'Just got the bus in time,' Annie said. She and her mother didn't have the smoothest relationship, but she found she was glad to see her. 'Dad working?'

Her mum gave a small nod, lips pursed, and Annie snaked her hand through the crook of her arm, letting her know she understood things weren't always easy at home. She was pleased when her mother smiled at her.

Jack was at the front of the church now, still biting his lip. He had a friend by his side — also in police uniform — and Annie was glad he wasn't alone because he looked so worried. Was he really frightened that Lily wouldn't turn up? Or was he just concerned about his pregnant wife-to-be?

As Annie watched Jack, his face broke into a huge smile and everyone in the church turned to see Lily and her father, Mick, appear at the door of the church. Mrs Briars, the church organist, played a loud, slightly off-key, chord and the congregation rose to its feet as she began a rousing version of 'Here Comes the Bride'.

Lily was glowing. She was smiling so broadly that Annie wondered if her cheeks would hurt later, and she was wearing a simple white gown that suited her unfussy beauty. Annie knew lots of women in the village had donated clothes coupons to Lily to buy the fabric for her dress and she felt a rush of affection for this friendly place where everyone looked out for everyone else. Almost everyone, she thought as her eyes met those of Elizabeth Barlow, who was still stepping out with Oliver Skilbeck. Elizabeth nodded at Annie without smiling. Annie didn't respond. If Elizabeth chose not to believe what Oliver had done to Annie, then that was her business.

Lily was gliding down the aisle, her eyes fixed on Jack's as though they were the only two people in the room, but as she reached Annie, she turned her head and grinned at her friend.

Annie grinned back, trying not to look surprised at the size of Lily's belly. Her baby was due to arrive any day and they were lucky that Reverend Thirlby had agreed to marry her and Jack before she gave birth.

'These are strange times,' he'd told Lily, and she'd told Annie. 'We should take our happiness wherever we find it.'

And it certainly seemed like Lily and Jack were doing just that. The ceremony was beautiful and Annie wasn't ashamed to say she sobbed buckets throughout the vows. Not just because she was happy for her friends — though she was. But

4

also because she was thinking of her Edward and how they'd never say those words to one another, or start their lives together. Because Edward was dead and Annie's heart was broken. It had been more than half a year since that awful day when they'd found out Edward's ship had been sunk. But while Annie knew she'd never stop loving Edward, the pain didn't seem as raw as it once had. Except on days like today of course. Sometimes it was hard to come face-to-face with the happiness of others.

After the ceremony everyone piled into the Woolpack, where Lily's cousins Jed and Larry Dingle were the temporary landlords, minding the pub for Jonah and Dot Dingle who'd travelled to South Africa before the war and got stuck there. Annie avoided the beer that was on offer; partly because she was never sure where Jed got his stock and partly because she knew she had to catch the bus back to base quite soon.

'I'm so pleased you're here,' Lily said, coming up behind her and grabbing her for a hug. 'It wouldn't have been the same without you. Have you seen Meg? She's over in the corner, talking to Nina. She'll be happy to see you. She's been right miserable since they moved the POW camp.'

Annie squeezed her friend tightly, trying not to squash her belly.

'I'll catch up with her in a minute. Let me look at you, first. You look wonderful.'

'Fat.'

'Blooming.'

The women laughed.

5

'Are you well?' Annie asked. Lily was clearly blissfully happy but Annie couldn't help notice how pale she was, and the occasional grimace that crossed her face.

Lily winced. 'I've been fine, up until now,' she said in a low voice. 'I'm just having a few cramps. I think I've been on my feet too long.'

'Then let's find you a chair,' said Annie. She bustled round finding somewhere for Lily to sit.

'How are you?' Lily said, looking straight into Annie's eyes as Annie cleared a pile of coats from a bench.

Annie pinched her lips together. 'I'm fine.'

'Really?'

She gave a small nod. 'I'm getting there.'

Lily took her hand and they smiled at one another.

'Sit,' Annie said.

Gratefully, Lily sank down on to the bench and then shot back up straight away, looking alarmed. 'Oh heavens, Annie, I think I've wet myself!'

Annie looked down at the pub floor where a large puddle was gathering. 'Lily, love, your waters have gone. The baby's coming. That must have been what your cramps were.'

Lily's face was even paler than before. 'It's too soon.'

Worried her friend was on the verge of panic, Annie took both her hands. 'Look at me, Lily,' she said. 'Take a deep breath. You're only a couple of weeks early, the baby will be fine.' She hoped she was right. She knew more about calves and lambs than she did about babies. 'We need to get you away from all these people.'

Lily looked like she was going to cry.

'Find Jack,' she begged Annie. 'And Nina. Get Nina.'

Annie scanned the room. She saw Meg disappearing out of the door — perhaps she had to get back to her adopted children — and then she spotted Nina by the door, chatting to a group of people. Nina was easy to see because she was tall and elegant and wearing a bright mustard-yellow blouse with a pretty pussycat bow.

'I see her,' she told Lily. She ducked through the busy pub and gently touched Nina's arm.

'Sorry to interrupt,' she said. 'Could I have a word?'

Nina let Annie draw her to one side and raised an eyebrow quizzically. 'Everything all right?'

'I think Lily's gone into labour.'

Nina gasped. 'Oh bugger.'

Annie managed a smile at that. 'She's over by the window. Can you get her home?'

Larry Dingle, Lily's cousin who ran the pub, was collecting empty glasses and eavesdropping brazenly.

'Is Lil having the baby?' he asked, his Irish accent more pronounced than ever. 'Take her upstairs.'

Annie nodded gratefully. 'You get Lily and I'll find Jack,' she said to Nina.

'And the doctor,' Nina said over her shoulder as she headed towards Lily, followed by Larry. Annie hoped he wouldn't invite himself upstairs too — she didn't think he'd be much use.

She found Jack and told him what had happened and he dashed off upstairs without so much as a second thought, while Annie ran through the village to Dr Black's little cottage, where he was just sitting down to a plate of what looked like rabbit pie.

'Go,' said his wife. 'I'll keep this warm.'

With the doctor upstairs with Lily, and Jack nowhere to be seen — presumably upstairs too, pacing the floor — Annie allowed herself to breathe again. She hoped Lily would be all right, and the baby too. Again she felt a wave of despair at the thought of Lily getting married and becoming a mother, while she — Annie — was left to grieve for Edward and the life they'd planned to live together.

Suddenly she needed air. She weaved through the remaining wedding guests, who didn't seem to have noticed the disappearance of the bride and groom thanks to Jed's beer, and went outside. It was still raining, though not as persistently, and the village was quiet. Annie settled herself on a low bench by the pub window, sheltered under the roof, and took a few deep breaths. What a day. And she would have to leave soon if she was going to make it back to base in time. She wondered if the baby would arrive before she had to go.

'Annie?' The voice made her jump. It was Jacob, her Edward's brother, and the reason Edward had gone to war. Annie glared at him.

'Hello, Jacob.'

'Annie, I'm glad to catch you.'

'Got something else on your conscience that

8

you need to confess?' Annie was surprised how angry she still was with Jacob. He and Edward had drawn straws to decide who would enlist and who would stay to work the farm and Jacob had later confessed he'd tinkered with the straws to make sure Edward went. Deep down Annie knew Edward had been keen to enlist. Being desperate to see the world beyond Beckindale, Edward would not have been happy if Jacob had gone, but Annie still resented Jacob. Without his tampering, perhaps Edward would still be here.

'No more confessions,' Jacob said softly. 'I actually wanted your advice about the farm — you know us better than anyone else.'

Annie wasn't expecting that. She stared at Jacob for a second, then relented. 'Sit down,' she said.

Jacob sat at the other end of the bench, leaving a gap between them. 'We're having a hard time,' he began.

'We?'

'Ma and me. We're not coping. We had the chap from the War Ag round the other day.'

Annie made a face. The War Agricultural Committees oversaw all the farms now, making sure they were growing the crops that were most useful, treating their animals well, and generally making the most of the land. They could be helpful — advising farmers which fields to plough or suggesting other crops to try — but they held a lot of power and could even take over farms if they thought they weren't being run properly.

'What did he say?'

Jacob chewed his lip.

'The animals are all fine, especially since we've got rid of the sheep and we've just got the dairy cattle and chickens. But he wants us to put flax in two of the fields at the top, and more potatoes down the bottom.' He shook his head. 'We're all right for now, but I just don't see how we'll manage come the spring.'

'I thought you had help?'

'We did, we had the POWs, but they moved the camp to make way for another training camp, and now it's just us.'

Annie made a face. Emmerdale Farm was large and it was a lot of work for Jacob and his mother, Maggie. But even so . . .

'I can't stay,' she said.

'No,' Jacob answered quickly. 'That's not what I'm asking.'

'Then what?'

'Ma's being bullish, insisting she coped with the farm during the Great War and she'll cope now. She doesn't want me to get more help.'

'She had help last time,' Annie pointed out, thinking of Hugo, the conscientious objector who'd been sent to work on the farm. 'And she was a lot younger.'

Jacob rolled his eyes. 'I know,' he said. 'I don't want Ma to wear herself out. She's been getting so tired recently. I think she's doing too much.'

'She's not ill?' Annie didn't like to think of Maggie being under the weather.

'Not sure,' Jacob shrugged. 'Don't think so. Some days she's better than others.'

'So what are you thinking?'

'A Land Girl.'

Annie drew a breath.

'That's a great idea, but . . . '

'But?'

'Will Maggie feel like you're replacing her. A POW, a man, is one thing, but another woman?'

'That's what I'm worried about,' said Jacob. He chewed his lip again, suddenly looking like he had when he was a little boy. Annie felt herself softening towards him, very slightly.

'It's grand you're looking out for someone else for once,' she said. 'Getting help for the farm is a very good idea and you need to do whatever you think is right for your family.'

Jacob nodded. 'Thank you,' he said.

Annie stood up. 'I have to go and get the bus.'

'I'm glad we caught up,' said Jacob.

They looked at each other for a moment, and Annie nodded. 'Please give my love to Maggie.'

As she turned to go, the door of the pub opened behind her and Jack appeared. He'd lost his uniform jacket; his dress shirt was crumpled and his hair was standing on end but he looked happy.

'Annie,' he called. 'Annie, the baby's here.'

Annie beamed. 'Is everything all right?'

'It's wonderful,' Jack babbled. 'It's a girl. She's a girl. We've got a girl.'

Annie threw her arms round Jack and hugged him tight. 'Congratulations. What are you going to call her?'

Jack smiled. 'Hope,' he said. 'She's Hope Dingle Proudfoot.'

'Hope,' Annie repeated. 'Hope is exactly what we all need.' She smiled at the proud new father. 'That's perfect.'

1

FEBRUARY 1942

Audrey Atkins was having the best day of her life. Admittedly, up until now, her life had been fairly dull so there wasn't much competition, but she hoped now she was officially a Land Girl that this was just a sign of things to come.

She was travelling in the back of a rickety old farm truck, perched on a bag of grain, being thrown from side to side as the lorry navigated the winding country lanes, and she'd honestly never been happier.

'All right in the back?' the driver shouted. He was called Smithers and he owned the land next to the farm that Audrey had been matched with.

'Going to Sugden's?' he'd said, as they'd all waited nervously in the small town of Hotten. Audrey had nodded, wondering if this large, red-faced man was her new boss. But when she'd asked if he was Sugden, he'd shaken his head and grinned at her.

'I'm Smithers. Jacob's got his hands full today and he asked if I'd drop you off. Climb in and get yourself comfortable. I've just got to go and pick up some paperwork, then we'll be off.'

She'd clambered up into the truck with the two girls going to Smithers' farm and smiled shyly at them.

'I'm Audrey,' she said, tucking her left arm in her pocket.

'I'm Tilly, and she's Ginny,' said one of the girls, who had her hair tied up in a scarf and looked like she'd been born to wear the bib-front overalls they'd all been given. Audrey still felt slightly self-conscious wearing trousers and kept imagining her mother tutting at the sight of her daughter wearing what she'd no doubt deem to be men's clothes. But her mother wasn't there. Audrey grinned at Tilly. 'I like your scarf.'

'My hair goes wild in the wind if I let it blow about,' she said. She prodded the other girl, who was rummaging around in her kit bag, looking for something. 'Ginny, find that other scarf. The blue one.'

Ginny rummaged some more and pulled out a square headscarf which she waved in the air like a flag.

'This one?'

Tilly took it and held it out to Audrey. 'Here.'

'I can't take that, it's yours.'

Tilly shrugged. 'The girl I shared a room with at training left it behind. Thought it might come in handy. Shall I do it for you?'

She'd bounced over to Audrey and deftly tied the scarf round her head. Audrey paid close attention to what she was doing, working out a way for her to do it herself later.

'Thanks.'

'Found it,' Ginny muttered, peering into her cavernous bag. 'Finally.'

She produced a tube of lipstick. Audrey's eyes nearly burst out of her head.

'Beauty is your duty, ladies,' Ginny said, mocking the propaganda posters Audrey had seen around. She slicked on the bright red lipstick without even checking her face in a mirror and pouted at Audrey and Tilly. 'It's called Victory Red. Bobby bought me it.'

Tilly rolled her eyes. 'Bobby's a GI,' she said to Audrey. 'He's always buying things for Ginny.'

'I pay him back in other ways,' Ginny said, waggling her eyebrows and cackling. Tilly joined in and, shocked as she was, Audrey found herself laughing too. These girls were so energetic, so full of life, that she couldn't help herself.

When Smithers reappeared and they set off towards their new jobs, the laughter continued. Tilly and Ginny had trained together across the Pennines in Lancashire, while Audrey had done her four weeks — which seemed so quick now she thought about it — near to Leeds, which was about as far away as she could go from her Sussex home. They regaled her with tales of the other girls' antics, and all the mistakes they'd made with the horrible rubber udders they'd had to use to learn how to milk, and Audrey laughed until her stomach ached.

'Nearly there,' Smithers shouted from the front.

'What's your story, then?' Ginny said, nodding to Audrey. 'What made you join up?'

Audrey made a face. 'Promise you won't think I'm odd?'

'No odder than anyone else,' Tilly reassured her.

'You know the poster? For a healthy, happy job?'

The other two nodded.

'Course.'

The posters were all over the place, promoting the Women's Land Army. They showed a young woman in a smart green jersey and brown britches, holding a pitchfork in one hand and her jacket in the other, gazing out over some neatly tended fields.

'I kept seeing it and I kept thinking that the woman in the picture looked like me,' Audrey said.

Ginny frowned. 'No she doesn't.'

Audrey took a breath. It wasn't easy to explain. 'In the picture, she's holding her coat, you see? And you can only see a bit of her hand?'

'Yes?' Tilly and Ginny were both looking bewildered.

'First time I saw the picture, I thought her hand looked like mine. Obviously, I realised straightaway that she was holding something, but it stuck in my head. Because look . . . '

Audrey eased her left arm out of her pocket and showed her new friends. She was missing the lower part of her arm and her hand.

'Blooming heck,' said Ginny. 'Were you in an accident?'

Audrey shook her head. 'Born like that. My arm just didn't grow properly.' She looked at the other girls' worried faces. 'It's fine, honestly. I can do lots of things, if I'm given a chance to prove myself. That's how I got through the medical, by showing the doctor what I could do.'

'And you didn't fancy doing something easier, like reading to injured soldiers, or knitting socks?' Tilly looked impressed.

Audrey shook her head. 'Where's the fun in that?' she said. 'And actually, knitting's one thing I really can't do.'

Tilly looked horrified. 'Oh God, I'm so sorry.'

But Audrey chuckled. 'I'm good with a crochet hook,' she said, and Tilly laughed in relief. Audrey felt relieved too, as though she'd successfully navigated one hurdle on her journey to becoming a Land Girl.

They were travelling through a village now. Audrey caught a glimpse of the sign that said they were in Beckindale, and felt a lurch of nerves. 'This is me,' she said. 'This is where my farm is.'

'Nervous?' Ginny asked.

'Really nervous.'

'Me too.'

'Me three,' added Tilly and they all laughed again.

'Sugden's farm is just up here,' Smithers called as he turned off the main road and on to an unmade track.

Audrey grimaced at the other girls and Tilly looked concerned. 'Do they know?' she asked. 'About your hand?'

Audrey shook her head. 'I thought it was best to meet them first, and show them that I'm capable. I've learned that people underestimate me.' Especially her parents, she thought, though she didn't say it.

Tilly grinned at her. 'I bet they only underestimate you once,' she said.

Pleased with the support from her new

17

friends, Audrey felt more confident than she was expecting to as Smithers pulled up outside a large stone farmhouse. She hoisted her kitbag on to her shoulder, said goodbye and good luck to Tilly and Ginny, and jumped down from the back of the truck.

'They're expecting you,' Smithers said as Audrey went round to the driver's window to thank him for the lift. 'Reckon they'll be pleased to see you. They need the help.'

Audrey hoped she'd be what the Sugdens were looking for. She waved to Smithers and the girls, and drawing in a deep breath, she lifted her chin and knocked on the wooden door. Immediately a dog started barking and she smiled. She loved dogs, and she was looking forward to learning more about farm animals. Animals didn't judge her the way humans did, or have preconceptions about what she could or couldn't do. She smiled in delight as a black and white sheepdog came flying round the corner of the house, barking loudly.

Audrey bent down and the dog came to her, sniffing her curiously, and growling. She rubbed it behind its ears and was thrilled when it stopped barking. *You'll do,* she imagined it thinking. *You're fine.*

'Oh Ben, you're the worst guard dog there could ever be,' said a voice. Audrey stood up to see a middle-aged woman standing by the door to the farmhouse. She was dressed similarly to Audrey, with bib-front trousers, though she looked tired and gaunt.

'I'm Maggie Sugden,' she said, without

18

smiling. 'You must be our Land Girl.'

Audrey gave Ben another rub. 'I'm Audrey Atkins,' she said. She stood up and offered Maggie her right hand to shake.

Maggie gave Audrey an appraising look from the tips of her toes up to the top of her head and back down.

'You know farms?'

'I've done all my Land Army training.'

'But do you know farms? Are you from a farming family?'

'No,' Audrey admitted. 'But I grew up in a village in Sussex and my best friend's family were farmers. I spent a lot of time running around there, helping with the harvest and whatnot.'

Maggie nodded. 'Why did you join the Land Army? I've heard that girls think it's an easy option.'

Audrey snorted. 'They'd soon change their minds when they started training.'

'It's hard work.'

'I know. I like hard work.' Audrey looked round, at the farm buildings and then out to the fields, feeling a stirring of excitement. 'I like being outside. Doing something real, you know?'

Maggie gave the first glimmer of a smile.

'I do,' she said. 'Come on, Audrey, I'll introduce you to Jacob and show you where you'll be sleeping.'

Audrey followed her inside, feeling oddly like Maggie had just approved her, as the dog had done.

The farmhouse was large, with stone floors

and a warm kitchen. Ben ran ahead, joined by another dog who was slightly smaller but just as friendly. Sitting at the table was a dark, surly-looking young man, a bit older than Audrey, who also looked tired. He nodded at Audrey as she entered.

'Hello.'

'I'm Audrey,' she said.

'Jacob.' Like his mother, he didn't smile. Instead he drained the cup of tea he was drinking and then stood up. 'We're glad to have you.'

Audrey studied him. He didn't look glad. Instead he just looked sad and a bit defeated. The smaller of the two dogs went to him and laid its head on his knee as though it understood he needed some affection, and he caressed its ears gently.

Audrey took a breath. 'It can't be easy, having a stranger coming to live in your home. I just wanted to say that I love farming, and I'm a really hard worker, and I'll try my hardest not to get under your feet, or in your way. I'll just do my job.' She'd thought quite hard about what to say when she arrived and practised in her head on the train, but the words were a bit garbled because she was nervous.

From the corner of the room came a snort that might have been laughter, and for the first time, Audrey noticed an older man sitting in a chair by the window. She almost gasped in surprise as she saw his face was horribly scarred on one side, but managed to stop herself reacting badly. He must have been injured in the last war,

20

Audrey assumed. She'd seen enough former soldiers in her time to recognise his horrible injuries. Poor family, she thought. What a lot to go through.

'That's my father, Joseph,' Jacob said. The older man raised his hand in greeting and Audrey did the same.

'Did you practise that speech?' Jacob said, and Audrey thought she could see a glint of amusement in his dark eyes.

She lifted her chin again. 'No.'

'Really?'

'A bit.'

Jacob chuckled. 'Edward would have done that, wouldn't he, Ma? Practised beforehand.'

Maggie gave a sad smile. 'Course he would. Not like you getting by on a wing and a prayer.'

Audrey wasn't sure who Edward was, but she didn't like to ask when Maggie looked so sad. Instead she smiled.

'Shall I put my things in my room?'

'I'll take your bag,' Jacob said.

'Honestly, it's fine.'

But he took hold of the strap of her kitbag and pulled it from her shoulder, forcing her to untuck her arm from the pocket of her trousers and revealing her missing hand. There was a moment of silence as the Sugdens all looked at her. Audrey let Jacob take the bag, then tucked her hand away firmly once more.

'Upstairs is it?' she said.

2

Jacob left Audrey in her room with a slightly awkward nod of his head, and she unpacked her few belongings into the sturdy chest of drawers. It was a nice room, with a large window that overlooked the fields behind the farmhouse. The sheets on the bed were well darned and had obviously been split down the middle and re-sown with the edges together to hide any wear and tear, but it was comfortable and clean. She sat down with a sigh on to the coverlet, suddenly feeling exhausted. What had she expected, really? She should have been upfront about her hand from the start and then it wouldn't have been a shock to the Sugdens. She'd simply hoped she could get to work first before they spotted it, but she realised now that that had been naïve.

She wondered what would happen. It seemed like a lovely farm but it was big, and there was no question that the Sugdens needed her. Would they send her away or would they give her a chance?

'Come on, Audrey,' she said out loud. 'Chin up.' She knew she could do good work at Emmerdale Farm and she hoped Maggie and Jacob would realise that. Perhaps she should go and speak to them? Make sure they understood that she was capable and willing to learn. Yes, that's what she'd do. She'd say she was just going for a walk into the village and on the way out wanted to reassure them that she was up to the job. That way she could make an excuse and leave them to talk about her, which they would obviously want to do, and hopefully decide she was worth the risk.

She took a deep breath and stood up, picking up her coat.

'Right then,' she muttered. 'Let's go.'

She drew her shoulders back and walked down the stairs, intending to go back into the kitchen and ask if she could have a word. But as she approached the kitchen door, she heard her name. She was clearly too late; they were discussing her already.

'It was your idea to employ Audrey,' Maggie was saying. She sounded irritated and Audrey's heart sank. She knew Jacob was the one she'd been dealing with but it was clear Maggie was really in charge. If she couldn't win her over, what chance did she have?

'It was my idea to get a Land Girl,' Jacob replied. 'But I thought we'd get one who was . . . '

Audrey flinched. Was he going to say 'normal'? She shrunk back against the wall, feeling wounded.

'Who was?' Maggie snapped. Jacob didn't reply and Audrey was glad. She knew her mother would say eavesdroppers only hear bad about themselves but somehow she couldn't move from the hall.

Jacob sighed. 'It's hard work, farming. We've got the War Ag breathing down our necks. We need to plough those other fields and plant the

23

flax. Not to mention getting those potatoes sorted. Our livelihood's on the line, Ma. What if she's not up to it?'

Maybe now was the time? She could walk in to the kitchen and tell them how strong she was, how since she'd been a little girl she'd worked out ways to lift with one hand, and use her other arm for balance, how she could do almost anything she was asked. But then she'd have to admit to listening in on their conversation and she wasn't sure the Sugdens would like that.

She heard a rumbling deep voice, Joseph she assumed, though she couldn't make out exactly what he was saying; she still struggled with York-shire accents sometimes and his speech sounded stilted and hesitant.

'She did seem nice, Pa,' Jacob replied and Audrey smiled to herself. 'But what if she's more trouble than she's worth?'

Maggie gave an exasperated sigh. 'For pity's sake, Jacob,' she said. 'You're never happy. She's here now. Let's see what she can do before we write her off, shall we?'

'You've changed your tune.' Jacob sounded like a sulky schoolboy.

'I have,' Maggie admitted. 'There's something about that girl that reminds me of myself. A bit of grit about her. I think we should give her a chance.'

'Flaming 'eck, Ma,' Jacob grumbled. 'I never know where I am with you. She's only got one bleeding hand or did you forget that? No amount of grit is going to make up for that when we need her to milk the cows or bring in the harvest.'

Audrey had heard enough. Wanting to clear her head, she turned and fled out of the front door and across the yard to the lane.

Upset and annoyed, she marched down towards the village, thoughts swirling in her head. She could get in touch with Ginny and Tilly, she thought. Perhaps Smithers would need another girl? Or he might know of another farmer locally who could do with the help. Or maybe one of the girls she'd met while she was training could put a word in for her. She'd like to stay in Yorkshire now, she'd fallen in love with the countryside and the people and though she'd not been here long, it felt like home. She'd thought she could grow to love Emmerdale Farm and it was a shame it wasn't going to be the place for her.

She marched on, through the village, going nowhere in particular and taking no real interest in her surroundings, until she reached the pub. It was called the Woolpack, and outside was a young man with thick hair and a chiselled jaw worthy of a Hollywood star. He was about Audrey's own age and he was unloading a sack of something from a small van. Audrey slowed down her march and watched as he hoisted the sack on to his broad shoulders and, as though it weighed no more than a few pounds, carted it into the pub. After a couple of minutes he came out again and leaned into the back of the van. Audrey found her eyes were drawn to him, admiring the way the muscles in his arms tightened as he pulled another sack out. But as he yanked it free from the van, the hessian split and large potatoes spilled out and rolled across the street.

The man swore softly under his breath, then he looked up to where Audrey stood across the road and directly into her eyes.

'Don't just stand there gawking,' he said good-naturedly. 'Give us a hand.'

He grinned suddenly and Audrey felt her cheeks flame. He had such a lovely smile she wasn't sure where to put herself.

'Come on.'

'Oh, right, yes,' she gabbled. She darted across the road without even checking there was nothing coming — fortunately the street was quiet — and arrived at the man's side, panting slightly. 'What do you need me to do?'

He gave her an amused smile. 'Pick up the spuds.'

Audrey wanted to kick herself but instead she crouched down and started picking up potatoes, deftly cradling them in her left arm and collecting them with her right hand. The man pulled an empty sack out of the van and as she dropped the spuds inside, she noticed his eyes flicker to her missing hand, then back up to her face. She pretended she hadn't spotted his glance and carried on picking up the potatoes, which had gone surprisingly far. She helped him hoist the new sack on to his shoulder and watched him carry it round the back of the pub.

'What are the potatoes for?' she asked when he came back. She was curious about what need a pub had for spuds that were, in her opinion, not good for eating — they were green, and some had started to sprout and seemed more useful for feeding to the pigs.

The man glanced round to see if anyone was in earshot. No one was nearby other than a young girl sitting on a wall a little way down the road but he still leaned towards her before he spoke. Audrey felt a shiver run through herself as he got closer.

'Jed wants them,' he said. 'They were meant for the pigs, but he reckons he can make something.'

'Make something?'

The man looked round again. 'Some sort of drink I think. Pretty potent, from what I hear. But not strictly legal, if you know what I mean?'

Audrey tried to look like she was absolutely on-board with illegal alcohol being made from potatoes, when in actual fact she'd only been in a pub for the first time when she did her training less than a month ago.

'I do know what you mean,' she said earnestly, hoping to appear worldly and clearly failing because the man was looking at her, that same amused look in his eye.

'I'm Ned,' he said. 'Ned Barlow.' He went to stick out his right hand for her to shake, checked himself, realised it was fine and that Audrey could shake with her right hand, and grinned again.

Audrey grinned back. She liked how unembarrassed he was about her missing hand — people often tried to pretend they hadn't noticed, or fall over themselves trying to help her, which was sweet but awkward. The way Ned had of accepting her the way she was made her missing hand seem less important.

'Audrey Atkins,' she said, shaking his hand vigorously.

'Can I buy you a drink?'

'A drink?'

Ned tilted his head towards the Woolpack.

'In there.'

Audrey bit her lip. Was it acceptable for Land Girls to go into pubs with strange men? She had a feeling it was perhaps not the done thing. Ned saw her hesitate.

'We could sit outside? It's cold but we can wrap up. I've got a jacket in the van and your coat's warm enough.'

Audrey nodded. 'Outside would be perfect.'

She asked for a ginger ale, which seemed safe enough, and took up a seat on one of the wooden benches outside the pub. It was getting dark now but the young girl Audrey had noticed across the road earlier was still sitting on the wall, kicking her feet against the stones.

Ned reappeared with a ginger ale for Audrey and a beer for himself. He drank a long gulp and settled himself next to her. She felt the heat of his leg on her thigh, even though they weren't touching. Half of her wanted to move further along the bench away from him, and the other half wanted to slide up so her leg and his were closer. She'd never been so aware of someone else's physical presence before. It was an odd feeling.

'Sad story that,' Ned said.

Audrey blinked. 'Pardon?'

He nodded towards the girl on the wall. 'Susan, her name is. She came up from London to live with her gran — Rita Roberts, she lives across the way. I don't know all the details, but she's on her own. I think she lost her mother in the Blitz.'

'Oh my goodness,' Audrey breathed. 'That is sad. The poor girl. Why is she sitting outside? She must be frozen.'

Ned shrugged. 'That's the vet's place. P'raps they're friends. She's new in the village too. Well, new-ish. Been here a few months.'

'She?' Audrey was impressed.

'Apparently.' Ned raised an eyebrow. 'Women are doing all sorts nowadays. I've even heard they're trying a bit of farm-work.'

'Is that right?'

They smiled at each other for a long minute and Audrey felt a rush of warmth from the top of her head to the tip of her toes, despite the frosty evening. And then suddenly the moment was broken as Audrey heard her name being called.

She looked round to see Jacob Sugden striding towards her, the little dog at his heels, and sighed.

'Don't reckon I'll be doing farm-work for long,' she said under her breath to Ned. 'Not if he has his way.'

'Didn't expect you to be here,' Jacob said, looking down at Audrey and Ned where they sat. He wasn't smiling. 'Making friends?'

'Jacob,' Ned said. Was Audrey imagining it or did Ned sit up a bit straighter. 'Have a seat.'

Jacob hesitated for a second, then he sat down.

'Heard you leave,' he said to Audrey. 'That door slams.'

She looked down at her feet but didn't reply.

'Did you hear Ma and me talking?'

Now she looked up. She met his gaze and was pleased to realise he looked vaguely sorry. 'I did.'

Jacob grimaced. 'You weren't supposed to.'

'Then you shouldn't talk about me when I'm in the house.'

There was a pause.

'I'm just not sure . . . ' he began.

Audrey glared at him. 'You've not even given me a chance.'

'But your hand.'

'Let me show you what I can do.'

Jacob took a breath. 'We're in a bad way, Audrey. The farm's on its last legs and we need to act fast or the War Ag will take it off us. And on top of that is the feeling that we're letting everyone down — God knows everyone needs the food we can produce. I'm just not sure we've got time to see what you can do.'

Audrey felt her shoulders slump. How could she argue with that? But then she felt the back of Ned's hand brush her leg ever so gently.

'She's strong as an ox,' he said.

Jacob looked at him.

'How do you know?'

'I had a bag of spuds that split. Audrey was walking past and she helped pick them up — quick as you like — and when they were back in the sack, she lifted it on to my back without even flinching.'

Jacob stared at Audrey. 'You did that?'

'S'pose.'

'How d'you pick 'em up?'

Audrey rolled her eyes. 'With my hand.' Then she relented. 'I used my other arm like a basket,' she said. She put her hand down and stroked the dog's head.

'Bella likes you,' Jacob said, watching the dog lick Audrey. 'She doesn't like everyone. We got her from Old Man Butler when my last dog died. He's sometimes a bit rough with his animals and she can be skittish. But she likes you.'

Audrey smiled, sensing him softening. 'I can do all sorts, Jacob. I can dig, and plant, and milk. I'm good at working out ways to adapt and I find I can do most things. Except victory rolls.'

Jacob looked blank.

'I can't do fancy stuff with my hair,' she explained, giggling at his expression. 'It's why I keep mine short.'

Jacob smiled. It changed his face and made him look much younger.

'Don't care what your hair looks like,' he said. 'Are you coming back then? We've got an early start in the morning.'

Audrey got to her feet, pleased as punch with how the conversation had turned out.

Jacob took a couple of steps away from the pub then turned to Ned. 'Potatoes?' he said.

Ned grinned. 'Potatoes.'

'Jed?'

'What do you reckon?'

Jacob let out a sharp bark of laughter and, hands in his pockets, sauntered off. Audrey followed, smiling to herself. As she reached the

31

lane, she looked back at Ned and raised a hand to wave.

'Thanks for the drink,' she called.

'See you again, Audrey,' he replied with a wink.

Cheeks flushing, she headed off after Jacob.

3

Nancy Tate was exhausted. She'd been up to Smithers' farm to look at a cow with an infected hoof, and because her car was in the garage she'd had to cycle all the way carrying her heavy bag. It had taken twice as long as usual thanks to her having to puff and pant along on the bike, and she was worried she might have missed any walk-in patients while she was out and that meant she was worried about how she was going to pay Mick Dingle for mending whatever was wrong with her car. Mind you, she thought, she wasn't going to be able to run her car much longer. She'd have to keep it just for emergencies or take it off the road altogether because of the petrol rationing. Hardly anyone in the village had a car anymore. Everywhere she went she saw vehicles tucked under tarpaulins, waiting for the war to be over. So she'd do well to get used to cycling. Seemed she was going to be doing more of it.

With heavy legs, she turned the pedals slowly as she rode into the village raising a hand from the handlebars briefly to acknowledge Jacob Sugden as he walked past with a young woman in Land Army uniform. She must be working up at Emmerdale Farm, Nancy thought. That was good. She'd only been up there once but it was obvious that things were rough for the Sugdens; they could do with the help.

Ned Barlow was getting into his van and he nodded at her, too. Nancy smiled to herself. It certainly wasn't easy being Beckindale's new vet — and the first ever woman to hold the job — but she'd been there for a couple of months now and she was beginning to feel more at home. As long as she didn't think too much about what had brought her there in the first place.

Her heart sank, just a little, as she spotted the figure sitting on her wall. Susan Roberts. Nancy felt so sorry for the gawky young woman, but she was beginning to get fed up of her hanging round the whole time.

A bicycle bell behind her made her jump and she turned on her own saddle to see Ruby Dobbs charging past her.

'Hello, Miss Tate!' Ruby called as she sailed past and came skidding to a halt next to Susan. 'How's the bike?' Ruby loved cycling and was always pleased to see other people joining her.

For a second, Nancy felt as though her exhaustion would overwhelm her. Ruby's relentless enthusiasm and Susan's quiet presence were the last things she needed when she felt like this. But she tried to smile. 'The bike's great, thanks,' she panted at Ruby as she pulled up by the surgery and wearily slid off. 'Hello, Susan.'

'Need a hand?' Susan asked. Nancy looked at her. She was around fifteen, Nancy thought though she wasn't an expert on schoolgirls and it seemed like forever ago that she'd been one herself. She had long legs and a skinny, ungainly frame. Nancy, like everyone else in the village, knew she had ended up in Beckindale because of

34

some tragedy in London, and felt desperately sorry for her. But something about the girl made her also feel awkward and worried about saying the wrong thing.

Ruby, though, seemed to feel nothing of the sort. She was a couple of years younger than Susan, but very much in charge. She rested her bike against the stone wall and eyed Nancy carefully.

'You look whacked,' she said.

Despite herself, Nancy laughed. 'I am.'

Ruby nodded briskly, the gesture making her look very much like her adoptive mother, the village schoolteacher Meg Warcup. Nancy didn't know Meg very well but she'd seen her around and heard — with a great deal of admiration — how she'd taken in Ruby and her brother Stan when their mother was killed. Knowing that about her made Nancy feel awkward too. Meg must have been so determined, strong and capable to suddenly become a mother to two heartbroken children, while Nancy was struggling to cope with animals. She sighed and Ruby looked at her with sympathy.

'Right then,' the girl said, sounding much older than her years. 'Let's get you inside and Susan and I will make you tea.'

Too tired to argue, Nancy unlocked the front door and let the two youngsters steer her into the house. She lived in Smithy Cottage, which had, once upon a time, been the blacksmith's forge. The blacksmith himself, a dour chap called Leslie Jackson, had a new place on the other side of the village and after years of seeing his business decline was enjoying a boom in trade now everyone was using horses again and mending old farm machinery. The cottage was next door to the vet's surgery which had a reception area at the front, a treatment room behind and space at the back for the animals to stay overnight if they needed to. It even had a small kitchen for making tea, and an operating theatre, which Nancy hadn't used yet. It was very well equipped and Nancy often thought how lucky she was to have been given the chance to take it on.

But it was into Smithy Cottage that she and the girls now trooped.

'Meg always says there's nothing a brew can't make better,' Ruby said, tramping up the hall clutching Nancy's bag.

Behind Nancy, Susan made an odd noise, like a sigh and a sob all at once and Ruby gasped.

'Sorry, Susan,' she said. 'Meg also says I don't think before I open my gob.'

Nancy's head was spinning with the chatter. She sat down on the saggy armchair that had become her favourite, and pulled off her coat and boots.

'Where have you been?' Susan asked Nancy quietly as Ruby set about making up the fire, and lighting it, bringing some much-needed warmth into the room.

'Cow with an infected hoof.'

Susan nodded. 'Was it all right?'

'It should be. Caught it early enough.'

Nancy liked how the girl cared about the animals. She was always asking after them and checking up on creatures Nancy had been treating. It was sweet, really. She had to remember that, because Nancy knew she could be sharp-tongued and standoffish, especially when she was tired and when there was so much at stake.

'No animals next door today?' Susan asked.

Nancy shook her head. 'It's quiet.'

She felt another wave of worry that she didn't have enough patients to keep the practice afloat while the village vet, Michael Walters, was off helping the war effort. He was an older gentleman — well into his fifties — but he'd joined the Royal Army Veterinary Corps and was working with dogs, as far as Nancy knew. His wife had gone to live with her sister in Scotland while he was away. Nancy was holding the fort while Mr Walters was gone, but she knew lots of local people weren't happy he had let a woman — and a young woman at that — take on the practice, and so things were quiet. Then again, she was barely coping as it was, rushing from appointment to appointment. If things did pick up, how would she manage? She swallowed down her concerns and forced herself to smile at Susan.

'We should be glad the animals are all fit and healthy,' she said.

Susan nodded. 'I'll put the kettle on,' she said.

Nancy let her head roll back on to the back of the chair as the two girls made tea. She was starving but she'd have a cuppa first then decide what to eat. If she had any food in. She had no idea what was in her cupboards and she couldn't actually remember if she'd had breakfast that day.

In the kitchen, Ruby was jabbering away.

'I've put new pedals on my bike, did you see? Lily showed me what to do. She's so nice and her baby's so sweet, have you met her?'

Nancy didn't hear Susan's reply. She wondered if the girl minded Ruby jabbering on about family.

'Hope, she's called,' Ruby went on, seemingly undeterred by Susan's lack of response. 'Bit of a weird name, but it's nice I reckon. Meg likes it. She says we all need a bit of hope right now.'

There was a pause and Nancy heard the kettle whistling and then water being poured.

'Lily's been teaching me about bikes,' Ruby said and finally Susan replied.

'She's taught you ever such a lot.'

'She really has.' Ruby sounded delighted. 'She's been lovely. But Meg reckons Lily's missing getting her hands dirty at the garage. Her dad won't let her work on the cars while Hope's so little, but she's been doing bits with the bikes and she never minds me hanging round.'

'Loads of people cycle round here,' Susan commented. 'Loads do in London too but there ain't so many hills down there.'

Ruby chuckled. 'Hills are the best bit.'

She appeared in the doorway to the lounge with three mugs of tea on a tray and — joy — a plate of biscuits.

'Susan found these in a tin,' she said. 'Do you know how long they've been there?'

Nancy blinked. 'No idea.'

Susan bobbed up behind Ruby. 'Think they're from Christmas,' she said. 'The tin had holly on it. Maybe someone gave them to you as a present?'

Nancy was none the wiser — Christmas was a blur in her memory because she'd stayed in Beckindale instead of going home to see her family. She'd told her father she couldn't leave so soon after arriving and that she had no one to cover, which was true but she hadn't told him she didn't want to see him. She'd ended up going out to put down a horse that had broken its leg and it had been a pretty horrible day all told. But the horse's owner had been nice at least . . .

'Yes!' she said triumphantly to a startled Susan as the memory resurfaced. 'Mrs, erm, whatsit, in the big house at the far end? She gave them to me on Christmas Day. Her son sent them from America.'

'Mrs Lacock,' Ruby said. 'American biscuits? I've never had one of those.'

She looked hopefully at Nancy, who couldn't help but laugh. These girls with their endless energy and never-ending questions may have been exhausting but they did bring life into her quiet home and that was something.

'Dig in,' she said. She sipped her tea gratefully and took a biscuit for herself.

'So, Ruby, you've been working on some bikes with Lily?'

Ruby started chattering away, talking about saddles and spokes, and Nancy felt her eyelids growing heavy. It was so cosy in her small lounge, with the fire toasting her toes and the mug of tea warming her fingers. She could just drift off, right here.

'That's the most brilliant idea, isn't it, Nancy?'

Nancy jerked back to consciousness. Susan and Ruby were both looking at her.

'Sorry,' she said, embarrassed. 'What were you saying?'

'I was saying that Susan really loves animals.'

Nancy nodded. She'd assumed as much from the way Susan hung around. 'Do you have a pet?' she asked.

Susan's face clouded over and Nancy cursed herself inwardly. Of course the poor girl didn't have a pet if she'd lost everything in the Blitz. Though didn't her grandmother have a cat? Yes, a big fluffy elderly tom called Clifford. Nancy always remembered people's pets — it was the people themselves she found it harder to put names to.

'Gran's got a cat called Clifford,' Susan said, and Nancy felt a momentary triumph at getting the name right. 'He's really old now though and he just sleeps most of the time. And I had a dog . . . '

She trailed off and Nancy let her. But Susan hadn't finished, she was just finding the words.

'When the war happened, really early on, they said we had to . . . ' She swallowed and Nancy suddenly realised what she was going to say.

'Oh God,' she said.

'What?' Ruby was none the wiser. Susan looked wretched so Nancy stepped in.

'They thought there would be food shortages and rationing,' she explained. 'And they told people it would be . . . ' she choked on the word ' . . . kindest . . . to have their pets euthanised.'

Ruby looked blank.

'Put down,' Nancy said.

'No.'

'I'm afraid so. Lots of us were openly against it and many vets refused to do it. I was still training at the time, so I wasn't asked but I would have said no.'

Susan's face was white. 'I had a dog called Scruff and he was the sweetest little thing. He was just a mongrel. Mum got him for me when he was a pup and I loved him so much. But my dad said he had to go.'

Nancy felt awful for the sad, awkward girl in front of her, but didn't really know what to say. Ruby, though, looped her arm through her friend's and leaned her head on to her shoulder.

'Your dad probably thought he were doing the right thing at the time,' she said. A shadow crossed her thin face. 'I don't always understand why adults do what they do, but I reckon they're all just doing their best.'

Susan gave her a small smile and Ruby turned her attention to Nancy.

'So seeing as Susan loves animals so much we had an idea . . . '

'Which is?' Nancy was short. She was too weary to follow Ruby's wandering conversation.

'You know how I've been doing bits and pieces for Lily and she's been teaching me about bikes and that?'

'Yes?' Nancy's tired mind was struggling to work out where Ruby was going with all this.

'I think it would be good if Susan helps you out downstairs, with the animals.'

41

Nancy shook her head. 'Oh, Ruby, I don't think so.' She knew the girls were trying to help but she was finding things tricky enough, running the practice on her own, making ends meet, and trying to convince the locals she was a proper vet and not some silly girl who was pretending, without having to train Susan or worse, find money to pay her.

But Ruby wasn't listening.

'You're worn out,' she said. 'Look at you, dozing off on the couch like an old lady. You can't do everything on your own, Miss Tate. Let Susan help you.'

'I can't afford help.'

'You wouldn't need to pay her. She'd be learning. That's enough.'

'What about school?'

Ruby rolled her eyes. 'After school, and at weekends and in the holidays.'

Nancy was about to say no again, more forcefully this time, when she caught a glimpse of Susan's face. For the first time since she'd come to the village, she was smiling a proper, genuine smile. She looked hopeful. Nancy sighed.

'You might need to do some mucky stuff or the boring things like filing and typing up bills.'

Susan nodded eagerly. 'I don't mind that.'

'And when she's done the boring stuff you can teach her about being a vet,' Ruby said. 'Helping each other, you see. That's what it's like in Beckindale.'

Nancy raised an eyebrow. 'Really?'

'Really, it is. Took me ages to realise it when we first got here, but now I see that everyone looks out for everyone else. Like Meg looking out for me and Stan even though we didn't like it at first, or Lily teaching me about bikes and me helping her. Susan can help you and you can teach her. It's perfect.'

Susan was sitting up straight, her jaw tense as she waited for Nancy's answer. Nancy knew when she was beaten, and Ruby was right; she could do with a hand.

'Fine,' she said. 'Susan, you can come and help out. I can't pay you, but I'll teach you what I can.'

Susan looked like she might cry with happiness. 'Thanks, Miss Tate,' she muttered.

Nancy gave them both a tired smile. 'Now, you two, I want a quick wash and an early night, so get off, will you?'

The two girls scrambled to their feet and Nancy showed them out. She hoped she hadn't just made a big mistake.

4

Audrey wiped the sweat from her forehead and stood back to admire her handiwork. She was digging over a plot in the farm's garden to plant more vegetables and it was hard going, but she'd achieved quite a lot so far. Maggie was keen to grow more veg, and was also planning to get a beehive so they could produce honey which Audrey thought was a great plan. So she was digging another bed ready for planting. She was on her own at the farm today because Jacob and Maggie had both gone to find out more about planting flax, which would be turned into thread and used to make things like parachute harnesses, although Audrey wasn't totally clear how that would work. She was looking forward to finding out more when the others came back. She didn't mind being on her own actually. She knew the ropes at Emmerdale Farm now, having been there almost a month, and she was pleased the Sugdens trusted her enough to leave her behind. Though Jacob had taken a bit of persuasion at first.

'I could see if Ned Barlow's around and he could come and help,' he said. 'He's busy with his family's fruit and vegetables but he's normally up for a bit of extra work.'

Audrey had felt her cheeks redden at the mention of Ned's name but while she was keen to see the burly farmhand again, she wasn't so eager to catch a glimpse of him that she'd let Jacob think she wasn't capable of doing her job on her own.

'It's fine,' she'd said. 'All I'm doing is digging, it's not hard. I'll get that whole bed done today if you let me get on with it.'

Jacob had looked like he was about to argue then, wisely, thought better of it. 'If you're sure.'

Audrey had nodded firmly. 'I'm sure.'

So here she was, alone. The sun was shining, which was a welcome relief after the harsh winter, and though the light was weak there was a hint of warmth in its rays. Audrey had even taken off her jacket and was just working in her short-sleeved shirt. She thought she'd work a bit longer then head inside to have the lunch Maggie had left for her and make sure Joseph was all right. He mostly stayed in his chair, now, looking out over the farm, and he didn't say much, though he'd told her to call him Joe. Audrey wondered if he might like to sit outside now the weather was looking better. She'd ask Maggie about it later.

She tilted her face up to the sky and let the sunshine soak into her skin. It was lovely to be out here, in the quiet stillness of the countryside. She could hear birds singing and somewhere, far down the hill, a tractor purring along. She had been so right to join the Women's Land Army, she thought. So right. She just wished her mother could understand that.

She pushed the spade into the earth again and turned over a clod and there on the air, thought she heard a cry. She raised her head to listen but

45

nothing; she must have been mistaken. But as she started to dig again, she heard another wail. She froze, her heart pounding. Was it a child? A woman? Where was the sound coming from?

There it was again, a keening, heart-rending cry, but actually now she could hear it better she realised it was more animal-like than human and it was coming from the lower field — where the cows were.

Throwing down her spade, she ran towards the sound, jumping over the stile, and barrelling into the field where the large-eyed cows all turned to her. Audrey was a bit frightened of the cows, she couldn't lie. She'd not had much to do with animals growing up, and the milking lessons she'd had at her Land Girl training were all on rubber udders rather than the real thing. But Maggie was patiently helping her grow bolder, asking her to feed the cattle sometimes or fetch something from the field. And Audrey had seen the newborn calves teetering around on their spindly legs and been rather taken with them.

Now though, she was standing by the hedge, breathing heavily, as half a dozen huge, black and white jerseys — who were very protective of their little calves — all waved their enormous heads in her direction. And there it was again, that horrible sound, cutting through the quiet morning.

'There, there,' Audrey breathed, holding out her hand and wondering if the cows understood she was there to help. 'What's happening, ladies? What's gone wrong?'

The cry came again and this time, Audrey saw

where it was from. In the corner of the field, away from the others, a cow was lying on her side in the grass, kicking out with her legs.

'Oh my goodness,' Audrey said to herself. 'Is she having a calf? I thought all the calves were here already.' She dodged the swaying jerseys and ran around to the other cow, which was crying louder and louder.

Tentatively she reached out her hand and stroked the back of its head. It was damp with sweat and her eyes were white with fright as she looked at Audrey. Audrey knew nothing about cows or calves but it was obvious something was wrong. She knew Jacob and Maggie kept a watchful eye on their cows when they were in labour, letting them do what they had to do naturally, and only intervening if something wasn't right. But she couldn't leave this one to go it alone, that was clear.

'I'll get help,' Audrey said, no idea whether the cow knew what she was saying. 'I'll get the vet.'

She stood up and gazed down towards the village. Should she run? It was quite a distance. And what if something happened to the cow in the meantime? Her eyes alighted on the farmhouse and she made a sudden decision. Quickly, she raced past her newly dug vegetable patch and into the kitchen. Joseph, sitting by the window, jumped as the door crashed against the wall.

'Sorry,' Audrey said, her words tumbling out in her panic. 'Joe, I need you. There's a cow in trouble and I need to get the vet. Will you stay with her? Make sure she's all right?'

Joseph looked up, frowning.

'In trouble?' His words were slow but Jacob had told Audrey his father wasn't as simple as people assumed and it seemed he was right.

'She's calving and something's wrong.'

With some difficulty, Joseph got to his feet. Audrey had never seen him stand before.

'In t'bottom field?'

'Yes, in the corner. You'll see her. I'll run to the village.'

Joe looked at Audrey, eyes narrowed, sizing her up. 'Bike?' he said.

'Can I ride one?' Audrey tucked her left arm behind her back, and lifted her chin. 'Of course.'

Joe raised a bushy grey eyebrow and Audrey shrugged.

'I'm all right if I'm careful and as long as I don't go too fast because I can only use one brake,' she added.

Joe gave her a sudden, lopsided smile. 'Jacob's bike . . . in barn.'

'I'll get it.' Audrey turned to go then turned back to the frail farmer. 'Will you be okay, here by yourself?' she asked. He seemed so vulnerable.

'Fine,' Joe said. 'Go.'

He shuffled off towards the field and Audrey watched him go for a second. Then she followed him out of the back door and went in the opposite direction, round the side of the farmhouse to the barn where she found the bicycle leaning against the wall. It was a bit creaky and obviously hadn't been ridden for a while. With a certain amount of trepidation, she got herself on. She could rest her left forearm on the handlebar for balance and use her right hand to brake and steer. It wasn't perfect, and she knew she had to be careful and not try to go too fast because she might come a cropper, but after a few wobbly turns around the farmyard, avoiding chickens, she found her rhythm and headed off down into Beckindale.

She was almost enjoying this, she thought as she swished — slowly — down the lane. She was terrified the cow would die, and her heart was hammering against her ribs. But she felt exhilarated and full of energy. She just hoped the vet was around and not out on another job, because she wasn't sure what she would do if that happened.

She slid to an uneven halt by the village signpost and leapt off the bike, not even stopping to pick it up when it clattered to the ground because she'd not secured it properly. She dashed over the road to the vet's surgery and was so relieved when the woman was there that she almost hugged her.

'You're the vet?' Audrey panted, trying to catch her breath.

The woman, who was about five or even ten years older than Audrey, with glossy dark hair and a sharp stare, nodded, unsmiling.

'Nancy Tate.'

'I'm from Emmerdale Farm. There's a cow having a calf, but something's wrong. She's in trouble.'

Nancy frowned. 'I was just up there last week. I thought all the calves were here?'

Audrey shrugged. 'Apparently not. You need to come.'

Nancy looked down at the large diary that was open on the desk where she stood.

'I'm meant to be going to check on the Braithewaites' ducks, and then I've got an appointment to look at some chickens that Mr Whittaker's buying,' she said, almost to herself. 'Perhaps I could stop in on the Braithewaites on the way . . . '

The leggy girl that Audrey had seen sitting on the wall the evening she met Ned appeared from the back room, making both Audrey and Nancy jump.

'God, Susan, I didn't know you were here,' Nancy said, irritated. 'Did you come in the back way? Shouldn't you be at school?'

'Got off early,' Susan said. 'Want me to rearrange your appointments?'

Nancy looked annoyed but then she glanced at Audrey, who was twitching, eager to be off back to the cow, and nodded.

'Can you tell Mrs Braithewaite that I'll check on her ducks later? And I'll do the chickens tomorrow if there's a space.'

'Will do,' Susan said cheerfully. 'Hope the cow's all right.'

'My car's outside,' Nancy told Audrey. 'I've got a tiny bit of petrol left so we can drive up the hill.'

On the way back to the farm, Nancy fired questions at Audrey: what was the cow doing? How did she look? Was she moving? Was she still? Audrey tried to answer as best she could, but she had been so panicky when she left the animal that she wasn't sure if she was right.

Nancy pulled into the farmyard and both

women jumped out.

'Just over here,' Audrey said.

To her surprise, when they reached the field, Joe had managed to shoo the other cows away to the far side. He was standing by the pregnant beast, who he'd got on her feet again, rubbing her ears and talking to her.

'Joe, we're here,' Audrey called.

'About time,' he grumbled. 'She's in . . . pain. Breech.' He took a breath, looking as though he was going to carry on but Nancy jumped in.

'I know what to do,' she snapped. 'I'll take it from here.'

Joe made a face at Audrey and she gave him a small smile in return, feeling uncomfortable at Nancy being rude to the farmer. The new vet definitely wasn't the friendliest person Audrey had met in Beckindale. She just hoped she knew what she was doing.

'Joe, you look worn out,' she said. 'Why don't you go back inside? That's okay, isn't it, Miss Tate? We don't need Joe now?'

Nancy barely looked up from where she was rummaging in her bag and said, 'No.' Then she added, as an afterthought, 'Thanks.'

Audrey gave Joe's arm a grateful squeeze and he gave her his funny crooked smile again, then shuffled off back to his chair inside. Audrey hovered by Nancy, not knowing if she should go or stay.

'Should I . . . '

Nancy pulled on some gloves and stood up. 'No, I need you. What's your name?'

'Audrey.'

'I'm Nancy.' The women nodded at each other, neither smiling. Nancy carried on: 'Audrey, you need to stand at the head and keep her calm. Do you know cows?'

Audrey grimaced. 'Not really.'

'Fine. Just put your hands either side of her neck, like this.'

Nancy reached out and before Audrey had time to pull away, the vet took her wrists in her fingers. Both women flinched as Nancy realised that Audrey had a missing hand and, embarrassed, loosened her grip.

'I can do it,' Audrey said. 'I can keep her calm.'

She positioned herself at the front of the cow. The poor creature was still wailing, a sad, shrill moo that made Audrey shiver. She must know her calf was in danger. Maybe even dead already.

The animal didn't protest as Audrey put her arms either side of her huge face and held her gently but firmly.

Nancy watched and then nodded. 'That's it exactly. Now she might move a bit as I examine her.'

Down the other end of the cow, Nancy did what she had to do. The creature's mooing got louder and Audrey kept her eyes averted from whatever the vet was doing.

'Good girl,' she cooed. 'Good, brave girl.'

'I can turn the calf but I need you to keep her really calm,' Nancy said. 'If she kicks out, I'm in trouble.'

'Is the calf alive?'

Nancy took a deep breath. 'Not sure. It's

unlikely, I've got to be honest.'

'Oh God,' Audrey said. 'Maggie said the War Ag aren't impressed if anyone loses livestock. What if the Sugdens get into trouble because of this?'

Nancy looked grim. 'These things happen,' she said. 'But whether the calf is alive or dead, she needs to give birth.'

Heart pounding, and feeling close to tears, Audrey kept a firm grip on the animal as Nancy worked to turn the calf. It felt like hours, but was probably only a few minutes, when she finally said, 'That's it, I think. I've got the hooves.'

The cow was bellowing now, and stamping on the grass. Audrey was struggling to keep her still but she grasped her neck and kept talking as Nancy delivered the calf.

It slithered out on to the grass, and lay horribly still. The cow bellowed again.

'Let her go,' Nancy said. 'Let her see the calf.'

Tears streaming down her face, Audrey loosened her grip on the cow's neck and watched as the poor creature turned to her baby, licking it and nudging it, calling to it softly.

'I can't bear it,' Audrey said, turning her head away. 'I can't watch.'

But Nancy took her hand and squeezed it. 'No, look.'

On the grass, the calf was squirming, trying to stand up on its spindly legs.

'Ohh,' Audrey breathed. 'It's all right. It's alive.'

Nancy grinned, her whole face lighting up. 'It's alive,' she said. 'I'll give her a minute then check the calf over. But it looks all right to me. A good, strong male.'

'You saved them both,' Audrey said in awe. 'You did this.'

Nancy shrugged. 'It's my job.'

'Audrey!' A shout from nearby made them both turn and look as Jacob strode across to the field, face like thunder. 'What the bloody hell's going on? Dad said there's a cow in calf.'

'There was,' Audrey said, proud as punch. 'She's had it. Nancy delivered the calf.'

Nancy's smile disappeared. 'Calf was breech,' she said briskly.

Jacob climbed over the gate and came over to where they were standing, gazing down at the calf as he suckled like two new parents.

'Audrey,' he said. 'All our calves have been born.'

'I know,' said Audrey.

Jacob tutted. 'Look at the tag on the cow's ear,' he said. 'What colour is it?'

'It's blue,' Audrey said, no idea what was going on.

'And what colour are the tags on all the other cows' ears?'

Audrey looked round. 'They're yellow . . . ohhhh.'

'Ohhhh,' Jacob mocked.

There was a pause and then he gave an exasperated groan.

'You blithering idiot, Audrey. This isn't one of our cows.'

5

Nancy hadn't had much to do with Jacob Sugden since she'd arrived in Beckindale, but she'd heard — from Ruby's chitchat mainly — that he was quick to anger and now it seemed she was about to see for herself.

She looked at him now, red-faced and spluttering.

'Did you not think to bloody check?' he was shouting at the Land Girl, Audrey. 'Did it not occur to you that all our calves are here already so this one might not be ours? Before you landed me with a bloody bill for a cow that's not even mine? For Christ's sake, Audrey, you're supposed to be helping us but you're a liability. I knew you weren't up to the job.'

Audrey, who'd impressed Nancy with her calm head during the dramatic delivery, looked devastated. She tucked her arm — the one with the missing hand that to Nancy's surprise, hadn't held her back at all — behind herself, and stared at her feet.

'I'm sorry,' she muttered.

Jacob took a breath. 'Yeah,' he said. 'Well maybe you should have thought before you acted. Honestly, Audrey, I'm so annoyed . . . '

Nancy was tired and emotional after saving the calf, and she was suddenly filled with rage at this belligerent man who'd come along after the drama was over, to share his opinion.

'Oh, shut up,' she said.

Jacob stopped talking immediately, his mouth open in shock.

'That's better,' Nancy said. Next to her, Audrey gave a little squeak that could have been surprise or perhaps an attempt at muffling laughter.

'I've met some rude men since I got to Beckindale, but you're the worst so far, Jacob Sugden,' she told him. He was about her age, but she felt like a schoolmistress, scolding him for being cheeky. 'May I point out that your own father, who's worked this farm for years, didn't notice the colour of the cow's tag so it seems a bit unfair to criticise Audrey, who's only been here five minutes, for not spotting it either.'

Jacob opened his mouth and then closed it again without speaking. Nancy was pleased; she hadn't finished yet.

'That cow would have died if Audrey hadn't acted as fast as she did. The cow would have died, and the calf too. And on your land, which would have caused all sorts of ructions, with the owner and the War Ag, I imagine. Whose cow is it?'

Jacob looked sulky. 'It belongs to Paul Evans.' He tilted his head over towards the farmhouse. 'He had a few fences down the other day when the storm brought down a tree. I reckon his cow must have wandered off and found herself in with ours when we moved them for milking. We don't always count them in and out because we're so small.'

Nancy nodded. 'We need to tell him what happened. Explain how Audrey acted quickly

56

and cycled down to the village to fetch me . . . '

'She cycled?' Jacob cut in.

Audrey nodded. 'Took your old bike from the barn.' Then she gasped, her hand across her mouth. 'And I left it down by the pub, sorry.'

'I'll get Ruby to bring it back,' Nancy said. 'It's not important.'

Again Jacob looked like he was going to argue, but he didn't. Nancy went on, 'She cycled down to the village to get me, and in doing so, she saved the lives of Paul Evans's cow and calf. He'll be very glad she did what she did. In fact, he'll owe you a favour. And don't worry about the money; I'll send Paul my bill.'

'Fine.' Jacob was still annoyed, but Nancy was crosser.

'And now I think you should apologise to Audrey,' she said.

'What for?'

'For being so rude. She did absolutely nothing wrong. She kept her head, and she kept the cow so calm it made things much easier for me. She's got a real aptitude for farming that one.' Nancy thought about mentioning Audrey's hand, saying that despite her disability she was coping well, but then thought better of it. Instead she smiled at the Land Girl, who was still looking shaken and teary. 'You're lucky to have her, Jacob,' she said. 'You'd do well to remember that.'

To give him his due, Jacob looked a bit shamefaced. 'We are,' he muttered. 'Sorry, Audrey.'

Audrey gave him a quick, sudden smile. 'S'alright,' she said. Then she narrowed her eyes and looked at him at an angle. 'Reckon you've learned your lesson yet?'

'What lesson's that?'

'Not to underestimate me.'

Jacob let out a bark of laughter which made Nancy jump. 'I reckon I might have,' he said.

★ ★ ★

Nancy drove home via the Braithewaites' house to check on their ducks, which were laying so well Mrs Braithwaite gave Nancy two large eggs to take home for her tea. Her mind was full of organisation. She could tick off the ducks, but she still had to fit in the chickens, and she really needed a morning to herself to sort out her paperwork and do all the invoicing she'd not had time for; goodness knows she needed the money if she was going to keep this practice running.

She let herself into the surgery and found Susan still there, sitting at the desk with a cat on her lap.

Nancy felt a flutter of irritation, seeing the youngster in her space. She was still riled by Jacob's reaction to the cow and she really wanted some quiet to calm down and get organised.

'Still here?' she said, more rudely than she should have. She dropped her bag on the floor with a loud thump and felt bad when Susan winced at the sound. She was jumpy, generally, Nancy had noticed. Nervous about sudden noises or bangs. Feeling guilty made Nancy even more irritated and she tutted. 'Thought you'd have gone by now.'

Susan though, now she'd recovered from the thump of the bag, seemed unperturbed by Nancy's shortness.

'I was just about to go when this chap strolled in from outside and made himself comfortable,' she said with a grin. The cat was asleep on her lap, snoring loudly. 'I didn't want to disturb him.'

'Your grandmother will be wondering where you've got to,' Nancy said, trying to get rid of the girl without being too blunt about it. Then she paused, looking at the papers on the desk where Susan sat.

'What's this?'

'Oh, I popped round to see Mr Whittaker to rearrange your appointment. And then when I came back to write the new time in the diary, the cat came in too and I didn't want to move him. While I was sitting here, I saw all this paperwork needed sorting so I went through it.'

Again Nancy felt that prickle of annoyance at the thought that Susan had been through her private papers. But the girl was still talking.

'This pile is invoices that have been paid — you've got a lot of cheques to put into your account, Miss Tate. I ticked them off in your ledger and then here . . . ' She produced a sheet of paper covered in her rounded handwriting. 'Here are all the ones that are late paying. You should chase them.'

Nancy stared at her. 'You've just saved me a morning's work,' she said, astonished.

'It wasn't hard,' Susan said. 'You need someone to do this for you. You can't possibly keep up with all this paperwork and look after the animals by yourself. I bet you've been really worried about money, because you've just not had time to pay in those cheques.'

Nancy felt a weight had been lifted from her shoulders by this gawky, sad schoolgirl.

'I have,' she admitted. 'I feel really silly.'

Susan waved a hand. 'You're good with the animals,' she said. 'You need someone to help with the other stuff.'

Nancy looked at her. 'Do you want to do it?'

But Susan laughed. 'No,' she said. 'I want to be a vet, like you so I need to stay at school. I'd rather help with the animals. You just need a receptionist, that's all.'

Nancy pulled out a chair from under the desk and sat down heavily.

'You know I've been up at Emmerdale Farm with the Land Girl?' she said. Susan nodded, looking at her curiously, obviously not sure where this story was going.

'Did you notice her hand?'

Again Susan nodded. 'She's only got one.'

Nancy looked up at the ceiling. 'She was really helpful today. Calm, thoughtful, capable. But when Jacob came home he was annoyed with her.'

Susan tutted.

'I know,' Nancy agreed. 'But the girl — Audrey — she gave him what for. Told him off for underestimating her. I was furious on her behalf but she stood up for herself too.'

'I liked her,' Susan said.

'Me too.' Nancy paused, trying to think of a

way to say what she wanted to say, without thinking too much about the betrayal that had sent her fleeing to Beckindale. 'My father is a vet, you know?'

'I didn't know that.'

'He is. But he never really believed I could do it. He always underestimated me.'

'You've proved him wrong now, though.'

Nancy thought of the unpaid invoices, and the uncashed cheques and the missed appointments and wondered if Susan was right.

'Maybe,' she said. 'But more importantly, I've done the same as him. I've underestimated you.'

Susan gave the little thin smile that Nancy was growing to recognise. 'Have you?'

'I have.' She took a breath. 'And I'm sorry.'

Susan's smile grew marginally wider.

'S'alright,' she said.

'Truth is, Susan, I need some help here. You're right that I need a receptionist and once I've paid in those cheques I should be able to afford to employ one.'

Susan chuckled. 'And would you carry on helping with the animals? I can't pay you, but it would be good experience and I can help with your schoolwork in return.'

Susan's eyes gleamed with pleasure and she looked genuinely happy. The thought that it was because of her made Nancy feel warm inside and soothed some of her worries.

'I'd like that,' Susan said. 'Can I come tomorrow afternoon?'

'Great.'

They smiled at each other and then

reluctantly, Susan stood up and the cat woke with a start and yowled crossly. Nancy opened the surgery door and without a backwards glance, the puss stalked off.

'Do you know Nora Prendagast?' Susan asked as she pulled on her blazer. 'She's friends with my gran.'

Nancy shook her head. 'Don't think so. Does she have animals?'

'She's got two daughters.'

Nancy laughed. 'I can't help with those.'

'They're grown-ups, the daughters. And Nora was at our house yesterday talking about her older daughter, Betty. She's ever so pretty, Betty. She's always got her hair done and that. But she hates her job — she works in a factory in Hotten I think. And she hates it because she doesn't have enough to do so she's bored, and she doesn't get to chat to people. She's a real gossip, is Betty.'

'Is she?' Nancy was already thinking about a cup of tea and some proper dinner for once. Maybe she'd boil those duck eggs and have them with some toast.

'She'd be a good receptionist, I reckon,' Susan said patiently.

The penny dropped, finally, for Nancy.

'Betty Prendagast?'

'She lives in the house with the red door, by the post office,' Susan said. 'I think she'd bite your hand off for a job like this. She hates everything about that factory — she even hates getting the bus to work, I've heard her complaining about it. But she knows everyone in

62

the village and she's clever, her mum says. She's always saying Betty's so sharp she'll cut herself.'

Nancy grinned. 'Sounds like she'd fit right in here,' she said. 'Maybe I'll call in on her later.'

6

Audrey sat at the bus stop. Jacob had given her the day off, much to her delight. She thought he felt guilty about how rude he'd been the other day when they'd had all the drama with the cow. But that had all worked out fine in the end. Paul Evans, the farmer who owned the cow and her calf, had been so grateful for their help that he'd promised to help out at Emmerdale Farm if they ever needed him. He ran the local pig club — where people all clubbed together to buy a piglet and cover the cost of rearing it — and as a thank you he'd sent the Sugdens one of his home-cured hams. Thinking about the salty meat now made Audrey's mouth water. Maggie had served up a few slices, then packed it away for now.

'We need to make it last,' she'd said sensibly, but to Jacob and Joe's obvious disappointment. Jacob had slapped Audrey on the back and said she should have an extra slice because they only had it because of her. Maggie had expressed admiration at how well Audrey had done riding the bicycle and much to Audrey's surprise, she'd suggested Jacob show Audrey how to drive the tractor, and after the tiniest hesitation, Jacob had agreed to give her a few lessons in the weeks to come. And then he'd given Audrey today off. So all in all, the frightening dash down to the village to find Nancy the vet had been worth it.

'What are you smiling about?' Startled by the

voice, Audrey looked up, and saw Ned Barlow giving her a broad grin. Her stomach twisted in a not unpleasant way and she found she couldn't help smiling back.

'I'm looking forward to seeing my friends,' she said. 'I'm going to meet them in Hotten.'

'Other Land Girls?'

He sat down next to her and she took a deep breath, pleased to have him near her.

'Ginny and Tilly,' she told him. 'They work for Smithers, over the hill.'

Ned nodded. 'I've done some work over there. Nice bloke is Smithers.'

He turned to face Audrey and she found herself gazing into his dark eyes.

'I've been hearing stories about you,' he said.

'About me?' She couldn't tear her gaze away.

'That you delivered a calf and it wasn't even one of yours.'

Audrey chuckled. 'None of them are mine,' she pointed out. 'They all belong to the Sugdens. But yes, this cow had wandered into their field. And no, I didn't deliver it. The vet did. I just fetched her, that was all.'

'Picking up spuds, delivering calves, charming farmers,' Ned said. 'What else can you do, Audrey?'

Audrey swallowed, her mouth dry suddenly. 'Charming farmers?' she said. 'What do you mean?'

'Well, you've obviously got grumpy Jacob Sugden wrapped round your finger,' he said. 'And you've charmed me too.'

Audrey gave him a mischievous look. 'But you're not a farmer,' she said. 'You're a farmhand and a greengrocer.'

Ned made a face. 'You've got me. I thought I'd make myself sound more important so I'd impress you.'

Then he looked at her sideways. 'How do you know that, anyway?' he said, a teasing note in his voice. 'Been asking about me?'

Audrey felt her cheeks redden. 'Maybe.'

'I've been asking about you, too.'

'What have you found out?'

He wrinkled his nose, which Audrey thought was very sweet.

'Nothing really.'

She laughed. 'There's not much to find out.'

'Tell me anyway.'

'I'm nineteen. I grew up in Sussex and now I work at Emmerdale Farm.'

'And that's it, is it?'

Audrey shrugged. 'Not much, I told you.' She scuffed the toes of her boots on the ground and looked at Ned. 'What about you?'

'I'm twenty. I grew up here. My parents have the greengrocers over there . . . ' He pointed. 'They grow lots of their own fruit and veg too, now. I help them out and I work all over. Wherever they need me.'

'Why haven't you enlisted?' Audrey said, then regretted it as Ned looked away, his confident demeanour suddenly vanishing.

'Failed the sight test, didn't I?' he muttered. 'Had measles when I were little and it affected my eyes.'

Feeling bold, Audrey reached out and patted his hand, glad he'd sat on her right.

'You're doing the same job I am, and it's really

66

important,' she said. 'People need food.'

He turned back to her. 'You think?'

'I know.'

He grinned, the swagger back as fast as it had gone. 'You got a sweetheart?'

Audrey flushed again at the direct question. 'No,' she said. 'You?'

'Nope.'

There was a pause. Audrey looked down the road, hoping the bus wasn't coming. She was rather enjoying this conversation. Luckily there was no sign of it. Just a young mother, looking slightly flustered, pushing a baby in a pram.

'There's a dance,' Ned said. 'Saturday night, in Hotten. Lots of folk from the village will be there. My sister Sarah and her husband Ray Merrick, and her friend Meg Warcup, and the Prendagast sisters, and Seth Armstrong and Ernie Hudson.'

The names meant nothing to Annie but it sounded exciting. Ned carried on: 'Thought maybe we could go. Together, like.'

'Together,' Audrey said.

Ned grinned again, sending her stomach into those twisting, squirming knots. 'Together.'

Audrey was thrilled. She'd never been to a dance before. And she'd certainly never been asked to a dance by a man. She wondered what it would be like to feel Ned's arms around her on a dancefloor, and thought she'd absolutely like to know for sure.

'I'll need to check with the Sugdens,' Audrey said. 'But if they don't need me, then yes please.'

Ned looked chuffed. 'Great stuff,' he said.

'Good. I'll come and fetch you on Saturday.'

He stood up, and slightly awkwardly put his hands in his pockets.

'See you then,' he said. Kicking at a stone, and raising his hand in greeting to the young mother who was approaching the bus stop, he sauntered away without looking back.

Audrey watched him go, her eyes tracing the shape of his broad back and narrow waist. She hugged herself, already looking forward to Saturday night. What should she wear? Thank goodness she was going to see Tilly and Ginny. They'd know what outfit she should choose and how she should act.

Next to her, the young mother sat down with a sigh. 'Ned Barlow, eh?' she said, a touch of wistfulness in her voice.

Audrey didn't know what to say. 'Do you know him?' she asked, wondering what the woman meant.

The woman gave her a quick smile. 'Known him for years.' Then she nudged Audrey so unexpectedly that she nearly fell off the bus stop bench. 'He's a real catch, is Ned Barlow.'

Audrey's cheeks flamed again. 'We're not . . . ' she began but the woman laughed.

'I'm teasing,' she said. 'It's lovely, meeting someone new and going to the pictures or to dances.'

Audrey smiled. 'I've never done anything like this before.'

'Old news for me,' the woman said, nodding her head at her baby, who was sleeping peacefully in the pram. 'This one's put a stop to all that.'

'She's lovely,' Audrey said politely, though actually she thought all babies looked the same. 'How old is she?'

'She's five months and she's a holy terror,' said the mother. 'She's lucky she's so adorable.'

The woman was sitting on Audrey's left — and now she turned and stuck out her left hand for Audrey to shake.

'I'm Lily,' she said. 'And this is Hope.'

Awkwardly, Audrey showed her left arm and instead offered her right hand. The woman — Lily — looked horrified.

'God, I'm sorry. I didn't notice.'

'Don't be,' Audrey said, shaking her hand. 'I'm Audrey and honestly, it's fine. You weren't to know.'

'There I was being all envious of you, planning a night out with Ned and the whole time you're . . . ' She trailed off.

'It's fine,' Audrey said firmly. There was a small, uncomfortable pause. 'Why don't you come to the dance?' she said suddenly. 'Ned said lots of people from the village are going.'

Lily sighed. 'Oh, I'd love to,' she said. 'My husband Jack used to enjoy a dance too.' She looked proud when she mentioned her husband.

Audrey adopted the same teasing tone the woman had used with her. 'You could have a night out with Jack,' she said. 'A romantic evening, just the two of you.'

Lily smiled, like she was remembering something special.

'How long have you been married?' Audrey asked.

Lily screwed up her nose and looked at the baby. 'A while,' she said vaguely, colour rising in her cheeks. 'But things are different now we've got Hope.'

'Maybe someone could watch her for you?' Audrey said. She was quite taken with Lily, who seemed to be torn between love for her daughter and nostalgia for life before she was a mother. 'What about your mum?'

Lily grimaced. 'My mum died, few years back,' she said and it was Audrey's turn to feel bad.

'Sorry,' she muttered.

'But my stepmother might be persuaded. She adores Hope.'

Audrey was pleased. 'There you go, then. Your stepmother can have the baby and you and your husband can have some fun.'

Lily looked thrilled and worried at the same time. 'Do you think it would be all right for me to go to a dance?' she asked. 'Even though I'm married, and a mother. Is it proper?'

Audrey had absolutely no idea if it was proper or not, but Lily seemed very far from her own mother, who was anxious and rather resistant to fun so she nodded. 'I think it's important for Hope to have a mum who knows how to enjoy herself,' she said.

Lily beamed at her. 'Then yes, if Nina can look after Hope, Jack and I will come along. It'll be great to have a night off.' She looked at Audrey. 'Who are you?' she said. 'Why are you sitting at the bus stop, making me feel better about things?'

'I'm a Land Girl,' Audrey said, laughing at her

new friend's quizzical expression. 'I work at Emmerdale Farm with Jacob Sugden, and I didn't mean to make you feel better, but I'm glad I did.'

Lily looped her arm through Audrey's and grinned at her. 'I'm glad too,' she said. 'Now while we're waiting for this blasted bus to show up, tell me everything about you and Ned Barlow.'

7

Ginny and Tilly were, predictably, terribly overexcited about Audrey going to the dance with Ned.

'I can't believe it's been arranged on our weekend off,' Tilly grumbled as they wandered down the main street in Hotten after Audrey had got off the bus.

'I know, it's rotten luck,' Audrey said. 'But there will be another one soon, I'm sure. There are so many training camps round here, and the men will need to blow off steam.'

'I've heard there are GIs coming,' Tilly said, with a glint in her eye. 'They'll throw a dance for them, definitely.'

'Tilly, you've already got yourself a GI. Leave some for the rest of us.'

Tilly made a pretend cross face at her friend and Audrey laughed, pleased to be back in the company of the other Land Girls.

They crossed the street and went into a tea room recommended by Maggie. 'The woman who runs it is a miracle-worker,' she'd said. 'One taste of her fruit cake and you'd forget there's a war on.'

She was right, too. The cake was delicious, and the tea just as Audrey liked it. And, of course, the company was wonderful. Audrey thought she'd never laughed as much in her whole life as she did that afternoon. She'd told her friends all about the drama with the calf and they'd hooted with mirth.

'Imagine going to all that effort, for a cow that wasn't even from your farm,' Ginny chuckled.

'Honestly, Gin, if you'd seen me flying down the lane to the vet. Riding Jacob's bicycle, and wobbling all over the place . . . ' Audrey was laughing too. 'I was terrified.'

Tilly looked at Audrey over the top of her tea cup. 'Bet you weren't,' she said. 'Nothing seems to scare you.'

Audrey flushed at the praise, but she shook her head. 'Jacob bloody Sugden scares me. He's nice enough, but he's a right grumpy one when he wants to be.'

'Is he nice looking?' Ginny looked interested and Audrey made a face.

'No.' Then she thought. 'Well, he's nice enough, I suppose. He's sort of dark and brooding. But I'd stick with the GIs if I were you, Gin.' She grinned at her friends. 'What's Smithers like?'

'Ginny's got him wound round her little finger,' Tilly said.

Ginny gave her a firm nudge, spilling her tea. 'He's a sweetie,' she said. 'He reminds me of my dad.'

Audrey felt a pang at the mention of fathers. She missed her own dad terribly and often thought of things she'd like to tell him. But she knew it was just too difficult at the moment, so she stored up her news in the hope that one day she'd get to share it.

'So,' Ginny said eventually, 'tell us about this chap who's invited you to the dance.'

'Ned,' Audrey said. A little thrill ran through her just saying his name. 'He's a bit older than me, tall, very strong . . . '

'Not married?' Tilly said shrewdly. 'Farmer, is he? Why's he not enlisted?'

'He's a greengrocer,' Audrey said. 'At least his family are greengrocers. He helps them on their vegetable plots and works at some of the farms locally. But he's not enlisted because he failed the sight test.'

Ginny nodded approvingly.

'Do you think he'll be a good dancer?' she asked, a dreamy look in her eye. 'Because, in my experience, men who dance well do other things well too.'

Audrey's cheeks reddened again at the thought, and she was grateful when Tilly saw her discomfort and stepped in.

'What are you going to wear?'

'I've got a frock I brought from home, that I think will do,' Audrey said. 'I might see if I can make the skirt a bit fuller. Maybe add some ribbon round the neck and make it fancier, if I can.'

'You could pin some little flowers in your hair,' Ginny suggested, looking at Audrey appraisingly. 'As you can't wear it up. Pick some primroses from the verges. They'll look gorgeous. And . . . ' she leaned down to pick up her handbag and rummaged through it. 'Take this.' She held out a tube of lipstick. 'It's coral pink. It'll suit you.'

Audrey was so pleased, she could barely breathe. 'Honestly?'

'There's not much left. But take it.'

Audrey took the tube and opened it. Inside was a short stick of bright coral lipstick, well-used of course, but still more than enough. She thought she might even be able to make it last for years if she used it sparingly.

'This is beautiful,' she said. 'Are you definitely sure?'

Ginny grinned. 'Take it, use it, enjoy it, and get that handsome, short-sighted greengrocer to kiss it all off.'

'Ginny!' Tilly chided, but she was smiling too. 'Have fun, Audrey.'

★　★　★

The lipstick was perfect, Audrey thought as she got ready for the dance on Saturday evening. She'd never been one for worrying about how she looked or fretting over her hair or cosmetics, but she'd really enjoyed getting everything sorted for the dance. Maggie had let her have a look in her 'bits and bobs bag' as she called it. It was full of material scraps, buttons, ribbons and fasteners. To her delight, Audrey had found a bright yellow ribbon — from an Easter bonnet from years ago, Maggie told her. 'Did Jacob make it?' Audrey had asked, unable to imagine Jacob as a little boy in a silly hat.

Maggie had frowned for a moment and then smiled. 'I think it was Edward who made that one,' she said sadly. Audrey knew now that Edward was Maggie's son, who'd been killed in action the previous year, so she'd immediately held the ribbon out to the older woman.

'You keep it,' she said.

But Maggie had shaken her head. 'No, no point in it gathering dust in my bag. Edward would want you to have it.'

And so, Audrey had trimmed the neckline of her dress with it. She was quite a competent hand sewer, as long as someone threaded the needle for her, and she was pleased with the result which freshened up her old frock a treat. Then, as Tilly had suggested, she'd gone out to find some primroses; the bright yellow flowers filled her heart with gladness as she saw them blooming on the grass verges. With a bit of help from Maggie, she'd pinned them into her hair, and then slicked on the coral lippy. And now she was ready.

'You look pretty as a picture,' Maggie said. Much to Audrey's surprise, she leaned over and gave her a quick hug. 'It's nice having another woman around the place again.'

Audrey wondered what Maggie meant by 'again' but she was too distracted with nerves and excitement about the dance that she didn't ask.

'Is Ned coming to fetch you?' Maggie said.

Audrey made a face. 'No,' she said. 'He was supposed to be, but there was some trouble with the cabbages, or something. So he said he'd meet me at the bus stop.'

Maggie smiled. 'I'll take you down in the trap, if you like? You don't want to be walking and getting yourself dusty from the lane.'

'That would be wonderful.' Audrey beamed at Maggie, who she was starting to grow rather fond of.

★　★　★

Thanks to Maggie's transport, Audrey arrived at the bus stop earlier than she'd arranged with Ned. She was happy to sit and wait though, so she waved off Maggie's offer to stay, said thank you and wandered over to the shelter where she could linger until Ned arrived. She felt a delicious fluttering of butterflies in her stomach, as though she was on the brink of something thrilling. Like a child waking up in the morning and realising it was Christmas Day, or when she'd walked into the county office to join the Land Army.

She bounced a little on her toes, wondering if Ned would be a good dancer. She wasn't particularly light on her feet, but she could manage a passable waltz. At school dances Audrey had often been left sitting by the side of the room, while her friends were asked to dance. She'd assumed it was because the boys felt awkward about her missing hand and weren't comfortable dancing with her. And, oddly enough, she hadn't minded really. She understood that young men were gawky and uncomfortable at the best of times, so adding a missing hand into the mix made things a hundred times worse. She'd enjoyed sitting there, soaking up the atmosphere, listening to the music, and dancing when she had the chance. But her mother had spoken to one of the chaperones, discovered that Audrey was left out, and stopped her going to any more dances despite her protests. More fun she'd missed out on, she thought now resentfully. But not anymore. Audrey

Atkins was going dancing and she was going to blooming well enjoy every second.

'Are you Audrey?' said a voice. Audrey turned to see a woman, about her age or a bit older, looking at her. She looked vaguely familiar.

'Yes?' she said. 'Who are you?'

'Elizabeth Barlow,' the woman said. 'I'm Ned's sister.'

So that was why she looked familiar. She shared the same eyes as her brother, though hers were narrowed as she looked at Audrey.

'Is there a problem?' Audrey asked politely, wondering if Ned had sent his sister to find her. 'Is Ned all right?'

Elizabeth shrugged. 'Not seen him since this morning,' she said. 'He's been sorting the cabbages.'

'I heard.'

There was a pause. Elizabeth sat down at the bus shelter. Audrey stayed standing. She was a bit wary of this prickly Barlow sibling. Ned had told her he was closer to his oldest sister Sarah than he was to Elizabeth, even though she was closer in age to him. But she thought she should make an effort with her, so she forced a smile. 'Are you going to the dance?' she asked.

Elizabeth sighed. 'I'm supposed to be, but my Oliver is keeping me waiting as usual.' She let her head fall back, dramatically. 'Aren't men just the worst?'

Audrey rather liked most of the men she knew, but she wrinkled her nose, shrugged her shoulders, and hoped Elizabeth would think she was agreeing with her.

'You know who's the absolute worst?' Elizabeth said. She brought her head back up and gave Audrey a piercing stare.

'Who?' said Audrey cautiously, sensing that she wasn't going to like the answer.

'Ned.'

There it was. Audrey didn't want to ask for more details, but it seemed Elizabeth was going to give them anyway.

'He's got a different girl on his arm every week,' she said. 'He's definitely one for a pretty face.' Slowly and deliberately she let her gaze run from the primroses in Audrey's hair down to her feet in her battered old party shoes. Elizabeth kept her stare on Audrey's missing hand for a second or two longer than was polite and Audrey felt herself bristle. But she didn't want to get into an argument in the street with Ned's sister of all people so she stayed quiet.

'Yes, he's definitely got an eye for the ladies, has our Ned,' Elizabeth went on. She gave a little laugh that Audrey suspected wasn't genuine. 'Of course, you're new in the village so it's no wonder he's snapped you up. You're about the only girl this side of Hotten who's not stepped out with him.'

Audrey felt queasy. Ned hadn't seemed that way at all in the short time she'd known him. Was he the sort of man who chopped and changed sweethearts more often than he changed his shirt? She hoped not. But this was his sister, surely she knew him better than anyone . . . She took a breath, wondering what to say.

'Audrey,' said a voice behind her and there, to her relief, was Ned, looking clean and smart in a shirt and jacket. She couldn't stop herself smiling, despite the horrible things she'd just been hearing.

Ned came to her and took her hand. 'You look beautiful,' he said and Audrey felt the butterflies again.

'So do you,' she said and laughed at herself for calling this burly man beautiful. Ned's eyes shone with pride, and then his expression changed as he looked over Audrey's shoulder and saw his sister at the bus stop.

'Elizabeth,' he said.

She gave him an unfriendly smile. 'I was just getting to know Audrey.'

Ned's grip on Audrey's hand tightened. 'I thought you were meeting Oliver Skilbeck?' he said to his sister.

'I am.'

'Well, reckon he's forgotten because I've just seen him going into the Woolpack.'

Elizabeth gave a frustrated sigh, gathered up her belongings and marched off across the village to the pub.

Ned and Audrey sat down where Elizabeth had been and Ned gave Audrey a cheeky smile. 'I've not seen Oliver all day,' he admitted. 'I just wanted rid of her. She's always been on the miserable side, but she's been horrible since she started going with Oliver. She's snappy and irritable and always on the defensive. He's a nasty piece of work but she won't listen, just lashes out at anyone who seems happy.'

Audrey felt a wave of sympathy for Elizabeth. 'Poor her,' she said.

Ned made a face. 'Hopefully he'll ditch her soon enough and she'll get back to her normal grouchy self,' he said. He smiled at her and Audrey's butterflies fluttered madly in her stomach. 'But let's not worry about her,' he said. 'Let's just have some fun.'

8

'Do you know, I don't think that's half bad?' Betty Prendagast gave her sister's lips a final dab with a brush and passed her a hand mirror.

Margaret, pouted at her reflection, showing off her dark-red mouth. 'It's worked brilliantly, hasn't it? Who'd have thought beetroot would do instead of lipstick?'

Betty rolled her eyes. 'Who'd have thought we'd be painting our legs with gravy browning? We're going out dressed as a plate of Sunday lunch.'

Margaret chuckled. 'Here, you sit and I'll do your lips for you. And you never know, maybe we'll meet a handsome GI tonight, with a bag full of silk stockings and lipsticks.'

Betty pursed her lips as Margaret dabbed the brush into the bowl of boiled beetroot and then on to her mouth. 'You might meet a GI,' she said, trying not to move her lips. 'I'm taken, remember?'

Margaret scoffed. 'Seth Armstrong isn't the one for you, Betty. He's running rings around you while you follow him round like some daft ha'porth.'

Betty bristled, snatching the mirror from her sister and admiring her reflection. 'Seth's good to me.'

'When he wants to be. When he's not up to no good with that Ernie Hudson.'

'Ah, he and Ernie are thick as thieves, that's all. It's nice he's got a good friend.'

Margaret scoffed again and Betty ignored her, patting her hair into position. Thing was, deep down she knew her sister was right. She adored Seth, who'd been her sweetheart for years, and she knew he felt the same about her. At least she hoped he did. Because that was the trouble, you see Seth never really showed how he felt about Betty. They had a lovely time when they were together but he was never exactly falling over himself to spend time with her. He was a gamekeeper up at the Miffield Hall estate and he loved it. Betty even suspected his boss, Mr Verney, had pulled some strings to keep Seth working on the estate instead of being called up. She was pleased about that mind you, so she didn't want to ask too many questions. But no, Betty was in no doubt that Seth's job came first. Well, his job and playing the fool with his friends. And his ridiculous all-consuming love/hate friendship with Ernie. She sighed. Maybe Margaret was right; maybe Seth wasn't the one for her after all.

As if sensing she was feeling gloomy Margaret tugged at her sleeve. 'Can you show me that jive again. I can't get it right.'

Betty grinned. She knew her very well, did Margaret, and she realised that the one thing always guaranteed to lift her mood was dancing.

'Put the wireless on,' Betty said. She slid down from her seat and waited for Margaret to fiddle about with the dial until she found some music.

'It's tricky because you go backwards and

forwards, and side to side,' Betty showed her sister the moves, and Margaret wailed in despair.

'How do you just pick it up straight away?' she said.

Betty chuckled. 'I'm just lucky.'

Margaret jumped about the room a few times, trying to get to grips with which way her feet should be going until their father shouted up the stairs that they were making the whole ceiling shake and could they please stop thumping about.

Laughing, the girls checked their appearance one more time and headed downstairs to catch the bus to Hotten.

Their mother, Nora, came out of the lounge to see what they were wearing and nodded in approval. 'You look lovely, girls,' she said.

Betty gave her a twirl. 'We're doing our bit for the war effort,' she joked.

Nora smacked her gently on the bottom with her magazine. 'Don't be so cheeky, Betty,' she said light-heartedly and the girls giggled. 'Now geroff or you'll miss the bus.'

They had to run for the bus, which was already at the stop when they left home, but they caught it just in time. It was full of local Beckindale people heading to the dance hall. There was an excited atmosphere as the sisters climbed aboard and the buzz of conversation was loud. Betty waved hello to Meg Warcup and her friends, and nodded at Ned Barlow who she'd gone to school with. He was sitting next to a pretty young woman wearing bright coral lipstick who Betty didn't recognise.

84

She pretended she wasn't looking for Seth but she was really, so she was delighted when she spotted him towards the back of the bus.

'Betty!' he called. 'Saved you a seat.'

She skipped down the aisle, ignoring Margaret's huffing and puffing behind her, and plonked herself down on the seat next to him. He kissed her cheek and she breathed in the smell of his hair oil, feeling dizzy just from being close to him. He looked so handsome in his checked shirt, with his hair slicked back. She would be proud to be on his arm tonight.

Margaret, in the seat behind, leaned forward and tapped Seth on the shoulder. 'Aren't you going to ask Betty about her new job?'

For a second, Seth's face was blank, then he grinned as he realised what Margaret was talking about.

'At the vet?' he said. 'You got it?'

Betty clapped her hands excitedly. 'I did. I'm the new receptionist and I start on Monday.'

'Ee, that's great,' said Seth proudly and Betty beamed. 'What's she like? That new vet? She's not been up to Miffield Hall yet, least not when I've been there. But I've heard she's proper difficult.'

Suddenly deflated, Betty lifted her chin. 'She's very nice, actually. Clever as anything. And she wanted me special. She'd heard about me in the village and thought I'd make a good reception-ist.'

'She doesn't smile much,' Margaret said thoughtfully.

'She's got a lot to think about,' said Betty,

85

though she wasn't completely sure what a vet would have to think about other than . . . well, dogs that were sick and sheep that had nosebleeds, but she'd find out. She was just pleased she didn't have to go back to that awful factory where they worked in silence and there were no windows.

'Well, good luck to you,' said Seth. 'Reckon you'll need it.'

Annoyed that he'd made her feel bad about her news, Betty pretended to stare out of the window as the bus wound its way into Hotten. Really she was watching Ned Barlow and the girl he was with in the reflection in the glass. They were chatting animatedly, their eyes fixed on each other. The girl's coral lips were gleaming and Ned couldn't take his gaze from her face. They were completely focused on one another, as though the smelly bus barking out black clouds of fumes, and its noisy passengers, didn't exist.

Betty sighed again. She and Seth had never been that way with each other, not really. They'd just kind of grown together; it hadn't been a sudden lightning bolt or a clash of drums and cymbals. Just familiarity and, yes, she thought, love.

Next to her, Seth shifted in his seat and feeling a flush of affection she took his hand in hers. He squeezed her fingers and smiled at her.

'You look beautiful tonight, Betty my love,' he said. Betty's stomach flipped over with joy. She hoped Margaret had heard. That would teach her to think Seth wasn't the one for her.

She went to tell Seth that he looked lovely too but before she could speak he let go of her hand and leaned into the aisle.

'Ernie,' he shouted. 'Ernie, whatever you drink tonight, I reckon I can drink more.'

Up at the front of the bus, Seth's best friend and sometime rival, Ernie, grinned. 'That sounds like a challenge to me.'

Betty groaned. If Seth was on the sauce tonight, then chances were, she'd be dancing alone.

The bus pulled up at the stop by the hall where the dance was being held and nearly all the passengers hurried off, eager to get started. Betty was chuffed when Seth took her hand and led her inside, and gave Margaret a little triumphant glance over her shoulder. Margaret stuck her tongue out from between her beetroot-red lips and Betty laughed. She loved dances and parties and being in a crowd of happy people having fun.

Seth was full of beans tonight too — he liked being out on the town, as well — and as soon as the band struck up, he whirled Betty on to the dancefloor. He was quite light on his feet, her Seth, for such a burly man, and he tried his best, but Betty knew he wasn't as good as she was. She didn't mind, though. She kept the steps simple and just enjoyed being with him, feeling his arms round her and his hands warm on her back through the thin fabric of her dress.

On stage, the band had been joined by a singer. She was about Betty's age, but looked older because she was dolled up in a way that made Betty's heart ache with envy. She looked like she'd stepped out of the screen at the pictures with her smooth, powdered skin, her glossy lips and her hair twisted into shiny victory rolls. She was wearing a dress similar to Betty's but it hung better and draped elegantly round her knees in a way that made it clear hers hadn't been made from an old tablecloth.

'Look at her,' Betty said to Seth. 'Her up on stage. Isn't she wonderful?'

Seth glanced at the woman and then back to Betty. 'She's not a patch on you,' he said and Betty felt a warm glow inside.

The band struck up a jive, and Seth grimaced. 'This one's not for me,' he said. 'I'm off to find Ernie, see what the old bugger's up to.'

He gave Betty one last twirl and headed off. Betty was disappointed for a second but her feet were twitching and as always, Margaret knew what she was thinking as she appeared by her side.

'Come on then,' she said, taking Betty's hands. 'Show us what you can do.'

All the practising in their bedroom paid off as Margaret and Betty kicked and hopped their way across the dancefloor, breathless and laughing with the sheer joy of it. Other couples made room for them and some even stopped to watch — Betty saw Jack Proudfoot and his new wife Lily standing by and clapping as they whirled past and gave them a quick wave. And when the number came to an end, everyone applauded and Betty thought she'd never been happier in her whole life. Which was silly really, when she thought about how she'd felt the first time she'd kissed Seth, or when he'd asked her to be his girl.

'I need a drink after that,' Margaret said. Her cheeks were red from dancing and a strand of her hair had escaped from its roll.

'I need to go to the ladies,' Betty said. 'Can you get me a cider?'

She gave Margaret some money and weaved her way through the dancers to the lav. Much as she disliked covering her legs with gravy browning, she couldn't help thinking it was much easier to deal with than actual stockings were. As she was washing her hands, she caught the eye of the woman next to her in the mirror. It was the girl who'd been with Ned Barlow on the bus. Betty grinned at her.

'I know you,' she said. 'You're from Beckindale.'

The girl smiled back. 'I am. I live at Emmerdale Farm.'

'Ah,' said Betty, remembering her mum had said something about Maggie getting some help. 'The Land Girl?'

'That's me,' the girl dropped a jokey curtsey. 'My name's Audrey.'

Betty did a full-on theatrical bow, doffing an imaginary top hat. 'Betty.'

Audrey looked amused at Betty's performance. 'You're a wonderful dancer,' she said. 'I saw you out there. Everyone was watching.'

'I love dancing.'

'I can tell. You should be on the stage.'

Betty laughed with delight at the compliment.

'I'm serious,' Audrey said. 'I grew up in Worthing and you're just as good as the dancers we'd have in the shows on the pier. Better, even.'

'I'd have loved to have been a dancer,' Betty admitted. 'When I was a little girl, it was all I wanted to do. I used to put on shows for my parents in the front room and charge them entry. I'd make my sister Margaret take the money on the door but I never shared the proceeds with her.'

Audrey chuckled. 'That sounds very inventive.'

'Not sure Margaret would agree,' joked Betty. She admired her new friend in the mirror. 'I love your lippy,' she said. 'Is it real? A real lipstick?'

'My friend Ginny gave it to me,' Audrey said. She dug in her handbag and pulled it out to show Betty. 'She's got a boyfriend who's a GI.'

'Nice,' Betty said. 'My sister Margaret was hoping to meet a GI tonight, but there aren't any here.'

Audrey shrugged. 'I bet they don't all have bags full of lippies anyway.'

Together they wandered through the hall until Audrey saw Ned and skipped off to join him. Betty found Margaret, still at the bar. She was chatting to a very tall, skinny man in RAF uniform and seemed completely enthralled so Betty decided to give them a minute before she interrupted. She looked for Seth, but couldn't see him, so she stayed put at the side of the dancefloor, swaying a little to the music.

'You're a dancer?' a voice said behind her. She turned to see the singer she'd admired earlier.

'Me?' Betty spluttered. 'A dancer? Not really. I

90

mean, I did lessons with Miss Diana in Hotten for years, but I'm not a dancer. I'm a receptionist for a vet. At least, I will be, come Monday. I've not started yet . . . ' She realised she was babbling and trailed off. 'Sorry,' she said. 'I always get a bit giddy at dances.'

'I'm Pamela,' the singer said. 'Nice to meet you.'

'Betty,' said Betty, shaking Pamela's hand vigorously. 'You sing so beautifully.'

Pamela ducked her head in modesty. 'Thank you,' she said. Then she looked at Betty as though she'd just had an idea.

'I'm with ENSA,' she began. Betty obviously looked blank because Pamela carried on, 'The Entertainments National Services Association? We do concerts and shows for the forces.'

Betty breathed out slowly. A whole association dedicated to entertainment? She hadn't even known such a thing existed.

'Like Vera Lynn?'

Pamela chuckled. 'Sort of. There are lots of us. We're based nearby for a few weeks and I wondered if you might be interested in helping us out. Costumes, make-up, that sort of thing? We're always short of backstage crew and it's a good way to get some experience in the entertainment world. I thought you might be interested in that sort of thing.'

'Really?' Betty could honestly not think of anything else she'd like more.

'Really,' said Pamela. 'But not if it's going to be a problem with your new job. It would mostly be evenings.'

91

Evenings were when Betty spent time with Seth. Still, Pamela had said it was only a few weeks.

'I can make it work,' Betty said. 'Absolutely no problem at all. When do you need me?'

9

Betty was all over the place on Monday morning. Nervous about starting her new job, excited that she wasn't getting the bus into Hotten to go to the horrible factory, and underneath it all, still giddy about her conversation with Pamela at the dance. She'd given Betty a piece of paper, on which she'd written the address of the base where the ENSA performers were working for the next few weeks, and asked her to come along on Wednesday week to help sort through some costumes. Betty had agreed, thrilled to bits at the idea of seeing what went into a proper stage production.

She'd told Margaret all about it, but she'd not mentioned it to Seth. She didn't really know why other than she was still smarting about his negative reaction to her new job. She couldn't bear it if he did the same with this ENSA volunteering, too.

'Right then, Elizabeth,' she said to her reflection in the mirror. She was wearing a smart dress that had once been her mother's and had been altered to fit. Her mum had sewn a pussycat bow on to the collar and Betty thought it made the dress look much younger, but still smart enough for a receptionist in a vet's surgery. She straightened her skirt, picked up her bag, and headed off downstairs to see if there was any tea in the pot before she went across to start work.

The vet's surgery was in chaos when she arrived at nine o'clock, just as Nancy had asked her to. There were already two people waiting to see the vet; a man with a dog, and one older woman — Mrs Roberts, who was Susan's grandmother — with a carry basket on her lap. Betty could hear a bird screeching in the back room and another dog barking, and Nancy was on the phone, leaning over the desk, and scribbling something in the appointments diary, upside down, as she spoke.

'I could be with you about eleven,' she was saying. 'I'm really sorry, I can't do anything earlier than that.'

Betty took a step into the waiting room, her nerves threatening to get the better of her and gave Nancy a small wave to show her she had arrived. Nancy looked flustered and relieved at the same time and made a gesture towards the waiting animals and their owners, that Betty couldn't quite interpret.

Taking a deep breath, Betty put her bag down on the desk chair, and turned to the owners.

'Who's first?' she said.

'Hello Betty,' said Mrs Roberts, who Betty could now see had a fat orange cat on her lap in the battered basket. She lifted the lid and a pitiful mew floated out. 'I think it was me. My Clifford's got an infected gum. He's not himself.'

'Oh dear,' said Betty faintly. She wasn't sure this was exactly how she'd thought her new job would be. She thought she should probably say

94

thank you to Mrs Roberts for putting a word in for her with Nancy, in a roundabout way, but somehow she couldn't find the words.

Nancy was still talking, looking worried.

'If you prefer to go to the larger surgery in Hotten, that's up to you, Mr Chesham,' she said. She pointed to Clifford and then to the examination room behind them and Betty nodded.

'Could you take Clifford through and Miss Tate will be there presently?' she said to Mrs Roberts.

'Will do, Betty love.' Mrs Roberts took her yowling cat through the door and Betty breathed a sigh of relief.

'I can assure you, I'm every bit as qualified as Mr Walters,' Nancy was saying. 'I'm just looking after the practice for him while he's in the army.'

Betty reached over the desk and turned the appointment book round so she could see what was written there. 'Felix?' she said.

The dog's ears pricked up.

'We're just here to pick up some medicine,' his owner said. He was a farmer from the other side of the village who Betty knew by sight.

Betty looked round and saw a cupboard by the desk with a neatly handwritten sign saying 'medication' on the door. She unlocked it, with the key that was in the lock, and found a packet of pills with Felix's name and the farmer's details on the label. Pleased, she handed them over, urging the owner to read the instructions, and off they went.

As the farmer left, Nancy was finishing her

95

conversation. 'Well, I don't know exactly when Mr Walters will be back,' she said. 'That rather depends on Herr Hitler.' She slammed down the phone receiver, looking aghast. 'Another patient lost,' she said. She'd run her fingers through her hair so much that her once-neat roll was dishevelled, and she only had make-up on one of her eyes. 'What an awful morning. I overslept and then there were patients here as soon as I opened the door.'

Betty gave her what she hoped was a sympathetic smile. 'Better off without that one, I reckon,' she said. 'Why don't you go and sort out Clifford's gums. I'll make some tea, and get myself familiar with everything. And I think I'll start half an hour earlier from now on — so I can be here before the patients.'

Nancy stared at her and for a second Betty thought she might cry, but instead she nodded, firmly. 'That sounds excellent, thank you.'

Betty soon discovered that the vet's surgery was in a mess. Someone — she assumed it was Nancy — had tried to organise a few things, sorting out invoices and writing down appointments, but it was clear they needed a proper system. She made tea and took a mug into Nancy, who had examined poor Clifford's gums, and was now looking at the wing of the squawking budgie.

'It's looking much better,' she was cooing to the bird. 'Much better, you pretty boy.'

Betty put the mug down on the side. 'There's tea there for you,' she said.

Nancy barely acknowledged it, just glanced

over her shoulder and then back at the bird. Betty bristled, just slightly. 'Everything's in a right old mess, if you don't mind me saying. I can sort it all out, but you need to let me get on with it all. Is that going to be all right?'

Nancy looked round again, as she let the bird jump off her hand and on to the examination table. 'Whatever you need to do,' she said.

'It's not going to be easy.'

'I know.' Nancy bit her lip, suddenly looking much younger and Betty felt a rush of sympathy for her. She wasn't much older than she was herself, and here she was in a strange place, trying to run her own business.

'Listen,' she said. 'I'm quick to learn, and I'm organised, and I know everyone in this village. I can have this whole place running smoothly in no time at all. How about you concentrate on the animals and I do everything else.'

Nancy picked up her mug of tea and took a large gulp. Again, Betty saw that look on her face, like she was about to cry, and again Nancy gathered herself before she spoke. 'That would be excellent.' She paused. 'Thank you.'

Thinking Nancy was warming up, Betty leaned against the wall of the treatment room. 'What brought you to Beckindale, then?' she asked. 'Someone in the village said you're from over Scarborough way?'

Nancy glared at her and Betty regretted trying to make conversation. 'I'm just looking after the place for Mr Walters,' Nancy said shortly, which Betty obviously knew already. She opened her mouth to ask another question but Nancy gave her such a look that she shut it again without saying what she was going to say.

'I'll get on then,' she muttered. Betty turned to go, as the budgie, which had decided to test its poorly wing by going for a swoop around the room, landed on her shoulder.

'Oooh,' she said in surprise. 'Hello there.'

Nancy smiled for the first time that morning. 'Maybe you should do the animals too,' she said wryly.

Betty chuckled, pleased to see her new boss was human after all. 'Ah no, I'll stick to the paperwork,' she said. 'I'm not right good with fur and feathers, me.'

She looked round at the budgie, which was still perched on her shoulder, and watched in disbelief as it did its business right there, leaving a trail of white goo all down her mother's dress.

Betty looked at Nancy, who was — to Betty's surprise — trying very hard not to laugh. 'Paperwork,' she said, beginning to giggle herself. 'And maybe I'll bring a coat to wear over my clothes while I'm here?'

'Leave it with me,' Nancy said, sounding much more cheerful than she had all day. 'Thanks for the tea.'

★ ★ ★

Nancy wasn't all bad, Betty thought later that day. She was just overworked and frightened of failing. Any fool could see that if they took five minutes to think about why the new vet might be

98

grumpy. She remembered that it was her Seth who'd told her about Nancy's moods, and felt bad for thinking of him as a fool. But even though she could see why the new vet wasn't the cheeriest soul, she still felt that working here was going to be a bit of a battle. Better than factory work, though, she reminded herself.

She'd had a look through the appointments book, horrified at the mess that things had been in up until now. After a lot of scribbling and rubbing out, she had come up with a way for Nancy to organise her time — doing appointments at the surgery in the morning, and visits to farms after lunch. From three o'clock each afternoon, there was to be nothing scheduled so Nancy could deal with emergencies, or do any other treatments she had to fit in.

Betty had a pile of cheques to pay into the bank, which she decided she'd do the following afternoon, once Nancy had given her the right paying-in book. And she'd typed up five outstanding invoices. Luckily, given how chaotic the rest of the place was, it was quite straightforward because someone — again she assumed it was Nancy — had marked which ones had been paid and which hadn't.

The door to the surgery opened and a schoolgirl came in. She was the evacuee, Susan Roberts, the granddaughter of the lady with the fat orange cat. Everyone had been talking about her when she first arrived in Beckindale because she always seemed so sad. She'd lost someone in the Blitz, apparently. Betty couldn't bear thinking about it. Margaret was a pain sometimes and her parents could drive her mad, but she couldn't imagine losing any of them. It must have been awful.

'Are you Betty?' the girl said and Betty jumped, hoping she hadn't been staring. She gave Susan her most dazzling smile.

'I am indeed. And you must be Susan. I've had your gran in here this morning, with Clifford. She was telling me how much you love animals.'

Susan dropped her schoolbag on one of the chairs. 'I want to be a vet,' she said. 'I've been helping Nancy after school. Did you see what I did with the invoices?'

Realisation dawned on Betty. 'That was you?' She was impressed. 'Goodness, that was really helpful. There's a lot of work to do here but it would have been a lot worse if it wasn't for you. You're a clever old thing, aren't you?'

Susan looked pleased. 'Is Nancy here?'

Betty shook her head. 'Gone up to Emmerdale Farm to look over their calves and check on one of the cows who's got mastitis.' She stumbled over the unfamiliar word and grimaced, but Susan just nodded, like it all made perfect sense.

'I'll go and see the animals out the back. Is the budgie still here?'

Betty gestured to her shoulder where the evidence of the budgie was still apparent, even though she'd sponged it off more than once. 'It's still here.'

Susan gave a quick smile that lit up her whole face. 'Nancy got me a white coat to wear while

I'm here. I love it. It makes me feel like a real vet.'

She perched on the edge of the desk, looking earnest. 'Nancy's really kind,' she said. 'I know she can be hard to work with, Betty. But she's got a lot on her plate. She's snappy and that but she doesn't mean it. Honestly.'

Betty tried to smile at the girl but found she couldn't. 'She's not the friendliest person I've met,' she said.

Susan looked worried. 'You're not thinking of going back to the factory?'

Was she? Betty wasn't entirely sure. When she'd taken this job, she'd pictured herself sitting behind a neat desk, maybe with a pair of glasses perched on her perfect nose — Betty didn't wear glasses but she thought secretaries needed them — as she typed letters on a large typewriter and answered phone calls. But instead her hair was messy, she had budgie business on her shoulder, she was mentally exhausted from rearranging Nancy's diary and she'd made so many cups of tea, she may as well have applied for a job in a café instead. Susan was looking at her anxiously.

'Are you?'

Betty looked at the piles of admin on her desk after just one day in the job, the ink stains on her hands and the stain on her dress. She thought about Pamela, the glamorous woman from the dance, and wondered if she'd ever been messed on by a budgie. She very much doubted it. Pamela's world was very different from Betty's but that was just how it was. Betty could do a good job here, and she'd see more of Seth if she

101

was working locally, plus she still had the chance to go and help out with the ENSA show. It was all good.

'I'll stay,' she said. 'For now.'

10

'Thanks for all your hard work today, Betty,' Nancy called as her new receptionist skipped off down the path from the practice front door. Betty waved gaily and danced across the road, narrowly avoiding Ruby who was charging towards the garage on her bicycle. Nancy watched her go. She really was something else, that Betty. She was going to be a very good receptionist, Nancy thought. She was quick-thinking, funny, and full of life. Her good temper seemed to rub off on everyone, calming down a frantic farmer on the telephone who was worried about a horse, and even squeezing a laugh out of grumpy Mrs Baxter — owner of the budgie who'd mistaken her shoulder for a toilet.

'Is it all right if I get off too?' Susan said. 'I'd really like to get home and check on Clifford.'

Nancy tried not to be irritated by the girl's eagerness. Of course it was all right for her to go home. Nancy didn't own her. Determined to not snap at Susan again, and horribly aware the poor child bore the brunt of her bad moods, she gave her a tired smile and tried to be extra kind.

'Of course it is. Give him an extra tummy rub from me. And let me know if you're struggling with that biology homework. I can go through it with you tomorrow.'

Susan picked up her schoolbag and darted off, and wearily Nancy went back inside, sat down at

Betty's desk and picked up the ledger. Betty had spent the afternoon going through the accounts — she had a head for numbers, apparently, judging by the scribbled sums and neat figures she'd written in the books. Suddenly longing for a soft sofa and a cup of tea, Nancy took the heavy paperwork in her arms and went upstairs to her little flat. Predictably, there was no food in the house to speak of, so she toasted a couple of slices of stale bread and spread it thinly with some jam that one of her patient's owners had given her. Then she sat down, with her tea and toast, and read through all Betty's work.

It made grim reading. Really grim. So grim, in fact, that the last mouthful of toast turned to sawdust in her mouth and she had to wash it down with a gulp of tea. Things were not looking good.

Nancy had been telling the truth to the annoyed client on the telephone this morning. She was only taking care of the practice while Mr Walters was away. He'd handed over his business — the business he'd been running for ten years with some success — to her so he could go and join the Royal Army Veterinary Corps. Nancy was paying him rent for the premises, and running her own business there, on the understanding that she'd leave as soon as he got back. She'd jumped at the chance to take it on, even though she'd been daunted by the enormity of the task, because she was struggling to find a job elsewhere. She'd been doing shifts covering vets who were away from their practices since she graduated from university — one of just two female vets in her year. But no one seemed to want to employ a woman permanently. She had a lot to prove — to Mr Walters who'd taken a chance on her, to the vets who'd turned her down for jobs, to her university lecturers who'd thought she would give up, like Heather Allen — the other female vet in her year — had, and more than anything else, to her father. She felt the weight of expectation on her shoulders. But the way these figures were looking, she'd be closing the doors on the surgery before the year was out. And what would that prove other than that all the people who had doubted her, were right?

With a sigh, she threw her head back against the sofa cushion. The walls of this tiny flat were closing in on her and she wanted to get out. She'd go for a walk, she thought, just as raindrops splattered against her window. She rolled her eyes. What timing. Still, there was no such thing as bad weather, her mother always said. Just the wrong clothing. Feeling worn out, Nancy dragged herself upright, pulled on wellies and a waterproof jacket and headed out into the rain.

Unsurprisingly, the village was deserted. It was getting dark and the rain was teeming down. Nancy put her hood up, and hunched into her jacket as she walked, without any real destination in mind.

She tramped down the main street, past the pub, intending to take a loop round the village, past the pub and the post office, and then round the back of the church and through the graveyard, to get back home.

As she approached the garage, though, she heard raised voices and walked a bit more slowly so she didn't interrupt whatever was going on.

'It's just not right, Lily,' a man was saying. His Irish accent told Nancy that it was Mick Dingle speaking. 'You can't do both and nor should you.'

'You're not being fair,' Nancy heard Lily reply. She sounded less angry, and more upset. 'This isn't what I expected.'

'I'm not being fair? What about you? Are you being fair to little Hope?'

'Dad . . . ' Lily said. But Nancy heard a door slam and saw Mick disappear round the back of the garage, obviously heading home. She felt an odd relief that it wasn't just her family that was less than perfect, and almost immediately felt guilty for feeling that way. She went to carry on her way, past the garage, but this time was stopped by someone calling to her.

'Hello!'

She turned and saw Lily Proudfoot — who'd been one of the people arguing in the garage — waving to her. She was also dressed for the wet weather, in a sou'-wester and matching hat, and she was pushing a pram with a see-through rain cover.

'Nancy!' she called.

Nancy didn't know Lily very well. She'd only ever spoken to her in passing, she felt awkward about having eavesdropped on the row she'd had with her father, and she wasn't in the mood for company. For a brief moment, she thought about pretending she hadn't heard and carrying on her solo walk. But she'd turned now, and paused, and it seemed she had to respond.

'Hello!' she called back, hoping that was it. But Lily wasn't done. She splashed up behind Nancy,

'Nice weather for ducks,' she said.

Nancy grimaced. 'Ducks don't actually like the rain.'

Lily looked surprised. 'Really? Well, you should know I suppose, being a vet.'

Suddenly ashamed of being so prickly, Nancy caved.

'Of course they like the rain,' she said, forcing a smile. 'I was just being silly.'

'Oh,' Lily said. There was an awkward pause, then she spoke again. 'I saw you out here in this weather and wondered if you fancied a cup of tea? I've got the keys to the garage and you can get out of the wet. This one's asleep and I should make the most of it.'

Nancy glanced into the pram where Lily's baby girl was snoozing peacefully, cosy under a blanket and with the cover keeping the rain off. She thought about saying no, she just wanted to be on her own, but Lily looked slightly desperate — as though she needed the company — and Nancy remembered someone once telling her that when times were tough, the best thing to do was to help someone else. Perhaps giving Lily a bit of her time would help her sort out her own troubles.

She smiled again, more genuinely this time. 'I'd love a cup of tea.'

'Follow me,' said Lily.

They walked back the way Lily had come, then down the little side street that led to Lily's father's garage. Lily unlocked the door and they went inside, relieved to be out of the rain.

Lily filled the kettle and put it on to the little stove her father kept in his office, she uncovered the pram, and checked on the baby, and then peeled off her own waterproofs. Nancy took her jacket off too, impressed by how efficient Lily was.

When they both had steaming mugs of tea in their hands, Lily sat back against the battered sofa Mick used for customers, and looked at Nancy.

'You seem to be carrying the weight of the world,' she said, intuitively. 'I saw you wandering through the village and I recognised the slump of your shoulders. That's why I called out to you. I thought we could have a moan to each other.'

Nancy nodded. 'That's why I said yes to a cuppa, even though I wanted to be on my own.'

Lily chuckled. 'Go on then,' she said. 'Spill. What's up?'

Nancy sighed. 'I'm making a complete mess of the surgery,' she said. 'I'm either rushed off my feet, or sitting twiddling my thumbs. Business is so erratic and I'm worried there won't be anything for Mr Walters to come home to.'

Lily frowned. 'That's not true, surely? I've heard nothing but good things from people who have brought animals to you.'

'The few people who have brought animals to me.'

'Are you struggling for clients?'

Nancy nodded. 'Lots of local farmers moved to the big practice in Hotten when they found out I was taking over,' she said. 'They don't want to trust a woman with their animals.'

Lily sighed. 'I've heard that before. These types don't like to trust a woman with their cars, either.'

'I can't cope with the clients I've got because I've been trying to be a vet, a nurse and a receptionist all in one,' Nancy explained. 'Plus I'm really worried because I'm not making enough money. I've just taken on Betty Prendagast as a receptionist, which will help with organising my time, but now I need to pay her wages, too. And unless I get more clients, I'm going to go under. Then . . . '

'Then?'

'My father will have been right.'

Lily looked interested.

'Did he not want you to be a vet?'

'He did and he didn't,' Nancy said. 'He's a vet himself. He's got a successful practice, not far from here.'

'So why don't you just work with him? Like I work with my dad. Sometimes.'

Nancy groaned. 'Because he betrayed me.'

'That sounds awfully dramatic,' said Lily. 'How did he do that?'

'He signed over the practice to my brother Nigel.'

'He's a vet too?'

Nancy threw her head back against the sofa cushion. 'No,' she wailed. 'Not a vet. He runs a haulage company transporting goods round the country. He's very successful. My father thought that Nigel's business sense made him more of a safe bet to run the vet's practice than me. Even though I am actually a vet. He said . . . ' she paused as the anger she'd felt when her father had told her threatened to rise up again. 'He said I would get married soon and want to stop working so it made more sense for Nigel to be the boss. He said because Nigel's married with a son, that he needed the security.' She screwed her face up. 'Nigel's not even working there at the moment, because his company got a big contract — I'm not sure what it is. Something hush hush and terribly important for the war. So, Dad's taken over again for now. He said he'd give me a job but I was so angry I turned him down.'

'Good for you,' Lily said.

'Well, yes, good for me. But then I went and took on this job instead because I was desperate and so was Mr Walters because he wanted to go and work with the dogs because he'd been asked specially by the veterinary corps. But it's been a big mistake. And instead of proving my father wrong, I'm going to prove him right.'

'It doesn't look that way from where I'm sitting,' Lily said. 'I see a woman who's doing her best in difficult circumstances.'

Nancy rolled her eyes and Lily gave her a sympathetic smile.

'I want to go back to work in the garage,' she said. 'It's perfect. I can work round Hope, and round Jack.'

'But?'

'But Dad won't let me.'

'I heard you arguing, just before we bumped into each other,' Nancy admitted. Lily gave an exasperated sigh. 'Dad thinks mothers shouldn't work,' she explained. 'He thinks my Jack has a good job with a steady income and why would I work if I don't need to?'

'So why do you want to work?' Nancy asked with interest. She couldn't imagine giving up the job she'd worked so hard for, but she wasn't a mother. Perhaps things would change if she ever had a family of her own.

'Because I'm bored being at home with Hope,' Lily said in a hurry. 'Does that sound awful? Oh God, it sounds awful.'

Nancy looked over at the pram where Hope was still sleeping. She didn't look like the most exciting companion.

'I think it sounds normal,' she said. 'I expect lots of mothers feel that way.'

Lily looked doubtful. 'Really? Everyone just says how wonderful it is.'

Nancy leaned towards her and lowered her voice. 'Everyone lies, Lily. My sister-in-law had a terrible time when my nephew Frank was born. She was crying every day. Baby blues, they called it. She's better now, but I don't think she's in a hurry to have another one. She's quite honest about how tough those first few months were.'

'Really?'

'Really.'

'Maybe I should have just adopted older children like Meg Warcup did with Ruby and

111

Stan,' Lily said with a wry smile. 'Skipped this bit.'

A thought struck Nancy. 'Maybe you could pitch it like you're doing your dad a favour?'

'What, adopting older children?'

'No, silly.' Nancy was pleased to see Lily smiling again. 'Working at the garage.'

'He doesn't need me. He's got another mechanic as well as himself.'

'What if you did something different? What if you did the bicycles?'

Lily looked thoughtful. 'Like a sideline?'

'Exactly. Ruby says you've been teaching her about hers, and she's also told me there are loads of cycling enthusiasts round here. Not to mention all the people who have to cycle now petrol rationing's what it is.' She grimaced, thinking that she'd be joining them soon, wobbling all over Beckindale with her vet's bag on her back. But she pushed away her own self-pity and concentrated on Lily.

'What if you took on all the bicycle repairs?' she said. 'You'd be doing your dad a favour — getting Dingle's Garage a name for pushbikes as well as cars — and you'll be able to get out of the house and have some time out from being a mam. I'll bet you'll appreciate Hope much more if you have a break a couple of times a week.'

Lily stared at her and Nancy was afraid she'd said something wrong.

'That's brilliant,' Lily said. 'Simple and brilliant.'

Nancy beamed. It had been so long since she'd smiled like that, she'd almost forgotten how. It felt good to help someone else.

'I've got an idea too,' said Lily.

'Really?'

'All the farmers round here bring their tractors and trucks and that to Dingle's Garage.'

'Yes?'

'How about we spread the word about you? Do you have some leaflets I could hand out? Maybe we could even do a discount thing — ten shillings off their first visit if they say I recommended you? And vice versa. Plus, sad fact is, if my dad recommends you, they're bound to listen. They take more notice of a man than of a woman.'

Nancy nodded. 'You're not wrong there,' she said.

'Let's do it then,' Lily said. 'Bring some flyers round — get Ruby to do them if you've not got some already. She's quite good at drawing. And Susan's got lovely writing. Once we've got them I'll start handing them out. We can put a few up around the village, too — on the board by the post office, and in the pub.'

Nancy felt slightly overwhelmed, in a good way. 'Thanks Lily,' she said. 'I really appreciate you helping me like this.'

Lily gave Nancy a nudge. 'Don't fret,' she said. 'It's what we do here, isn't it? Help each other out.'

Nancy nodded. 'I'm starting to understand that.'

11

Audrey was in her bedroom, watching out of the window as Ned talked to Maggie in the farm garden. They were putting in the new beehive that Maggie had bought and were getting ready to transport a colony of bees inside. Audrey was frightened of the creatures, having been badly stung as a child, so she'd sneaked off inside to hide away before Ned and Maggie arrived.

But she couldn't help watching.

The garden was looking lovely now the worst of winter was over. There were daffodils all over the place, waving their heavy golden heads in the spring breeze, tulips jostling for space among them, and pansies in small clumps by the path. Audrey was enjoying watching the seasons change which sounded silly being as seasons had been doing just that for all of her nineteen years. But it seemed different this time because she was a part of it all. Part of the cycle of sowing seeds, growing and harvesting.

She knelt up at the window to get a better look at Ned. He was talking earnestly to Maggie, gesturing with his arms. Audrey knew he was rather interested in beekeeping and wanted his own hives one day, so he'd been glad to help Maggie. She was glad too. She liked him being around Emmerdale Farm.

When she'd chatted to Ned's sister before the dance, the things Elizabeth had said made

Audrey feel unsettled and silly. Was she really just the latest in a long line of adoring girls on Ned's arm?

When they got on the bus, she'd sat awkwardly for a couple of minutes, horribly aware of Ned's presence next to her but not sure what to say. Eventually, as the crowded bus set off towards Hotten, he turned to her and said, 'I reckon our Elizabeth's been telling you I've got lots of girls on the go.'

Audrey had flushed. 'Pretty much.'

Ned rolled his eyes. 'Don't know what's up with her lately.' He took Audrey's hand. 'I've danced with plenty of lasses and I've been to the pictures with a couple but I've never had a proper sweetheart before. I never wanted one really; I've always liked doing my own thing. Ploughing my own furrow, my pa would say.'

Audrey had nodded, biting her lip. What was he trying to say?

'But when I saw you in the village that evening . . . ' He paused. 'When I saw you, I thought to myself, 'Oh there she is, the girl I've been waiting for'. And now I understand what all the fuss is about.'

Audrey had stared at him, astonished. 'That's exactly what I felt,' she said. 'Thank goodness, eh?'

And they'd both laughed, pleased as anything that they had shared their feelings.

They were stuck like glue to each other for the whole evening. Audrey had barely spoken to anyone else for the first hour or so, simply wanting to hear Ned's views on farming, his family, the war

— everything. And share her own stories, too. They had so much to talk about. Later on, Audrey had gone to the ladies while Ned went to get them some drinks, and got talking to a woman from Beckindale called Betty who was thrillingly glamorous and full of life. Audrey thought she might like to be friends with Betty and hoped she'd see more of her around the village.

As she emerged from the lav, Audrey watched Betty across the dancefloor. Her face was glowing as she chatted to the singer from the band. Betty was just as pretty as the woman who'd been on stage and she'd obviously loved being the centre of attention when she and her sister were dancing. Audrey shuddered at the thought of everyone looking at her. She was quite happy stepping out with Ned round the edge of the dancefloor.

'Who are you looking at?' Ned had appeared at her shoulder, holding two drinks. He handed one to her.

'Betty.' Audrey tilted her head in the other woman's direction. 'I just got chatting to her in the loo.'

Ned had laughed.

'Betty is such a chatterbox,' he said. 'She was always in trouble at school for jabbering on when she should have been quiet.'

'I liked her.'

'She's a good lass, is Betty.' He shook his head. 'Wasted on Seth Armstrong, though.'

Audrey made a face. 'Is he rotten to her.'

'Not rotten, really. He just doesn't appreciate her.'

'She could be a film star one day, I reckon,' Audrey said. 'Did you see her dance?'

'Betty Prendagast, a film star?' Ned said, hooting with laughter. 'When did you ever see a film star who came from a little village in Yorkshire, like ours?'

Audrey grinned back at him. 'Anyone can do anything,' she said, mock-sternly. 'Look at me.'

Ned put his arm round her waist and drew her close.

'Oh, I've been looking at you all night, Audrey. And I like what I see.'

She had felt the warmth of his body against hers and for a moment her legs went weak and she thought she might topple over. Was he going to kiss her? She'd been kissed a couple of times before, by boys she wasn't overly interested in, and found it a thoroughly uninspiring experience. But the way her whole body reacted when Ned was nearby made her think that perhaps being kissed by him would be totally different.

She leaned towards him, enjoying the closeness, as she tilted her face up to his, and he bent towards her and . . . the lights in the hall went on.

Blinking, Audrey looked around and saw the other dance-goers doing the same. 'I guess the evening's over, then,' she said, disappointed.

Ned grinned at her. 'There will be more evenings like this one,' he'd said. 'Lots more.'

Now, watching Ned from her bedroom window, Audrey hoped they could spend another evening together soon. He and Maggie had finished with the bees and were standing back to

117

admire their handiwork. But as Audrey watched, she saw Maggie turn slightly away from Ned as he looked at the hive, and grimace. She was holding her stomach and she looked pale, as though she was in pain. At the window, Audrey stiffened. Should she go and help? But then Maggie straightened up and her face cleared. And Ned looked up at where Audrey sat and gave her a wave that suggested he'd known she was there all along.

Her cover blown, Audrey decided to go and see him before he had to leave. So, all thoughts of Maggie's odd moment forgotten, she leapt up from her seat at the window and bounced downstairs.

She found Ned and Maggie in the kitchen, brewing tea.

'Hello, where have you been?' Maggie said. 'Fancy a cup?'

'I'd love one, thanks,' Audrey said. She smiled at Ned. 'Hello.'

He grinned back at her, and for a second, he was all Audrey could see. 'Hello.'

'You two have a seat,' Maggie said. 'I'll bring it over.'

She began taking mugs from the cupboard, but as she reached up she winced. Audrey was by her side in a flash.

'Are you all right?' she asked, concerned. But Maggie gave her a reassuring smile.

'Just pulled a muscle,' she said.

Audrey looked at her, wondering if that was the whole truth but Maggie smiled again and handed her two mugs.

'Take those to the table.'

Ned was chatting to Joseph, who was in his chair by the window as usual. His speech was stilted and slow but Ned patiently waited for him to finish, never jumping in to finish his sentences as Audrey was always tempted to do. He was a good man, Audrey thought, gazing at Ned. A good, hardworking, honest, kind . . . strong, handsome man.

'Mugs, Audrey,' Maggie said with a chuckle.

Jolted out of her daydream, Audrey flushed and put the mugs down on the table so Maggie could pour the tea.

They sat and chatted for a while, Ned and Maggie explaining how they thought the beehive would help the vegetable garden to bloom as well as giving them honey for the farm.

'If it works well, we could get another hive next year,' said Maggie. 'We've got the space.'

'Maybe the war will be over by then,' Ned said and Audrey felt an odd pang. She wasn't enjoying the war, of course. It was a horrible thing casting a shadow over everyone, but if the war ended, what would she do?

From his chair, Joe snorted. 'No . . . chance,' he said in his funny stilted way. 'This time . . . next year.' He paused to take a slurp of his tea. 'We'll be sat here . . . saying same.'

Ned nodded but Maggie gave her husband an odd, worried glance. 'I thought Jacob would have come for a brew,' she said, picking up the teapot. 'I'll freshen the pot in case he shows himself.'

As if he'd heard his name and come running, Jacob came through the back door.

'Hive looks good,' he said to Maggie, then he noticed Audrey and Ned sitting at the table and his expression went from its usual slightly dour appearance to a sullen look with a curled lip.

'Ned,' he said. He turned to Audrey. 'I need you to mend the trough in the middle field.'

'Now?' she said, disappointed. She wanted to spend more time with Ned, but she knew having spent the last hour hiding from the bees she was pushing her luck.

'If it's not too much trouble.' Jacob's voice was heavy with sarcasm.

'Maybe we could go for a walk tomorrow?' Ned said to Audrey as she got up from the table and went to rinse her mug out in the sink. 'After church?'

'Can I?' Audrey looked at Jacob, checking it was all right to say 'yes please' and he shrugged.

Maggie, though, gave her an encouraging smile. 'Course you can, love,' she said. 'You deserve a bit of time off.'

'I'll meet you at church,' Ned said and Audrey nodded. She was pleased to have the chance to spend more time with Ned, but somehow she felt like the shine had been taken off their arrangement now. She gave Ned a small wave and said goodbye and threw Jacob a withering glance as she headed out of the door to look at the trough. But he didn't notice.

12

When Wednesday evening finally arrived, Betty was so excited she could barely stand still. Earlier that day, she'd told Nancy about helping out at the ENSA show and to her surprise, Nancy had been really nice about it.

'Sounds like a lot of fun,' Nancy had said. She took the appointments book from Betty's desk and opened it to the right page, nodding as it clearly confirmed what she'd been thinking.

'We're clear from three o'clock this afternoon and there are no animals waiting for treatment,' she said. Betty smiled, pleased her new system of organising the appointments was working already.

'That means, if there are no emergencies, you can catch up on some paperwork,' Betty said pointedly, looking at the stack of drug orders and other admin that she'd left for Nancy to sign.

Nancy smiled. 'It means, you can head off early if you like.'

Betty had been delighted, and jumped at the chance to get home so she could choose what to wear for her big night.

She'd told Seth, eventually, about what she was doing. She'd half expected him to simply nod in his usual distracted fashion, like he did when she told him stories about work, and go back to joking around with Ernie. But he hadn't. Instead he'd looked at her over the top of his pint and frowned.

'That lass that was at the dance?' he'd said.

'Pamela.' Betty had nodded. 'She was so nice. She said I was a good dancer.'

'You're a great dancer, Betty love,' Seth said, his thick eyebrows knotting together. 'But what's that got to do with you being a skivvy for some girls who are no better than they should be.'

Betty had felt her heart sink. 'What does that mean?' she snapped. She'd drained her gin and orange and put the empty glass down on the bar with a thud. 'I'm not going to be a skivvy.'

Seth had reached out and taken her hand, stroking her skin gently with his thumb just the way she liked it.

'I mean you're better than those girls,' he said. 'Them with their fancy hair and their lips all red, wandering around in their undies.'

'You seem to know a lot about it.' Betty, who rather admired fancy hair and red lips, had raised a wry eyebrow and Seth snorted.

'Get away, love,' he'd said. 'I know what men are like and I don't want the likes of them looking at you like they look at those girls, when they're up on stage, prancing about, showing them what they've got.'

Betty had felt the tiniest flicker of irritation at Seth telling her what to do, but then he pulled her towards him and gave her a kiss and she melted.

'I'm not being a skivvy, I'm just helping with costumes,' she'd said. 'I know it's not important but it's still war work.'

Seth had looked dubious but he let her carry on.

'And I won't be wearing my undies nor

122

prancing about on stage so you've got nowt to worry about Seth Armstrong.'

They'd not talked about it again. Seth had simply rolled his eyes when Betty had said she couldn't go for a drink tonight because she was off to the ENSA camp.

And so not long after four o'clock, she was on the bus heading towards Hotten. The training camp wasn't too far away — just the other side of the town — so before long she was walking up to the gates, nerves jangling.

'Betty Prendagast,' she told the soldier at the gate. 'I'm here to see Pamela Marks. She's part of the ENSA.'

The soldier gave Betty an approving nod. 'You part of the entertainment?'

She flushed. 'Me? No, I'm just helping out backstage,' she said.

The soldier grinned, looking disarmingly young under his helmet. Betty had a sudden, awful realisation that he would soon be given a gun and sent to France, or Africa, or somewhere else miles from here, to kill other boys just like him. The war often seemed far away from her safe life in Beckindale but then every now and then it rushed back into her consciousness like someone pulling a rug from under her feet. Now she stared at the sweet-faced soldier and forced herself to return his smile.

'Just backstage,' she said again.

'Shame,' he said, looking her up and down. Betty preened — just a bit. She was happily involved with Seth, after all, and it wouldn't do to flirt too much.

'Is it this way?' she said and the soldier nodded and pointed.

'Hut at the far end on the left,' he said. 'Maybe I'll see you later.'

'Maybe,' said Betty. She walked away, feeling his eyes on her and deliberately putting a little swing in her step, knowing her skirt hugged the curves of her bottom and legs in a very flattering way.

Confidence boosted, she found the hut at the end, and went inside. Calling it a hut was a bit of a misnomer. It was a large, corrugated iron structure, with a hubbub of activity inside. There were people wandering around in dancewear, others half in costumes or half out of them. Somewhere, someone was singing and at the far end, she saw Pamela, carrying a large pile of fabric.

'Pamela,' she called and she was pleased when Pamela dropped what Betty could now see were costumes, and came rushing over. She was wearing uniform, which surprised Betty. She hadn't expected theatrical types to be clad in proper army garb.

'It's ugly, isn't it?' Pamela said, reading Betty's mind. 'And so horribly itchy. But it makes it easy deciding what to wear when you get up in the morning.'

Betty, who rather liked women in uniform because they looked so smart and official, said nothing.

'Anyway, thank goodness you're here,' Pamela said dramatically. 'We're so desperate for another pair of hands.'

Betty waved her palms at Pamela jokingly. 'They're all yours.' She looked round the room. 'What do you need me to do?'

'I was just going to go through some make-up,' Pamela said. 'Could you give me a hand with that, first of all?'

Betty was pleased. She liked cosmetics. 'Do you have stage make-up?' she asked Pamela as they sat down together to sort through a large box.

'Some, but it's hard to get hold of now. We just make do, like everyone's doing. Same as with the costumes. We have some bits donated from old London theatres but mostly we just do what we can with what we've got and adapt things as we go along. Have a root through the box and if there's anything that really can't be saved, chuck it.'

'You don't have people to do the costumes for you?'

'A couple but mostly we all pitch in. It's why we need people like you.'

'I'm happy to help,' Betty said. She examined a cake of mascara that was almost entirely used up except for a ridge of black round the edge of the pot. 'Can you get any more out of that?'

Pamela made a face. 'Chuck it.'

'My sister and I have been trying beetroot for lipstick,' Betty told her. 'it's rather good.'

'That's a smart idea,' Pamela said. 'God, I miss proper make-up.'

'Me too. I'd kill for a new kohl pencil.'

'Apparently girls in the munitions factories get a make-up allowance,' Pamela said. 'That's what I've been told.'

Betty thought about it. 'I'm not sure that makes up for how awful the work is. I've heard some of them are turning yellow because of the chemicals.'

'Crikey,' Pamela said. 'That's not good.'

'I'd much rather be here.'

Pamela chuckled. 'I know. We're all a bit ramshackle, unfortunately. But every day I thank my lucky stars that I'm here and not nursing or driving an ambulance or something like that. I'd be so miserable.'

'Were you a singer before the war?'

'I wanted to be, but I'm from North Wales and there's not much opportunity for performers there. It's mining, mostly. I was saving up to go to London when I saw the ad for ENSA and joined up.'

Betty felt a rush of envy as she watched Pamela bend over the make-up box, her shining hair falling over her perfectly painted face.

'And now you're singing every day.'

'I am. It's wonderful. I'm singing and I'm travelling. I've been to France, and Belgium, and there's talk of us going to North Africa in a few months.'

'Are you nervous about going so far away?'

'Not really. We're not allowed to go where the fighting is, because we're civilians officially. And it's not as frightening for us as it is for the troops.'

Betty was full of admiration for this beautiful, confident woman. 'It sounds thrilling.'

She threw a hollowed-out lipstick tube on to the empties pile. 'What's next?'

'Are you any good at sewing?'

'Not as good as my mother, but I can do a fair job.'

Pamela smiled in relief. 'These are the dancers' costumes,' she said, gesturing to the pile of clothes she'd been carrying when Betty arrived. 'They all need bows sewn on the back. Could you do that?'

'Of course,' Betty said. 'Just give me a needle and some cotton, and somewhere to sit, and I'll crack on.'

Pamela glanced round at the chaotic room and then gave Betty a small wink.

'Tell you what, come with me,' she said. She and Betty both gathered up the costumes and the ribbons that would become the bows, then Pamela led Betty through to the back of the ENSA hut and out another door, collecting a sewing basket on the way.

'I've got to go and practise my songs with the band,' Pamela said. 'But I thought you might like to sit at the back of the rehearsal room while the dancers are going through their act? Could be more fun than sitting in a corner elsewhere.'

Betty beamed at her. 'I'd love that,' she said.

And she really did. She sat on a comfortable chair and sewed bows on to each costume as neatly as she could, trying to push away the voice in her head pointing out how small the outfits were and reminding her what Seth had said.

While she sewed, she soaked up the atmosphere. She watched the dancers going over their routine, breaking it down into sections, and going over any tricky moves. It wasn't that different from the dances she'd learned with Miss Diana. She found herself marking out the steps while she sat, and then standing up and, still clutching her needle and thread, following along with the dancers.

Eventually, she put down the costumes and just danced, tucked in the corner of the room where she thought no one could see her. As the music came to an end and the dancers in the room finished with a twirl, so did Betty — and she came face to face with an amused-looking Pamela.

'You've picked up the steps already,' she said, astonished.

Betty felt a bit silly. 'Sorry, Pamela. I'll finish those bows now. I just got carried away with the music.'

Pamela didn't look in the least bit annoyed. 'Don't apologise, you're a good dancer.'

'I love it,' said Betty dreamily. 'I've learned a lot just watching the girls here.'

'Stay here,' said Pamela. She dashed off and Betty sat back down and finished sewing the final bow on to the costumes.

Pamela arrived back, looking very pleased with herself. 'You're going to need another bow,' she said.

Betty glanced up, counting the dancers in her head, and then counting the bows she'd sewn. 'They're all here.'

Pamela was almost bouncing, she looked so excited.

'I had a word with Daphne — she's the dance leader here — and she says you can dance with the girls this evening, if she likes you. But she will. You're marvellous.'

Betty's jaw dropped. 'No,' she said. 'I can't.'

'Of course you can,' said Pamela. 'It'll be a hoot. Come and meet everyone.'

She dragged Betty across the room to the dancers.

'Everyone this is Betty,' she announced. Betty felt her cheeks flame, as the other girls all greeted her gaily, but she also felt a flicker of excitement. She was going to dance on a stage, in front of an audience. It was like a dream come true.

Daphne, the dance teacher, a rather severe-looking woman wearing ballet shoes with her uniform, turned to Betty.

'Pamela's told me you're rather good,' she said. 'Can you show me what you can do?'

'Right now?' Betty said. Her skirt was a bit too tight, and her shoes too stiff for proper dancing. 'Could I change?'

'I've got a spare practice dress,' said one of the dancers. She pulled a scrap of pink material from her bag and threw it at Betty.

'Come on then,' said Daphne. 'We don't have all evening. We're on stage in an hour.'

Feeling self-conscious, Betty slunk into the corner, wriggled out of her skirt and blouse and pulled on the practice dress, which was — like Seth had warned — like underwear. For a second, she thought about putting her own clothes back on and saying she didn't want to dance for Daphne but then she pulled her shoulders back, kicked off her shoes and darted back to the centre of the room. Daphne sat down at the piano, counted her in and, taking a deep breath, Betty danced.

As the music finished and she ended with the twirl, there was silence in the room. She pulled down the skirt of the borrowed practice dress, which was slightly too short, and waited to be told she was hopeless and to get dressed and get back on the bus to Beckindale.

But instead Daphne smiled for the first time.

'Lovely,' she said. 'Let's run through it from the top. Betty, you slot in there, between Eleanor and Vi. And Maeve, can you help find Betty a costume when we're done here?'

Betty was overwhelmed; she couldn't quite believe what had just happened. Was she truly going to dance on stage at a proper show? She'd done performances before, of course, at the village hall and a couple of times at the summer fete in Hotten but this was in another league. Seth, she thought, would be horrified. Disappointed in her. Ashamed. Angry even. She felt a sudden stab of nerves. What on earth was she thinking?

'Erm, what time will the show finish?' she asked tentatively, casting around for an excuse. 'It's just I need to get the bus . . . '

Daphne waved an elegant hand. 'We'll have someone drive you home,' she said. 'There are always soldiers around who are happy to get out on the road for a bit. I think they like having time on their own.'

From the back of the room, Pamela clapped loudly. 'This is marvellous,' she said. 'I knew

130

you'd fit right in. I can't wait to see you dancing with the others.'

There was a pause as everyone looked at Betty. 'Dancing with the others,' she repeated quietly to herself. She felt a flicker of excitement. 'Dancing with the others.'

'Are you in?' Daphne asked briskly. Betty looked from her to Pamela and then down at her own bare legs in the too-short practice dress.

'I'm in,' she said, her head still reeling from everything that had happened. She walked over to where the dancers were arranging themselves into their positions for the start of the dance, and smiled a nervous hello at Eleanor and Vi, on either side of her.

'Ready?' said Daphne. 'Let's go.'

13

The show was a rip-roaring success. At least as far as Betty was concerned. Yes, the scenery was a bit wobbly, the costumes weren't all perfect and there were some too-long gaps between sketches, and a couple of forgotten lines, but in Betty's opinion it was perfect. And the audience enjoyed it too. The soldiers whooped their way through the dances, and their reaction seemed to breathe life into Betty as she danced. She started out unsure and nervous, keeping her movements small and tight, but as the applause reached her, she grew in confidence and began dancing for the crowd. Every shout and every cheer gave her more energy. It was a wonderful experience.

Afterwards, in their makeshift dressing room, Betty took her time over removing her costume and make-up, listening to the chatter from the other dancers, and joining in as they critiqued their performances. She'd never really felt part of something before. She was fine at school but she wasn't bookish or overly interested in learning so she often sat at the back and made the other children laugh instead, feeling very much on the sidelines. At the factory, she'd disliked the serious atmosphere, and the lack of chitchat. But now, here among these women who felt the same way about dancing and performing as she did, she felt like she belonged.

'I've found my people,' she murmured and

then laughed at herself for being so pompous.

Pamela, who'd brought the house down with her songs tonight, appeared behind her, her pretty face glowing with pleasure and pride.

'Betty, you were marvellous,' she said. 'I'm so pleased we didn't waste you on costumes. You're a born performer. You were a real hit with the crowd.'

'So were you,' Betty said, turning around and taking Pamela's hands in hers. 'Oh, I loved it, Pamela. I loved every single second.'

'It showed.' Pamela squeezed Betty's fingers. 'I'm chuffed to bits.'

Betty caught a glimpse of her own face in the mirror. She was flushed and her hair was a bit dishevelled, but she could see her eyes were dancing with happiness. Seth always said he could tell her mood was obvious from her eyes, and he was right. But the thought of Seth brought Betty up short. How could she have enjoyed herself on stage so much when she knew what Seth would say about it? How could she have drunk in the cheers of the soldiers, knowing Seth would be cross if he saw them whooping and shouting at her? She felt an unfamiliar squirming sensation in her stomach. Guilt, she thought. That's what guilt feels like. She gave Pamela a little smile and started getting changed into her normal clothes.

Eleanor, who had danced next to Betty in the line, was standing next to them, bending and flexing her knee. 'It's not right,' she called across to Daphne.

Daphne came over, a worried frown on her

face. 'Well done, Betty,' she said as she passed. 'Let's have a look, Eleanor.'

Eleanor sat down and let Daphne examine her knee.

'It's a bit swollen, I think. Let's get some ice on it.'

'It really hurts,' Eleanor said. 'I think it needs resting but we've got so many performances coming up, how can I rest?'

She ran her fingers through her hair and then looked at Betty, thoughtfully. 'What about Betty?' she said.

'What about me?'

'What about you covering me in the dances, while we're here?'

Betty was taken aback. 'Oh, I don't know,' she said.

'You'd be great.'

'But I'm not in ENSA. Would I even be allowed?'

'Would she?' Eleanor asked Daphne. She screwed up her face, thinking and then shrugged.

'Don't see why not.'

'Will you do it, then?' Eleanor asked. 'I could really do with time off my feet.'

Pamela was thrilled and clapped her hands again, and Betty was also filled with excitement. But she was wary of saying yes immediately, no matter how tempting it was. She knew she should really talk about it with her parents, and Nancy. And Seth.

'I'd like to,' she said cautiously. 'But I have work, and there are things to think about.'

'We're here for ten weeks, though our stints are sometimes extended so it could be longer,' Daphne said. 'We're doing performances at this base, as well as a couple of others nearby. And there are a few civvy performances too — like the dance where you met Pamela, and a couple of factories. I'll give you a list. We'll need some more rehearsals, too.'

Her head spinning, Betty swallowed. Could she do this? Should she do this? 'Give me the list and I'll see what I can do,' she said.

Eleanor beamed at her and Pamela squeezed her hand again.

'This is marvellous,' she said, and Betty nodded, but she wasn't completely sure. Was it?

She was driven home by one of the soldiers — another baby-faced young man who made her heart twist with fear for him. But as she clambered out of the car she waved goodbye cheerily and he leaned out of the window. 'Thought you were great on stage,' he said as he pulled away.

Feeling like she'd done something good — bringing joy to young lads like that was surely worthwhile, whatever Seth thought of it — Betty quietly let herself into the house and crept up the stairs to her bedroom. She was exhausted, but happy. It was after midnight, so everyone else was asleep and she was horribly aware she had to get up for work at her usual time and not enjoy a lie-in to recover from all the excitement.

As she tiptoed to her bedroom, Margaret's door opened. 'You're back so late,' she hissed. 'Where have you been?'

'Shhh,' Betty said, pulling her sister into her bedroom and closing the door softly. She sat on the bed, still in her jacket, and took off her shoes.

'I've been with the ENSA girls.'

'Did you go out?' Margaret said suspiciously, flopping on to Betty's bed. She narrowed her eyes at her sister. 'Your face is all pink. Have you been drinking?'

'No, I've not been drinking,' Betty said. 'But I've been having the most wonderful time.'

She stood up and wriggled out of her jacket and hung it up, then did the same with her skirt and blouse. She always took care of her clothes; they weren't expensive but she knew they looked better if they were well cared for. She took her time about it, knowing Margaret was desperate for more information.

'Betty,' Margaret groaned. 'Where have you been?'

'Oh, just dancing in the show,' Betty said casually, over her shoulder, as she slid her blouse into her wardrobe.

Margaret stared at her. 'No!' she said.

'Yes!'

Unable to keep her excitement hidden any more, Betty jumped on to the bed beside her sister and felt under her pillow for her nightdress.

'I was watching them all rehearse and I learned the steps,' she said, poking her head through the neck hole.

Margaret gave Betty a friendly thump on the arm. 'You're so blooming fast at picking up steps. I knew it would come in handy one day.'

Betty grinned. 'They asked if I wanted to join them on stage.'

'Just like that?'

'Well, I had to show the woman in charge that I could dance first. And when she realised I could keep up, she let me join in.'

'Ohh, Betty,' Margaret breathed. 'You are so bold. I'd never have been brave enough to dance on a stage like that.'

'Get out of it,' said Betty, pleased with her sister's admiration. 'Course you would.'

'What was it like on stage? Did you get it all right? Who was watching? What did you wear?'

Betty arranged the bedclothes over them both and they snuggled down together, like when they were little girls.

'It was amazing,' she began, keeping her voice down so they didn't wake their parents. 'Incredible. I was so nervous, Margaret, but as soon as I realised the audience were enjoying it, I had this huge rush of energy.'

'Adrenaline,' Margaret said. 'Fight or flight. Or dance.'

Betty blinked at her. 'I don't know what that means but it sounds right,' she said. 'And the end, when they were all cheering, was just wonderful. Like I was meant to be there.'

'Oh, you're definitely meant to be on a stage,' said Margaret with the weariness of a sibling who'd grown up watching her sister perform for her. Betty chuckled and squeezed her sister's arm.

'And,' she said dramatically.

'There's more?'

'They've asked me to fill in for one of the girls who's injured,' Betty said. 'Just while they're in Yorkshire.'

'Oh my goodness.' Margaret sounded delighted. 'Another show?'

'More than one.'

Betty leaned out of the bed and found her handbag, then she pulled out the list Pamela had given her.

'Four more shows at bases, and one fundraising thing where they need dancers. One at a factory. A couple of dances. All over Yorkshire in the next few weeks.'

'Are you joining the ENSA?' Margaret asked. 'What about your new job?'

'No, don't fret. I'm not joining them. I belong here with you, Mam and Dad, and Seth,' Betty said. 'I would just be helping out while they're local. I could do the shows and keep working. At least, I think I could.'

She felt another stirring of doubt as she looked at the list. There were a lot of shows. And she wasn't a professional dancer. Her legs were aching after tonight's performance — could she even keep up? And what if she had to miss work for rehearsals? No one had mentioned her being paid for dancing with the ENSA girls. She couldn't afford to lose her job at the vet's because she was spending all her time dancing. And then there was Seth? He'd been more than clear when he told her what he thought about ENSA dancers. He'd never agree to her dancing in the shows. And even if he did, all that extra commitment would mean she'd never see him.

He worked odd hours up at the estate, learning to be a gamekeeper. And between that and his nights out with his mates, she'd be lucky if she remembered what he looked like by the time ENSA rolled out of Yorkshire again.

'I'm not sure, you know Margaret,' she said now.

'Not sure about what?'

'About doing these other shows.'

'You're a good dancer, Betty. You'd be great.'

'I know. But I'm not a professional, am I? All the other girls do this as their job; I'm a receptionist.'

'A receptionist with twinkle toes,' Margaret joked.

'But still just a receptionist.' She turned her face into the pillow and groaned. 'I can't do it, Margaret. What about Seth?'

'What about him?'

'What will he think of his girl being up on stage every night?'

'It's not every night,' Margaret said, deliberately — and frustratingly — misunderstanding.

Betty sat up. 'I wore this polka-dotted outfit — not more than a swimming costume really. It had a bow on the backside, Margaret.'

'Bet you looked wonderful in it,' Margaret said longingly. 'With your legs.'

'Well, yes, it did look smart,' Betty agreed. 'But Seth would not be happy to know I was parading in front of hundreds of soldiers dressed like that.'

'Shouldn't think he'd even notice.'

Betty pinched her sister's arm.

139

'Ouch,' Margaret said. 'We're not ten, Betty. You don't need to pinch me. Why don't you ask Seth what he'd think?'

'I don't have to. He already told me. He said the ENSA performers were prancing about in their undies. And I said it was fine because I was just helping with the costumes and not going on stage.'

Margaret grinned, suddenly. 'So tell him that then,' she said, a glint in her eye. 'Tell him you're helping with the costumes. Or rather, don't tell him, just let him assume.'

Betty shook her head. 'I don't think I'd feel right, lying to him.'

'Not lying,' Margaret said. 'More not telling the truth.'

'Is there a difference?'

'A big difference,' said Margaret, yawning. Straightaway Betty did the same.

'When do you have to decide by?' Margaret asked, closing her eyes, pulling the blanket over herself, and settling down in Betty's bed.

Betty kicked her. 'Don't get comfy here, Margaret. Go back to your own bed. I said I'd let them know by the end of the week.'

Sleepily, Margaret slid out of the bed and padded to the door on her bare feet.

'I think you should do it,' she said. 'And I think you should do it whatever Seth blimming Armstrong says. G'night.'

Betty blew her a kiss, and turned out the light. Could she do it? Could she really perform in front of hundreds of soldiers, like a real dancer? Pamela had said that being on stage with the

140

ENSA dancers could be the start of a career in entertainment, which sounded wonderful. But what sort of career could she have here in Beckindale? To do that, she'd have to leave and go to Leeds or even London. And Seth, her lovely, handsome, funny Seth would never want to do that. Being a gamekeeper was all he'd ever wanted. And if she wasn't going to have a career as a dancer, was there any point in doing the shows now? Knowing how that would annoy Seth and maybe even upset him?

Her head swimming with thoughts and plans, Betty closed her eyes, and went to sleep.

14

After all the excitement at ENSA, Betty was quiet for the rest of the week. She barely said a word on Thursday, hoping that because Nancy knew she'd been working on the ENSA show the previous night, she would chalk it up to her being tired.

She was still in a funny mood on Friday, though and it seemed Nancy had noticed because when the initial rush of Friday morning had calmed down and there was a lull in between patients, she wandered into the reception area and offered to make Betty a cup of tea.

'That would be nice,' Betty said, surprised. 'But it's my job, let me do it.'

'Nonsense. Your job is to keep things organised,' Nancy told her. 'I don't remember saying anything about putting the kettle on in your interview.'

Betty smiled. 'Thank you.'

Nancy made the tea and, instead of taking hers back into the treatment room, she stayed in the waiting area, looking a bit uncomfortable.

'Is everything all right?' she asked. 'You seem to be in a strange mood.' She paused. 'I just wanted to check you're happy. You're not thinking of leaving?'

Betty smiled. 'No,' she said. 'Though I admit, it's been a baptism of fire.'

'Baptism of budgie business,' said Nancy. Betty laughed. It wasn't often that Nancy made jokes — she was always fretting about something. But she'd definitely been a bit happier recently. Or at least, she'd been happier until now when she was back to fretting.

'Just got a few things on my mind,' Betty told her, wanting to reassure her boss that her mood was nothing to do with her.

Nancy nodded, sipping her tea, and Betty had a sudden hope that this clever, focused woman might be able to help her make her own decision.

'Your dad is a vet, isn't he?' she said.

'He is.'

'How did you know it was what you wanted to do too?'

Nancy sat down on one of the waiting area chairs. 'It was less that I wanted to be a vet and more that I simply couldn't imagine doing anything else.'

Betty was startled at Nancy's words. 'That's it, exactly.'

'Is it?'

'Did he help you? With your training and that.'

Nancy gave a snort. 'Up to a point.'

'What does that mean?'

'It means while I was at school, he thought it was marvellous. I was like a pet project for him. He'd take me along on jobs and quiz me, and get me to examine animals with him. He loved it when the farmers were impressed by how much I knew.'

'That's so sweet,' said Betty, though Nancy's

143

face suggested it was anything but. 'You didn't like it?'

Nancy pinched her lips together. 'Let's just say it all got a bit complicated and I didn't end up working with him like I'd always imagined. I came to work here instead.'

Betty chose her words carefully, understanding that this wasn't easy for Nancy to talk about. 'And was your dad pleased about that?'

Nancy made a face. 'Not really.'

'But, you wanted it so badly, you did what you had to do, even though it was difficult?' Betty said thoughtfully.

'I suppose so.'

'What did your dad say?'

'It didn't matter to me what he said. I just thought that it was happening and he needed to accept it.'

'Woah,' Betty said. 'You don't mind that you upset him?'

Nancy thought about it. 'I mind a bit,' she said. 'But I've come to realise that I was waiting for him to make my decisions for me. I thought I could only be a vet if my father allowed it to happen. If he wanted it to happen and if he helped it happen. But that's not how it is. I'm responsible for my own life and there is little point in sitting around waiting for other people. My father let me down when I needed him to believe in me. Now I just rely on me.'

She looked at Betty with a defiant expression, as though she was expecting her to disagree. But Betty was impressed with the fiery approach of her new boss. And, she had to admit, she was even more confused than before.

Nancy wasn't finished. 'Do you know what I think?'

Betty shrugged.

'I think that this war is a terrible thing,' Nancy said. 'It's awful and when I think about those boys off fighting it makes me want to weep.'

'I saw this soldier at the base the other night,' Betty told her. 'He was so young, a real baby face, you know? And I suddenly thought of him in France, or somewhere with a gun in his hand and . . . oh Nancy, it made me cold.'

Nancy nodded. 'I was up at Emmerdale Farm the other day, and the sadness in Maggie Sugden's eyes is obvious.'

'He was such a nice lad, Edward Sugden was.'

They were both quiet for a moment and then Nancy carried on. 'The war is terrible, but it's bringing opportunities for us women that we might not have had otherwise,' she said. 'I wouldn't be here if it weren't for Mr Walters taking that job with the Royal Army Veterinary Corps.'

Betty nodded. 'And there wouldn't be an ENSA,' she said.

Nancy looked interested. 'Did it go well? Your time with the dancers?'

Betty cupped her chin in her hand and looked dreamily into the distance as she remembered the magical evening. 'Very well,' she said. 'I got to dance.'

'On stage?' said Nancy, sounding impressed. 'In front of all those soldiers?'

'They loved it,' Betty said, more to herself

than to Nancy. 'They loved it and so did I.'

'Wonderful.'

'You said you thought you could only be a vet if your dad wanted it to happen,' Betty said, her mind racing. She could see Nancy was bewildered by the way she kept jumping from one thing to another but it was helping her sort things out. 'But here you are.'

'Here I am.'

Betty stood up suddenly. 'Could I take the rest of the day off? I need to speak to Seth about something.'

Nancy nodded, clearly realising Betty was going whether she agreed or not. 'Go ahead.'

Betty didn't even stop to pick up her jacket, she simply raced out of the door without looking back and then she half ran, half walked up the hill to the estate to find Seth.

Fortunately, she found him easily enough — the estate was huge so she had been worried it would take her ages. He was talking to his boss, Mr Verney, and looked surprised — but not annoyed — to see her.

'Sorry for interrupting you at work,' she said, still out of breath from her mad dash up the hill.

'It's a nice surprise,' he said and Betty felt her heart swell with love. It swelled even more when he proudly introduced her to one of his colleagues who was nearby, and to Mr Verney himself.

'Have you got time for a bit of a walk?' Betty said, stretching the truth just a bit. 'It's quiet at the vet's so I thought I'd come and see you.'

'Go on, Seth,' Mr Verney said. 'You've been

146

busy this morning. I'll come get you if you're needed.'

Seth offered Betty his arm, and she took it. They strolled off round the estate. It was a beautiful spring day, with daffodils in clumps at the edges of the fields, and the wind gentle against their faces. Betty felt optimistic and excited about what was to come, but nervous and worried about how to start the conversation with her fella.

'It's glorious up here, isn't it?' she said, as they walked.

'It is that.' Seth paused in his walking to take in the view. 'Look the estate stretches right down there, as far as you can see.'

'What a lovely place to work.' Betty felt like she was building up to telling him about dancing with ENSA but she didn't know how to broach the subject.

Seth turned to her, his eyes shining. 'It's my favourite place in all the world.'

Betty smiled at him — his enthusiasm was infectious. 'I can see that.'

'When I was just a tiny lad, I used to come up here with Ernie,' Seth said. Betty nodded. She'd heard this story more times than she could remember, but she always liked hearing it. 'We'd run around in the woods and build dens and I always used to say I wanted to live here, even if it was only for a day.'

She squeezed Seth's arm a bit tighter. She loved how passionate he was about the country-side and nature and his beloved estate.

'I was over the moon when I got this job,

Betty. Over the blooming moon. Every day I'm thankful for it.'

Betty looked up at him, the man she loved. His eyes were shining and full of happiness. 'Do you think you'll stay here your whole life?'

Seth turned to her. 'Everything I need is right here. Where else would I go?'

Suddenly and inexplicably, Betty felt suffocated, despite the countryside spreading out every way she looked. 'Right,' she croaked. 'Where else?'

Taking a breath, she thought for a moment. 'You know when you said if it was only for a day, you'd still do it?'

Seth nodded. 'This is what I was born to do, Betty. If I could only have done it for a day or a week or a month, I'd still have taken the chance, just so I'd done it at all.' He frowned at her. 'Why all the questions?'

She gave him her best, most dazzling smile. 'Just thinking about some things, that's all.'

'Oh you don't want to be thinking, Elizabeth,' Seth said. 'Just be. That's best. Just be.' He gazed out over the estate, contentedly. Betty watched him, feeling that flicker of nerves again.

'I've been asked to help with ENSA while they're nearby,' she blurted out. 'It's for ten weeks.' She swallowed. 'Ten weeks at least. I want to do it.'

Seth turned to her and frowned. 'Don't they have their own people to help?'

'I'd be filling in for someone.'

'Oh I don't know, Betty. Sounds like they're taking advantage of your good nature.'

'They're not,' Betty said. 'I want to do it.'

But Seth shook his head. 'It's not right, you running around after women like that.'

'Women like what?' said Betty. Seth's reaction had annoyed her.

'Women who are only concerned with their looks,' he said. 'Women who want men to stare at them and goodness knows what else with them.'

'They're nice,' Betty said. 'And I wouldn't be running around. It's all very well organised.'

Seth snorted. 'Well if you want to be a seamstress for a gaggle of shrieking tarty women, that's up to you.'

Betty lifted her chin. 'You're right.'

'About the women?'

'About it being up to me.'

Seth glared at her. 'Ain't right, Betty,' he said.

Betty realised he was digging his heels in, and decided to use charm instead of arguing more. She looped her arm through his again and gazed up at him.

'Oh Seth,' she said in a light voice. 'You know it's only silly me, with my love of dancing and nice clothes. Helping with ENSA is a little hobby for now. That's all it is. Just me using the few skills I have to help our troops.' She smiled at him, and looked at him through her eyelashes. 'And I know it's going to get in the way of us spending time together, but we'll just have to make the moments we have really count, won't we?' She pressed her body up against him for a second, and then pulled away. 'But if you don't want me to do it, you just say . . . '

Seth drew her closer again and kissed her. 'Oh Betty,' he murmured. 'Don't be so dramatic. Of course you can help out if you want to.'

Betty relaxed into his embrace, wondering what he'd say if he knew the truth.

★　★　★

Later on that same day, Betty went to the bus stop. She wanted to get to the base and tell Pamela what she'd decided. She'd thought of telephoning, or sending a telegram even, but she thought it was best said in person.

Seth had said he'd be in the pub after work and to pop in if she fancied a drink. Betty had said she might, but now she didn't even glance in the direction of the Woolpack as she dashed to the bus stop.

She was convinced now that joining the ENSA dancers for the short while they were in Yorkshire was the best thing to do. Like Nancy had said, she had to do what was right for her. Seth may not like it, but he didn't need to know what she was really doing. It was his fault he'd assumed she'd be helping with the costumes, not hers. And it was only for a couple of months. One day, she'd be able to tell her grandchildren about getting up on that stage and dancing for the troops. And, maybe now when she thought about that baby-faced lad on the gate, she'd not feel awful about what might be in store for him but rather feel proud that she'd brought him joy for a few hours.

She didn't wait long for the bus, which was

good, and soon she was at the base feeling butterflies whirling madly in her stomach, and trying to wipe her sweaty palms on her skirt without anyone noticing.

Today the gate was being manned by a different soldier. He wasn't so baby-faced, but he had a lovely upturned nose and freckles which reminded Betty of a lad she'd known at school and that twisted her heart just a bit. She was definitely doing the right thing. He let her in and she hurried off to find Pamela.

She tracked her down in a quiet corner, clutching some sheet music and singing softly to herself.

'Sorry to disturb you,' Betty said as she approached. Pamela looked up, annoyance crossing her face first but then her expression changing as she saw it was Betty.

'Hello,' she said. 'I didn't think you were coming until tomorrow?'

Betty grinned. 'I wasn't supposed to, but I wanted to tell you in person that I'm going to cover Eleanor while she's injured.'

Pamela looked delighted. 'That's wonderful news, Betty. I'm so glad.'

Betty beamed at her.

'I was just going to have a cuppa,' Pamela said. 'Fancy one?'

'Yes please,' said Betty.

Pamela led the way to the mess hut, jabbering at Betty all the way. 'I'm so pleased you're going to get an idea of how wonderful ENSA is,' she said. 'People can be a bit cynical you know? They think it's frivolous.'

'I can imagine.'

Pamela made a face. 'My mother thinks I should be nursing,' she said. 'I'd be a terrible nurse. I faint when I see blood and I've got no patience.'

Betty laughed.

'Two teas, please,' Pamela said to the woman serving behind the counter.

'You could have joined the WRVS,' Betty said in an undertone as the woman gave them their drinks with a cheery grin.

Pamela shuddered. 'That's definitely not for me. I'm a hopeless cook, I can barely boil an egg. And I once tipped a full bottle of milk down the sink just because I wasn't concentrating.'

'I worked in a factory, making parachutes,' Betty said as they sat down at a table to drink their tea. 'I hated it.'

'Not surprised.'

'Still felt guilty when I left though,' Betty admitted for the first time. 'I told myself I was still doing my bit, working at the vet's because Nancy — that's my boss — she's taken over the practice while Mr Walters is off in the army. But dancing with ENSA is better.'

'Do you know what some people say it stands for? ENSA?'

Betty shrugged. 'No.'

'Every night something awful,' Pamela said with a hoot of laughter. 'What a cheek.'

She looked serious for a second. 'Honestly though, I know we're not always word perfect, and the costumes are a bit haphazard, but there are some really talented performers among us.

152

And if the critics could see how much the troops love it, they'd soon change their minds.'

'The audience was astonishing the other night,' Betty agreed. 'Seeing them clapping and hearing them singing along and cheering gave me so much energy. It was the best thing about it all.' She sighed. 'I just love being on stage, Pamela. I love having an audience and I love to dance.'

Pamela grinned. 'Anyone can see that. You're a born entertainer, Betty. I shouldn't wonder if this spell with ENSA leads to bigger and better things.'

Betty smiled, humbled by the praise but loving it all the same.

'Honestly,' Pamela went on. 'You should think about joining ENSA for real. It's such good training. I'm hoping to get an agent when the war's over. Maybe get a job in the West End.'

'In London?' Betty was impressed.

'Why not?' Pamela said. 'It gives me something to aim for. Something to look forward to, for when this horrible war finally ends.'

She looked sad for a second, as though her mind was elsewhere. Then she gathered herself and gave Betty an over-exaggerated wink. 'You should come too,' she said. 'We could share a flat. Work in a theatre. It would be a blast.'

It would be, Betty thought. It could be. But it wasn't going to happen, she knew that. Pamela, though, wasn't finished.

'You could be a Tiller Girl,' she said, looking at Betty appraisingly. 'You've got such long legs and you can kick higher than any of the other dancers.'

Betty had seen the Tiller Girls on newsreels at the flicks but never in real life. She thought they were wonderful with their slick movements, all in perfect time with one another. And their matching outfits took her breath away. But that wasn't for girls like her, Yorkshire girls with loving families, and sweethearts like her Seth.

'Get away,' she said good-naturedly.

'I'm being serious. Especially if you get some experience here first.'

Chuckling, Betty drained the dregs of her tea and stood up. 'I won't get any experience if I don't go and find Daphne and tell her I'm going to take the job,' she said.

'She's in the rehearsal room,' Pamela said. 'She'll be really pleased. Come and find me when you're done.'

Betty nodded, nervous and excited about what was to come.

'And think about joining ENSA properly,' Pamela said. 'You're the perfect fit.'

15

When Betty disappeared to talk to Seth, about what, Nancy didn't quite understand, the surgery seemed very quiet. Nancy busied herself with tidying the surgery, re-stocking the medicine cabinet, cleaning some cages, and generally getting organised. She felt, for the first time, a slight flush of pride in the Beckindale practice, rather than the helpless despair she'd become used to feeling since she'd taken over. She knew she wasn't out of the woods when it came to the finances, but she felt less hopeless.

Susan arrived at the surgery later on in the afternoon. Nancy was arranging some instruments on a metal tray when the girl came into the treatment room so quietly that Nancy didn't hear her approach.

'Hello,' Susan called, and Nancy, caught unawares, jumped with surprise and dropped the large metal tray with an enormous clatter, scattering instruments and the tray itself across the surgery floor.

'Oh, bother,' she said. But as she bent to pick everything up, she caught sight of Susan who'd dropped to her knees and curled into a ball, hands over her ears.

Very gently, Nancy put her hand on the girl's shoulder. 'Susan?' she said. 'Susan, it's me, Nancy. I just dropped a tray. Are you all right?'

Susan looked up, her face frightened, and as

she focused on Nancy tears welled in her eyes.

'Oh, Nancy,' she said. 'I'm so sorry.'

Nancy held out a hand to help her up, and Susan took it, getting to her feet with some effort.

'I just got a fright, that's all,' the girl said. She looked embarrassed, almost. 'I'm not good with sudden noises.'

Nancy felt foolish. Of course the poor girl wasn't good with noises — it must have been terrifying in London with bombs dropping night after night.

'Come and have a seat,' she said, steering Susan out of the treatment room and into the waiting area. 'I'll get you a glass of water.'

She could feel Susan trembling all over as she took the girl by the shoulders and sat her down. Her employee management skills were really being tested today. Her father would be impressed, she thought resentfully. If he ever got to hear of it, that was.

She filled a glass with water from the sink, and gave it to Susan who sipped it gratefully.

'Feeling better?' Nancy asked.

Susan nodded. 'Just a bit silly.'

'Nonsense, you got a fright. Don't feel silly.'

'When it happened, the bomb, there was no warning,' Susan said suddenly. 'It was just a huge thump out of nowhere. The siren hadn't gone off. It was dark, but not as late as some of the raids had been.'

Nancy didn't know what to say. Susan had been so quiet and now she was talking and Nancy didn't want to say the wrong thing and stop her. Instead she just took the girl's hand.

'We were having tea. Mum had just got home from the factory and she was knackered, so I'd sort of taken over. I was watching the little ones and making sure they was eating everything.'

Nancy was almost afraid to ask. 'The little ones?'

'My sister, Cass. She was ten. My brother, Andrew, who was six. And Eric, the baby. He was almost three and he could be a right bugger when he wanted to be. He was messing around in his high chair, laughing like a drain. He picked his bowl up and he chucked it on the floor. You know like they do?'

Nancy remembered her nephew, Frank, doing just the same thing when he was a toddler. She nodded.

Susan swallowed. 'He threw his bowl and Mum sort of sighed so I said I'd get it, and I crawled on the floor under the table to pick it up, and Eric was laughing . . . ' she paused to gather herself. 'And then there was this huge crash and I don't remember nothing else until I woke up in the hospital. Mum, and Cass and Andrew and little Eric . . . ' her voice caught and she paused again. 'They'd gone.'

'Oh, Susan,' Nancy breathed, feeling sick. 'All of them?'

Susan nodded, her lips pinched tightly together. 'I like to remember Eric laughing.'

Nancy felt sick but she managed to give the girl a small smile. 'That's a nice memory,' she said. She felt so sad for the poor, poor girl losing her whole family like that. 'What about your father?'

157

Susan shrugged. 'Dunno where he is. He joined up — he's in the Navy though. Lord knows why because he'd barely even seen the sea before — but we've not heard nothing for more than a year. Gran reckons he might be a POW but we don't know for sure.'

'Oh, Susan.'

Susan forced a smile. 'I'm lucky to have my gran. She's great.'

Nancy thought of Mrs Roberts with her fat cat and her warm heart and smiled too. 'She's a good woman.'

'I'm lucky to have you, too,' Susan said. 'I can't tell you how much it means to me, working here. I miss Scruff ever such a lot and being around the animals really helps.'

Moved by this girl, who'd suffered so much and who still carried on, Nancy could only nod and squeeze Susan's hand once more.

'I'm lucky to have you,' she eventually managed to say in a squeaky voice.

'Oh, I never told you,' Susan said, sitting up a bit straighter, and breaking the sombre mood. 'I got top marks in my biology test. All that help you gave me really paid off.'

'Well, that really is something,' Nancy said, feeling a flush of pride she'd only ever felt in herself before. 'Well done, Susan.'

She thought for a moment.

'Mr Harden gave me some of his wife's fruitcake the other day,' she said. 'It's pretty solid but I reckon it'd do nicely with a cup of tea as a celebration. Shall I put the kettle on?'

'I'll do it,' Susan said. 'You have a sit down.'

158

Nancy watched Susan walk through to the kitchen area to put the kettle on. The youngster was really coming out of her shell, she thought. Opening up about her family, and chatting much more than she'd ever done before. Nancy felt quite pleased with herself. She was finding her feet, making a living, even — sort of — making friends. She liked Lily Proudfoot a lot, and Betty was fun to be around, and the Land Girl, Audrey, always stopped for a chat when she passed by. It wasn't all as disastrous as it had seemed just a few weeks earlier. Maybe she was starting to belong in Beckindale — finally.

16

Sometimes Audrey wondered if her brain was getting bigger with all the new knowledge she'd shoved into it since she arrived in Beckindale. Her muscles were definitely bigger — her legs were lean and sinewy from all the physical work and her shoulders were broad and sturdy. She rather liked it. She'd never felt strong before; her mother had always worried about her too much to let her do much physical exercise. She'd never played hockey or learned to swim but now here she was, hoisting bales of straw onto her shoulders without hesitation, learning to ride a horse — which she loved — and the other day she'd even climbed a ladder on to a barn roof to mend a broken tile without even thinking twice about it. But it was hard work. Really, really hard. And things weren't all smooth sailing at Emmerdale Farm.

Jacob was tricky. He was a good teacher and he encouraged her to try lots of new things. But his moods were unpredictable and he wasn't exactly one for praise. If it wasn't for his occasional nods, Audrey never knew whether she was doing the right thing. She didn't always mind. She was happy in her own company and generally she and Jacob rubbed along quite well. But on the days when she was finding it tough or struggling to learn something new, Audrey longed for a pat on the back or a 'well done' from her surly boss.

She knew now that he'd lost his brother, Edward, in the war. That made her feel more kindly towards him. Perhaps his short-temper and sharp tongue were his grief talking. It didn't always make it easy for Audrey to cope with though.

She'd hoped Maggie would be warmer but though she was at first, the older woman had become distant and distracted. Audrey thought she might be ill — she remembered seeing her pain when she and Ned were sorting out the beehive — but she didn't think it was appropriate for her to ask. And some days Maggie seemed better.

But all in all, life at Emmerdale Farm wasn't quite as fun as Audrey had hoped. Every day she heard her mother's voice in her head, telling her she couldn't do the physical work demanded of her, that she should be careful, stay at home, and not tire herself out. It was getting harder to ignore that voice and sometimes, when she lay in bed worrying about the next day, she wondered if she should just give up and go back home.

Ned, though, was the one thing that stopped her packing her bags. She'd been spending more and more time with him recently. He was coming by later to take her to the pictures in Hotten in fact. Audrey loved every moment she shared with Ned. They talked about everything and she'd even told him her worries about the farm. He was definitely a bright spot in an otherwise gloomy time.

But still, she was learning a lot. Expanding her brain along with her muscles. Today she was watching Jacob as he tried to show her the best way to get the cows into the milking parlour. She may have been understanding more about farming, but Audrey was still a bit nervous around the cattle and Jacob was determined to get rid of her worries so he'd dragged her out of bed at this ungodly hour — the sun wasn't even properly up yet — to come and help with the milking.

'They're big, but they'll do as you tell them,' he told her as he slapped one cow gently on the rump to get her to move. 'There you go, girl.'

Audrey mimicked his tone, speaking calmly but firmly to the cow nearest her. 'In you go,' she said. 'In you go, girl.'

The cow turned and gave Audrey an appraising look from under her long eyelashes, and then stayed exactly where she was.

'In you go,' said Audrey. Again, the cow stayed still. Audrey looked at Jacob in despair.

'She's not listening.'

'They're just not used to you yet,' Jacob said. 'Try again.'

Audrey gave the cow a firm slap on the rump. 'Go on, girl.' But no. The huge beast dug her hooves into the muck and stayed put.

'Go on,' Jacob said, prodding the cow gently. She swung her head round, as though checking it was him and not Audrey who was trying to get her to move, and then obediently trotted up the small ramp and into the parlour, followed by the other cows.

'Infuriating,' groaned Audrey.

Jacob frowned. 'They're like women,' he said. Was he joking? Jacob Sugden didn't joke very often. He smiled and, realising he had indeed been light-hearted, Audrey chuckled.

'At least I don't have to milk them all by hand,' she said, raising her left arm and gesturing with her stump. 'It would be like painting the Forth Bridge — I'd be milking until it was time to start this evening's session.'

Jacob gave her a look that she couldn't quite read. 'You do all right, Audrey,' he said.

Pleased with what was, for Jacob, rare high praise, and still feeling put out that she couldn't handle the cows, Audrey flushed with pride. 'Do you need help with the milking machine?'

He shook his head. 'Ray's inside to keep an eye on the cows,' he said, talking about one of the older farmhands who worked for a few different farmers when they were needed. 'I can get it started, if you want to go and get some breakfast. I'll be down in a minute.'

Suddenly starving hungry, Audrey nodded. She wandered down to the farmhouse to find some food. There was no sign of Maggie, nor Joe, but there was a loaf of bread on the dresser and a pot of homemade jam. Audrey wondered where Maggie had gone. Perhaps she'd taken herself off to rest. She did that more and more now, when before she'd been full of energy. But she'd obviously been around this morning because she'd left the bread here for Audrey and Jacob. Audrey filled the kettle, trying not to think that she'd failed because she couldn't get the cows into the shed. She'd try again tomorrow, she thought. It would be fine. It had to be.

Awkwardly, she put the bread onto the board, and picked up the knife, but perhaps because she was distracted or tired from her early start, as she went to slice the loaf, the knife slipped and cut her left arm. It wasn't a bad cut, but it stung and as Audrey watched the blood dribble, she began to cry. This was too difficult, she thought as she tried to find a cloth to dab away the blood. Jacob was mean and Maggie was distant, and Joe was sweet but barely there, and she couldn't do anything Jacob asked her to do and now this. Filled with self-pity she held a cloth to her cut, leaned against the sink and sobbed her heart out.

'Now then, what's this?' Jacob came into the kitchen, looking uncomfortable as he saw her tears. 'What's upset you? Are you hurt?'

Embarrassed, Audrey took the cloth from her wound and showed him. 'It's not bad,' she said. 'I slipped when I was cutting the bread.'

He looked at her and then, without speaking, he leaned past her and opened a cupboard. For a second, Audrey thought he was going to get a mug and make himself breakfast around her, but actually he pulled out a first aid box.

'Sit yourself down,' he said, not unkindly. 'I'll have a look.'

Audrey obeyed, plonking down on a kitchen chair. Jacob washed his hands and then sat next to her, gently taking the cloth away and looking at her cut.

'I'll just put some antiseptic on it, and cover it

164

so it doesn't get mucky,' he said. Audrey watched him silently as he dealt with the cut. She liked that he didn't balk at touching her left arm — lots of people shied away from her missing hand. And she tried not to wince when he dabbed it with antiseptic that made it sting.

'Good as new,' he said. 'You sit there, I'll make the tea.'

Deftly, he filled the teapot, sliced some bread and put it all on the table in front of Audrey. She sighed, still feeling sorry for herself.

'What's the matter now?' Jacob said, his surliness never far from the surface.

'You did all that in about two minutes, without cutting yourself,' she said. 'I couldn't do that, and I couldn't do the cows. I'm hopeless.'

Jacob gave her that same odd look he'd given her by the cow shed. 'You're very capable,' he said.

Audrey laughed in a humourless way. 'That's what every girl dreams of being called, isn't it? Capable.'

Jacob rolled his eyes. 'I just mean that you've proved me wrong, haven't you? All those worries I had when you first arrived and now look at you.'

'I feel like you were right,' Audrey admitted. 'That it would have been better for everyone if I'd gone home then. Or better yet, not come here in the first place.'

'Really?' said Jacob. He sounded surprised. 'Is that how you really feel?'

'Yes, it is.'

'But you're such a help,' Jacob said. 'And we

love having you around. Even Pa is fond of you, and he doesn't like anyone.'

Audrey gave a small, genuine chuckle. 'Honestly?'

'Honestly,' Jacob said. 'You've done well.'

Audrey looked down at her plate, embarrassed to feel more tears spring into her eyes.

'Oh now, don't cry,' he said, looking awkward. 'Is it better if I'm cross with you?'

Audrey gave him a watery smile. 'No, it's nice when you're nice,' she said. 'I'm just being silly.'

Jacob shrugged. 'Ma says I'm too hard on you.'

'You're not,' Audrey said. 'Not always. I'm learning so much.' She wiped away another tear. 'I just . . . my mother . . . it's difficult.'

Jacob shifted in his seat. 'Bet your mother's proud of you.'

Audrey let out another sob and Jacob looked horrified. 'What did I say?'

She didn't want to tell him about her mother and the difficulties she'd had, not really. But he was being so nice, and somehow she found she started talking and couldn't stop.

'When I was born, my parents were devastated about my arm,' she said. 'Mum said the doctor apologised to her. Apologised, can you imagine?'

'It can't have been easy for any of you,' Jacob said, pouring them both another mug of tea.

Audrey shook her head. 'Not easy, no. People still make assumptions about me because of my arm. And my mother, God love her, is the worst.'

'How so?'

'She smothers me,' Audrey said. 'She treats me

like I'm about to break. And I understand why, because when I was small, Mum had to fight to get other parents to let their daughters play with me, or to let me join in games.' She swallowed a sob, remembering how some parents would bustle their children away, telling them to leave the 'poor little girl' alone and not bother her. 'She was really protective of me, and I'm grateful, I am. But the older I got, the worse it got. I made friends, but she didn't want me doing anything with them. She wouldn't let me skate on the pond when it froze like everyone else. She didn't let me go camping, or on the trip to the summer fair with my class. She wouldn't let me join the Girl Guides.'

'That's kind,' Jacob said, his face taking on a more sullen guise. 'It's nice to have a mother who loves you like that.'

'I know she was only doing it because she loves me. But I don't want to be treated like I'm special,' Audrey said fiercely. 'I'm not special, I'm just like everyone else. I'm good at some things and hopeless at others and I can do my bit for the war effort too.'

'What did she say when you told her you were joining the Land Army?'

Audrey laughed.

'I didn't tell her.'

'What?' Jacob looked impressed but also slightly disapproving.

'I joined up, which wasn't easy. I had to really talk the enlisting officer into it. And then once it was all arranged, I told them. I chose to do my training as far away as possible from home and I didn't tell my mother where I was going. I send her letters via my schoolfriend, Janet. She's my go-between.'

'That's cruel,' Jacob said bluntly and Audrey winced. It was cruel, she knew that. But she also knew if she hadn't done it this way, she'd have been living at home with her parents, living a sort of half-life, forever.

'If my mother knew where I was, she'd round my father up and they'd come and get me,' she said.

'Bet they miss you.'

'I miss them,' Audrey said, honestly. 'But this was the only way.'

Jacob tutted. 'You don't know how lucky you are, to have a mother who cares so much.'

'Maggie cares about you,' Audrey said, annoyed that he'd not seen things her way.

Jacob snorted, back to his usual grumpy self. 'Does she?'

Audrey had clearly hit a nerve. 'She's proud of you,' she said, thinking of conversations she'd had with Maggie since she'd arrived. 'She's always telling me she doesn't know what she'd do without you.'

'Is she?' Jacob looked like a little boy as he said it. Audrey wondered why he was so convinced his mother didn't care. It certainly didn't seem that way from what she'd seen around the farm.

'She is, she's told me so.'

Jacob snorted again, but Audrey thought he looked pleased. Talking of Maggie, though, made her think. 'I've not talked to your mum much recently. She's been a bit distant, don't you think? Taking herself off.'

Jacob nodded. 'I had noticed. Like she's got something on her mind? I thought she was just thinking about Edward, but you've seen it too?'

'I have,' Audrey said. 'Maybe you should check in with her? Make sure she's all right?'

Jacob made a face. 'Not sure about that. We're not really much for mother-son chats.'

Audrey frowned at him. 'Well, do something about it,' she said.

Again Jacob gave her that odd look and she suddenly realised what it was. It was admiration. The knowledge made her sit up a bit straighter and pull her shoulders back.

'See?' Jacob said. 'Capable. You don't see obstacles, do you? You just climb right over them and keep on going.'

Audrey grinned. 'Wouldn't life be boring if it was too easy?'

Jacob drained his mug of tea and stood up. 'We need to go and check on the cows,' he said. Obviously their first proper conversation was over.

'Will you speak to Maggie?'

He looked at her. 'Maybe.'

They smiled at each other, and Audrey felt a weight lift. She'd been wary of Jacob, but now she felt she understood him a bit better. She liked him, she realised. He was a good farmer, and an excellent teacher.

'What about you and Ned Barlow, eh?' Jacob said as they trudged back towards the milking shed.

Audrey blushed. 'We're friends.'

169

'Just friends?'

Growing up, Audrey had always longed for a sibling, and as Jacob teased her she had a sudden glimpse of what it would have been like to have had a big brother. She found she liked it. She leaned towards Jacob and nudged him with her shoulder.

'Leave it,' she said. 'None of your business.'

'Ah,' said Jacob.

'Ah what?'

'That means there is something going on.'

'Cows should be ready to go back to the field, now,' Audrey said. She walked faster, leaving Jacob behind. 'Come on, Sugden. Look lively.'

The welcome sound of Jacob's laughter followed her into the milking shed.

17

'I can't believe Jacob was so nice to you,' Ned told Audrey later as they rumbled along the lane in his dad's van. 'He's not nice to anyone.'

'He's sad about his brother, I think,' Audrey said. 'That would make anyone grumpy.'

'He was surly long before Edward went away,' Ned pointed out. Audrey made a face.

'I think there's all sorts going on between him and Maggie,' she said. 'Lots of unspoken grudges.' She sighed. 'That's probably true of all families, to be honest.'

'Definitely true in mine,' said Ned. 'Except our grudges are spoken.'

Audrey knew he was still annoyed with his sister for saying those things about him before the dance, but she wasn't bothered. Ned had made it quite clear that Audrey was the girl for him.

In fact, as they drove along the lane heading home after their night out at the pictures, his fingers were resting gently on her leg. She liked feeling the heaviness of his hand and the warmth of him through her cotton frock and when he took it off to change gear, her leg felt cold.

She was disappointed when they reached Emmerdale Farm. She wanted to ask Ned to come in for a cup of tea but she didn't know if anyone would still be up. Jacob usually went to bed early, because he had to be up at the crack of dawn, but Maggie often stayed up reading in the kitchen. Audrey couldn't tell if there was a light on because of the blackout curtains at the window.

'That's me,' she said. 'Thanks for a lovely evening.'

Ned put his hand on her face and she gazed at him, taking in his eyes and his crooked front teeth, and his smile.

'Thank you,' he said. He leaned over and kissed her gently on the lips. Audrey felt her whole body melt as their kiss grew deeper. Kissing Ned was definitely nothing like kissing the boys at school. When she kissed Ned, it was like her whole body responded to his touch. She even felt tingling in her toes. It was wonderful.

They stayed in the van kissing slowly for a few minutes, but then reluctantly broke apart. Ned had to get the van home and Audrey knew Jacob would be annoyed if she was tired in the morning.

'Bye!' she called as she hopped down from the passenger seat. Ned blew her a kiss then he pulled away. Giddy with joy, Audrey danced into the kitchen, shutting the door firmly behind her so no light escaped. To her surprise though, the room was empty. The lamp by the chair was on, there was a half-drunk mug of tea on the side table and a pad of paper and a pen discarded next to it. But there was no one around. Odd.

'Like the *Mary Celeste*,' muttered Audrey. She went to the mug of tea and felt it with her hand — still warm. And then her eye was caught by the writing on the notepad. It was a letter in Jacob's handwriting and it began 'Dear Annie . . . '

Knowing she was doing wrong, but somehow doing it all the same, Audrey picked up the pad and began to read.

'Dear Annie,' she read. 'I know you are still angry with me and I am not surprised because what I did was terrible. So I don't expect you to reply to this letter, just like you haven't replied to the others.'

Audrey bit her lip, wondering what Jacob had done. Slowly, she sank down into the chair and carried on reading.

'I wanted to tell you that Audrey, our new Land Girl, is working out well. She is a hard worker and has made a real difference. I don't need to worry about the War Ag — for now anyway. We have got the flax growing well and in spring, Ma bought a hive of bees.'

Audrey read on. Jacob had written a friendly, chatty letter all about the farm and the village — even mentioning Lily Proudfoot at the garage and Sarah Barlow, Ned's other sister who Audrey liked enormously.

'I hope things are going well in . . . ' the letter finished. Jacob had obviously stopped writing in a hurry. Audrey turned the paper over but there was nothing on the other side. And then it was snatched out of her hand and she looked up to see Jacob looming over her, his face twisted in fury.

'What the bloody hell do you think you're doing?' he roared.

Audrey scrambled to her feet, her heart thumping. 'I'm so sorry,' she said. 'I wanted to see if your tea was still warm because I didn't know where you were, and your letter caught my eye.' She swallowed. 'I saw my name.'

'That doesn't give you the right to go through my stuff,' he shouted.

'I know,' Audrey said. 'I really am sorry.'

But Jacob was still angry. 'That's private. You can't go around reading other people's letters. How dare you?'

Jacob was bigger than Audrey and now he seemed even larger as he stood in front of her. She was trembling with fear, but she was angry too.

'You shouldn't have left it lying around then,' she said.

'Fox got into the hen house,' he said. 'I had to run.'

Audrey was aghast. 'Oh God, are they all right?'

Jacob shrugged. 'Only got a couple. I chased him off before he could do much damage.'

'Thank goodness.' She looked at him, trying to gauge if his fury had subsided. She thought it had, a bit. 'It's a nice letter,' she said. 'Chatty.'

Jacob glared at her.

'She doesn't reply?' Audrey went on, ignoring his sullen stare. 'This Annie you're writing to? She doesn't answer your letters?'

Jacob's shoulders slumped. 'No,' he said. 'But I keep writing.'

'You should,' urged Audrey.

Jacob glared at her again. 'What do you care?' he snapped. 'And what right have you got to tell me about writing letters, when you don't even tell your own mother where you are. Maybe you should write to her. Properly, I mean.'

Audrey's jaw dropped. How dare he speak to her like that?

'That's none of your business,' she said.

'Yeah? Well my letters to Annie ain't none of yours,' Jacob said, waving the paper in her face. 'So just . . . ' he cast around for the words. 'Sod off.'

'You sod off,' said Audrey back. She'd never said such aggressive words before.

There was a pause and they both glowered at each other. Someone was going to have to back down. Audrey clenched her hand into a fist and breathed out slowly. Come on, Audrey, she told herself. Be the bigger person here.

'Shall I make you another tea?' she said, her eyes still on Jacob's red, angry face. 'That one's been sitting there for a while.'

She thought Jacob was going to say no, but he sighed. 'That would be nice.'

Audrey freshened the pot and made them both a mug, then she brought the drinks over and settled herself into the other chair by the fire.

'I'm sorry for reading the letter,' she said.

Jacob gave her a sullen look. 'I'm sorry for shouting.' He sounded sulky like a child caught out doing something wrong.

'So,' Audrey said, curiosity getting the better of her. 'Who's Annie?'

'None of your business,' Jacob said. But he said it mildly. His anger had definitely calmed down.

'Might help to talk about it,' Audrey said.

'Rather than bottling it all up.'

Jacob screwed his nose up, but he didn't speak.

'Is she your girl?'

'No,' he said quickly. 'She was Edward's girl.'

'Tell me,' Audrey said. 'Tell me about Edward.'

Jacob slurped his tea and took a deep breath.

'He didn't have to enlist,' he said, looking at a point somewhere over Audrey's head. She could see his eyes were sad. 'Neither of us did. But we decided one of us would go and the other would stay here and run the farm. We drew straws.'

'That seems a fair way to do it.'

'It does, doesn't it? Except it wasn't. Because I messed around with the straws and made sure Edward got the short one.'

Audrey was shocked, but she tried not to show it.

'Jacob,' she breathed. What did you do that for? 'Were you scared of going?'

Jacob looked at her properly now. 'No,' he said firmly. 'That wasn't it. I did it because I was in love with Annie Pearson.'

'Annie in the letter,' Audrey said.

He nodded. 'Annie was Edward's sweetheart — and I thought if he was away, she'd choose me.'

He swallowed, and blinked away what might have been tears. Audrey pretended not to see.

'He wasn't supposed to die.'

Feeling sorry for him, Audrey reached out and gave his hand a gentle pat.

'And then it all got really complicated,' he

said. 'Things haven't been right with Ma and me since. Edward was her favourite, you see?'

'I'm sure that's not true.'

But Jacob nodded. 'It's to do with stuff that happened way back, during the last war. I know she loves me, but I know if she had to pick, she'd choose Edward.'

Audrey wasn't having it. 'I really don't think that's true,' she said.

Jacob shrugged. 'Don't matter,' he mumbled.

'So you write to Annie and she doesn't reply?' Audrey asked, wanting to know more about this woman.

'I write every week or so.'

'Why doesn't she reply?'

'Because she blames me for Edward being killed. I told her, you see, what I did with the straws.'

Audrey couldn't really blame Annie for being angry. But she also understood just how sorry Jacob was.

'Where is she, this Annie? Where has she gone?'

'She's in the Wrens,' Jacob said. 'Portsmouth.'

'Do you still love her? Has she come back to Beckindale since she left?'

Jacob kept his eyes fixed on the point above Audrey's head.

'I've only seen her once since she went. Not for a while though. She came to Lily and Jack's wedding.'

'And?'

'And nowt. She was Edward's girl. That's all water under the bridge.'

Audrey opened her mouth to ask more questions but Jacob raised his hand to stop her speaking.

'Nowt,' he said again. 'It's over and done with.'

Audrey's heart twisted in sorrow for him. He was carrying so much upset and guilt — no wonder he was grumpy all the time.

'I might go to bed,' she said. 'Busy day tomorrow.'

She stood up and then, on a whim, she dropped a kiss on to the top of Jacob's head.

'Never give up,' she said. 'Goodnight.'

Jacob nodded. 'Goodnight.'

18

Later the next day, Audrey cycled down into the village to make an appointment with the vet. One of the horses had a bite on its ear that had got infected and Jacob wanted Nancy Tate to look at it.

'Can you go down and see when she'd be free?' he'd asked Audrey.

'Are you scared of her?' she teased. 'Because she shouted at you?'

'No,' said Jacob. Then he grinned. 'Bit.'

'You should be,' Audrey said. 'She's right scary.'

'Listen to you, sounding like a Yorkshire lass,' Jacob said. 'Now, get off or you'll see how I can be right scary too.'

Audrey had jumped on to Jacob's old bike, which she used often now, and cycled off down the lane towards Beckindale. It was a glorious day, warm but with a soft breeze, and the hedgerows were in full bloom. She was much more confident on two wheels now and as she cycled, slower than that awful day when she'd had to fetch Nancy in a panic, but far more controlled, she thought about how she'd love to show her mother what her life was like here. Show her how she could cycle, and ride a horse — almost — and dig vegetable patches, or carry straw. She'd written to her this morning about how much she was looking forward to harvest time. She'd considered writing her address on top of the letter, and posting it straight to her parents' house — Jacob's reaction to how she kept herself away from her parents had made her understand that she was being cruel. But in the end, she'd sent it via Janet as usual. Perhaps, though, she thought now, her mother just needed to see what she was doing to understand how able she really was? Or perhaps she would be horrified if she saw her balancing on the back of Jacob's horse and drag her home to Sussex to roll bandages and read to injured soldiers. Not that there was anything wrong with that, but it wasn't what Audrey wanted to be doing.

Plus, of course, she'd miss Ned terribly. He was such a nice man, that's what everyone said about him. He was so funny and kind, and never once had he made a big thing of her missing hand. And the fact that he was very handsome with broad shoulders, thick arms and dreamy brown eyes that she could look into for hours didn't hurt.

She wobbled on her bicycle as she thought about going to see *The Maltese Falcon* last night, and the way Ned had kissed her when he dropped her home, so perfectly that her head had spun and her heart had pounded.

She wobbled again, as she hit a bump in the road and nearly went right over the handlebars.

'Concentrate, Audrey,' she told herself crossly. It wouldn't do to fall off her bike because she was thinking about her boyfriend. Was Ned her boyfriend? They'd not said anything formally, but she was beginning to think of him as that. Maybe she'd bring it up when they saw each other later.

She managed to reach the vet's surgery without any further mishaps and propped the bicycle up against the wall. Inside, it was heaving. There were people and animals everywhere and barely any empty seats.

'Hello,' she said to Betty, who was looking completely in control, sitting behind the reception desk, and wearing a white coat.

'Hello, Audrey,' she said. 'What can I do for you? Mrs Armitage, you can take the kittens in now.'

One of the women in the waiting room stood up and took a large cat basket into the treatment room.

'It's so busy,' Audrey said, impressed.

'I know. Nancy did some sort of deal with Lily Proudfoot and now we've almost got too many patients.'

'I need to make an appointment for Jacob's horse,' Audrey said. 'I hope you can fit it in.'

Betty ran her finger down the appointments book and told Audrey when Nancy could fit her in. Audrey agreed and jotted down the times in her own diary.

'That was easy,' she said.

Betty grinned.

They chatted for a few minutes about the farm, then they both looked up as Mrs Armitage left the treatment room and Nancy poked her head out.

'Just going to the loo,' Nancy hissed at Betty. 'Give me five minutes before you send in the next one.'

'Will do,' said Betty. She looked at Audrey.

'Five minutes for you to tell me all your news,' she said, a knowing look on her pretty face. 'What's the latest on you and Ned.'

'Betty,' Audrey grumbled. 'I didn't come here to be interrogated. Anyway, it's you who looks full of life and happiness. Is it Seth who's made you smile like that?'

A shadow crossed Betty's features, then she gave Audrey what seemed to be a rather forced laugh. 'Seth's wonderful,' she said. 'He's such a sweetheart.'

'But?'

'What?'

'It sounded like you were going to say, 'he's such a sweetheart, but . . . ''

Betty looked alarmed then she smiled. 'You're right, I was.'

'So what was the but?'

'I was just going to say, he's not why I've been so happy recently.'

Audrey leaned closer. 'Betty, you've not met someone else, have you?'

'No!' Betty was shocked. 'Never. Seth's my fella.'

'Then what?'

'I've been helping out with the ENSA dancers,' she said. 'All over Yorkshire. It's wonderful.'

'Sounds right up your street,' Audrey said. 'What are you doing? Costumes and props and that?'

Betty turned her chair slightly so she was facing away from all the people in the waiting room and spoke in a low voice.

'At first,' she said. 'Then I started dancing.'

Audrey was thrilled. 'I remember seeing you at that dance in Hotten. You're a good dancer, Betty. It sounds perfect.'

Betty looked dreamy. 'It really is. I love every second. And they've extended their stay now so I get to do it for longer.'

'So what's that got to do with Seth?'

Betty grimaced. 'I haven't told him.'

'That you're dancing?'

'He just thinks I am doing costumes, and I've never told him the truth.'

Audrey waved a hand. 'Look,' she said. 'I don't know much about romance but I reckon what he doesn't know won't hurt him. So what if you're sewing frocks or dancing? You're helping out either way.'

'I suppose.'

'There you go. No harm done.'

'You're right,' Betty said, nodding. 'No harm done.' She gave Audrey another dazzling smile, but Audrey couldn't help noticing it didn't quite reach her eyes.

Nancy reappeared and nodded at Betty before she dashed back into the treatment room. Betty raised her voice, 'Mr Salinger, Miss Tate should be ready for Percy now.'

An elderly man clutching a budgie in a cage, nodded to Betty and went through to the back.

'Nancy will see Jacob tomorrow, then,' Betty said to Audrey. Obviously their conversation about ENSA and Betty's dancing was over.

'If you ever fancy a cup of tea,' Audrey began. 'Or something stronger? You know where I am.'

This time Betty's smile did reach her eyes. 'I'd like that,' she said. 'Thank you.'

It was interesting, Audrey thought as she left the surgery, how even the people who seemed to be happy and settled with their lot sometimes had other things going on that you'd never know about. She walked down the path and sighed in frustration as she saw her bicycle had a flat tyre. She must have got a puncture when she wobbled over that bump on the way to the village. That would serve her right for mooning over Ned when she should have been concentrating on the road. Now she'd have to walk all the way home, wheeling the bike.

'You should take it to Lily.' A voice made Audrey look up, and there was Susan in her school uniform, a heavy bag of books slung over her shoulder.

'Pardon?'

'Lily Proudfoot,' Susan said. 'She's doing bike repairs now at the garage. She's not there all the time, because of her baby, but she's there now — I just saw her.'

'She is?'

'I think it was Ruby's idea,' Susan said proudly. 'Well, Nancy's idea and Ruby's.' Audrey didn't doubt it, she knew Ruby was a real force to be reckoned with.

'I'll take it over there now,' she said. 'Thanks, Susan.'

Susan waved and went off towards the surgery, while Audrey wheeled her bike across past the pub and over to the garage. Susan was right; Lily was there, working outside the garage itself. She was wearing overalls and had her hair tied in a scarf and she was putting a wheel back on a very fancy-looking bicycle with dropped handlebars and gleaming paintwork. Beside her was her baby's pram and every now and then she glanced into it.

'Lily,' Audrey said, hurrying over.

Lily looked pleased to see Audrey, which was nice. Audrey had been so busy up at Emmerdale Farm over the last few weeks that she'd not had time to catch up with the woman she hoped would become a friend.

'Hold on,' Lily said. She gave the wheel one final push and it snapped on to the bike frame. She smiled in satisfaction.

'All done. How are you?'

'I'm really well, thank you,' Audrey said. 'Which is more than can be said for my bicycle.'

She showed Lily the flat tyre.

'I can sort that for you in no time,' Lily said.

Audrey perched on the wall by the garage and pecked into the pram. Hope was asleep, her little cheeks rosy red.

'She looks like she's blushing,' she said.

'Teething,' said Lily, pulling the tyre off Audrey's wheel in one swift movement. 'Nightmare.'

Her eyes softened as she gazed at her daughter. 'She's been in such pain, some nights, I've just wanted to take it away for her, poor lamb.'

Audrey remembered once hearing her mother saying she wished she could swap her daughter's misshapen arm for her good hand, and felt a flush of guilt about how she'd treated her parents.

'So you're doing all the bike repairs?'

Lily beamed. 'I am. It's going very well.'

'I've seen lots of cyclists around, so you must be busy.'

'Getting there,' Lily said, nodding.

Audrey was pleased for Lily, who looked happier than she had ever seen her.

'How are things up at Emmerdale Farm?' Lily asked.

'Good. Busy.' She paused. 'Jacob was telling me about Annie Pearson,' she said casually.

Lily looked up. 'What did he tell you?'

'That she was his Edward's sweetheart.'

'They were always together, those two,' Lily said fondly. 'She misses him something terrible. She did the right thing, getting away.'

'Jacob misses her.'

'Really?' Lily sounded doubtful. 'He was never very nice to her. I always thought he was jealous of her and Edward.'

Audrey didn't say that Lily had been right about that. It was Jacob's business, after all. Instead she asked what Annie was like.

'Lovely,' Lily said. 'Hardworking, caring, funny. But lately she's not been herself. She's had a lot to cope with, losing Edward. And . . . ' She trailed off. 'She did the right thing getting away,' she said again.

'Maybe she'll come back one day,' Audrey said, wondering how anyone could leave Beckindale forever. It was such a nice place to live.

'Maybe,' said Lily, but she didn't sound very sure.

Audrey swung her legs out in front of her, and Lily watched. 'You look good,' she said. 'Healthy and strong. You're brown as a berry and look at the muscles in your arms. Farming obviously agrees with you.'

Audrey grinned. 'It's really hard. Much harder than I expected it to be,' she said. 'But I enjoy being outdoors, and creating something so important. It feels good doing my bit for the war effort, too.'

'Good for you.' Lily frowned at Audrey's tyre. 'Here's the hole,' she said. 'I could patch it, but I've got a spare inner tube. I'll swap it for you. How did it happen?'

'I hit a bump when I was cycling down,' Audrey said, feeling her cheeks flush as red as baby Hope's. 'I wasn't concentrating.'

'Thinking about Ned, were you?' Lily grinned. She stood up and wiped her hands on her trousers. 'I'll just get that tube, hang on.'

Audrey sat in the sunshine, watching little Hope snoozing peacefully. She could hear men talking outside the pub, and children shouting from the cricket ground. It was so peaceful here, and the horrors of the war seemed very far away. She lifted her face towards the sun and closed her eyes, enjoying the warmth of its rays heating down on to her skin.

But while she sat there, warming herself, a shadow fell across the village as a plane flew in front of the sun and she shivered suddenly. Things were good now, but the war was always there, no matter how far away it seemed.

The roar of the plane's engines made Hope whimper. Audrey leaned over the pram and looked at the little girl.

'It's all right,' she said, stroking her cheek. 'It's all going to be all right.'

19

NOVEMBER 1942

The weather was wild as Betty left home. The wind whipped the front door out of her hands and slammed it shut, rattling the hinges, and she pulled her thin coat round her and tied the belt more firmly.

'As soon as this bloody war is over, I'm going to buy a new coat,' she muttered. There was no point in trying to put up an umbrella, despite the rain, because the wind would simply turn it inside out as soon as she lifted it above her head, so instead she rammed her hat down past her ears, hoping it would stay put.

'Well, don't you look a picture,' said Seth coming up behind her. She turned to greet him, smiling.

'I don't want to get my hair wet, because my curls will drop.'

'You're beautiful even with dropped curls,' he said. He kissed her and she melted in his embrace, as always.

'Get away,' she said affectionately. 'Where shall we go?'

'Pub?'

Betty didn't really want to go to the Woolpack; she wanted to spend time with Seth on his own, rather than sharing him with others. It was a while since she'd finished her stint with ENSA but she still felt she hadn't properly caught up with him.

But the rain was teeming down, it was cold, her hat was threatening to fly off, and the Woolie was just over the road, looking warm and welcoming in the autumn gloom, so she smiled.

'Pub would be good.'

She was pleased when Seth found a cosy corner table for them, and when he went to get their drinks, he didn't chat to anyone at the bar, other than a quick jovial exchange with Jed Dingle. He brought the drinks over and sat close to Betty.

'Hello, love,' he said, giving her another kiss. Betty beamed, feeling a rush of love for her kind, funny, genial boyfriend.

'Hello.'

'Feels like we've not done this for ages,' he said. 'Just sat and had a drink and a chat.'

'We've not,' she pointed out. 'You've had a lot of work on with Miffield Hall turning its grounds over for vegetables and that.'

Seth nodded. 'Mr Verney reckons it'll stop them requisitioning the house, but I'm not so sure.'

'It's big enough to be a hospital,' Betty said. 'He should probably just let them get on with it.' She saw Seth's stricken face at the thought of his job disappearing and hurried to change the subject. 'We've both been busy.'

'More than four months you were with that ENSA lot in the end,' Seth grumbled, not for the first time. 'Four blooming months. They were lucky to have you with them for so long. That's what those theatre types are like — they take advantage of folk like you and me.'

'They were nice,' she said. 'Just people like us, doing their bit for the war effort.'

Seth snorted, which put Betty's back up. 'Load of shirkers.'

Betty prodded him. 'Oh Seth, you should see how much the soldiers love a bit of entertainment,' she said. 'Those lads don't have much to look forward to, do they? So having some dancing to watch, or silly sketches to laugh at, gives them a bit of light relief.'

She thought Seth would argue, but instead he smiled. 'You're right,' he said. 'Must be tough for them. It's good you were there to help.'

Betty had a sudden memory of finishing a routine on stage, to the whoops and cheers of a group of RAF pilots who had finished training and would be heading to their base — and their first combat flights — the following day. She remembered the smiles on their faces and the happiness the ENSA entertainers had brought with them and she nodded.

'It is good,' she said.

'I'm proud of you, Betty,' Seth said, lacing his fingers through hers. 'I know you were only doing costumes and that, but you really did your bit.'

Betty squirmed in her seat, uncomfortable that he was praising her for helping with costumes when she'd actually been prancing about on stage. She thought of Audrey saying there had been no harm done, and wondered if that was right. Four months was a long time.

191

'Bet you're glad to have some free time again, though,' he went. 'I know that vet works you like a dog . . . ' he chuckled at his own joke ' . . . but I've not seen you for ages and you must be worn out.'

Betty shook her head. 'I'm tired, yes, and I've missed you. But I'll miss ENSA too. It's been wonderful.'

'Well, that's over and done with now, in't it?' Seth said. 'Now it's back to normal. Just you and me.'

He kissed her again and Betty felt content. It had been the right thing to do, giving ENSA a go, that was certain. Perhaps she had felt a pang as she watched Pamela and the others pack up their kit ready to move on across the Pennines to Lancashire where their next bunch of shows were. But she belonged here in Beckindale, with Seth.

Before she left, Pamela had tried again to get Betty to join ENSA.

'Why not have a word with Daphne?' she had said. 'What harm could it do?'

Daphne had ears like a bat, and heard them talking. 'What about me?' she asked.

'Betty's thinking of joining up.' Pamela had jumped in before Betty had time to answer.

'Joining ENSA?' Daphne said.

Betty had hesitated for a second, then nodded. 'We'd be glad to have you.'

'Not as glad as the soldiers would be,' Pamela had joked. 'Betty always gets the biggest cheers when she dances.'

Chuffed to bits, Betty had let her pride lead

her to Daphne's office where she picked up the recruitment forms.

'It's a bit different from enlisting in other services,' Daphne had explained. 'You need to apply to the central registry in London and you should really go to the theatre in Drury Lane for an audition.' Betty had shivered with excitement at the very thought of going on stage in a London theatre. 'But actually, because you've done the stint here, I can write you a reference instead.'

She'd looked stern. 'It's very competitive,' she said. 'At one point they were auditioning 500 performers a week.' Then she smiled. 'But given your experience and your talent . . . ' Betty had looked at her, exhilarated and terrified by what she was about to say.

' . . . I'd say you're a shoo-in.'

Despite Daphne's cajoling, Betty didn't fill in the forms right there and then. Instead she brought them home and stuffed them in the drawer of her dressing table. She told Margaret all about it, and her sister was encouraging but by then Betty's confidence had deserted her and she was no longer sure it was the right decision.

'I've done my bit,' she'd said. 'I don't want to spend my days travelling round the country, living out of a suitcase, far from you and Seth. It's not the life for me.'

Margaret had looked at her through narrowed eyes.

'Really?'

'Really,' Betty said firmly.

She'd made the right decision. Definitely. Almost definitely. The touch of Seth's lips on hers now had convinced her. Just about.

'You and me,' she echoed.

Seth grinned at her.

'I'll get us some more drinks,' he said. He headed off towards the bar, nodding hello to people as he passed, and Betty sat back in her seat, happy that she'd made the right decision.

'Betty?' A voice startled her out of her thoughts, and she looked up to see Audrey Atkins, the Land Girl, standing by her table, clutching a gin and orange.

'Hello, Audrey.'

'On your own?'

Betty looked round for Seth but she couldn't see him.

'Seth's here somewhere. He's gone to the toilet. You?'

'Waiting for Ned, but he's been held up. I hate being in the pub by myself. I can hear my mother's voice in my head, telling me how unbecoming it is.'

Betty chuckled.

'Men, eh? Leaving us dangling. They don't know how good they've got it.'

'Mind if I sit down for a bit, so I don't look like a lemon stood at the bar with all the men?'

'Course not.'

Betty moved her coat and Audrey sat down.

'Where's Ned, then?'

'Helping to move some cows that were in a barn that's blown down up at Tall Trees Farm,' Audrey said. 'He sent a message with Danny, over there.' She gestured to one of the farmhands who could often be found propping up the bar at the Woolpack.

'That's nice that he let you know,' Betty said. When she and Seth had been courting a while, she'd spent a few long evenings waiting for him alone in the bar. Until she got fed up and started going home. Funnily enough, he'd always managed to get there on time after that.

'He's really thoughtful, my Ned,' said Audrey. Her eyes were soft as she talked about her boyfriend. 'I told him Maggie had been feeling a bit under the weather, and he brought her a carrot cake his mam made.'

'That's sweet.'

'That's Ned.' Audrey's happiness was shining from her pretty face and Betty felt an uncomfortable flush of envy. Did she look like that when she was talking about Seth? She thought that she had done, once upon a time, but now? She wasn't sure. She forced herself to smile.

'It's going well, then? You and Ned?'

Audrey sighed happily. 'He's the nicest man I've ever met.'

Betty laughed. 'And the most handsome?'

Audrey giggled like a little girl. 'That too.'

She leaned towards Betty. 'Jacob's being so funny. He keeps checking that Ned's being good to me, and the other day he told him to make sure his intentions were above board.'

'Never,' Betty said, surprised by what she was hearing. 'Grumpy Jacob Sugden looking out for someone else apart from himself? What have you done to the lad?'

'Ah Jacob's not so bad,' Audrey said. 'He's had a lot to deal with.'

Betty wasn't so sure about that; she'd never had much time for the older Sugden brother who had never been, in her opinion, as nice as his brother. But she wasn't going to argue.

'So, what did Ned say when Jacob quizzed him about his intentions?' she asked.

'He told Jacob that they were absolutely above board and that he could trust him,' Audrey said.

She giggled again. 'But I told Ned later that I didn't mind if they weren't.'

Betty laughed too — Audrey's joy was infectious.

'Ooh, you filthy beggar.'

'I'm thanking my lucky stars I was posted to Emmerdale Farm,' Audrey carried on. 'I've met such wonderful people — not just Ned,' she said as Betty gave her a knowing look. 'There's Lily, and you, and Nancy. Even Jacob. And my Land Girl friends, Tilly and Ginny. It's like a whole new world for me. And I know I'm doing something worthwhile.'

Betty understood completely. 'That's exactly how I felt about my dancing,' she said. 'I felt blessed to be able to do something I loved so much, and to know it was doing some good.'

Audrey nodded vigorously, sipping her gin.

Betty glanced round checking to see Seth wasn't approaching, and wasn't surprised to see him sitting at the bar, laughing with his friend Ernie. She rolled her eyes and shifted a bit closer to Audrey.

'I'm thinking about joining ENSA properly,' she said in a quiet voice. Though ten minutes ago, she'd been determined she wasn't.

Audrey's eyes lit up. 'Oh Betty, that's a wonderful idea. Nancy would miss you, though. And have you told Seth?'

'No,' Betty wailed. 'I don't know what to say.'

'I reckon he'll be really proud of you,' Audrey said.

Betty glanced over at Seth. 'Perhaps,' she said.

The door to the pub opened, bringing with it a gust of wind and some leaves, and Audrey looked up hopefully. But it wasn't Ned, it was another farmhand, an older man called Harry.

'You Audrey?' he called.

Audrey nodded.

'Ned's stuck. They sorted the cows but there's fences down now and the pond's overflowing. Reckon they'll be there for a while.'

'But it's dark,' Audrey said.

'Even more reason to make sure the animals are secure,' Harry pointed out reasonably and Audrey nodded, looking sad.

Betty felt cross suddenly. She'd only come to see Seth and he was busy with Ernie, while Audrey had been let down too — though that wasn't Ned's fault. She drained her drink. 'I'm going to get off,' she said.

'Be careful, lass,' Harry said. 'The rain's really coming down now. Reckon the river will be high.'

'Do you think it could flood?' Betty remembered it flooding when she was a small girl. She and Margaret had thought it was all an enormous adventure, huddled in the front bedroom upstairs as the water rose. Now, of course, she could understand that it had been terrifying for her poor mother, who'd stayed at home with the girls while her father joined the other men in the village stacking up sandbags and bailing out water.

Harry nodded. 'Few more days like this and it could burst its banks, mark my words. So you watch yourself, Betty Prendagast.'

Betty felt prickly because old Harry had been the one to warn her to be careful, and not her Seth, but she smiled all the same.

'I'll watch myself,' she told him.

'I'll come too.' Audrey said. They both bundled up in their coats and headed to the door. Betty called out to Seth to say goodbye but he was larking around with Ernie and he didn't hear her. Embarrassed by his lack of attention, she turned to Audrey.

'I saw Maggie the other day and she looked very thin. Is she all right?'

'I'm worried about her,' Audrey admitted as they bowed their heads against the wind. 'She's not been right for months. Jacob had a word with her and she said she was fine, that she was just missing Edward, but I'm not sure. I mean, of course she misses him, but this seems physical. She was so energetic when I first came to the farm, and now she's tired all the time.'

Betty made a face. 'Maybe she needs a tonic. You could ask Mrs Wetherby at the chemist.'

'Good idea,' Audrey said.

They walked along together and then Betty paused. 'Are you walking back up to the farm?'

Audrey shrugged. 'I suppose so. Hadn't thought about it.'

Betty tugged her sleeve. 'Come back with me. You don't want to be walking back in this weather. You can stay at ours. You can have my bed and I'll go in with Margaret.'

'This rain is awful,' said Audrey. 'I hope Ned's all right.'

'Ned will be fine — he's a big boy,' Betty said. 'Come and dry off at ours. No point in risking the walk if you don't have to.'

'If you're sure?'

'Of course I'm sure,' Betty said. 'What are friends for?'

20

Nancy woke with a start, feeling something wet on her neck. For a moment, she wasn't sure where she was and then she realised she was at the surgery, with her head on Betty's desk. Groggily, she rubbed her eyes and straightened up, feeling a crick in her neck. And then, plop, another drop fell on to her head.

She looked up. There was a large dark patch on the surgery ceiling and it was dripping.

'Oh no,' she groaned. 'That's all I need.'

She'd been up half the night, answering emergency calls. Not many of the farmers around Beckindale had phones at home but there seemed to be some sort of efficient messaging service between those who had and those who hadn't when it came to emergencies. Her car was out of action now, so at a loss as to how to get to where she needed to be, she had dashed across the street to where a man named Paul Oldroyd lived. He was in the Home Guard and Nancy thought they might be out supporting people who had been affected by the weather and could help her get around. She was right but fortunately she managed to catch him at home, wolfing down a sandwich in between dashing around between flooded farms. Paul offered to take her to her calls in one of the Home Guard cars. They spent hours driving through flooded country lanes in the pitch black of the rain-sodden night, to farms where animals had got into trouble. Paul would drop her off, drive off to make sure everyone nearby was coping all right, and then come back to pick Nancy up and take her to the next place.

She'd checked over a terrified, soggy dog who'd fallen into a swollen pond and declared him fit and well. She'd helped pull three sheep out of a boggy field and made sure they weren't injured, and then she'd had to euthanise a horse who'd got scared when a tree branch blew down, bolted and broken a leg. She'd come back to the surgery to make a note of everywhere she'd been and apparently fallen asleep where she sat.

Blearily she blinked at the ceiling. The drips were getting larger by the second, splattering on to paperwork on Betty's desk and smudging ink.

'God,' she said, rubbing her cheeks vigorously and giving them a gentle slap as she tried desperately to wake herself up. 'What do I do about that?'

Another drip sploshed on to the desk and, alarmed at how much water had already fallen, Nancy darted into the back room and found the metal bucket she used to wash the floor. Back in the reception room, she put her bottom to the desk and shoved it along far enough to avoid the drips, and put the bucket under the wet patch. Immediately the room echoed with the sound of the water falling into the metal container and Nancy shuddered. Would this rain ever end?

She went to the window to check what the weather was like and to her horror, saw a group of people gathered by the surgery door. More patients? She wanted to cry with fatigue and she definitely wanted to go home, have a wash and perhaps something to eat. But instead, she walked to the door and unlocked it. As people piled in, she ran an expert eye over the animals' injuries — or the worried looks on the people's faces — mentally sorting them into things that needed to be dealt with immediately, and things that could wait, and sighed in relief as Betty arrived too.

'Lord, it's wild out there,' Betty said, shaking out her umbrella and looking round at the chaos in the waiting room. 'What's happening?'

'The roof's leaking, yesterday's invoices are soaked, Mrs Crow's pig has the flu, and I'm so tired I can't see properly,' Nancy said in an undertone, that had an edge of panic. 'I don't know what to do first.'

'Start checking over some animals and I'll make appointments for you to get to the farms when you can,' said Betty, pulling on her white coat and then peeling it off again as she realised it had been soaked by the drips coming through the roof. 'We'll have to leave the leak for now.'

'Right,' said Nancy. 'Good.' Her nerves were jangling and she felt slightly light-headed, but she took a cat with an injured paw through to the treatment room.

'My fence blew down and he stepped on some splintered wood,' the owner explained. Nancy stroked the moggy's head and pulled the splinter out, to the sound of its outraged yowls.

'He'll be fine now,' she said. 'I'll just dab a bit of antiseptic on there.'

But as she turned to fetch the ointment, the treatment door burst open. 'You need to come,' said Betty.

'Excuse me,' Nancy said to the cat's owner, annoyed at Betty's rudeness. But she followed her out to the waiting room, which seemed even busier than it had five minutes ago.

'Stanley's had a fall, and I didn't know what to do.' Meg Warcup stood there, holding her adopted son — Ruby's little brother — rather awkwardly in her arms, his legs dangling down by her hip. 'Dr Black is out on a call.'

She looked dangerously close to tears. Little Stanley — who was really too big now to be cradled like a baby — was pale and his eyes were closed. On his forehead was a huge lump, oozing with blood and his arm was hanging at an odd angle.

'I'm a vet,' said Nancy helplessly. 'I can't treat a little boy.'

'Oh please, Nancy. I think he's broken his arm.'

Stanley opened his eyes. 'It's def'ly broken,' he said, almost triumphantly. 'I heard it crack.'

Nancy's legs turned to jelly and saliva filled her mouth. For a second she thought she might be sick. But with a huge effort she managed to swallow, and give Stanley and Meg a reassuring smile. 'I'll have a look,' she said.

Susan appeared at her side — obviously she'd come through the back door again. Her pigtails were wet and she looked nervous.

'What's happened?' she gasped. 'Is Stanley all right?'

'Not now, Susan,' Nancy snapped.

'There's a cat in the treatment room,' Susan said nervously. 'Shall I give it some ointment?'

Nancy barely looked at the girl, so worried was she about little Stanley. 'Please,' she said.

Susan disappeared and, confident Betty was dealing with the queue of patients, Nancy turned her attention to Stan. 'What happened?' she asked.

'School's closed because part of the roof has fallen down and the halls are flooded,' Meg said. Nancy glanced at the bucket on the surgery floor which was filling up rapidly and felt a faint worry that the same thing would happen here. She nodded and Meg carried on. 'But we went anyway, just in case any children turned up. Stanley decided to climb up on a pile of debris from the roof, except it wasn't stable, it collapsed under his weight, and he fell.'

Nancy sat down next to the little boy and gently took his arm. He let out a wail that made her jump. 'It hurts,' he said sternly. 'Be careful.'

'I will,' she told him, trying not to show that she had no idea what she was doing. 'I can't do much more than splint it,' she said to Meg. 'He needs to go to hospital but that will help until you can get him there.'

'I'll take you, lass,' said the cat's owner, who'd emerged from the treatment room. 'I've got enough petrol.'

Meg looked like she might cry at the unexpected kindness. 'Thanks so much,' she whispered.

Nancy left Stanley cuddled on his mother's knee, and went into the treatment room to gather what she needed. Susan was there, still looking worried.

'I did the cat's paw,' she said.

'Well done,' Nancy said, opening a cupboard to look for bandages that might work for Stanley.

'What should I do now?'

'I don't know, Susan,' Nancy said. Ah, there were the large ones. She knew she had some somewhere. 'Empty the bucket? Help Betty with appointments? I don't much care.'

Susan squeezed her lips together and, had she not been so edgy about what she was about to do to poor Stanley, Nancy might have felt guilty.

Back in the front room, Nancy quietly told Meg to cuddle Stan a bit tighter and quickly she splinted his arm and tied it up neatly with a bandage to hold it still. She hoped she was doing it right because a boy's arm was very different from a dog's leg, but she did her best. Stanley's bravado had deserted him and he was crying softly as Meg stood up, still holding him in her arms

'Thank you so much,' she said.

Nancy nodded. She didn't want thanks.

'Susan, Ruby was waiting at the school to make sure no other children arrived,' Meg said.

'Why don't you go and find her?' Nancy said, wanting the schoolgirl out from under her feet.

But a sudden crash from outside made them all jump and Susan went pale.

'Tree branch,' said Betty, peering out of the window. 'Nothing damaged.'

'I'd rather stay here for now,' Susan said in a wobbly voice.

Nancy sighed inwardly. But she could hardly turn the girl away into the rain and wind.

'Fine,' she said. 'Give Betty a hand.'

'Let's go, love,' said the cat owner to Meg and Stanley. And Nancy watched them head outside, heads bowed against the gale.

The rest of the morning went more smoothly. Nancy dealt with the few animals that were still waiting to be seen, and then she went up to look at Mrs Crow's pig. She was absolutely weak with tiredness by the time she got back to the surgery so she was relieved to see there was just one patient waiting to be seen — Jacob Sugden's dog, Bella. She was shivering, her ears drawn back, huddled against Jacob's legs.

'Poor girl,' Nancy said when she saw her. 'What's happened?'

'We were moving the cows late last night, because the barn they were in lost a bit of its roof and the water was coming in at a rate of knots,' Jacob began. 'Bella was such a help, bless her. But she must have got really cold because she's not stopped shivering. Thought she'd be okay after a good feed and a sleep but she was the same this morning.'

'Bring her through,' Nancy said.

Susan was in the treatment room, reading a biology textbook and drinking tea. Nancy was irritated to see she was still there, and she didn't acknowledge her, simply glanced in the girl's direction, then looked away again. Susan got to her feet as Nancy and Jacob entered but sat down quickly and watched in silence.

Nancy picked Bella up — the dog didn't even wriggle in protest, just limply allowed Nancy to hoik her on to the table — and ran her hands over her body.

'Just checking if she's hurt anywhere,' she told Jacob. She paused as she got to the dog's belly, which was swollen, and felt more slowly and deliberately. Bella turned her head and gazed at Nancy as though she knew what was going on.

'Good girl,' Nancy said. 'I think you've got some explaining to do.'

Jacob looked slightly disgruntled at this exchange between Nancy and his dog so Nancy smiled.

'She's pregnant,' she said.

Jacob's jaw dropped. 'She never is.'

Nancy took his hand and ran it over the dog's belly. 'Feel that?'

Jacob's face was a picture of wonderment and surprise. 'I can't believe I didn't realise.'

'You didn't breed her deliberately?'

'Nope,' Jacob said, rolling his eyes. 'I guess she had some fun with Smithers' sheepdog while I was up seeing about the cows.'

Nancy chuckled. 'You have to be careful.'

Jacob rubbed Bella's ears. 'What a good girl you are, working so hard when you should be resting,' he told her. Bella weakly licked his fingers.

'She's probably just exhausted,' Nancy said. 'Not surprising really. Leave her with us for a few hours. We can warm her up, give her some special food, and generally make sure she's doing all right, and then you can pick her up later.'

'She'll be all right though?' Jacob chewed his lip.

'Should be.' Nancy glanced round at the schoolgirl who was looking on, her face etched

207

with worry about the mutt. This would keep her out of Nancy's hair. 'Susan will look after her; she loves dogs.'

'I do,' Susan said eagerly. 'I'll look after her, I promise.'

Jacob thanked them both, and headed back out into the rain.

Nancy and Susan bustled round, finding a blanket for Bella to snuggle up in, and giving her some of the dense food that Nancy hoped would give her a burst of energy. The dog was skittish and nervy but Susan was calm and it was clear Bella trusted her. She was being rather useful, and Nancy felt herself start to relax.

'Do you know the birds fly lower in the sky when a storm's on its way?' Susan said cheerfully as they worked.

'I thought that was just an old wives' tale.'

Susan shook her head. 'Old Harry was telling me. He said he knew the weather was going to be bad because of the birds. And he said the squirrels started burying their nuts earlier this year, and they built their nests higher in the trees, so he could tell there was a storm on its way.'

Nancy raised an eyebrow. 'Is that right? He could have warned everyone else.'

Susan chuckled. 'Animals are clever,' she said.

'They are,' Nancy agreed. She cocked her head on one side, listening for movement in reception.

'It's quiet,' she said. 'Is the waiting room empty?' She was hoping the worst was over now — that everyone had taken whatever precautions they needed to against the rain, despite Harry's lack of warnings, and that all the animals were safe.

Susan stuck her head round the door. 'It is,' she said. 'Why don't you go and grab forty winks while there's nothing happening? I'll stay with Bella and make sure she's all right and Betty's here if anyone comes in.'

Nancy was tempted. She looked at her watch; it was just after three o'clock. Perhaps she could nap for an hour? She was so exhausted that surely even the tiniest amount of sleep would help?

'Are you ready for more?' Betty said, coming into the treatment room with her notepad. 'There are three jobs for you.'

Nancy felt weak suddenly, and leaned against the table for support. 'Three?' she said.

Betty's brow creased and she took a step towards Nancy. 'Is it too much? You're exhausted, Nancy.'

Nancy forced herself to stand upright, despite the dull ache in her legs and the spinning sensation in her head. 'It's fine.'

Betty put her head to one side and regarded her carefully. 'You don't look fine,' she said bluntly. 'You're pale and I bet you haven't eaten.' She thought for a moment. 'Why don't I call the big veterinary centre in Hotten? They can take on some of these jobs and you can have a break.'

'No,' Nancy almost shouted. She knew if any of her patients went to the big vets, they'd never come back to her. She had to keep going despite how tired she was.

Betty tapped her pencil against her notepad as she looked at her. 'If you're sure,' she said eventually and Nancy nodded.

'It's fine,' she said again.

She saw Betty exchange a glance with Susan, but she didn't comment on it. Instead, she took a deep breath.

'I'll pack my bag. Betty, can you let the clients know I'm on my way. And Susan, it's a bit steamy in here, can you open the door a fraction, just to let some air in?'

Susan did as she was asked. Outside it was still raining, and through the open door Nancy could hear panicked shouts. She wondered if there was more flooding to contend with; Betty had said it was possible that the river could burst its banks which sounded frightening.

Wearily, she picked up her bag, and started filling it with drugs, bandages and anything else she thought she might need while she was out. Susan tried to help, but Nancy just wanted to get out, do the job and get back. With tiredness blurring her vision and her nerves on edge, she found Susan's kind efforts just annoyed her.

As she zipped her bag up, a gust of wind blew through the open door and into the treatment room, where it slammed the door through to the waiting area shut, making Nancy jump and her heart thump. And poor Susan, who was crouching down by Bella, shrieked in fright at the loud noise — right in the dog's face.

Bella, being skittish enough already, scrambled to her feet and quick as a flash, darted out the door and off into the rain.

'Bloody hell, Susan, you silly girl,' Nancy shouted. 'What on earth are you doing?'

Susan, still trembling after her shock, stood up and stared at Nancy, her breathing ragged. 'Sorry,' she said. 'Sorry Nancy. I'll get her.'

She turned and dashed off after the dog, without so much as stopping to put her coat on.

'Bugger,' said Nancy. Her chest tightened as she thought of how she'd snapped at poor Susan, who was just trying to help. And now she was out in the torrential rain.

Nancy pulled on her waterproof jacket and went outside.

'Susan?' she called. There was no sign of the girl, or the dog. Nancy skirted the side of the surgery and emerged into the main part of the village, but she still couldn't see them.

Up ahead was a group of men, including the village policeman Jack Proudfoot, Ned Barlow, Seth Armstrong, and others Nancy only knew by sight.

'Have you seen Susan? she called to them. The rain was loud on the hood of her jacket and she had to raise her voice to hear herself — and make herself heard by the men.

Jack turned. 'Not recently. Have you lost her?'

Nancy sighed. 'She chased after a dog that escaped, but she didn't take her coat. She'll be soaking, bless her.'

Jack made a face. 'Hope she didn't go near the river. It's about to go. We're heading there now to try to shore it up a bit. If the banks collapse, the whole village could flood.'

'Is she in her school uniform?' said Seth's

211

friend, Ernie. Nancy thought for a moment — she'd really not been paying much attention to Susan that morning — then nodded.

Ernie grinned. 'I saw a lass in uniform heading up Mrs Roberts's path a few minutes ago.'

Nancy knew she should check that Susan was back home — with Bella too — but the rain was showing no sign of easing and she was aware she had the other animals to get to. Susan was a smart girl. She would have caught Bella and gone to shelter at home, getting out of the rain as soon as she could.

'Thanks,' she said to the men. 'That's a relief.'

She just hoped she was right.

21

Keeping her hat pulled down tightly over her ears, Audrey darted from Maggie's battered old farm truck into the vet's surgery. She had volunteered to come and pick up Bella, as Jacob was trying to mend a hole in the cow shed roof before the weather got even worse, and Maggie had said she would drop her off. She had an appointment in Hotten, she said, though she hadn't volunteered any more information than that and Audrey hadn't asked. She thought Maggie was perhaps seeing a doctor, and she didn't want to pry. Though, as she'd got out of the van, she'd paused with her fingers on the handle.

'I hope your appointment goes all right,' she'd said, slightly awkwardly. 'You know if there's anything I can help with, you just need to ask.'

Maggie had nodded, but not spoken, and Audrey had got out of the van and headed into the gloomy, rain-drenched village. It was almost dark, though it wasn't long after four o'clock and there was no one about as she dashed up the path to the surgery and through the front door, where she stood on the mat for a while, letting the drips run off her mac.

'Hello Betty,' she called.

Betty, who'd been putting some folders into a filing cabinet, turned and looked at her in, what seemed to Audrey, to be alarm.

'Audrey,' she said, slamming one of the cabinet drawers shut. 'You're here.'

'I'm a little bit earlier than Jacob said, but Maggie was going to Hotten so she dropped me off.'

'Nancy's not here.'

'Does she need to see Bella before I take her? I'm so excited we're going to have puppies. What a lovely surprise.'

Betty shifted from one foot to the other, avoiding Audrey's gaze.

'It's good news,' she said, sounding as though it was anything but. Audrey frowned.

'Is everything all right? Is something wrong with Bella?'

Betty took a breath, but as she opened her mouth, Nancy came through the door.

'Audrey,' she said in the same tone Betty had used. 'You've come to get Bella.'

Audrey was bewildered. 'Yes,' she said. 'Is that a problem?'

Nancy took off her wet raincoat and hung it up. Audrey saw her glance at Betty.

'No problem,' Nancy said. 'We just had a small incident.'

'What kind of incident?' Audrey was beginning to worry. She'd just seen Meg Warcup getting out of a car with little Stanley whose arm was in an enormous plaster cast, there was a tree down in the middle of the village and there were people everywhere, trying to keep the water away from their front doors.

'We had Bella here, but she erm, ran off,' said Nancy. Audrey's jaw dropped.

214

'What?'

'I'd opened the door and she got spooked by something and ran outside.'

'But she's fine, I think,' Nancy said hurriedly. 'Susan went after her and Ernie said he saw her going home.'

'You think?' Audrey was furious. How could a vet lose a dog?

A huge clap of thunder made them all jump.

'The weather's getting worse,' Betty said, worried. 'Seth popped in while you were out, Nancy. He's gone with some of the others to check on the river. They were hoping that they could stop it bursting its banks near the village. But Seth reckons it might be too late.'

'But where's Bella?' Audrey said, not wanting to be distracted.

'I'm not exactly sure,' Nancy said. Audrey noticed the normally well-turned-out vet had large purple circles under her eyes and unwashed hair and felt a small glimmer of sympathy. 'I was hoping she'd have brought her back by now.'

'Well, she obviously hasn't.' Audrey snapped.

Lightning flashed outside, making the surgery lights flicker, and then another roll of thunder happened almost immediately.

The door to the surgery swung open and as they all turned to look, Ruby came in, shaking her wet hair.

'What are you all staring at?' she asked with a cheeky grin. 'I've been round to see Mrs Roberts to check if Susan showed up. I waited ages though and she didn't come so I thought she might be here.'

215

Nancy looked stricken. 'You're wearing your school uniform,' she said to Ruby.

Ruby looked at Nancy as though she was mad, and carried on. 'I just wanted to check Susan was all right. She hates thunder; she gets so scared. Once she was round at our house when there was a storm and she disappeared. Meg found her, hiding behind the sofa.' She chuckled. 'Is she through the back?'

Audrey looked at Nancy, whose eyes were wide in her pale face.

'Ernie saw you going up the path, not Susan,' she said. 'It was you.'

Ruby made a face. 'What are you talking about? Where's Susan.'

With a sinking feeling, Audrey realised what had happened. 'Tell her,' she said to Nancy.

'Susan went out to look for Jacob's dog,' Nancy said quietly. 'She's not back yet.'

Ruby frowned. 'Went out in this weather?'

'She went out before the thunder started.'

'And she's not back yet?'

'Not yet.'

'So where is she?'

Ruby was looking from Nancy to Audrey to Betty and back.

'Where is she?' she asked again, her voice sounding shrill. 'Where's Susan?'

'I don't know,' Nancy admitted.

Ruby was only a child, but she was tall after a recent growth spurt. She drew herself up, lifting her chin, and stared at Nancy.

'Why did you let her go?' she growled. 'She'll be soaking wet and scared to death.'

Audrey wasn't sure what to do. She was annoyed too, but Nancy seemed close to tears, and she thought Ruby getting angry wasn't going to help anyone.

'I'm sorry,' Nancy was saying. 'I was going to go after her, but I had patients to see, and I couldn't work out what to do first.'

'She's just a little girl,' said Ruby, sounding much older than her own years. 'You're a grown up. You should have looked after her instead of snapping at her all the time. You should be ashamed.'

'I know,' Nancy whispered. 'I am.'

Betty stepped in between Ruby and Nancy. 'You're right,' she said to Ruby soothingly. 'We've made a mistake but we'll put it right, you'll see. Come and sit down and I'll make you a cup of tea. Susan will be back in no time, you mark my words.'

But Ruby didn't want tea. She held her hands up to Betty, as though to ward her off.

'Susan's scared of loud noises,' she said, stressing each word like Betty was simple and wouldn't understand what she was saying. 'She is afraid of thunder. She won't come waltzing back in, because she will be terrified. Thunder makes her think of the Blitz.' She looked round at Nancy and Audrey and, in a sarcastic tone, added: 'Remember the Blitz? The Blitz that killed her whole family?'

Nancy looked at her feet and Audrey stepped forward.

'Ruby, don't upset yourself,' she said, putting out a cautious hand and patting Ruby's arm.

217

'Have a sit down, like Betty said.'

Ruby whirled round. 'No, I won't,' she said. 'I'm going to find my friend, seeing as none of you care two hoots about her.'

She made to leave but Nancy reached out and grabbed her arm.

'No,' she said firmly. 'Absolutely no way. It's awful out there and I've already got Susan's disappearance on my conscience. You stay here with Betty and Audrey and I'll go.'

'But she's my friend . . . ' Ruby began but Nancy's bullish expression made it clear there was no arguing and Ruby sat down suddenly on one of the hard chairs.

'Please find her,' she said, looking very young. 'She'll be so scared and it's getting dark.'

Nancy nodded. 'I will,' she said, pulling on her still-wet jacket.

Without planning to speak, Audrey found herself jumping in. 'I'll come too,' she said. 'Bella knows me. And you need someone to be with you, Nancy. I really think it's foolish to go out in this storm by yourself.'

'Like Susan did,' Ruby said pointedly.

'Like Susan did,' Audrey agreed. She turned to the angry girl. 'I know you're upset, Ruby, but you need to stay here with Betty in case Susan comes back.'

Ruby's chin was set in a defiant grimace, but she nodded.

'Shall I tell her gran?' she said. Audrey looked at Nancy, who shrugged, and then to Betty who thought for a second.

'Let's not worry her yet,' she said.

Audrey had a thought. 'What about Jacob? We should tell him what's happening because he'll want to come and look for Bella, I bet.'

Betty nodded. 'I'll find someone who can go up to Emmerdale Farm.'

'Maybe wait a while,' Nancy said. 'There's no point in panicking everyone if we find Susan quickly. Give us an hour or so and if we're not back by then, start telling people.'

Betty looked dubious, but she agreed.

'Where should we start? Audrey said, mentally picturing Beckindale and wondering where a scared girl might go to shelter from a storm. 'Should we check the cricket pavilion? Or perhaps the churchyard . . . ?'

'She might be in the woods,' Ruby said suddenly.

'Why do you think that?' Nancy asked.

'It's quiet in there,' Ruby said, again speaking as though Nancy needed everything spelling out. 'She's scared of loud noises, and she likes the woods because they're quiet. Not the bit up by the estate, or the other side near the training camp, because the gun shots make her edgy. But the bit down the bottom. There's a little hut there that we found. It's by . . . ' Ruby trailed off.

'By the river,' Betty finished for her.

Audrey's heart sank. Surely if the river burst its banks and flooded the village, the wood would flood too. Would the trees be enough to stop the waters rising? She doubted it. She tugged Nancy's arm.

'Let's go,' she said. 'We can't wait any longer.'

She looked at Betty. 'Do you have a torch here? It'll be dark soon.'

Betty nodded and opened her bottom drawer, where there was a large torch. She gave it to Audrey, who passed it to Nancy.

'I need to keep my hand free,' she said apologetically. Nancy nodded and took the torch without commenting further.

In silence, the two women pulled up their hoods and headed out into the murky afternoon. It was so grey that it was already difficult to see through the gloom, and Audrey felt a lurch of fear. What if they didn't find Susan? There was water running down the path and the rain was still hammering down. Thunder clapped again, and a flash of lightning lit up the pub opposite.

'I've never known rain like this,' she said to Nancy, who was walking beside her, hunched into her coat. 'It's just relentless.'

Nancy glanced at her, her face lined with worry. 'Do you think we'll find her?'

Audrey felt sick, but she forced herself to give Nancy what she hoped was a comforting smile.

'If she's with Bella, she'll be fine,' she said. 'That dog is as loyal as the day is long and she'll look out for Susan.'

She left unsaid the possibility that Susan was alone and Bella was elsewhere. She found herself shivering — half with the cold and half with fear — so she looped her arm through Nancy's for comfort, and together they trudged on towards the edge of the village, past the cemetery, splashing through puddles that were spreading to merge with other puddles.

'This is bad,' Audrey muttered. 'It's really bad, Nancy.'

Nancy glanced at her. 'I know.'

Audrey's heart was racing and her legs were wobbly. But she forced herself to keep going as they got closer to the humpback bridge, where the children paddled in the summer. The little hut Ruby had told them about was on the other side, so they had to get across somehow. As they got nearer, they could see the water was black and angry.

'Look how high the water is,' Audrey said in shock. 'It's almost touching the bottom of the bridge.' Her voice was trembling as much as her hands.

'It's going to flood,' Nancy said. 'It's so swollen, it has to. Oh God, this is awful.'

'We need to find Susan.' Audrey was beginning to panic. 'We need to find her before the river bursts its banks because if we don't she's going to drown.'

Nancy let out a whimper. 'This is my fault,' she said.

'There's no time for blame, we need to hurry.' Audrey tugged her arm to pull her up over the humpback bridge and on to the other side. Neither of them looked down into the swirling fierce water — they were both afraid of what they might see.

On the other side, as they approached the woods, they could see figures down on the riverbank on their right, towards Butler's Farm — it was the men from the village, trying to act before the water got too wild.

They slowed for a moment, watching the men work. They were trying to create a channel for the flood water to follow, obviously hoping to give it somewhere to go other than the village, but the river was rushing too fast and as the women watched, one of the men slipped and almost fell into the swollen currents. Both Audrey and Nancy gasped as one of the other men grabbed his arm and pulled him to safety.

'There's nothing they can do,' Nancy said shrilly. 'The water is too powerful.'

Audrey shuddered as the men all stood, gazing down into the river, talking to each other and shaking their heads. One of them straightened up and she saw with a rush of horrified recognition that it was Ned. Her Ned.

'Oh,' she gasped.

Nancy followed her gaze.

'We don't have time to stop and talk,' she said, pulling Audrey away. 'He's strong and young, and more than anything he's smart. He won't get into trouble.'

'I should go and speak to him,' Audrey said.

'You'll only distract him. We need to find Susan.'

'What if they've seen her?'

'They'd have taken her home.'

Audrey knew that was true — the men wouldn't have let a young girl wander round in this weather. But she felt a sob in her throat as she let Nancy pull her along, down off the road on to sodden ground and into the woods. She glanced back over her shoulder as they went and she was pleased to see the men were picking up their tools. They'd obviously decided to call it a day. With a shiver, she realised that meant if the river did burst its banks, there was nothing anyone could do about it.

'We need to hurry,' Nancy said. 'Come on.'

Inside the woods, it was slightly drier because the trees sheltered them from the worst of the weather. But any last leaves had been blown away in the storm and so heavy was the rain, that they were still getting wet. And it was dark. Really dark.

'Put the torch on,' she said. Nancy took it out of her pocket and switched it on. The light shone through the trees, but not far. It was better than nothing, Audrey supposed. She thought of Susan alone in this gloomy, frightening place and quickened her pace.

'Come on,' she said. 'Come on, Nancy.'

'Aren't you meant to stay away from trees in a storm?' said Nancy as they hurried along, calling out for Susan and Bella as they went.

'Because of the lightning,' Audrey agreed. 'I think you're more likely to be struck if you're under a tree.'

A sudden flash lit up the sky, making the branches in front of them stand out like bony fingers, and they both jumped high in the air, and shrieked.

'Susan will be so frightened,' Nancy said, almost to herself, as they got themselves together. 'She was scared when I dropped a tray. She's going to be terrified.'

'I'm sure we'll find her,' Audrey lied. Her breath was coming in small shallow pants and she couldn't seem to get enough air. She was actually beginning to think they weren't going to find the girl. They had more chance of getting lost themselves and then what would happen? She wrapped her arms round her own torso and jammed her hand under her left armpit. Drips were running down her neck, and she couldn't feel her toes any more. She was really panicking now, but she didn't want to show Nancy how she felt.

'Come on,' she urged. 'Susan! Susan are you there?'

They walked a bit further and then Nancy clutched her arm.

'What's that? Can you hear something?'

Audrey listened as a faint roaring noise grew louder. It wasn't like anything she'd heard before and it made her heart thump in fright.

'What is that?' she said, her voice shaking. 'What's that roaring?'

Nancy's pale face gleamed in the half-light. 'It's the river,' she said. 'I think it's the river.'

'Oh God,' breathed Audrey. 'It must have burst its banks and it's flooding. Should we go back? What should we do?'

'Calm down,' Nancy was firm, though her face was etched with fear. 'We can't go back, we have to find Susan.'

They looked at each other for a second.

'She's all alone, Audrey.'

More than anything, Audrey wanted this to be over. She wanted to be next to the fire at Emmerdale Farm, chatting to Maggie and Jacob. But she knew that however scared she was,

Susan would be feeling worse. She took a deep breath, and pulled her shoulders back.

'You're right,' she said, 'But please let's hold on to each other. We need to be careful.'

They gingerly made their way along the soggy path. The river was to the right of them, still a little way away, but they knew that up ahead it widened and looped round so the path ran alongside it. They were already slopping through an inch or so of water, and Audrey was certain it was just going to get worse as they got closer to the river — or it got closer to them.

They were still holding hands, with Nancy on Audrey's right and then suddenly, Nancy let go of Audrey's fingers, the torch went out and Nancy wasn't there anymore.

Audrey shrieked. 'Nancy?'

There was no sound.

'Nancy?' Audrey was almost crying with fear.

Then to her utter relief, Nancy spoke. 'I'm here, I'm all right.'

Audrey tried to squint through the gloom but she could only make out a darker patch that she thought was Nancy. The torch switched on again, and Audrey could see her friend sitting in the water.

'What happened?' she said, dashing over to help her up.

'Tripped over a root or something.' Nancy's voice was trembling, and when she took Audrey's outstretched hand and heaved herself up, Audrey could feel her whole body was shaking.

'Are you hurt?' Audrey's breath was coming in

ragged pants, because she was so frightened. She'd never done anything like this before. If her mother could see her now, she'd have a fit. 'Oh you're bleeding.'

'Where?' Nancy put her hand to her forehead where there was a smear of blood and a lump beginning to grow. 'Oh, it's nothing, I whacked myself with the torch when I fell.'

'Are you sure you're all right?' Audrey looked at Nancy carefully.

'Just a bit wet,' Nancy said, obviously trying and failing to sound upbeat. She made an odd face, like she was attempting a smile. 'And really scared. And guilty.'

She clutched Audrey's arm. 'What if Susan's . . . '

'Don't,' Audrey croaked. 'Don't think like that.' She took a deep breath, and let it out slowly, trying to calm herself down and stop her heart thumping quite so hard against her ribs. 'We're fine. We've got the torch. You're all right. The water is still only ankle-deep. We can do this, Nancy. We can find Susan and Bella.'

'We can,' Nancy said faintly, then more determinedly, 'We can do this.'

Audrey didn't want to think about how they'd get back to the village if Susan was in the hut. If the river had burst its banks, the road by the humpback bridge would be impassable. But she wasn't going to worry about that now. Instead she gave Nancy a nudge.

'Come on,' she said.

They sploshed on a little further, clutching each other so hard that Audrey was sure Nancy's fingers would leave bruises on her arm, and then it was Audrey's turn to hear a sound.

'Shh,' she said. Nancy stopped. The roaring sound was still there, but ever so faintly above the rushing of the river, there was another noise.

'Is it . . . ?' Nancy began.

'I think so,' Audrey said. 'I think it's barking.'

'Bella?'

'Perhaps.'

Audrey took Nancy's hand in her good one, and squeezed her freezing fingers.

'Let's go,' she said.

22

Audrey and Nancy had been gone for a long time and Betty was starting to panic, though she was trying very hard to stay calm for Ruby's sake. The girl couldn't stay still. Betty had tried to persuade her to go home and see how Stan was after his trip to hospital, but she'd refused. 'He's with Meg,' she'd said stubbornly. 'Susan's got no one.' She'd let her tea get cold and now she was staring out of the windows of the surgery and fidgeting.

'It's raining so hard,' she said. 'And look how dark it's getting. It's really dark, Betty.'

Betty was sitting at her desk, trying to concentrate on some invoices, but failing.

'They'll be back soon,' she said, but she didn't really believe what she was saying and she could tell Ruby didn't either.

'Remember when Meg and me got lost that time?' Ruby said. 'When the Germans found us?'

Of course, Betty remembered. It was all anyone had talked about for months — the dramatic German plane crash, and the terrified airmen who'd grabbed Ruby, her brother Stan and her adopted mother, Meg, and held them hostage. Meg, the village schoolteacher, had been quite close to the German pilot who'd kidnapped her for a while when he was a POW at a camp nearby. Betty had felt a bit odd about that. She'd not seen him around though, since the POW camp had been moved and sometimes she wondered if Meg had kept in touch with him. She was a strange one, Meg. Prickly and often unfriendly, but there was no denying that she'd stepped up to take care of Ruby and Stan when they needed her. And judging by how Stan had been cuddled up to her today — goodness that seemed like years ago now — the children clearly loved her.

'Remember, Betty?' Ruby startled her out of her daydreaming.

'Like anyone would forget that,' Betty said.

'Everyone came looking for us,' Ruby pointed out. 'Lots of people came to help.'

'They did.'

'So we should go and look for Susan.'

Betty looked out of the window. The thunder was still rumbling and the rain was lashing against the glass.

'I don't think that's a very good idea. It's dangerous out there. I told you, my Seth reckons the river will flood tonight.'

Ruby went pale and Betty wanted to kick herself for mentioning the river.

'We have to do something,' Ruby said. She looked at the clock on the wall. 'It's been ages. I think we should at least go and tell Susan's gran. And Audrey said we should let Jacob know about the dog, too, if they weren't back.'

Absolutely the last thing Betty wanted to do was go out in this weather. She'd set her hair in curlers before bed last night and she knew she'd have to do it again tonight if it got wet. Her coat was threadbare and not nearly waterproof enough, and her wellingtons had a hole in them. But then she thought of sweet Susan, out there all alone, scared of the thunder and no doubt freezing too . . . well, she didn't want to think of what could happen. Instead she smiled at Ruby and reached for her hat.

'Come on, then,' she said.

They both wrapped up as best they could against the wild evening, but even bundled up they were wet through before they'd even got down the path from the surgery.

'Where are we going?' Ruby asked.

'To get help.'

They went to the Woolpack first. There weren't many customers there — the nasty weather meant all the farmhands who normally propped up the bar were otherwise engaged.

'Betty, what are you doing out in this rain?' said Larry, as they pushed open the door. 'And Ruby shouldn't be in here.'

'Susan's gone missing,' Betty said, not wasting time on small talk. 'We think she's in the woods — Ruby says there's a little hut she's fond of. Audrey and Nancy have gone after her.'

Larry looked alarmed. 'River's about to flood,' he said.

'I know.'

Old Harry was sitting at one end of the bar. Now he got to his feet. 'What do you need me to do?'

Betty could have kissed him. But instead she just barked orders. 'Do you have a car? Or a van? Can you get up to Emmerdale Farm and tell Jacob Sugden?'

Harry frowned. 'Why does he need to know?'

Betty didn't have time for long explanations. 'Susan went after Jacob's dog,' she said.

Luckily, Harry was a man of few words and even fewer questions. He nodded.

'Got the truck out the back,' he said. 'Right you are.' He pulled on his waxed jacket and hat, and headed out into the rain.

'Now we need to tell Susan's gran,' urged Ruby. Betty nodded.

'We'll get them to bring Susan here, when they find her,' she told Larry. 'She'll be cold and wet. Can you find blankets and keep the fire going?'

'Course I can,' Larry said. 'Lily's out back with the babby, shall I send her out? She might want to help.'

'Yes please,' said Betty.

'What's going on?' said a voice behind them, as Larry disappeared into the back room. It was Margaret — Betty's sister. This time, Betty did kiss her.

'Geroff,' Margaret said, squirming away. 'What are you doing?'

'What are you doing, more like,' Betty said. 'Why are you here?'

'Mam sent me to find you at the vet's,' Margaret said. 'She was worried you'd not come home. But you weren't there and then I saw you coming in here.'

Quickly, Betty explained what had happened. Margaret looked concerned.

'Poor girl,' she said.

'I've got the keys to Dad's truck.' Lily was there, dangling a heavy keyring. She spoke to

Ruby, sounding urgent. 'Larry told me Susan might be in the hut? That's at the far side, isn't it?'

Ruby nodded. 'Past the cricket pitch. Over the other side of the ford.'

'Well, let's go then,' Lily said. 'Shall we go round the back way? We can get across the ford in the truck, or if the water's really high, we can always try going over the footbridge, though it might be a bit of a squeeze. If the river's flooded, we won't get round by the humpback bridge. It's too wide there and the water will be too deep.'

Betty stared at her, trying to take in all the options she'd just been given. She hadn't for one minute considered they would get involved in the hunt for Susan, and she was frightened by the assumption that she was included in Lily's heroics.

'Where's baby Hope?' she stammered.

'She's fine. She's asleep and Larry's going to listen out for her.'

'But shouldn't we get one of the men to go? What about your Jack?' For the first time, Betty noticed Seth wasn't in his usual spot at the bar. 'Or my Seth?' she added, more tentatively.

'They're already all down by bridge,' Lily said. 'Trying to hold back the flood — though I don't fancy their chances.'

'Seth too?' Betty felt another lurch of fear. Her hands were sweating and she rubbed her palms on her thin coat. This was all too frightening and she really didn't want to go out into the storm.

Seeing her hesitate, Ruby tugged Betty's sleeve. 'We have to go with Lily,' she said, her jaw

232

set in determination. 'We need to find Susan.'

Ruby was right, but Betty's legs felt shaky just at the thought. She took a deep breath, again telling herself that however frightened she was by the idea of going into the dark woods in the storm, it couldn't be as scary as it was for Susan.

She turned to Ruby. 'Ruby, pet, you can't come with us,' she said firmly. 'I know Susan's your friend and you're worried, but I can't let you get cold and wet too.'

Ruby opened her mouth but Lily interrupted her before she could argue. 'Betty's right,' she said. 'This one's just for the grown-ups. I promise you, as soon as we find Susan we'll come and get you.'

Betty had an idea.

'It would be really useful if you could go and see Susan's gran,' she said. She turned to her sister. 'Margaret, can you and Mam take Ruby round to Mrs Roberts and tell her what's going on? Maybe stay with her and make sure she's all right?'

'We'll go right away.' Margaret put her arm round Ruby. 'Come on, Rubes,' she said. 'You need to show me the way because I'm never sure which house belongs to your gran. That cat of hers sits on the neighbour's fence, which always confuses me.'

Betty knew her sister had visited Mrs Roberts many times, and knew exactly which house she lived in, and she admired the way she'd got Ruby involved. Margaret was a very caring young woman. Far nicer than Betty was, in Betty's opinion. She watched their heads bob past the pub window and turned to Lily. 'Are you sure this is a good idea?'

Lily shrugged. 'We can't leave them out there by themselves. The truck won't go right into the woods but it's got more chance of getting through floodwater than we have on our own and if we need to get out, we can at least leave the lights on — they might hear the engine or see the headlamps, even though they've got the covers on for the blackout. It's better than no light at all.'

Betty knew Lily was right; they did have to do something. They called goodbye to Larry and heads bowed against the wind, they made their way to Mick's truck.

As they got close to the garage, they saw a group of men approaching from the opposite direction — Seth was among them. Thrilled to see him, Betty ran over and threw her arms round him.

'Ee is it good to see you,' he said. 'Though why you're out in this, Betty Prendagast, I don't know.'

'We're looking for Susan,' Betty told him.

'Nancy was looking for her, but that was hours ago,' Seth said. 'Ernie said she'd gone home.'

'There was a mix-up,' Betty said.

Seth frowned. 'You're not going into the woods are you?'

'Lily's going to drive in Mick's truck.'

'River's burst its banks,' said Ned Barlow, making a face. 'You can't get past the humpback bridge, not now.'

'We're going through the ford,' said Lily. Betty

looked at her. She'd always known she was bold — driving any vehicle that took her fancy, staying in the village when she found out she was expecting baby Hope rather than running off somewhere — but this was another level of bravery as far as Betty was concerned. Lily's eyes were bright and she had two red spots on her cheeks. She looked frightened, but determined. Betty tried to make her face look similar but it wasn't easy.

'I'm not sure you'll make it through the ford, even with the truck,' warned Ned and Betty's attempt to be brave fell apart.

'Is it really bad?' she said, her voice trembling.

'Worst I've known it,' Seth said, and Ned nodded his agreement. 'We couldn't stop the flood and the water's rising fast. We've come back to warn everyone here and start putting more sandbags out.'

'You think the water will come into the village?' Lily sounded alarmed. She took a step towards her Jack, who'd just arrived behind Ned and Seth with another small group of men. 'Jack, Hope's at the pub. Can you go and get her?'

Jack narrowed his eyes at his wife. 'Where are you going?'

'To find Susan,' she said. 'Seth'll explain. Come on, Betty.'

Her heart thumping so hard it almost hurt, Betty followed Lily, wishing she was as brave as her friend.

'I thought Jack might stop you going,' she said, as they clambered up into the truck.

Lily laughed. 'He knows better than that.'

She turned the key and the engine rumbled into life.

'I'm going to go down towards the river but I'll take it slowly,' she said to Betty, who was gripping on to the seat for dear life, even though they'd not started moving yet. 'The water will be rising and I don't want us to get into trouble.'

Betty tried to breathe normally as Lily eased the truck down the lane that led to the cricket pitch. It was getting really dark now. There were no streetlights, obviously, because they'd been turned off for the blackout, and the truck's headlamps were dim, because they were covered and angled towards the ground. Lily was right, though, that it was better than nothing and every now and then the lightning lit up the way ahead, showing that Ned had been right about the floods coming into the village.

The truck swooshed waves of water out to the side as they drove and Betty feared for Nancy and Audrey who were on foot.

They reached the ford. At least, Betty knew it had to be the ford because she'd lived in Beckindale all her life, but she couldn't see exactly where it was. In the headlights from Lily's truck, she could see the river swirling. It was far, far wider than it normally was.

'I'm going to go really, really slowly,' Lily said. 'We're high up so the water shouldn't come over the bonnet, but if it does, we might have to go back.'

Betty was so frightened she couldn't speak; she just nodded and gripped the seat even tighter. She was freezing cold, but still she felt sweat dripping down her back and in the reflection in the truck's window she could see her face was deathly pale.

Inch by inch, Lily edged the truck into the water. Betty could hear roaring, but she wasn't sure if it was the river or the blood rushing in her ears. As the truck went into the water, it slipped sideways and Betty gasped in fright. But Lily was in control.

'Easy,' she muttered to herself. 'Easy, Lily.'

Betty whimpered, and put her hand over her mouth to stop herself. She didn't want to distract Lily in any way.

Lily kept going, pushing her foot down gently on the accelerator. Betty felt sick with fright. What if they were washed away? What if the water started coming through the doors?

'Come on,' Lily said to herself. 'Come on.'

She revved the engine a fraction too hard and the truck slipped again, more violently this time. Betty shrieked and even Lily shouted in fear as the back of the truck slid sideways. This is it, Betty thought. We're going to be pulled down the river. But with steely determination, Lily held her nerve. She acted fast, and with a tug of the steering wheel she managed to straighten the vehicle again.

'Sorry,' she mumbled, hunching over the dashboard so she could see better. Betty was breathing hard. 'S'all right,' she managed to gasp as Lily pressed the accelerator again, more gently this time.

Terrified, Betty squeezed her eyes tight shut as they inched forwards. Then, with a whir of the wheels, they were on the other side of the river. Betty opened her eyes and for a frightening second, she thought they were going to plunge backwards into the water, as the tyres spun on the muddy ground. But then they gripped and Lily drove forwards to safety.

'Oh, thank goodness,' she said under her breath. Betty thought she'd be using much more colourful language than that if she were in Lily's shoes, but she didn't say so. She wanted to grab Lily and sob on her shoulder and shout in triumph that they were still alive, but actually she just patted her on the arm.

'Well done,' she said.

Lily drove on. The water was still halfway up the truck's wheels but they were on the path — at least they thought they were — so it was easier for Lily to drive. It was hard to see very far ahead, because the headlights were so dim, but Betty whimpered again, this time in relief, when they finally saw the small, ramshackle hut up ahead in among the trees.

Lily was frowning as the path narrowed. 'I don't think we can go much further,' she said. 'We're not going to get through. Let's get out, but leave the lights on for now.'

'Won't the battery get flat?' Betty didn't know much about engines but she did know it was bad to leave headlights on for too long. 'And what about the blackout?'

Lily looked up at the sky, and then shrugged. 'We'll have to risk it.'

Betty took a deep breath in. 'Right then,' she said. 'Let's get going.'

23

Nancy and Audrey were trying to wade through the flood as fast as they could to get to the hut up ahead. The water was right up to their knees now, and it was freezing. Nancy's head was throbbing where she'd hit it, and she was shivering violently, feeling the cold seeping into her skin through her wet clothes. Next to her she could feel Audrey doing the same.

'Susan?' Audrey was calling. 'Susan are you in the hut?'

They could still hear barking, but with the roar of the river it was hard to know which direction it was coming from.

'Susan?' Nancy shouted. But there was no reply.

The barking though was getting louder and more frenzied as they approached the hut.

'The dog is definitely in there,' said Audrey. Nancy nodded. She was horribly aware that they'd only heard the dog, not Susan. Was it Bella? Was Susan even with her? And if she was, why hadn't she called out?

The hut was close to what had been the river-bank. Nancy assumed it had been used by fishermen once upon a time, but it was ramshackle now and its roof was half off. She could see why Susan liked it though, when the weather was calmer. It was tucked away here, on the edge of the woods, and must feel like a little bolthole for Susan.

'Susan?' she called again. She and Audrey

exchanged worried glances. 'Where's the door?' she asked. It was so dark that it was impossible to see, and was she imagining it, or was the water past their knees now?

Suddenly they heard a shout from behind them and turned to see a shaft of light through the trees.

'What's that?' Audrey said. 'Who's that?'

'It's Lily,' Nancy said, recognising the figure silhouetted in the orangey light. She must have brought her father's truck. 'And Betty?'

'Betty too?' Audrey said, impressed. 'Good for her.'

The two women splashed towards them. Lily looked calm and in control, while Betty's face was white and she seemed terrified.

'I came in Dad's truck,' Lily called as they approached. 'Thought you might need some help.'

'Is Susan in there?' Betty said, her voice trembling.

'We've shouted but we can only hear barking,' Nancy said. 'We were just about to go in.'

Lily nodded. 'We should go, before the water gets higher.'

Nancy looked down. The water was almost at the top of her wellingtons now, whereas just ten minutes ago it had been ankle-deep. The realisation of how fast the water was rising made her gasp but she swallowed her fear. If Susan was in the hut, they had to get to her quickly.

'Come on,' she said. 'But go slowly and carefully. It's not easy moving through the water and we've already had one fall.'

Gingerly, the women all turned towards the

cabin. Nancy took a step forward and as she did so, a huge crack of lightning forked across the dark sky. With a roar, it arced on to a tall tree ahead of them, making them all scream with fear. The tree sizzled with sparks and then, with an ear-splitting groan, one of its top branches crashed down and into the front of the hut, tearing down one of its wooden walls and blocking the women's way in.

Betty was crying, whispering 'what will we do?' over and over, her eyes squeezed tightly shut. Lily and Audrey were clutching each other, both of them pale-faced with shock. Nancy's heart was racing, and she was shaking even more violently than she had been before. She thought she might scream so she clenched her jaw to stop herself before she spoke. 'Betty, shush,' she said. 'I have to think.'

'What if Susan was in there?' Audrey whispered. 'What if she was in there when the tree came down.'

'Susan?' Nancy called. 'Susan? Are you there?'

There was a terrible, eerie silence that stretched on and on. Betty moaned and someone — possibly Nancy herself — took a long juddery breath in. And then the barking started again, more frantic than before. Nancy thought it was the nicest sound she'd ever heard.

'The dog's there,' she said.

'And Susan?' Audrey asked, her voice hesitant.

'We won't know until we look inside, will we?'

Lily had been looking at the branch. 'Give me your torch,' she said to Nancy. 'I can see something.'

Nancy felt for Lily's hand in the darkness and put the torch in it, thanking her lucky stars she'd had the strap looped round her wrist when the tree fell. She'd been so frightened she'd let go of the torch as soon as the lightning struck.

Lily shone the torch on to the branch and the wrecked wall of the hut.

'There,' she said. 'At the back. Susan? Susan? Is that you?'

They all peered through the twigs and Nancy thought she saw a darker shadow right at the back of the hut.

'It's her,' she breathed. 'It must be her.'

She looked at Lily, frightened to put what she was thinking into words. 'Why isn't she replying?' she said. 'What if . . . '

'We need to climb over the branch,' Lily said quickly. 'Or move it out of the way.'

'We can move it,' said Audrey. 'Four of us together? We can lift that easily.'

'Are you sure?' Lily sounded doubtful. 'Betty's in a state.'

'I'm fine,' Betty said weakly. 'Honestly, I'm fine. I just got a fright. I can lift the branch.'

Nancy was impressed as Betty wiped her face with her gloved hand and threw her shoulders back. 'I'm fine,' Betty said again. 'I'll take this side, shall I?'

Lily went opposite Betty, holding the torch under her arm. Then Nancy and Audrey went to the other end of the branch. They had to reach into the cold water to get a grip of the wooden trunk, which made them all shiver but no one complained.

'Right,' said Audrey. 'We're going to lift it and move it round to the left, just enough to make a space for us to get through. On my count. One, two, three . . . '

Together, the women all lifted the branch and with a large splash, shifted it a couple of feet to the left, and dropped it back into the water, leaving the way into the cabin clear, just about. There were some jagged planks of wood sticking out from its walls, but with an appraising eye, Nancy thought she could get past.

'Someone hold the torch,' she said. 'I'm going in.'

With Lily lighting her way, Nancy carefully clambered over the broken wood and into the cabin.

'I'm right behind you,' said Audrey, and Nancy was grateful.

As they entered the hut there was a cacophony of barking and the sound of water splashing.

'Bella?' Audrey called. 'Susan?'

'Can you see anything?' Nancy hissed.

There was a splash and suddenly Nancy felt a dog's head nudging her thigh. She looked down and through the gloom she could make out the splodge of white fur that told her this was Bella.

'It's Bella,' she said joyfully. 'It's Bella, Audrey. Where's Susan, Bella? Where is she, girl?' She turned her head and called to Lily. 'Can you hold the torch higher? All I can see are the shadows of the branches.'

There was a pause and then the light lifted up and the hut filled with dim light.

'Much better,' Nancy said. Her eyes adjusting

to the gloom, she scanned the room and there, in the corner, was Susan. She was sitting on a wooden deckchair, obviously left behind by a fisherman, with her knees drawn up to her chest, her head lowered and her hands over her ears. The water was so high in the cabin, that it was lapping round her feet even though they were up on the seat of the chair.

'Oh, thank God,' Nancy breathed. Behind her, Audrey said the same.

'Susan,' Nancy said. 'Susan, sweetheart. It's me, Nancy.'

Slowly, and to Nancy's enormous relief, Susan raised her head and blinked at them. She didn't speak.

'Audrey, can you take Bella outside?' Nancy said. 'I'll get Susan.'

Audrey nodded.

'Susan, you've obviously looked after Bella really well,' Audrey said to the frightened girl. 'But I'm going to take her outside now. Betty and Lily are outside too. We need to get you home, my love.'

Susan didn't speak. She seemed frozen with fear.

Nancy picked up Bella, who was swimming in the cold water bravely, and the little dog nuzzled into her neck. She gave her to Audrey.

'Come back,' she said in a quiet voice. 'Get Betty to put Bella in the truck and then come back with Lily. I think I'll need you.'

Audrey nodded and disappeared out of the door with the shivering dog. Nancy heard voices and a little bark.

She took a sloshing step towards Susan, carefully feeling her way through the water in the gloom.

'Susan, love. Are you all right? Are you hurt?'

Finally, Susan responded. She shook her head slowly.

'I am so sorry I was horrible to you,' Nancy said. 'And we need to get you home.' Nancy held a hand out. 'Can you come?'

Susan didn't move.

Lily appeared behind Nancy, still holding the torch, and the light in the hut grew fractionally brighter.

'Susan,' Nancy said. 'Lily's here.'

'And Audrey,' said Audrey from behind Lily.

'And Betty,' said Betty. 'I'm here too. I've taken Bella back to the truck, Susan. She's doing all right. She's wrapped up in a blanket.'

Susan whispered something.

'What's that?' said Nancy, taking a sloshy step forward.

'Bella looked after me,' she said.

A clap of thunder made them all jump, and Susan curled up even tighter. The poor girl was shaking like a leaf, and Nancy wasn't sure if it was because of the cold, or from fright. Probably a combination of both.

'Bella's a heroine,' Nancy said. 'Come on, let's get you home so we can tell everyone about it.' She reached out to Susan and this time the girl gripped her hands tightly.

'I'm so sorry I frightened Bella,' she said.

'Nonsense,' Nancy said, trying to sound matter-of-fact when she just wanted to throw her arms round the girl and make everything all

245

right. 'It wasn't your fault. I'm sorry I shouted at you.' She looked at Susan. 'Are you hurt? Can you walk?'

'I'm not hurt,' said Susan, through chattering teeth.

Carefully Nancy supported her as she uncurled her legs and — grimacing — stood up in the water.

'It's so deep,' Susan gasped.

'The river has burst its banks,' Nancy said. 'We need to get a move on, because it's still raining and it's only going to get worse.' She'd noticed the water rising just in the few minutes she'd been with Susan, and she was inwardly panicking about how they were going to get back to the village.

'Come on, carefully now.' She was horribly aware that Susan wasn't wearing a coat, nor wellington boots.

She helped Susan wade through the water. She was virtually holding the girl up, she was so weak with fear and fatigue. When they reached Lily, she took Susan's other side, and then Audrey joined Nancy, and Betty took Susan's hand on Lily's side, and together, as though they were doing some strange, terrifying three-legged race, they reached the edge of the hut.

Nancy could feel Susan shaking.

'Nearly there,' she said. 'Lily's brought her dad's truck. It's just down by the edge of the wood.'

She hoped it wasn't too far and as though reading her mind, Lily said, 'Just a few more steps.'

Holding each other tightly, the women waded through the flood towards the truck. Susan was beginning to look more aware of what was going on, as though she was waking up from a long sleep.

'Are you all here because of me?' she said in wonder as they got to the truck.

'We were worried about you,' Nancy said. 'Well, it was Ruby really. She told us to get off our bottoms and start looking for you.'

'She can be very bossy.'

Nancy grinned. 'That's true.'

She put her arm round Susan and squeezed her tight.

'But she was right to worry. You'd have been in real trouble if we hadn't found you when we did.'

Lily opened the door of the truck and Bella barked in greeting. Lily reached inside and pulled out the blanket that Bella had been sitting on.

'Sorry, girl,' she said to the dog. Then she draped the blanket over Susan's shoulders. 'Get inside. You need to get warm.'

Nancy helped Susan climb up into the front of the truck and sighed with relief.

'Did you come across the humpback bridge?' she asked but Lily shook her head.

'Through the ford.'

Nancy breathed out. It seemed their ordeal wasn't over yet. 'Will we get back that way?'

'Only one way to find out.'

They all piled into the truck. Susan held Bella on her lap, the blanket over both of them. The dog seemed fine after her escapade, and Nancy was relieved. She remembered Jacob's adoring expression as he'd talked to Bella earlier and was happy she didn't have to tell him his dog had gone for good. Lily was driving, of course, with Nancy in the passenger seat next to Susan. And Betty and Audrey perched behind the driver's seat on a bench.

'You gave us quite a scare, pet,' Betty said to Susan, leaning over her shoulder.

Susan looked at her, a mischievous glint in her eye. 'I must have done, if you came out in this weather to find me,' she said. 'It's going to mess your hair up.'

They all laughed, louder than they'd normally laugh at a silly joke, but they were so relieved to have got Susan and Bella out of the water, they were all feeling slightly giddy. For now, at least.

Betty nudged Susan affectionately and Nancy exchanged a glance with Audrey over her shoulder, as Lily put the truck into gear and set off slowly through the water.

'What will we do if we can't get through,' Audrey said, voicing what everyone was thinking.

Lily grimaced. 'Not sure,' she said. 'If we can get out to the main road, we could go up the hill, towards Emmerdale Farm. But if the ford's impassable then I reckon the main road will be too.'

The women, and Susan, sat silently as the truck eased through the flood, all of them worrying about what was waiting for them.

But as they approached the ford, Betty sat up straighter. 'There's something there,' she said, trying to see out of the window, 'There's

248

something over the river.'

Lily squinted through the windscreen wipers, which were going ten to the dozen.

'It looks like a tractor,' she said. 'Who would bring a tractor out in this?'

She flashed the truck's lights and immediately the tractor put on its headlamps too.

Lily turned the truck slightly and its lights illuminated the vehicle on the other side of the water. Hanging off the tractor were Ned Barlow and Jacob Sugden. Beside it, upright and stiff-backed was Jack Proudfoot, and next to him was Seth and Seth's friend Ernie.

Lily brought the truck to a halt and leaned out of the cab.

'Evening boys,' she called. Nancy marvelled at her casual air after all they'd been through this evening. 'Jack, I told you to stay with Hope.'

'She's fine,' Jack shouted. 'She's with Nina and your dad.'

'Is Audrey with you?' Ned looked worried and Audrey clambered over Betty and stuck her head out of the other window.

'I'm here!' she shouted. 'Hello!'

'And Betty?' Seth stood up, balancing on the edge of the tractor to stay out of the water.

Betty squeezed underneath Audrey. 'We're all here,' she said. 'Susan too.'

'And Bella,' Audrey shouted to a concerned-looking Jacob.

'And Nancy,' Betty added, though no one — Nancy couldn't help but notice — had asked after her.

'We thought we'd come down in case you got

stuck,' Ned said. 'We've got ropes. If the truck gets into trouble, we'll yank you out.'

Nancy felt giddy with relief. It was going to be all right, she thought.

And it was. It took a while because the river had risen a lot and the water was powerful, but Lily was calm and in control the whole time.

The two vehicles formed a sort of strange procession and headed back to the village, splashing through the flood water.

'We said we'd go back to the pub,' Betty told Susan, Nancy and Audrey. 'Larry was getting blankets and keeping the fire burning. And I don't know about you, but I could do with a port and lemon.'

Nancy, who really only took a drink at Christmas, nodded vigorously. 'That's exactly what I need,' she said.

There was a bit of a party atmosphere at the Woolie. Susan's gran was there, emotional and teary. 'Not you too,' she kept saying as she hugged Susan tightly to her chest. 'Not you too.'

Margaret was there, and Lily's dad and stepmother, Nina. Old Harry was sitting at the bar. Maggie Sugden was pleased as anything to see Audrey back safe and sound, while Jacob was thrilled to bits to see Bella. Ruby was there with Meg and young Stan who was getting everyone to sign the cast on his arm.

'He's doing well,' Meg called out to Nancy. 'The doctor at the hospital said you'd done a good job putting the splint on it like that. He said it could have been much worse if you hadn't.'

Nancy waved off her thanks, but she felt absurdly pleased that she'd done something right today, before she'd shouted at poor Susan and sent her fleeing. She felt awful, still. She watched as Mrs Roberts settled Susan down in the corner, wrapped her in blankets and handed her a cup of tea. Bella nuzzled in next to her and Nancy thought now was the time to apologise. She sat down close to Susan, who still looked cold.

'I really am sorry for shouting,' she said. 'It's no excuse, I know, but things just got on top of me. I was horrible and I apologise.'

Susan smiled. 'I was in your way,' she said. 'Sorry for being a nuisance.'

Nancy reached out and took the girl's hand. 'You're welcome to come and be a nuisance at the surgery any time you like.' She paused. 'Can you tell me what happened?'

'When she ran away from the surgery, Bella went down the side of the graveyard,' Susan said. 'I think she wanted to go home. And I followed, thinking I could just make sure she was all right, and then walk her back up to the farm. But just as I got to her, the rain started coming down heavy again. I found a piece of string in my pocket and tied it to her collar and took her into the woods to shelter.'

'How did you end up in the hut?'

'When the thunder started, I was so scared,' Susan said. 'I just ran. Bella, bless her, came with me. We got to the hut, and then the water started rising and I was so cold and so frightened. I kept telling Bella to go, to go home, but she wouldn't.'

251

She looked at Jacob, who was hovering nearby. 'She's such a clever dog,' she said. 'She stayed with me the whole time. She heard Nancy and Audrey before I did. Her ears pricked right up and she started barking so loud. I was sort of frozen to the spot — not from the cold, really, more from being frightened — but Bella kept barking.' She stroked the dog's silky ears. 'She's a real treasure,' she said. 'I'm so sorry I almost lost her, Jacob.'

Nancy looked at grumpy Jacob Sugden, who had a reputation in the village for being surly and unpleasant, and was astonished to see tears in his eyes.

'You did good,' he muttered to Susan. Then he swallowed. 'All being well, we'll have pups soon, thought you might like one.'

Susan's face was a picture. She smiled more broadly than Nancy had ever seen her smile and suddenly grumpy Nancy Tate, who had a reputation in the village for being standoffish and snooty, was crying too.

'I think,' said Lily appearing at her elbow and handing her a hanky. 'It might be time for another port and lemon.'

24

It was a strange evening. The roads were flooded and with the blackout, it was too dark to get through safely, so people drifted off to stay with various friends and some people even settled down for the night at the Woolpack. Jacob was staying at the pub, and Maggie had gone straight home once she'd seen they were back safely with Susan.

'Would you like to stay at mine?' Nancy asked Audrey. Audrey was surprised by the offer because Nancy kept herself to herself most of the time, but she nodded.

'That would be great, thank you. I was worried I might need to curl up under one of the tables in the pub.'

Nancy chuckled. 'I'm so tired I could sleep draped on a washing line,' she said and Audrey agreed.

'It's been quite a day,' she said.

The rain was still falling, but Audrey thought it had eased off, at least a bit, as they walked across the village to Nancy's cottage.

Inside, they hung all their wet gear on Nancy's clothes horse, and Nancy lit the fire.

'Fancy some Horlicks?' she asked. 'I'm still cold and I could do with just sitting quietly for a while before I hit the hay.'

'That sounds good,' Audrey said. 'Need a hand?'

Audrey warmed the milk, while Nancy found extra blankets and made up a bed on the sofa and then they both settled down in the small lounge with their fingers wrapped round their warm mugs. Audrey sat under the blankets, while Nancy sat opposite, looking a bit stiff and upright, on a chair.

'I keep thinking about what could have happened today,' Nancy said. 'Susan could have drowned and it would have been my fault.'

Audrey made a face. 'I don't think it was your fault. It was just bad luck that Susan was spooked and scared Bella so she ran off. And then it was even worse luck that the thunder started up and Susan was terrified.' She paused. 'I suppose in some way you could blame Hitler. After all, it was his Luftwaffe that killed Susan's family and left her so frightened of loud noises.'

Nancy gave her a weak smile. 'I suppose. But I shouldn't have shouted at her.'

'You were tired and under pressure. Lots of people would have reacted in the same way. I know I would.'

'I doubt that.'

Audrey patted the sofa next to her. 'Come and sit here where it's more comfortable,' she said. Nancy obeyed and Audrey pulled a blanket over her, studying her carefully. 'You're very hard on yourself,' she said. 'You're doing a difficult job and you're doing it well.'

Nancy sighed. 'I feel like I'm making mistakes at every turn.'

'You've really won people over in Beckindale, though. The surgery is busier than ever.'

Nancy smiled properly this time.

'That's got a lot to do with Lily,' she admitted. 'She's been spreading the word. And we're doing this recommendation thing where we give customers discounts.'

'Maybe, but people wouldn't come back if they didn't think they could trust you,' Audrey pointed out. 'Those animals are their livelihoods, not to mention the only thing stopping the War Ag breathing down their necks, and they wouldn't let you loose on their cows and chickens if they didn't think you'd do a good job.'

Nancy nodded.

'I suppose.'

'Suppose nothing,' Audrey said. 'You know I'm speaking sense. How are you doing financially, if it's not rude to ask.'

'Better than I was, even with the discount. I'm hoping to be able to afford to employ a veterinary nurse in the new year, if things carry on this way.'

'Well there you go,' Audrey said. 'People are bringing their animals to you, you're doing fine money-wise — what is there to worry about?'

'I just need to prove I can do it,' Nancy said.

Audrey snorted. 'I know how that feels. No one thinks I can do anything when they first meet me.' She smiled as she thought of the one exception to that. 'Apart from my Ned, of course. He wasn't at all fazed when he noticed my arm.'

Nancy smiled. 'He's a treasure, your Ned.'

Audrey frowned. 'But everyone in Beckindale can see you're a good vet, Nancy. Who are you trying to impress?'

'My father,' Nancy admitted. 'I just want him to see I'm making a go of it.'

'How old do you think we'll be before we stop trying to please our parents?' said Audrey.

Nancy groaned. 'Fifty?' she said. 'Older?'

Audrey took Nancy's hand. 'Listen,' she said. 'You're just feeling the strain because you're so busy,' she said. 'And so what if you've made mistakes? Everyone does. Remember when I got you out to deliver the calf that didn't even belong to the Sugdens?'

Nancy chuckled and Audrey went on. 'Susan's safe because you went after her.'

'So did you.'

Audrey shrugged. 'I wasn't going to let you go by yourself, was I? You're my friend.'

Nancy smiled. 'I appreciate that,' she said. She eyed Audrey in a way that made Audrey feel slightly uncomfortable. 'How do you know so much?'

'I don't know anything really,' Audrey said. 'I just think people make assumptions because we're young or because we're women, or because I've got a funny arm, and we have to prove them wrong.'

'Who are you proving wrong? Jacob?'

'A bit. My mother though, mostly. So I understand how you feel about your father.'

'Bet she can't believe that you're wading through floods and clambering over cowshed roofs.'

'Hmm,' said Audrey, non-committal. She was too tired to start explaining that her contact with her parents was minimal at best. She drained her Horlicks mug and held it out. 'Now, I don't know about you, but I'm exhausted. So stop your yacking because I need to get some sleep.'

Nancy stood up and took Audrey's mug. 'Night then,' she said.

⋆ ⋆ ⋆

Both women were awake bright and early the next day. Nancy had lots of work to do and Audrey wanted to get back up to the farm to see what damage the storm had done and to check on the animals.

She thanked Nancy for putting her up and gave her a hug which Nancy returned, to Audrey's surprise. And then she pulled on her wet weather gear and headed outside. The rain had stopped but the village was a mess. There was an inch or two of dirty water which thankfully the sandbags had kept away from the houses, and Audrey could see the fields around were flooded too. The drains were gurgling as they worked overtime and there were tree branches down, and piles of leaves all over the place. One branch had broken a window in the post office, and there were people everywhere, surveying the damage and discussing what had happened.

She waved to Larry at the pub, and said hello to Betty who was dancing her way up the path to the surgery, despite wearing wellies, and looking as glamorous as she normally did, which Audrey thought was impressive, considering just last night she'd been soaked to the skin.

'Audrey!' She turned around and saw Ned splashing through the puddles towards her. Her heart leapt, just as it always did when she saw

257

him and she smiled broadly.

'Hello!'

'Glad I caught you,' Ned said. 'Are you heading back up to Emmerdale Farm?'

'If I can. I'm assuming the road's clear, but I don't know for certain.'

Ned nodded. 'It is, yes,' he said. 'Jacob went early this morning. You're lucky you're up the hill.'

'We are.'

'Thought you might like some company on the way up,' Ned said. He skirted round her so he was on her right, then offered her his arm and she took it. On impulse, she reached up and kissed his cheek.

'What's that for?' Ned asked.

'Just for being you.'

They splashed on through the village and then out on to the road, where the floods hadn't reached but where there were still large puddles and where the fields were soggy and forlorn. They chatted about the events of the night before, with Ned marvelling at how brave the women had been.

'I couldn't believe it when we heard you and Nancy had walked to find Susan,' he said. 'My head was spinning with worry. We'd been down at the river and Ernie nearly fell in . . . '

'We saw that,' Audrey said. 'We were crossing the bridge and we saw you all. I was so scared when I realised it was you standing right at the edge of the water.'

Ned grinned at her. 'We were both worried,' he said. 'When the river burst its banks, I was going out of my mind. And then when Lily said she was going to drive through the ford, I thought she was mad. Jacob and I wanted to go after her in the tractor, but Mick said she knew what she was doing.'

'She did.'

'I know that now.' Ned nodded slowly. 'Lily's always been bold, mind you.'

Audrey chuckled. Bold was certainly one way to describe Lily Proudfoot.

'You're all bold,' Ned added. 'You're all heroines, the way you rescued young Susan.'

'I don't know about that,' Audrey said modestly.

'I do. You deserve an award or summat. A bravery award.'

'When there are soldiers facing Nazis every day? I don't think so,' Audrey said. 'You're just biased because it's me.'

Ned grinned. 'There's a lad I know called George. He's a bit of an oddball, but he's a nice enough chap. Works for the *Hotten Courier*. I reckon, if I had a word with him . . . '

'Oh no,' Audrey said. 'No.'

'Oh come on,' said Ned. 'People should know about what you did. It's brilliant. If I speak to George, he can write an article about you for the paper.'

'Absolutely not.' Audrey was firm. 'What if my parents saw it? Imagine them finding out where I am in that way?'

Ned laughed. 'Your parents live in Worthing.'

'So?'

'So, they're hardly likely to be reading the *Hotten Courier* down in Sussex, are they?'

'I suppose not,' said Audrey. 'But even so, Ned. I'm not sure it's a good plan. We just did what anyone would have done. We don't need fuss and nonsense about it.'

Ned grinned at her, and her tummy flipped over again. She just loved being with him, even when he was being silly about newspapers and articles and reporters. They were approaching the farm now, but Ned stopped walking suddenly meaning Audrey had to stop too.

'Audrey,' he said. He fiddled with the collar on his jacket and then rubbed the back of his neck. 'Before you get home, I wanted to ask you something.'

Audrey felt worried suddenly. He seemed nervous and she was scared he was going to tell her something awful.

'What?' she said.

Ned cleared his throat. 'I wanted to ask if you'd be my girl, official like?'

Audrey laughed in relief. 'Really?' she said.

'Really.'

'I'd love that.'

She and Ned had spent a lot of time together over the past few weeks and they'd shared more than a few kisses, but now he bent his head and pressed his lips against hers in a way that made her head spin. Audrey responded, her breath almost taken away by the moment and her legs weak, until they broke apart and Ned grinned at her.

'My girl,' he said.

They started walking again, Audrey relieved to discover her legs still worked, because they were fizzing madly and she felt she was trembling all over.

'I'm going to tell everyone about you,' he said. 'I'm going to spread the word about how brave my girl and her friends were and how they rescued a young frightened schoolgirl.'

Audrey nudged him. 'People will get fed up of hearing about it, I reckon.'

'Never. It was incredible.'

As they approached the farm. Bella came out to greet them, her tail wagging, and Audrey gave her a delighted cuddle.

'Look at you,' she said. 'You're back to normal.'

'About bloody time.' Jacob appeared, holding a spade and a fork. He handed the fork to Audrey. 'Potatoes,' he muttered.

Audrey grinned at him and then at Ned. 'See, fed up of hearing about it.'

'What's that?' said Jacob.

'Ned was just saying he was going to tell everyone about our dramatic rescue of poor Susan,' Audrey said, hamming up the word 'dramatic'. 'But I said it was done now and no one cares, and then you arrived and proved my point.'

Ned made a face. 'You're not still going on about that, are you?' he said, deadpan.

Audrey looked at him, unsure if he was joking or not, then his face softened and he smiled.

'It was brave,' he said. 'I'm proud of you.' He walked past them and then paused and looked back. 'But those potatoes won't dig themselves.'

Audrey laughed out loud and kissed Ned goodbye. 'I'd better get on then.' She called out to Jacob to let him know she was just going inside for a quick wash and then she'd crack on and headed into the farmhouse.

It was quiet inside, and she could see Joseph asleep in his chair by the window as usual, but as she went up the stairs, she heard a moan.

'Maggie?' she called. 'Is that you?'

There was no reply. Perhaps it was the wind? But another moan told her she'd heard right the first time. She went along the hall to Maggie's bedroom and knocked on the door gently.

'Maggie?' she said. 'It's Audrey. Are you all right?'

She pushed open the door. Maggie was sitting on the side of the bed, bent in the middle and holding her stomach.

'Oh, Audrey,' she said, looking up and smiling — in an unconvincing manner. 'I didn't hear you come in. What can I do for you?'

'I heard you moaning and I wanted to see if you were all right.'

'I'm fine,' Maggie said. She stood up but her legs went from under her and she slumped to the floor.

Audrey gasped and rushed to Maggie's side. 'Maggie?' she said. She felt her heart thumping in her chest and couldn't believe that things were going wrong again.

'I'm all right,' Maggie said. She tried to sit up but couldn't. Audrey's heart lurched with fear. What was wrong?

'I'm going to send for Dr Black,' Audrey said.

'No,' Maggie protested. But then she gripped her stomach. 'Actually, perhaps he could give me something for the pain.' She breathed in, a shaky gulp of air. 'Can you help me up?' she said. 'I think I'll feel better if I can get into bed.'

Audrey helped the older woman to her feet — it obviously took her considerable effort to get upright — and guided her to sit down on the side of the bed. Then she took off Maggie's slippers and lifted her legs so she was lying down, and pulled a blanket over her to keep her warm.

Maggie's face was thin and drawn and she looked scared. Audrey felt awful that this had been going on so long, that she'd known things weren't right, and she hadn't been more forceful about checking up on her boss.

'I'm going to send Jacob for the doctor,' she said. 'I'll be back in a moment.'

Still scared about what was happening, Audrey dashed downstairs and out into the yard where she filled a worried Jacob in about what was going on. He barely let her finish before he was running to the battered old farm truck and jumping in.

'Stay with her,' he called as he swung the truck round the yard. 'Make sure she's all right.'

25

Dr Black and Jacob were back in no time at all. The doctor didn't seem surprised to see Maggie in such a state, which made Audrey feel even more guilty about letting things get as bad as they had. She and Jacob hovered outside the bedroom door until the doctor came out.

'She'll be fine,' he said. 'I've given her some pills to lessen the pain and she's got her operation soon enough. She just needs to rest.'

Jacob and Audrey exchanged an alarmed glance. Operation? Dr Black started downstairs. 'You check on Ma,' Jacob hissed to Audrey. 'I'm going to talk to him.' He hurried down the stairs after the doctor and with some trepidation, Audrey knocked on the bedroom door and went inside.

Maggie was tucked up in bed, looking slightly better than she had done.

'Has the pain gone?' Audrey said. The older woman nodded.

'Thank you for looking after me,' she said.

Audrey went to her and took her hand. 'What's wrong?' she said. 'What's happened?'

'I've got fibroids,' Maggie said.

'Fibroids?' Audrey turned the unfamiliar word over in her mouth. 'Is it serious?' she said, imagining all sorts of horrible outcomes. She swallowed. 'Are you going to get better?'

Maggie nodded. 'It's not serious and I'm not

going to die,' she said, reading the worried expression on Audrey's face. 'Some people don't even know they've got them. It's just mine are quite large and they've been causing me pain . . . ' she paused. 'And a lot of bleeding, which is why I've been feeling weak.'

Audrey looked at Maggie blankly. She looked pale, of course, but that wasn't out of the ordinary recently. But she couldn't see any sign of blood.

Maggie sighed. 'They're in my womb, Audrey,' she said, looking a little embarrassed. 'It's that sort of bleeding.'

'Oh,' said Audrey wincing inwardly. 'Poor you.' She paused. 'The doctor said you have to have an operation? Is that where you went yesterday?'

'I was at the hospital,' Maggie said. 'I've had some medicine for the fibroids, but it didn't work, so I need to have a hysterectomy.' She swallowed a sob and Audrey felt that lurch of fear again. She didn't know much about medical matters but she knew she was growing very fond of Maggie.

'That's a big operation, isn't it?' she said, remembering when a friend of her mother had one. 'You're going to take a while to recover.'

'But it'll be worth it in the end.'

Audrey looked at Maggie, once so energetic and strong and now tucked up in bed like a baby, and bit her lip. 'Why didn't you say anything sooner? Why didn't you tell Jacob and me?'

Maggie frowned. 'I've been silly,' she said. 'I realise that now. I thought if I ignored it, it would go away.' She sounded close to tears again. 'We've all been working so hard, and you being here's made all the difference. But the War Ag are always around and I didn't want to risk losing the farm.'

Audrey felt sorry for her, coping with all these worries on her own for so long. 'We'll step up,' she said. 'Of course we will. You just need to worry about getting better.'

'But we've got all those extra crops to think about now, the flax, and all the chickens, plus the vegetable garden.'

'Oh goodness, don't fret about us,' she said, in what she hoped was a brisk, capable tone. 'We can manage. We're not afraid of a bit of hard work, neither of us. There are a lot of people who'll help us out if we ask. Ned's around. And Smithers might lend us Tilly or Ginny for a day or two if we're struggling. And the chap from the War Ag knows us now.' She smiled at Maggie. 'You timed it very well — if it was harvest time we'd really be in trouble. Your job is just to concentrate on getting better.'

'Thank you,' Maggie said. Her forehead smoothed out as she relaxed a fraction. 'It's a relief knowing you and Jacob can work it all out between you.'

Audrey nodded, hoping they could cope. 'It's fine,' she said. 'Honestly. Have you told Joseph?'

Maggie shook her head. 'Not yet, but I will once I know when the operation is going to be.'

Audrey swallowed. 'Will it be soon?'

'Before Christmas, the doctor said. I'm glad. I don't want to wait too long,' Maggie said.

'Is it expensive?' Audrey knew the cost of some operations could really mount up and she didn't like to think of Maggie having to go without or having even more to worry about. But Maggie shook her head.

'It's covered, don't worry. I've got some savings.'

'When the operation's done, will you be better?' Audrey just wanted to know that the old Maggie hadn't gone forever. 'Will you have your energy back?'

'I certainly hope so.' Maggie smiled suddenly. 'That's what the doctor says, anyway.'

'Jacob's downstairs talking to Dr Black,' Audrey said. 'Do you want me to send him up?'

'That would be nice,' Maggie said. 'I don't want him to worry.'

Audrey knew Jacob was bound to worry anyway, but she nodded. Then she stood up and impulsively hugged the older woman tightly.

'I'll step up while you're in hospital and when you're recovering,' she said. 'I can even cook Christmas dinner if you need me to.'

Maggie laughed. 'I've not even begun to think about Christmas yet,' she said. 'Anyway, won't you be going back to Sussex?'

Audrey bit her lip. 'Maybe,' she said. Her parents had written to invite her but she'd not replied yet.

'We'd love to hear all about what you're doing,' her mother had written. Audrey had thought she really meant that she wanted to hear about it so she could stop it.

'I think I'd rather stay here,' she told Maggie.

'You'll need me around, especially if you're poorly.'

'We'd love to have you,' Maggie said.

Jacob took the news of his mother's illness surprisingly well. Like Audrey, he'd been imagining the worst so hearing that though she needed an operation, she should recover, was a relief.

'I can't believe she's suffered in silence all this time,' he told Audrey a week or so later. They were sitting on the fence by the cows, looking down towards the village, out over the fields that had been flooded but were now simply soggy.

'I think she was a bit embarrassed,' said Audrey, feeling her own face start to flush. 'You know, because it was a woman's thing.'

Jacob looked away, awkwardly. 'Well, she's got her op next week and then she'll be right as rain,' he said.

'She's going to have to take it easy for a while, don't forget,' Audrey warned and Jacob nodded.

'But she'll be better by the summer,' he said.

'I hope so.'

Audrey and Jacob had fallen into an easy friendship where they worked well together and chatted during their breaks. He told her more about Annie and what sort of person she was, though she still hadn't replied to his letters. Audrey was torn between wishing she could meet the woman who'd stolen the hearts of both Sugden brothers, and feeling intimidated at the very thought. Jacob made her sound perfect.

She told him about Ned and how sweet he was, and how much she was enjoying being his girl.

'You'll be Mrs Barlow before the war's finished,' Jacob teased and Audrey gave him a shove.

'I'm not in any hurry to tie the knot,' she said. But deep down she hoped Jacob was right.

A shout from the farmhouse made them look up. Maggie was in the doorway, waving something.

'She shouldn't be up and about,' said Audrey, cross. 'She needs to rest.' Maggie wasn't doing any work on the farm any more but getting her to stay put in her chair by the fire was easier said than done.

'What's that?' Jacob said, squinting. 'What's she got there?'

Audrey jumped down from the fence. 'No idea, but there's only one way to find out.'

She set off across the field to the house, with Jacob following.

'Get back inside,' Audrey scolded. 'It's freezing out here and you shouldn't be getting cold.' She bustled a protesting Maggie back to the fire.

'It's the *Courier*,' Maggie said as she sat down again. 'Look!'

'What about it?' Audrey asked. Maggie handed it over and there on the front of the newspaper was a photograph of Betty Prendagast, looking absolutely beautiful. Her eyes shone with unshed tears, and she had a worried expression on her pretty face — not too worried, of course. Not enough to crease her smooth forehead or create wrinkles around her eyes.

'Oh my goodness, she looks like a film star,'

269

said Audrey enviously. 'She's so funny, Betty. To look at her you'd think all she cares about is her looks, but she's such a kind person, that's not true at all. Why is she in the paper?'

'They've done a story about all of you rescuing Susan.'

'They never have.'

Audrey took the newspaper from Maggie and shook it out.

'Oh, they have.' She made a face. 'I bet this was Ned's doing, you know. I told him not to speak to the fellow he knows.' She wasn't really cross, though. Ned was so proud of her, she was quite enjoying the attention.

Amused, she read the story out loud. ' 'Four Beckindale women showed great bravery when they rescued schoolgirl Susan Roberts from last week's floods,' ' she read. ' 'Betty Prendagast (21) a veterinary nurse . . . ' '

She looked up at Maggie and Jacob.

'She's not a veterinary nurse, she's the receptionist.'

Jacob gave a bark of laughter. 'Sounds like Betty,' he said. 'Carry on.'

' 'Vet Nancy Tate (25), Land Girl Audrey Atkins (19) waded through the rising water to save the schoolgirl who'd hidden out in a riverside hut. They were helped in their daring rescue by Beckindale policeman's wife Lily Proudfoot . . . ' ooh Lily won't like being called a policeman's wife.'

She chuckled, reading it over again. 'They've made it sound like a film.'

'I bet that was Betty, giving them the lowdown,' Maggie said, but she said it affectionately because everyone was very fond of Betty.

'It's definitely Betty,' Audrey said. 'Listen to this, "I was frightened half to death,' said Betty, who describes herself as vet Nancy's right-hand woman.' She's hilarious.'

'She really should be on the stage,' said Maggie, peering over Audrey's shoulder at the story. 'Ooh look, there's a bit about you. What does it say?'

'Hang on, let me find it,' Audrey said. 'Oh yes. It says, 'Betty said her friend, Land Girl Audrey, deserves praise for undertaking the brave rescue. 'She's not been here long but she's become an important part of Emmerdale Farm.''

Audrey grinned at Jacob. 'An important part of Emmerdale Farm,' she said. 'It's written here in black and white. You should remember that next time you're grumbling at me.'

Jacob made a face at her. 'Today's news, tomorrow's fish and chip paper,' he said, making Audrey long for crispy fish and salty chips.

'You're right,' she said. 'It's just silly nonsense. I told Ned I didn't want to be in a story.'

'Are you annoyed?' Jacob looked at her curiously.

Audrey considered. Was she annoyed? She screwed her nose up. 'Not really,' she said. 'It's just a bit of fun.' She looked at the newspaper again. 'Can I keep this?' she asked Maggie, who nodded.

'Of course.'

'Reckon Betty will frame her copy?' Jacob asked with a smile.

'I'm positive,' Audrey said.

Jacob was right. Betty was thrilled to bits with the photograph and the write-up. She'd been so flattered when one of the reporters from the *Hotten Courier* had dropped into the surgery just a couple of days after the flood.

'I've heard you were involved in a daring rescue,' he'd said. Betty had thought him rather dishy, with his thick-rimmed specs. She'd got up from her chair and come round to perch on the desk so she was closer to him.

'Not just me,' she said. 'There was Nancy, that's the vet. She's out on a job at the moment. And there was Lily and Audrey.'

The reporter had run his eyes over her legs and smiled. 'Are they all as pretty as you?'

Betty had laughed. 'Stop it,' she said. But she tilted her head to give him the benefit of her best side and flashed him her special smile as she told him the whole story. And when the photographer had arrived to take her photograph and exclaimed at her bone structure and gushed about how easy she made his job, she'd been proud as punch.

Now, sitting in the quiet surgery, she gazed at the article, wondering if one day she'd see her photograph in magazines modelling the latest fashions, or starring in a film. But she knew it was doubtful unless . . . She reached down to where she'd left her handbag under her desk, and pulled out the ENSA application papers. She'd been carrying them round with her for months — since her stint dancing with them back in the summer. Maybe this was the right time to send them?

Quickly, before she had time to change her mind, she filled in the sheets and added her signature at the bottom. Then she slid them into an envelope, and gathered up the rest of the outgoing mail. If she was quick, she could catch the post . . .

Five minutes later, she was back at her desk, knowing that she couldn't change her mind now. The application form was on its way to London. Just like she might be one day. Maybe, if she got accepted by ENSA, it would just be the beginning and she could launch a career in showbusiness. How wonderful would that be? For a moment, she allowed herself to drift off into a daydream, where she arrived in Hollywood to take the lead role in a film. Maybe she could dance and act, like Judy Garland. Or act opposite Humphrey Bogart.

'Ee, you look beautiful there,' said Seth, startling out of her reverie. 'Like a film star.'

'Margaret thinks I look like Judy Garland,' she said, jumping guiltily as though he'd caught her doing something wrong. 'What are you doing here?'

Seth frowned. 'Not sure what Judy Garland looks like.'

Betty rolled her eyes. '*The Wizard of Oz?*'

Seth shrugged. 'Reckon she's not as pretty as you are,' he said.

Betty smiled at him. 'Why are you here?'

'Nice. Can't a man come and see his girl without a reason?'

'Seth . . . '

'One of the dogs up at the estate has eaten something it shouldn't have. He seems to be in a bit of pain and we're worried. Can Nancy come by and check it out?'

Betty sighed, and pulled the appointment book towards her.

'We keep afternoons for emergencies like this, so I can fit you in around four?'

'Sounds good. I'll let them know up at the estate.'

Slightly awkwardly, Seth bent and kissed her cheek and Betty waved him off half-heartedly.

As he was leaving, Nancy was arriving. She said hello and goodbye to Seth and came into the surgery.

'Apparently the *Hotten Courier* has done a write-up about us,' she said excitedly. 'Have you seen it?'

Betty reached down under her desk and produced a stack of the newspapers. 'I've bought ten,' she said.

Nancy gawped at her. 'What does it say?'

Betty cleared her throat and read out the story, in her best, most dramatic voice. Nancy sat on one of the waiting-room chairs, enthralled. She squealed at every mention of her name, and oohed and aahed at the frightening bits in a most satisfactory fashion.

'At the bottom there's a little box and it says: The *Courier* Thinks . . . ' said Betty when she'd finished the story.

'What does the *Courier* think?' Nancy asked eagerly.

Betty did a drum roll on her desk with two pencils. 'It thinks,' she said, 'that we four women are a credit to Beckindale.'

'That's so funny,' Nancy said, chuckling. 'But also very nice.'

'Should be good for business, too,' Betty said. 'That's what I thought when I spoke to the reporter.' She was only half lying. She had thought about the publicity for the vet's surgery as well as the publicity for herself.

'You did a good job,' Nancy said. 'Are we busy this afternoon?'

Betty wasn't interested in this afternoon's appointments. She was still thinking about the story.

'Do you know what you should do?' she said, an idea coming to her in a flash. 'You should send a copy to your dad.'

'No,' said Nancy. 'He wouldn't be interested in that.'

'He might be. And he'd see that you're a credit to Beckindale.'

Nancy screwed her nose up. 'You think?'

'Definitely.'

'I'm not sure,' said Nancy. 'I'll think about it. I don't want to seem boastful.'

Betty snorted. 'I'm getting one framed so we can hang it up in here,' she said. 'We should boast about it. We did a good thing.'

'And you look especially beautiful in the photograph,' teased Nancy.

Betty laughed. 'And that. Seriously though, you should send it to your dad. I bet old . . . ' she paused. 'What's your dad's name?'

Nancy tutted. 'Francis,' she said. 'His name's Francis.'

'I bet Francis would be chuffed to bits to see his little girl written about.'

Nancy shook her head. 'No,' she said. 'It's not really a Tate thing to talk about your achievements. But if you want to frame one, go ahead.'

She picked up her bag, and a copy of the paper, and went into the treatment room. Betty waited for the door to close and then picked up the telephone.

'Hello, operator?' she said. 'Could you connect me to Francis Tate, veterinary surgeon in Scarborough?'

There was a click as the connection was made, and then the phone at the other end rang.

'Francis Tate.'

'Sorry to bother you, Mr Tate,' Betty said in her best cut-glass accent. 'I'm phoning from a new company selling . . . ' she looked round for inspiration and spotted a bottle on the shelf. 'Flea treatments. I'd like to send you a catalogue. Would you be so kind as to give me your postal address?'

She scribbled down the address on an envelope, thanked Nancy's father for his time and hung up. Then she slid one of the newspapers into the envelope and dropped it into her bag. She'd post it on her way home, she thought. Nancy's father definitely needed to know how brave his daughter was.

26

DECEMBER 1942

'Lots of Christmas cards for you today,' said Norman, the postman a couple of weeks later. He handed Betty a big bundle of mail, gave her a jaunty salute and went on his way.

Betty leafed through the post. There were indeed many cards, from grateful animal owners, but there were other letters too. She waved them at Nancy.

'Applications,' she said. Business was booming and things had taken off in a big way since the article in the *Courier*, with an endless stream of new patients arriving at the practice.

The four women who'd rescued Susan from the flood were the heroes of the hour. People were stopping them in the street and saying 'well done' or expressing amazement at how brave they'd been. Nancy had found it uncomfortable at first, but she was rather enjoying it now. Everyone was so nice — wanting to chat about the flood, share stories and ask after Susan. Betty, of course, was loving every second and Nancy had even caught her signing autographs for a group of schoolchildren. Audrey and Lily were treating the whole thing with amusement and teasing each other rotten about it all. And Susan, bless her, seemed to be doing all right after her ordeal. She was very excited about having one of Jacob's puppies and was getting ready, even though the pups weren't even born yet and wouldn't be ready to leave Bella until after Christmas. And Nancy had noticed she was starting to talk more about her family, mentioning things her mother had liked, or telling stories about her siblings. She thought that was a good thing; Susan was healing.

With so much work on, Nancy had put an advert for a veterinary nurse in this week's edition. And judging by the pile of letters Betty was brandishing, it seemed there were lots of nurses out there who wanted to come and work at the surgery.

'Let's have a look,' she said. She pulled a chair up to Betty's desk and divided the pile between them. They both began opening envelopes and reading the applications inside.

'No,' said Betty putting her first one down on the desk. 'This is from Mrs Grayson, who lives out past the church.

'What's wrong with her?'

'She's at least seventy-five and she's halfway down the sherry bottle by noon.'

Nancy widened her eyes. She thought it was both hilarious and disconcerting how Betty knew everything about everyone.

'Really?'

'Really.'

'What about this one? Rebecca Johnson? She sounds good enough. Grew up on a farm, lots of hands-on experience,'

'Oh yes, Becky,' Betty said. 'She's good. Put her on the yes pile.'

'Not sure I can cope with a Betty and a Becky,' Nancy joked. 'Who else?'

'Cathy Charles,' said Betty thoughtfully. 'She lives in Hotten. I've never heard of her.'

'Yes,' said Nancy immediately. It would be good to interview someone without knowing their entire life story, via Betty, first.

They carried on sifting through the envelopes until Nancy recognised the handwriting on one and stopped with a gasp.

'What?' Betty said. 'My Seth hasn't applied, has he? He said he would but I thought he was joking.'

Nancy was gazing at the writing on the front of the envelope. 'No,' she said slowly. 'Not Seth. I think this is from my dad.'

Betty looked delighted. 'Your dad?' she said. 'Open it.'

Nancy felt queasy. Why would her father be writing to her? She got the occasional note from her mum, filling her in on little Frank's latest escapades, or other family news, but her father was rarely — if ever — in touch.

'I don't want to,' she said.

'Oh for heaven's sake,' said Betty impatiently. She snatched the envelope from Nancy's hand and slid it open with her letter opener. Then she pulled out the sheet of paper inside, smoothed it out and handed it to Nancy.

'Read it,' she demanded.

Nancy took the letter in her shaky fingers. 'My dear Nancy . . . ' she began. Betty clapped her hands.

'That's a good start,' she said. Nancy gave her

279

a withering look. 'Sorry, carry on.'

'I read with interest the story in the *Hotten Courier* about how you saved a young girl from the floods that recently ravaged Beckindale.' Nancy frowned. 'How on earth did he see that? They don't sell the *Courier* the other side of Yorkshire.'

Betty shrugged. 'No idea.'

Nancy eyed her receptionist with suspicion. She had a fairly good idea how her father had seen the paper, but she wasn't going to start quizzing Betty now. Instead, she turned her attention back to the letter.

'The regard the local people have for you is obvious from the article. And it seems you were courageous on the night in question — a personality trait that I would say you have always had in abundance. You were always fond of taking risks, even as a small girl, and never shied away from challenges.

'Never more did you show how bold you are, than when you stood up to me, turned down the offer of a job in my practice and went to work in Beckindale. I was convinced you would fail, and thought you weren't up to the job but I'm afraid that was due to my own short-sightedness.'

'He does go on a bit, doesn't he?' interrupted Betty. Nancy chuckled. She had gone from feeling sick at the thought of hearing from her father to euphoric.

'Are you going to let me finish?'

'Go on,' Betty said.

Nancy glared at her and she made a face.

'Okay then, just carry on. He was saying about

his short-sightedness . . . '

Nancy found the line and read on: 'I was judging you merely on being a woman, when I should have noted your tenacity, your intelligence and your competence. I was wrong, Nancy, and I hope you forgive me. You have more than proved yourself an excellent vet. I'm proud of you.'

Nancy's voice cracked on the last line. 'He's proud of me,' she whispered to Betty.

'And so he bloody well should be,' Betty said. 'Look what you've done here, Nancy. You've achieved so much and all without any help from him. I'm proud of you, too.'

Nancy grinned at Betty. 'Maybe I'll write back and invite him to come and see the practice,' she said. Her heart felt happier as though a cloud that had been overhead for months had blown away.

'You should definitely do that.'

'Did you send him the paper?' she asked.

Betty looked innocent. 'Do you think I'd have sent him one, after you decided you didn't want to?'

'Almost certainly.'

Betty caved. 'Yes, it was me. It was a good idea, though, wasn't it?'

Nancy reached over the desk and gave Betty a very un-Nancy-like hug. 'It was,' she admitted. 'Thank you.'

'This looks cosy,' said a voice. Audrey was there, in her Land Girl uniform, looking slightly harassed and shaking snow off her boots. 'It's freezing out there.'

'Nancy's dad's written to her,' said Betty.

'That's such good news.' Audrey was pleased, though Nancy noticed a shadow cross her face. She felt sad that Audrey wasn't on the best terms with her mother and wondered if they'd ever resolve their difficulties. She folded the letter up and tucked it into her pocket.

'What can I do for you, Audrey?' she asked.

'Jacob thinks the pups might be coming soon,' she said. 'Just wondered if you could pop up and have a look at Bella? Make sure everything's all right?'

'Of course,' said Nancy. She glanced at Betty, who was scanning the appointment book.

'You could go in on your way to see Smithers' cows later on,' Betty said.

'Would that suit you?' Nancy asked Audrey.

'Perfect,' said Audrey.

'How's Maggie?' Nancy asked as Audrey turned to go. She turned back again, running her good hand through her hair.

'In a lot of pain,' she said. 'She's going into hospital on Monday and we'll all be glad when her op's done. She won't be back on her feet for a while, though. Jacob and I are glad it's winter so there's not as much work to do on the farm.'

Nancy gave Audrey's arm a quick squeeze.

'Shout if you need anything,' she said. Audrey looked grateful.

'I will,' she said. 'Thank you.'

They all looked up as the surgery door opened again and Seth came in.

'No actual patients,' Nancy said cheerfully. 'Just people coming for a chat.'

'I'm a patient,' Audrey pointed out. 'Well, Bella is. And perhaps Seth is here to get you up to the estate because of some huge animal-related drama that only you can resolve.'

Nancy grinned. 'Are you, Seth? Do you need me?'

Seth smiled awkwardly. 'Not really,' he said, pulling his cap off. 'No.'

'Is it me you need?' Betty said, in a deep drawl, worthy of Katharine Hepburn as she leaned back in her chair and pouted at Seth. The women all laughed but Seth didn't even smile.

'I just wanted to let you know, that Ernie's joined up,' he said, turning his hat over in his hands. 'He's going on Friday.'

'No,' Betty said. 'But agricultural work is a reserved occupation.'

'He wanted to go.' Seth said. He looked devastated at the thought of losing his friend and Nancy, who'd treated his relationship with Ernie with a certain amount of disdain, felt bad for him. 'He said it's his duty.'

Betty looked alarmed. 'You're not going are you, Seth? You're not going to do something stupid and join up too?'

Seth shook his head looking miserable. 'Not now. With Ernie going we're right short of help on the estate. I can't leave them in the lurch. I don't know why he couldn't just join the Home Guard or something, if he wants to do his bit.'

'What's he going to do?' Betty asked. Ernie worked on the estate with Seth, but horses were his real love. She couldn't imagine him in a tank or on a boat.

'Apparently, some battalions are using horses in Palestine and around the Mediterranean,' said Seth.

'For fighting,' Nancy said, alarmed. 'That's not right.'

Seth shook his head. 'For transportation. But they need folk who know what they're doing. He says he can do a good job.'

Audrey stood up a bit straighter. 'I think you have to find the role that's right for you,' she said. 'Everyone's got something to offer and it seems Ernie's found his way to do it.'

Seth glared at her. 'We need him here,' he said.

Betty shifted in her chair. 'Audrey's right, love,' she said. 'If Ernie wants to go, then he should go.'

Nancy looked at Betty whose face seemed to be carefully expressionless and wondered, suddenly, what had happened about her passion for performing. She'd not mentioned it for ages.

'I suppose you're right,' Seth said, sounding like a sulky schoolboy.

Betty stood up, came over to Seth and gave him a kiss. 'Why don't we give Ernie a good send off, eh? Drinks in the Woolie on Thursday night? I'll have a word with Larry, see if we can put up some decorations.'

Seth gave Betty a small smile. 'That would be good.'

'Go on, then. You get back to work and I'll sort everything out.'

Seth nodded and said his goodbyes.

'I'd best be off too,' said Audrey. 'See you later, Nancy?'

But Nancy was watching Betty, who looked upset.

'I feel so bad,' she wailed. 'I've wanted Seth and Ernie to spend some time apart since I've been with Seth, but not like this. Poor Seth. They've been friends since they were little lads.'

'Seth will be fine,' Nancy said. 'He'll get used to Ernie being away, and he'll be so busy up at the estate he won't have time to miss him.' She paused, wondering whether to say what she was thinking, and then decided to plough on. 'What happened about your dancing?' she asked. 'You've not mentioned it for ages. I had a feeling you might decide to join up too, if you could perform. But then you didn't talk about it.'

Betty grimaced. 'Long story,' she said. 'I spent ages thinking about whether I should join ENSA. Months, in fact. I kept changing my mind, thinking I should stay here, then deciding to go. In the end I sent off the form the same day I wrote to your dad.'

'And now you're worried about what Seth will say if you go away too?' Nancy understood immediately.

'A bit.'

'You can't live your life on someone else's terms,' Nancy told Betty. 'If you want to join up, then you should do it.'

'Perhaps,' Betty said. But she didn't sound very sure. She looked sad for a minute, then she lifted her chin and smiled at Nancy. 'I suppose I'll get on with arranging this party for Ernie,' she said.

Nancy wondered whether to ask more about

ENSA but thought better of it. 'And writing letters to all the nurses we want to interview?' she said hopefully.

Betty groaned, but it was a light-hearted groan and Nancy was glad.

'Fine,' Betty said. 'But you're making the tea.'

27

CHRISTMAS EVE 1942

'Do you think it might snow?' Audrey said, peering out of the kitchen window.

Ned shook his head. 'Maybe up on the hills, but not down here.'

Audrey was disappointed. 'I so wanted a white Christmas,' she said. 'It never snows in Worthing.'

Ned crept up behind her, wound his arms around her waist and kissed her cheek. 'Who cares about snow?' he said. 'I've got everything I want for Christmas right here.'

Audrey melted. She turned around so she could kiss Ned properly, but pulled away quickly. 'We need to peel those potatoes,' she said. 'Because I think they might be the only thing saving this Christmas dinner.'

She looked glumly at the 'murkey' she'd prepared from a recipe in a Ministry of Food leaflet. It was a mock turkey made from sausage meat mixed with breadcrumbs — more breadcrumbs than sausage — and with two 'legs' fashioned from parsnips, donated by Ned's parents.

'It might taste better than it looks,' said Ned kindly.

Audrey snorted. 'Let's hope so,' she said. 'I really want Maggie to enjoy tomorrow, and not worry about a single thing.'

'How's she doing?'

'Not bad,' Audrey said with a shrug. 'Better the last couple of days, actually and glad to be home.' Maggie's operation had gone well and she'd only had to stay in the hospital for a few days. Now she was back and Audrey was spending a lot of time telling her to stay in bed.

'I can't believe this is the fourth Christmas of the war,' said Ned. 'Remember back in 1939, everyone thought it would be over by that first Christmas?'

Audrey rolled her eyes. 'Seems a long time ago now.'

'What were Christmases like when you were a child?' Ned said.

'Don't get chatting and forget those potatoes,' Audrey said, prodding him in the side. 'I'll cut them up once you've peeled them.'

Ned saluted her. 'Right away, ma'am,' he said. 'But tell me about Christmas.'

Audrey sighed. 'There's nothing to tell really,' she said. 'It was always very quiet. Just me and my mum and dad. Church, and dinner, and listening to the king on the wireless. Nothing fancy.'

'You didn't want to go home this year?'

Audrey swallowed. She felt guilty when she thought about her mum and dad, sitting either end of the dining room table and eating Christmas dinner without her. But she didn't feel guilty enough to go home.

'The Sugdens needed me here,' she said, slightly snappy. Ned realised she didn't want to talk about her family and instead went back to chatting about the celebrations.

'What was your favourite bit?'

'About Christmas? Carol singers, I think. I love carol singing. What about you?'

Ned thought for a while. 'All the food,' he said. 'Dinner plates overflowing with turkey and veg, and nuts in my stocking, and Christmas pudding.' He smacked his lips and rubbed his flat stomach and Audrey chuckled. 'More veg than turkey this year,' she said.

'I don't even mind,' said Ned. 'I just like everyone gathering round the table and chatting and laughing.'

Audrey looked at him fondly. He was so sweet, it filled her heart with joy. 'Will I see you tomorrow?' she asked. 'I've got you a little present.'

'You haven't?' Ned put his hand over his mouth, looking shocked. 'I feel bad now, because I didn't get you anything.'

Audrey tried to look like she didn't care. 'That's fine,' she said. 'Shall I get yours now?'

Laughing, Ned gathered her into his arms again. 'Of course I've got something for you,' he said. 'I was only joking.'

Audrey groaned. 'You get me every time.'

'I've finished those spuds,' Ned said. 'I need to get off to help Pa with the other veg deliveries before it gets dark. But come down to the village later? About eight o'clock? I've got a surprise for you.'

'Really?' Audrey was pleased.

'Really.' Ned kissed her goodbye, gave Bella and her puppies a quick pat, and headed outside, stopping to say hello to Jacob, who was just coming in from the field.

'It looks great in here,' Jacob said approvingly, looking at the paper decorations Audrey had hung up.

'Wash your hands outside,' Audrey scolded as he came towards the sink that was full of potatoes. He tutted but he obeyed, then came back into the kitchen and poured himself a mug of tea from the pot.

'Is Ma all right?'

'She ate more lunch today than yesterday, and she reckons she'll be well enough to sit downstairs with us for a while tomorrow.'

'She's improving every day.' Jacob looked pleased.

'It's a relief, I'll say that.'

'It is that. Reckon she'll be back on her feet in the spring.'

Audrey frowned. 'Don't rush her,' she warned, but then she smiled. 'Let's hope so, though.'

Jacob slurped his tea. 'Cold outside,' he said. 'I wondered if it might snow, but Ned says no.'

From his chair at the window, Joe snorted. 'That Barlow boy is too young to know,' he said slowly. He sounded stern but Audrey knew him well enough now to recognise the glint in his eye that meant he was teasing. 'Snow tonight.'

'Do you think?' Audrey was thrilled. 'I've never had a white Christmas. She flung her arms out dramatically. 'Isn't this wonderful?' she said.

Jacob was peering at the 'murkey'. 'Is it?' he said doubtfully. 'Thought we were having rabbit?'

'Maggie's not keen, so I did something different,' Audrey said. 'Saw it in a leaflet. It smells nice enough.'

To her surprise, Jacob looked up from the baking tray and gave her a sudden grin. 'It does.'

'Why are you so happy?' she said, suspiciously. 'What have you done?'

'Nothing,' he said. He glanced over at his father, who'd dozed off again, and lowered his voice. 'Got a letter.'

'A letter?'

'From Annie.' He sounded triumphant.

'She wrote back,' said Audrey, absolutely thrilled to bits. 'What did she say?'

Jacob rubbed his hair with the palm of his hand. 'Want to read it?'

'Do you mind?'

'It's nothing private.'

He dug into his pocket and pulled out a Christmas card. Tucked inside was a folded letter. He handed it over and Audrey unfolded it and smoothed it out on the kitchen countertop.

'Dear Jacob,' the letter read.

I was so pleased to hear Maggie's operation went well. I have written to her separately to wish her well, but please pass on my best wishes in the meantime. What a worry it must have been for you, her being poorly. I am sure your Land Girl is stepping up — it sounds as though she is being a big help. And don't worry about the War Ag. I bet you are doing a great job at Emmerdale Farm.

A bit of me hoped I would be home at Christmas, but it looks like I will be staying here. I don't mind really. It's good fun on the base with the other Wrens and there are three of us at our billet, so our landlady — Mrs Blake — can get creative with Christmas dinner as she'll have all our rations to combine.

I am sorry I haven't written sooner. It's been hard for me, getting used to being away from Beckindale and missing Edward. I am sure you miss him too, especially at Christmas time. Do you remember how he and you always used to fight over pulling the wishbone in the turkey? I don't expect there will be a turkey at your Christmas dinner this year, but if I had a wish it would be for the war to be over.

Please write again soon. I like to hear the news from home.

I wish you all a merry Christmas and a healthy 1943.

Annie.

Audrey breathed out slowly. 'What a lovely letter,' she said.

Jacob ducked his head, as though she was complimenting him. 'I know. She writes just like she talks. It's as though she was here.'

'I wish she was,' Audrey said. 'I'd like to meet her.'

Jacob beamed at her — a broad and most

uncharacteristic smile. 'She'd like you,' he said.

Audrey hoped so. She looked at Jacob, who was looking unusually dreamy.

'Are you finished outside?' she asked Jacob. 'Because I need some help with the decorations.'

★   ★   ★

Later, Jacob took Audrey down to the village in his pony trap to meet Ned.

'I can walk,' she'd told him, worried about Maggie being on her own for too long. But Jacob had insisted.

'Might call in at the church,' he'd mumbled as they set off down the hill. 'I'm not one for praying and that, but it's Christmas.'

Audrey had reached out and taken his hand. 'I know you must miss Edward,' she said. 'I'm sorry.'

Jacob hadn't replied, but Audrey thought he was grateful.

At the village, Jacob tied the pony up just past Mick Dingle's garage and threw a blanket over her.

'Won't be long,' he cooed. Then he looked at Audrey. 'Ned will bring you home?' he checked.

Audrey liked the way he looked out for her. She smiled. 'He will.'

'Keep warm,' Jacob said. He pulled his hat down over his ears, stuffed his hands in his pockets and sauntered off towards the church. Audrey watched him go, marvelling at how his spirits had lifted since he got Annie's letter. She obviously meant the world to him.

'Audrey?' Ned's voice made her turn round and she grinned to see him standing there, bundled up against the cold. 'Come this way, quickly,' he said. 'They're starting.'

He grabbed her hand and pulled her along to the centre of the village, where a group of people were gathering.

'What's going on?' she asked, totally confused.

'Shhh,' Ned said. 'Listen.'

Audrey listened. And there, through the freezing evening air, came the sound of singing.

'Carols,' she said, delighted. Still hanging on to Ned's hand, she wriggled through the crowd of people who'd gathered to listen, dragging him after her.

'Sorry,' she heard him mutter to people as they reached the front. 'Sorry.'

'The church choir does it every year,' Ned told her quietly. 'Singing carols outdoors.'

Audrey was rapt, gazing at the group of singers, each holding a candle that lit up the night around them. 'It's perfect,' she said.

And as the choir's voices rang out over the village, snow began to fall. Audrey was almost speechless with joy. Standing there as the snow drifted down, with Ned's arm around her to keep her warm and the carols filling the night sky, she thought she'd never been happier.

'Merry Christmas,' she whispered to Ned.

He looked down at her. His nose was red with cold and his eyes were watering in the icy wind, but she thought he'd never been so fine-looking. He whispered back, 'And a very happy new year.'

28

JANUARY 1943

'Jacob, can you pass the potatoes, please?' Audrey said.

'Easy, girl, you've already scoffed three,' Jacob teased as he handed over the plate.

Audrey stuck her tongue out. 'We've worked hard this morning. I've earned this dinner.'

Maggie smiled at them both bickering. 'I'm feeling much better now, hopefully you won't have to work so hard soon.'

Audrey gave her a stern look. 'Don't rush,' she said. 'I know you're feeling better but you're not completely recovered yet. And anyway, it's not been too bad, has it?' She looked at Jacob, who nodded. 'We've been lucky to have Ned helping out . . . ' she beamed at Ned who was sitting next to her at the table. ' . . . and Joseph's done his bit.'

At the far end of the table, Joe grinned. Maggie's illness had been tough on them all — especially poor Maggie — but it had really brought Joseph out of himself, Audrey thought. It had given him a real sense of purpose and he'd started helping round the farm more. Audrey was a bit nervous around him at first because his speech wasn't always easy to understand and he had a tendency to be grumpy, like Jacob. But she found he was impressed by her work, and they rubbed along quite nicely in the end. Joe wasn't up to much but he'd been happy digging over Maggie's vegetable garden and taking care of the bees. Jacob obviously enjoyed working with his dad, which was nice. He seemed much happier than he'd been when she first arrived in Beckindale — a whole year ago now.

'I've enjoyed being up here,' said Ned, cheerfully, helping himself to more carrots. 'It's been nice spending time with Audrey.'

Audrey blushed. She had loved having Ned around and the downside to Maggie being on the mend was that soon Ned could go back to working at the other farms around Beckindale where he picked up jobs as and when. He didn't like being tied to one place, normally, he'd told her. But he'd loved working with Audrey. Audrey had teased him about that, telling him he wasn't the drifter he pretended to be, but she'd been chuffed to bits inside.

A cacophony of barks made them all look up.

'What's upset them?' Jacob said. He got up from the table and went over to where Bella and her four puppies — all of them grown quite big now and ready to go to their new owners any day — were all nosing out of the window, and barking. Jacob looked over the dogs' heads and turned to the rest of them.

'Visitors,' he said. 'Man and a woman. Don't recognise them.'

'Debt collectors,' muttered Joseph.

'Salespeople,' said Ned.

There was a knock on the front door. None of their friends ever came into the farmhouse that way — they all used the kitchen door which led directly to where they were all sitting. So they were definitely strangers, then. There was another knock and Audrey sighed theatrically. 'We're not going to find out unless we let them in, are we?' she said.

She stood up and, stepping over a puppy, she went out into the hall to the heavy front door. It took a while for her to unbolt it. The locks were stiff from lack of use and it was tricky with just one hand. Eventually, though, she heaved it open and there, on the doorstep, looking terribly nervous, were her mother and father.

'Oh,' said Audrey stupidly. She stood there for a second, not knowing what to say. 'Hello.'

'Hello,' her parents chorused.

'You look well,' her mother said, as though she was making small talk at a cocktail party. 'Very . . . robust.'

'Robust?' said Audrey. 'Is that a good thing?'

Her mother put her head on one side, considering. 'I think so.'

'Then thank you.'

'Audrey,' her father said, firmly but not unkindly. 'It's very cold out here. Do you think you could possibly invite us in?'

'Oh, gosh, sorry,' said Audrey, completely thrown by their sudden and unexpected appearance. 'Come in.'

She stood back to let them enter, and then led them down the passageway to the kitchen. Everyone was still sitting at the table, except Jacob, who was clearing away the finished plates.

'Everyone,' said Audrey uncertainly. 'This is

my mother and my father.'

Four faces swivelled towards Audrey and her parents, and four jaws dropped in surprise. There was a pause and then it seemed Maggie remembered her manners.

'So lovely to meet you Mr and Mrs Atkins,' she said, standing up and smoothing down her skirt. 'Could I offer you a cup of tea?'

Audrey's parents accepted and they all sat down again round the table, as Audrey made the introductions.

'Well,' Audrey said once Maggie had poured the tea. 'This is a surprise.' Then she smiled. 'But it's nice to see you.' She was being honest. It was nice to see them after so long. Her mother's familiar face had a few more creases, and her dad's hair was speckled with grey and she thought with a pang of guilt, that it was probably down to her disappearing act.

Her mother frowned. 'It's a relief to see you. Are you all right? I've been so worried. Have you been working too hard?'

'I'm fine,' Audrey said, feeling a prickle of resentment already. 'How did you know I was here?'

Her mother bent down and from her bag, she pulled a copy of the *Hotten Courier*. 'We saw this.'

Audrey was astonished. 'How on earth?'

'Remember Mr and Mrs Tennant?' her mother began.

Audrey actually didn't. She didn't remember half of the people her mother talked about.

'You do,' her mother continued. 'Had a

daughter about your age. Sally, was it? Or Sarah? Anyway, they were in Bradford for some reason. A wedding perhaps?'

'No one would travel that far for a wedding in wartime,' said Audrey's father. 'That's madness. It wasn't a wedding.'

'Well, perhaps it was to see their son?' Audrey's mother carried on. 'I know he joined up and they were hoping to see him when he was on leave. Perhaps they had to come up here to catch him.'

Audrey wanted to scream in frustration. She exchanged a look with Ned, who was looking slightly bemused and forced herself to smile at her mum.

'It doesn't really matter why the Tennants were in Bradford, does it,' she said through gritted teeth.

'I suppose not,' her mother said thoughtfully. 'Anyway, they were here, and Mr Tennant — Peter — he had a toothache, and it couldn't wait until they were back in Worthing, so they found a dentist.'

Audrey had absolutely no idea where this was going. She waited, tuning out her mother's chatter until she needed to listen.

'And there, right in the waiting room was a copy of the *Hotten Courier*,' her mother said triumphantly. 'And of course, they recognised your name straightaway, and they brought it back home with them to show us, but what with one thing and another, it got forgotten until I bumped into Phyllis at the dentist again, funnily enough, and she said she had something for me, and brought it round.'

The bloody *Hotten Courier*, Audrey thought, shocking herself with how vicious her thoughts were. Bloody Betty Prendagast and her ambitions to be a film star. And bloody Ned Barlow, boasting about their escapades to anyone who'd listen and alerting the reporter to the story in the first place. She glowered at Ned, who looked down at the table, his usual cheeky grin vanishing.

'Your mother wanted to leave immediately,' Audrey's father put in. 'But I said no, that you'd be home for Christmas.'

Audrey looked down at the table, feeling an odd mixture of guilt and resentment.

'But you didn't come home,' Audrey's mother said accusingly. 'You stayed here.'

Her father put a hand on his wife's arm to calm her. 'We got the train from Brighton to London,' he said. 'And then . . . '

'More tea?' said Maggie, and Audrey wanted to hug her for stopping the endless chit-chat about nothing.

'Anyway, Audrey,' her father continued. 'Do you want to go and start packing? There's a train from Bradford at five o'clock, which we should be able to get if we leave now. Perhaps one of you would be kind enough to take us into Hotten? I assume you have transport of some kind? I can offer you a petrol coupon in exchange. Or would it be a pony and cart?'

Maggie paused in her pouring of tea, and Jacob, Ned and Joe all stared at Audrey's father. Audrey felt sick. Her whole life she'd been amiable Audrey, who'd gone along with her

300

mother's need to mollycoddle her. But now she knew what she could do, how capable she was, and she wasn't going to give in. Her life in Beckindale was too much fun, and the work she was doing with the Land Army too important for that.

She took a deep breath. 'I think I'm going to stay here,' she said in a small voice.

'Don't be silly, darling,' her mother said.

'I'm not being silly. I want to stay. If that's all right with Maggie.'

'Course it is, pet,' said Maggie.

Audrey's father shot Maggie a stern look and she pinched her lips together and didn't say anything else.

'Audrey,' said her mother, more firmly. 'This is ridiculous. Go and get packed.'

'No.' Audrey spoke a bit louder this time. 'I won't.'

Mrs Atkins, who'd always had a flair for the dramatic, put her hand to her forehead and closed her eyes.

'Go. And. Pack,' she said.

Audrey didn't move. Her mother looked at her husband in despair. 'You talk to her,' she said.

'You can't manage, Audrey,' Mr Atkins said, his voice full of concern. 'It's too hard for you. You only have one hand, for goodness sake. You can't work on a farm.'

Maggie spoke up again. 'We'd be lost without Audrey,' she said. 'She's been a treasure this last year.'

Jacob nodded. 'She's a blooming good farmer.'

Audrey's mother sighed, 'That's sweet of you,

301

but really there's no need to be kind. You've done more than enough for our girl.'

Audrey was generally a mild-mannered young woman. She was very rarely annoyed, or grumpy. But at that moment she was both.

'Did you read the article?' she asked her parents in a conversational tone. 'Did you actually read what it said?'

'Of course we did.' Her mother looked affronted to be asked.

'Then you'll have read how my friend Nancy and I waded through the flood water to reach the young girl who we rescued? And how Nancy, Betty, Lily and I brought her home safely?'

Her mother's eyes widened. 'I was horrified for you, my poor love. How dare that Nancy woman drag you along with her.'

Audrey sighed. 'She didn't drag me anywhere, Mum. I wanted to help. I can do all sorts of things, can't I, Jacob?'

Jacob nodded but he didn't speak.

'See?' Audrey said. 'I've done all sorts. I've mended the roof of the cowshed, and I've ridden a bicycle all over Beckindale. I've dug vegetable patches, and driven a tractor, and learned how to ride a horse, for heaven's sake. I've helped deliver a calf . . . '

'The wrong calf,' mumbled Jacob and Ned sniggered, obviously hoping it would lighten the mood. Audrey glared at them both. She was in no mood for jokes.

'I've made friends,' she carried on. Ned sat up a bit straighter, clearly thinking she was about to mention him but Audrey simply glowered at him again and carried on. 'I've really settled in here, Mum and Dad. And I'm staying.'

Her parents stared at her. Audrey wondered if she'd ever directly contradicted them before. She thought not. Certainly she couldn't remember a time she'd said no to them.

'Well,' said her dad.

There was an awkward pause and then Jacob cleared his throat. 'I can't lie, I was alarmed when I saw Audrey's erm . . . hand,' he muttered. 'But she's more than proved herself.' He swallowed. 'That calf would have died if she'd not jumped on my old bicycle and raced down to the village to fetch the vet. And that lass in the shed might have died too if she and Nancy hadn't got to her when they did.'

'Emmerdale Farm was in trouble before Audrey arrived,' Maggie added. 'We had the War Ag on our backs, and I've got no doubt they'd have taken the farm off us without her hard work. She saved us too.'

Audrey thought that was perhaps a bit dramatic but she was chuffed at the sentiment so she reached out and squeezed Maggie's hand in gratitude.

'She's . . . a good girl,' Joseph said hesitantly. Audrey beamed at him. He was a man of so few words that those he did say meant a lot.

'She is,' added Ned. 'I've got to know her rather well, and she's a real asset.'

Audrey ignored him, still cross about the *Hotten Courier* thing.

'Plus,' she said to her parents, who were looking quite taken aback at the onslaught of

303

praise about their daughter. 'I've signed a contract. I'm part of the Women's Land Army now. I can't just leave. I'd probably get sent to prison.' She looked at her mother's startled face and with a slightly devilish air, added, 'Or shot.'

Her mother gasped and Audrey went to her and took her hands.

'I'm doing something really good here, Mum,' she said. 'It's an important job and I love it and I'm good at it. And for the first time in my whole life, no one treats me differently because of my arm. No one is worrying about what I can't do — they're only interested in what I can do.'

Her mother gave her a weak smile and smoothed down Audrey's hair. 'I see you still have trouble with your hair,' she said.

Audrey grinned. 'I just tie it up in a scarf most of the time now,' she told her. 'My friend Betty tied a load for me and fastened them with elastic so I can just slide them on and off.'

'She did?' Her mum sounded impressed. 'That's a nice thing to do.'

'I'm happy here,' Audrey said quietly. 'I want to stay.'

Her parents looked at each other for such a long time that Audrey thought her bags were as good as packed. Then, finally, her father raised his eyebrows at his wife, and her mother gave him a small nod.

'All right,' she said with a sigh. 'Stay.'

Audrey threw her arms up in joy, and her father smiled at her. 'I have one condition.'

'Which is?'

'You write us a blinking letter once in a while.'

304

29

Maggie offered to take Mr and Mrs Atkins to the station in Hotten in the old farm truck. Audrey's mother had looked slightly alarmed at the state of her transport but knew better than to complain. Joseph wandered off to sleep in his chair, and Audrey, Jacob and Ned stood at the door of the farmhouse and waved them off.

They'd barely got to the end of the lane before Audrey turned on Ned.

'I told you what would happen if you spoke to the newspaper,' she said. 'I told you and you ignored me and did it anyway.'

Ned looked at her, astonished. 'But you liked the story. You laughed when you read it, and you kept a copy of the paper.'

Audrey snorted, annoyed that he was right. Ned reached out to take her hand and she pulled it away. 'It's all right,' he said, trying to soothe her. 'Everything's fine. They've seen how happy you are and they're pleased.'

Audrey, though, was still angry. 'But you didn't listen to me, Ned. I told you what I thought, and you decided you knew best and did it anyway.' She glowered at him. 'Getting away from people doing what they think is best for me was exactly why I left Sussex and came to Yorkshire.'

Ned looked taken aback. 'I'm sorry, Aud,' he said. 'I didn't think.'

Audrey nodded. 'I'm going to finish up that thatching,' she said to Jacob.

'I'll do that . . . ' he began but Audrey shut him up with a look.

'It's fine,' she said.

'I thought we were going to go to the flicks in Hotten,' said Ned.

But Audrey shook her head. 'Go home, Ned,' she said.

She turned around and went back inside, shutting the kitchen door firmly behind her. She was jumpy and out of sorts and she just wanted to be alone, though she actually had no intention of finishing the thatching. Joe was in his chair, snoring softly and Bella and all the pups were cuddled up in their basket. Bella lifted her head to acknowledge Audrey and she bent down to rub her head.

'Hello, Mum,' she said. 'You're doing a great job.'

Audrey pulled one of the cushions off a kitchen chair, threw it on the stone floor next to the dog basket and sank down. Almost immediately she was covered in puppies, making her laugh. She thought they should take pups into the hospitals where the wounded soldiers were, because they were bound to make them feel better than any medicine. Two of the puppies looked just like Bella with black and white patches, another — the one Susan had chosen — was all black. Susan said she was going to call her Midnight, which Audrey thought was rather nice. But Audrey's favourite was the smallest of the litter, a male pup who was black with a white patch on his eye and a crooked white tail. His front foot was misshapen so he walked with a bit of a list to one side. Jacob had told Audrey that had he not met her, he probably would have smothered the pup as soon as he was born, but now he knew her, he realised that problems like that didn't need to hold a person — or a dog — back. Audrey wasn't sure whether to be pleased or offended by that. But either way, she loved the little dog with his wonky tail and odd gait.

'He's really taken to you,' Jacob said, sitting down next to her and taking one of the other puppies from her.

'He's so sweet.'

'You can keep him, if you like.'

Audrey looked at Jacob. 'Really?'

He shrugged. 'Can't sell him with that gammy foot and I'm not going to get rid of him now, am I? Not now you're attached to him. You may as well have him.'

Audrey cuddled the little dog to her chest in delight. 'Thank you.'

'What are you going to call him?'

The pup looked at Audrey and she looked back at him. 'Winston,' she said.

Jacob chuckled. 'Suits him.' Then he gave her a nudge. 'Bit harsh on Ned, weren't you?'

'No.'

'I reckon.'

'I told him not to speak to the reporter,' she said, nuzzling the little dog's tummy.

'He was just proud of you. And you didn't mind when you saw the story.'

'Well, he should have kept his mouth shut.'

'Everyone was talking about it, Audrey.'

'I don't care. I told him what I was worried about and he didn't listen.' She sighed. 'My parents have never listened to me, Jacob. He knows that. He knows how that made me feel. And he did it anyway.'

Jacob gave her a stern look. 'Still think you're being hard on him. You're good together, you two. Don't lose him over this.'

'It's his fault,' Audrey said. But she cuddled the sleepy puppy a bit closer and her voice cracked. Jacob patted her knee.

'Thing is,' he said. 'Ned's heart is in the right place. He may have ridden roughshod over what you wanted, but he did it for the right reasons. He didn't think he was being silly. He was just telling people what you did. Because you did a good thing and he was proud.'

Audrey felt wretched. 'Do you think?' she whispered.

Jacob nodded. 'I'm certain of it.'

He took a breath. 'And the reason I'm certain of it is because I did the opposite.'

'What do you mean?'

'I mean, when I cheated on our drawing of straws to decide who went away, I didn't do it because I knew Edward wanted to go. I did it to get him out of the way so I could steal Annie. And I did it because I was angry with Edward because as far as I could see, my mother loved him more and Annie loved him more, and I thought he'd stolen what was mine.'

Audrey looked at him. He was frowning

deeply and she felt sorry for him. What a burden he was carrying.

'I don't know much about siblings,' she said. 'But I know the troubles Nancy's had with her father, and I've seen how Betty and Margaret are with their parents, and the way I see it is parents love their children differently, not equally.'

Jacob frowned. 'What do you mean?'

'I mean maybe it's not always even, because sometimes one will need more than another. Or sometimes there's other stuff going on. Maybe the mother was ill after the birth, or perhaps she found it tricky adjusting to being a mother . . . ' Audrey was thinking of Lily as she said this. 'And perhaps that affected how she feels about her child in a way. But it doesn't mean she doesn't love that child.'

Jacob looked away from Audrey and she thought she saw him wipe away a tear.

'Joseph's my father,' he said in a gruff voice. She didn't know what to say, because this was hardly news. But he hadn't finished. 'He's my father, but he wasn't Edward's.'

Audrey tried not to look shocked, but she was.

'My father was a bad sort, back then, so my mother says. He was violent and he was horrible to her and she was almost relieved when he went to fight.'

Audrey shuddered. She'd heard enough stories of the horrors of the Great War to know that things must have been really bad for Maggie to feel that way.

'While he was away, Mum had a conscientious objector here, to help on the farm. His name was

Hugo. He and Mum fell in love.'

Audrey couldn't believe what she was hearing. This was making her see Maggie in a whole new light. A not entirely favourable light.

'I know what you're thinking,' said Jacob. 'I thought the same for a long time after I found out. But don't let this affect how you think of my mother. My dad treated her badly, she was running the farm completely by herself, and this Hugo was kind to her.'

Audrey was surprised by Jacob's opinion and said so. He nodded. 'It has taken me a lot of thinking,' he said. 'A lot of time by myself in the fields, just being angry and sad and then angry again.'

'I'm not surprised,' she said. 'It must have been a shock. For Edward too.'

'When Edward was killed I felt guilty about that, obviously. Because it was my fault that he was there in the first place,' Jacob said. 'But I also felt guilty that I'd taken away my mother's last link to Hugo.'

'What happened to him?' Audrey said, gripped by this sad tale. 'What happened to Hugo?'

'He went to drive ambulances at the front. After the war, he came back to see Ma and they spent one night together.'

'Ohh,' breathed Audrey. 'And was that . . . ?'

Jacob nodded. 'That was when Edward was conceived.'

'Did Hugo know he had a son?'

'He died,' Jacob said. 'Here. He had Spanish flu and he died. He's buried down by the river.'

'That's so sad. Your poor mum. And poor

310

Edward. And you. And Joseph. It's sad for everyone.'

Jacob looked surprised. 'It is,' he said. 'I've never thought of it like that before.'

Audrey gave him an affectionate nudge with her shoulder.

'You see,' Jacob said, putting the sleeping pup from his lap into the basket and stroking its silky ears gently. 'Everything I've done has been from anger or hate or jealousy. I didn't think about my mother, or Edward and I certainly didn't think about Annie. But when Ned talked about how brave you were, he acted out of love.'

Audrey bit her lip. She thought he was right, but she also thought he was being hard on himself.

'Has Annie been writing more letters?' she asked.

He nodded. 'She has. But I'm not sure she's ever going to forgive me.'

Audrey thought for a moment. 'I think she'll see for herself how much you've changed when she comes home.'

'If she ever comes home,' Jacob said, gloomily.

'She will,' Audrey said. 'Beckindale's not somewhere you'd want to leave for good.'

She looked at Jacob. 'But I think before she forgives you, you need to do something else.'

'What's that?'

'I think you need to forgive yourself.'

Jacob gave her a weak smile. 'Well, I reckon you might be right about that. But I also reckon it's going to take a bit more time.'

'You'll get there,' Audrey said.

'Are you going to forgive Ned?'

Audrey made a face. 'Probably,' she said.

'You might want to go and tell him that.'

'I'll go tomorrow.'

'Then you might want to go and tell him that you'll tell him tomorrow.'

Audrey looked at him, confused.

'He's outside,' Jacob said with a grin. 'I told him to wait in the milking shed.'

'You have just done exactly what I was cross with him about,' Audrey said, annoyed. 'You've not listened to what I said, and you've dismissed my feelings.'

'But I've done it from love,' said Jacob.

Infuriated, Audrey punched his arm and he laughed.

'I'm sorry,' he said. 'But you should go and see him.' Then his face became more serious. 'Don't waste this, Audrey. Hang on to it, because it can be taken away at any time.'

Audrey screwed her face up, then she nodded. 'All right,' she said. She put her own sleeping pup into the basket, where he snuggled down against Bella, and stood up. 'I'll go and see him. But I'm still cross with you.'

Jacob chuckled and Audrey bent down and kissed his cheek.

'Cross,' she said again.

She pulled on her coat as she went outside because it was a cold evening and it was getting dark. She peered towards the milking shed and called, 'Ned?'

He appeared almost immediately. 'Hello, Aud,' he said.

'You were sure of yourself, waiting out here in the cold,' she said. 'I might not have come.'

He grinned. 'I was actually just about to leave.' He shrugged. 'Thought I'd blown it.'

'You nearly did.'

'I know.' He thought for a minute, clearly searching for the right words to say. 'I deserved to.'

'Jacob said you did it out of love.'

Ned looked surprised. 'Jacob Sugden said that?'

'He did. You'd be surprised how wise he can be when it comes to romance.' She took a step towards him, feeling her heart pounding in her chest.

'Is he right?' she asked, bolder than she ever thought she could be. 'Is he right that you talked about me to anyone who'd listen and told the chap from the *Hotten Courier* what happened, even though I'd asked you not to, because you love me?'

Ned took her right hand in his left, and clasped the top of her left arm gently.

'He's right,' he said. 'I love you, Audrey, and I'm so sorry I didn't listen to you.'

'Go on,' she said, beginning to smile.

'Isn't that enough?'

'Not nearly enough.'

Ned pulled her a bit closer to him.

'This last year, since you came to Beckindale has been the happiest of my life,' he said. 'I've always just bumbled my way through life, doing a bit of this and a bit of that. But suddenly I've got . . . ' he thought for a second, 'I've got a

313

reason for being. A purpose. And that reason is you, Audrey. I love you and if you'll let me, I'd like to listen to what you're saying for the rest of my life.'

She smiled at him and he smiled back. 'How was that?'

'Much better.'

'So?'

Audrey paused for a second, trying to look stern, then she gave up and threw herself into his arms, and squeezed him tight. 'I love you too, Ned,' she said. 'I love you and I love Beckindale. But if you ever do something like that again, I will be furious.'

'I know,' said Ned.

They kissed for a long time, until the sound of Maggie returning from Hotten made them break apart.

'I'm going to find a farm,' Ned said.

Audrey blinked at him. 'You won't need to look far,' she said. 'There are farms everywhere.'

But Ned looked serious. 'I've been saving up,' he said. 'For months. I reckon another year, and I'll have enough for a down payment. I can find a farm for us both to work on.'

'Sounds like a plan,' Audrey said.

'And then,' Ned added triumphantly. 'I'll ask you to marry me.'

Audrey was delighted. She kissed him again.

'And I might very well accept.'

30

MARCH 1943

There was warmth in the breeze today, Betty thought. A softness to the air that told her winter was definitely on its way out. It felt like hope, she thought. A promise of new beginnings and nice things to look forward to.

She needed something to look forward to. Because life at the moment was pretty rotten. No, not rotten as such. Rotten would almost be better because at least it would be something. Betty's life was just . . . nothing. She'd hoped that when Ernie went away, Seth would have more time to spend with her, but actually he'd just transferred his affections from Ernie to a couple of lads he worked with on the estate and now spent his evenings drinking with them instead. Betty carried on going to work, and helping her mother round the house, and sometimes going to dances with Margaret, but mostly she just felt . . . nothing. Sometimes at night, she would lie in bed and think about the few fantastic weeks she'd spent dancing with the ENSA, all those months ago. She would try to remember the cheers from the crowd, and the excited expressions on the faces of the soldiers watching, even though the memories were fading now. She'd done that, she would think. She'd made them all so happy. You just didn't get the same response from a sick dog, or a cat with a fur ball, even though she enjoyed her job.

She sighed, feeling a bit sorry for herself, despite the nice day. She'd popped out to get some milk because Nancy had been up half the night and had finished the bottle the milkman delivered yesterday on endless cups of tea. She was in a right state, was Nancy, because her parents were coming to visit. Her mother and father, her brother Nigel and his wife, and their little boy, Frank were all descending on Beckindale and Nancy was desperate to impress them. She'd cleaned the surgery to within an inch of its life, and her tiny cottage. She'd got Betty to go over the books with a fine-tooth comb in case her father asked to see them — Betty thought this very unlikely and had pointed out that Nancy could just say no, but she'd done it anyway. The surgery was actually in fine fettle. Business was going great, the new nurse — Cathy — was helping enormously despite Betty being a bit put out that Nancy hadn't employed someone she knew. And Nancy herself was like a new person. She was still sharp-tongued of course, but she was funny and she was never too busy to help young Susan with her schoolwork.

Betty stopped short as she approached the surgery. Seth was sitting on the wall, looking pale. Worried he was ill, she rushed over to him.

'Seth, love?' she said. 'What's up?'

He looked at her, and she was horrified to see his face was grey and drawn and, unless it was just the weak spring sunlight playing tricks on

316

her, his eyes full of tears.

'Betty,' he said.

She sat down next to him. 'What is it? What's happened?'

'Ernie,' he said. 'Ernie's been killed.'

Slowly, Seth explained that Ernie had been travelling from a camp in Damascus when there had been an attack.

'It wasn't directed at them,' he said. 'They weren't the targets, but a bullet caught one of the trucks and it blew up. The horse Ernie was on got hit by some shrapnel and threw Ernie off. He hit his head and that was it.'

'Oh God,' breathed Betty. 'His poor mother.' She reached out and took Seth's hand. 'I'm so sorry, love,' she said. 'I know he was very special to you.'

Seth nodded, his lips pinched together so tight they were white. They sat there for a minute or two, hand in hand, in silence. Betty thought about Seth and Ernie spending all their free time together when they were little lads, causing havoc at school, and annoying her by wanting to make mischief with each other rather than Seth spending romantic time with her, and she wanted to cry with the unfairness of it all.

Suddenly, Seth stood up. 'Right then,' he said. 'Best get on.'

Betty blinked at him. 'Are you all right?'

He didn't answer, he just bent and kissed her cheek. 'Woolie later?'

Stunned, Betty could only nod and watch as Seth pulled his hat lower down over his eyes and sauntered off up towards the estate.

★ ★ ★

Over at the vet's surgery, Nancy was on edge. She was so desperate to impress her father when he arrived that her nerves were jangling.

'I thought they were coming on Saturday?' said Cathy, the new nurse. 'It's only Monday.'

'I've started preparing far too early,' Nancy said, rolling her eyes. 'But I'm so nervous.' She gripped Cathy's arm as a thought occurred to her.

'What if it's all messed up again by the weekend? I'll have to stay late on Friday night and sort everything out.'

'It's going to be fine,' said Cathy in the soothing voice that was one of the many reasons Nancy was glad she'd employed her. 'Now, why don't you sit at Betty's desk and sort through the post? I'll put the kettle on and hopefully if Betty ever comes back with that milk, we can have ourselves a cup of tea.'

Nancy smiled gratefully and sat down. She sorted through some flyers from the ministry of agriculture, and some cheques paying invoices and then paused on one addressed to Betty.

'Ohhh,' she said. Betty had told her she'd sent her application into ENSA ages ago — not long after the flood. But she'd not mentioned it for weeks and Nancy had wondered what had come of it. But whenever she'd asked, Betty had said, 'It's not happening now,' in an offhand way. And eventually Nancy had stopped asking. But here were what looked like official papers, addressed to Miss Elizabeth Prendagast, and Nancy was absolutely thrilled.

'What's that?' asked Cathy.

Nancy beamed at her so eagerly, Cathy took a step back.

'Betty's a dancer,' she began and Cathy rolled her eyes.

'I know.'

Nancy chuckled. Betty danced everywhere, so it was hardly news. But this was. 'She did a short stint with ENSA when they were local and she wanted to join up officially.'

'Ooh like Gracie Fields?'

'Exactly. But it's been ages since she put in her papers and she'd not heard anything. It's different from other forces because they have to have people with a certain amount of talent.'

'Definitely not one for me, then,' joked Cathy. 'I sound like a strangled cat when I'm singing.'

Nancy grinned at her. 'Stay here with the actual cats then. I'll need you more than ever if Betty's swanning off round the world entertaining troops.'

Cathy hugged herself. 'She's going to be so excited,' she said. 'Where is she, anyway?' She peered out of the window and clapped her hands. 'Ooh, she's coming now.'

Nancy stood up, clutching the letter behind her back. 'I can't wait to see her face.'

Betty came into the surgery, holding a pint of milk. She'd not been happy recently but today she looked particularly pale and sad. Nancy felt a thrill knowing that she was holding something to cheer her up.

Without speaking, Betty handed the milk bottle to Cathy and then went towards her desk, barely registering that Nancy was standing there until she was almost on top of her.

Nancy bounced on her toes, impatiently. 'Betty, I've got a surprise for you . . . ' she began.

'Ernie was killed.'

Nancy stopped bouncing. 'Oh no.'

'Thrown from a horse when they were attacked.'

Nancy wanted to ask about the horses — she wasn't fond of animals being used in combat — but she knew this wasn't the time.

'His poor mother,' she said instead. 'He was a nice lad, Ernie. Always very sweet with the dogs at the estate.'

'Poor Seth,' said Betty. 'He and Ernie have been friends since they were in nappies. He's going to miss him so much.' Her voice wobbled. 'And I feel bad because I wanted Ernie to go so I could have more of Seth's attention. I'm a terrible person.'

Nancy put a slightly awkward arm round Betty's shoulders.

'No you're not,' she said. Over Betty's head she mouthed 'tea' at Cathy who took the milk she was holding and disappeared to fill the kettle. 'You're a good person, Betty. And of course you wanted Seth to yourself. He's quite a catch is Mr Armstrong — why would you want to share him?' Nancy was relieved when Betty gave her a small smile. 'This isn't your fault, Betty.'

Betty nodded. 'I suppose.'

'How's Seth doing?'

'He seems . . . normal,' Betty said frowning.

'He was upset when he first told me, but then he stood up and went back to work.'

'You know what fellas are like,' Cathy said handing Betty a mug of tea. 'They handle things different from us.'

'Seth's never been one to show his emotions,' Betty said. She took a sip of her tea. 'Gosh, another loss for Beckindale. We're only a small village and we've lost Edward Sugden and Ted Micklethwaite. And there was George Ransome. And Vi Pickles died in a bomb, during the Blitz.'

'There was the lad from the butcher's . . . ' Nancy said.

'Peter Harding,' Cathy said helpfully. Betty scowled at her. Nancy knew Betty hated when someone else knew more about the people of Beckindale than she did, especially newcomers like Cathy. 'And now Ernie,' Betty finished. 'I've heard some villages have lost twenty or more.'

Nancy shuddered. 'In some ways we're lucky that we're a farming community,' she said. 'It's not easy, by any means, and I firmly believe the farmers are fighting their own war right here, keeping the nation fed, but there's no denying it's saved some lives.'

'It has,' Betty agreed. She sighed. 'I suppose I'll just keep an eye on my Seth. Check he's coping all right. Not getting too glum.'

'Good plan,' Nancy said.

'What were you going to tell me?' Betty said suddenly. 'When I came in? You said you had a surprise.'

Nancy realised she was still holding the envelope. She tried to think of another surprise she could have been waiting to tell Betty because she wasn't sure she'd be as excited as Nancy had hoped, but her mind was blank.

'Erm,' she said. Betty looked at her expectantly. 'This came for you.'

She held out the envelope and Betty took it. 'It's from ENSA,' she said in a hushed voice. 'Finally.'

'Open it,' urged Nancy. 'Let's see what they say.'

Betty shrugged. 'No point, is there? How can I go now? Seth needs me here.'

Nancy wasn't sure Betty being here, miserable and out of sorts, would help Seth grieve for his friend. She held out her hand. 'Shall I open it for you?'

Cathy wasn't as interested in Betty's dancing career as Nancy. She gave Betty's arm a quick squeeze and disappeared into the treatment room.

Betty gave Nancy the envelope.

'Are you sure?' Nancy said.

Betty nodded and Nancy slid her finger under the seal and pulled out the papers.

'They want you,' she said. 'Obviously. You're to report to a place in Leeds next Friday or send a telegram if there's a problem.'

'Next Friday,' breathed Betty. 'That's so soon.'

Nancy looked at her. 'What are you thinking?'

'About what?' Susan said. She'd come into the surgery while the women had been concentrating on the letter. Her black puppy — growing fast — was squirming on the end of its lead.

'Sit, Midnight,' she said sternly and the pup

dropped onto his bottom, in an ungainly fashion. Immediately Susan bent down, rubbed his ears and told him how good he was. Then she stood up again. 'What are you thinking about what?'

Betty glared at her. 'Nosy.'

But Susan was undeterred. 'Interested.'

Betty gave her a small, sad smile. 'Got my ENSA call-up finally,' she said.

Susan looked delighted. 'That's wonderful.'

'But Seth's in a bad way,' Betty continued. 'Ernie was killed.'

Susan gasped. 'That's so sad.'

'It is. And how can I leave Seth now, when he's just lost the best friend he ever had?'

Susan bit her lip, looking at Nancy for advice on what to say.

Nancy shrugged; she was as out of her depth as their young friend. She thought for a moment.

'Why not sleep on it?' she said. 'You don't have to decide today or even tomorrow. You've got a few days. Why not just let it sink in and then you might find you know what's best.'

But Betty shook her head. 'No,' she said. 'I already know what's best. Seth's grieving and he needs me here with him.'

Decisively, she dropped the papers and the envelope into the waste paper basket by her desk.

'Is it all right if I go home?' she said to Nancy. 'I need to tell my mum what's happened, and then I'd like to check on Seth.'

'Of course,' Nancy said. She picked up Betty's bag and handed it to her. 'I hope Seth is bearing up.'

Betty nodded her thanks and hurried off out of the door of the surgery. Nancy watched her downcast head drift past the window, then scuttled to the bin and pulled out the papers.

'Nancy, what are you doing?' Susan said, shocked.

Nancy lifted her chin. 'Sometimes, people don't know what's best for themselves,' she said. 'Nancy knew that when I told her not to send the *Hotten Courier* to my father, and she did it anyway. And I know that Betty will regret throwing away these papers. Mark my words.'

She smoothed the papers out, folded them neatly and put them back into the envelope. Then she tucked the envelope into Betty's top drawer, underneath some other papers.

'Just in case,' she said to Susan. 'Just in case.'

31

Betty had never seen the appeal in spending hours in the Woolpack with Seth and his friends. She loved to chat and to eavesdrop on conversations and the men seemed to say very little. Or at least very little that Betty was interested in. She'd found she preferred to spend her time with other women, or with Seth on their own. But since the news of Ernie's death had spread around the village, she thought she'd tag along to the pub that evening and raise a glass to the poor lad. And be there if Seth needed her, of course. She'd never seen him as sad and deflated as he'd been that morning. Thinking about the tears glistening in his eyes as he told her what had happened made her sure she'd done the right thing when she'd thrown away those ENSA papers. She'd send a telegram to Daphne and tell her of the decision she'd made. In a few days. There was no rush to do it quite yet. After all, she wasn't due to report until Friday week. She'd wait until she knew Seth was all right and until all the panic about Nancy's parents visiting was over, and things had calmed down a bit. A week or so wouldn't hurt.

She straightened her hat in the mirror by the front door and pulled her belt in tighter to try to give the impression her curves hadn't all disappeared thanks to wartime rationing. Even if she was only going over to the Woolie there was no harm in looking nice. It wouldn't cheer Seth up to see his girl looking frumpy, would it?

'I'm really sorry about Ernie,' said Margaret from the top of the stairs. 'Is Seth right sad?'

'He is.'

'He's lucky to have you.'

Betty smiled. 'We're both lucky.'

Margaret didn't look too sure but she didn't argue. 'Still nothing from ENSA?' she said out of the blue.

Betty hesitated for a moment, still looking at her reflection and removing a fallen eyelash from her cheek with the pad of her forefinger, then she turned and smiled her best smile at Margaret.

'Nothing,' she lied. 'But it's for the best. I'm happy at the vet's, and Seth needs me here. Plus you'd miss me if I went, wouldn't you?'

Margaret gestured to Betty to come up the stairs to her. Betty scowled and shook her head.

'I'm going out. You come here.'

'No, come here,' Margaret hissed, pointing to the half-open door to the lounge where their parents were.

Intrigued, Betty went up to the top of the stairs. 'What?'

'I've applied to do nursing,' Margaret whispered. 'In Birmingham.'

'Birmingham?' Betty said in shock.

'Shhh.'

'Why Birmingham?' Betty asked, much more quietly. 'Why nursing?'

'Because I'm fed up with the factory too. And I've always loved looking after people.' Margaret paused. 'And because I thought if you could follow your dreams, I could too.'

Betty felt exhausted suddenly. As though she were responsible for Seth's happiness and Margaret's. If she joined ENSA, Seth would be unhappy. If she didn't, Margaret would think less of her. She forced herself to smile.

'I think that's a wonderful thing for you to do. You'll make an excellent nurse.'

'I've not told Mum and Dad, yet,' Margaret said. 'Not until it's definite.'

'They'll be really proud.'

'I hope so.'

Betty gave her sister a hug. 'I'm proud too,' she said. 'But I have to go and meet Seth. Tell me more about it tomorrow?'

Margaret frowned. 'If you hear from ENSA you will tell me, won't you?'

Betty gave her another dazzling smile. 'Of course.'

She blew her sister a kiss and went downstairs. Normally she skipped down every flight of stairs, but today her steps felt heavy.

And she felt the same as she trudged across the village to the pub. She wasn't the usual Betty, dancing instead of walking. Instead she just felt weighed down with the sadness of losing Ernie, of losing Margaret, and of losing opportunities.

She stood for a moment outside the pub, gathering herself. She pushed her shoulders back, straightened her spine, and flashed her best on-stage smile. That was better. Now she was more herself.

'Come on, Betty,' she murmured. 'You've still got your Seth and he needs you.' She tossed her head. Everyone would be sad in the pub. People would be mourning Ernie. And if there was one thing Betty Prendagast was good at, it was cheering up folk when they were feeling down. It was time to put on a show.

With a deep breath she pushed open the doors of the pub, and to her amazement, was greeted with gales of laughter. Seth was sitting in his usual position at the side of the bar, draining the last dregs from a pint. With a flash of annoyance, Betty wondered if he'd still be sitting there in twenty years' time. Or even fifty. Then she dampened down her irritation. He'd lost his best friend; of course he deserved some time to relax.

She fixed her grin to her face, and went over. 'How are you, love?'

Seth planted a smacker of a kiss on her cheek.

'Grand. Larry, a gin and orange for my Betty, please, and put another one in there for me.'

He shoved the lad next to him off the stool.

'Budge up for Betty.'

Betty took off her hat and perched on the stool, feeling a little like a spare part. Seth was in the middle of all his friends from the estate, and from nearby farms. Lads he'd known since school. The same lads he drank with all the time. She'd expected them all to be mourning for Ernie but it seemed life went on.

Obviously seeing her confusion, Seth leaned towards her and spoke softly into her ear.

'I'm really sorry about Ernie. I am. I can't believe he's never going to wander in here smelling of horse muck, and order a pint. We had a laugh, me and him. He was a good lad.'

Betty nodded, feeling close to tears as the loss hit her again. Poor, sweet Ernie with his love of horses and his awkward smile.

Seth patted Betty's knee. He looked away and Betty knew he was trying not to cry himself.

'It's all right to be sad,' she said quietly. 'It's all right to mourn for him. He was your friend and you'll miss him.'

Seth tipped his head back and looked towards the ceiling of the pub, blinking a few times. Then as Betty watched, he breathed in deeply, seemingly finding some inner strength, and clenched his fists. Then he looked at her.

'Ernie's gone,' he said. 'I reckon the best thing we can do is to get on with our lives. Not let this drag us down. Because if we do that, then they've won, ain't they? The Nazis. And I'm not having that. We need to live life and get back to normal as soon as possible. Isn't that right?'

Betty actually felt that the war meant that nothing was ever going to be normal again. Ernie going was bad, of course, and Edward Sugden and all the other losses. But not all of the changes were negative. Margaret was going to be a nurse. Nancy was a successful vet. Lily had baby Hope. Audrey had come to Beckindale . . . She tried to ignore the little voice inside her head adding that she'd had a taste of life on stage with ENSA. There had been good changes and there had definitely been bad ones but changes they were. Nothing was normal and she very much doubted anything ever would be.

Seth nodded in satisfaction as Larry put another pint in front of him, and handed Betty her gin. 'We should just get back to normal,' he said again

Betty felt dizzy suddenly. She took a swig of her gin but it burned her throat as it went down and bile rose up. She slid off the stool and gave Seth a kiss.

'I'm not feeling too well,' she said. 'If you're all right, I might head home. I need to see Margaret about something.'

Seth looked at her curiously. 'Are you sure?'

Betty gave him another broad smile. 'Of course. You raise a glass to Ernie for me, won't you. I'll miss him.'

Seth pulled her close and hugged her and she breathed in the smell of him, reminding herself why she'd fallen for him in the first place.

'You're a good girl, Betty,' he said into her ear. 'And I'm glad you're mine.'

Feeling happier, Betty wriggled out of his embrace and walked to the door, giving her hips an extra swing because she knew he was watching. He did love her, and he was a good man, her Seth. He was full of love, and kindness, and she thought she was lucky to have him. She would do well to remember that.

Outside the sky was turning darker. She would go home and have a proper chat with Margaret, she thought. She'd been so busy with Nancy's frantic preparations for her parents' visit — honestly you'd think they were the King and Queen the way she was carrying on — that she'd barely had time to catch up with her sister recently. And if Margaret was moving to Birmingham, then they had to make the most of every minute.

As she came down the steps from the pub, someone called out to her, and she turned to see Lily Proudfoot.

'Hello, Lily,' Betty said. 'Where's the little one?'

'In bed, I hope,' Lily said with a grin. 'Jack's on duty this evening. I've been at the garage working on a bicycle.'

'This late?'

Lily shrugged happily, her eyes sparkling in the twilight. 'I love it,' she said. 'Time flies when I'm working on the bikes.'

Betty sat down on the wall by the pub, feeling horribly and uncharacteristically envious of Lily. It seemed everyone was happy and things were working out for all her friends. So why not her? Then she caught herself. At least she was alive and Seth was alive, and Margaret was only going to Birmingham, not to where the fighting was.

'Are you all right?' Lily was looking at her strangely. 'You seem a bit . . . off.'

Betty tried to give her the special Prendagast grin, but her face wouldn't move. 'I'm fine,' she muttered. She wiped away a tear that had somehow fallen without her noticing she was crying.

'You don't look fine.' Lily sat down next to her.

Betty wanted to open up and tell her friend about all the rotten things that were going round in her head, but she found she couldn't speak about what was bothering her. What would Lily think if Betty confessed she was feeling gloomy because Ernie had died and she was annoyed that meant she'd be staying in Beckindale? Or that Lily's bicycle business was booming and Betty was jealous. Or that Audrey and Ned were spending every spare moment together and canoodling all over the place and Betty just kept thinking that she and Seth had never been like that. Not really. Or even that Nancy was excited because her brother was coming to visit, just when Betty's sister was leaving Yorkshire. Imagine Lily's face if she knew what a horrible, selfish person Betty was.

Lily, clearly realising that Betty couldn't find the words to say why she was upset, took charge. 'Do you remember how we used to think Nancy was grumpy and snooty?' she said, as though they were carrying on a conversation they'd started earlier.

Betty managed to nod. She knew more than anyone how prickly Nancy had been when she first arrived in Beckindale.

'But actually she was just scared,' Lily said.

Betty nodded again.

'And I felt like that too, when Hope was born.'

This time Betty did manage to speak. She'd always thought Lily swanned through life, facing up to awful things like her mother's death, with real grit. She'd never imagined her being scared.

'Really?'

'Absolutely terrified.'

'About looking after a baby?'

Lily looked up at the darkening sky, as though trying to remember.

'About having a baby, yes. But that wasn't half of it. I was scared about marrying Jack and

332

putting all that responsibility on to him.'

Betty knew that Jack wasn't baby Hope's father. Lily had fallen pregnant when she'd been working as a driver with the ATS and had a romance with an officer called Derek Mortimer. He'd been married and poor Lily had been left out in the cold, until she took up with Jack. But Lily never talked about her fling with the married man directly, so Betty wasn't about to start.

'It was a really big thing for Jack to do, marrying me,' Lily said thoughtfully. 'Huge. We barely knew each other — not really. It was such a risk.'

'It paid off,' Betty pointed out. 'You've been wed more than a year now and he seems a great father.'

'He's wonderful,' Lily said dreamily. 'I can't believe I was so lucky.'

'But you were still frightened?'

'Frightened Jack would change his mind, frightened everyone would gossip, frightened I'd be a terrible mother . . . '

Betty gave her a sympathetic half-smile.

'And being so frightened made me feel very low for a while. But starting the bike business at the garage made all the difference.'

'You're saying I should start a business?'

Lily chuckled. 'No,' she said. 'I'm saying, everything passes eventually. You might be feeling sad now, but something will happen and you'll start to feel better. I promise.'

Betty smiled at her. 'Thanks, Lily,' she said.

The women said their goodbyes and Betty

headed home to see her sister. Maybe something would happen to make her feel happier, just as Lily had said. She just hoped it would happen soon.

32

Audrey was walking Winston by the river. For ages after the floods she'd avoided the whole area past the cricket pavilion; she wasn't in any hurry to go back there. But since spring had come and the sun had come out, she found it was a nice part of Beckindale and perfect for dog walking.

Winston was thriving. He'd grown so much under Audrey's care, and even his crooked foot didn't give him too much trouble. He slept on Audrey's bed and followed her round like a shadow and she absolutely adored him. Every day she thanked her lucky stars that Jacob, the big softie, had let her keep him. She knew farmers all over the place had been forced to cull their sheepdogs when they stopped keeping their sheep. But though the Sugdens had got rid of their flock, Jacob had hung on to Bella. And then let her have Winston too, even though the pup was another mouth to feed. Jacob had a good heart, underneath it all, she thought.

She walked on, enjoying the warmth of the spring sunshine on her face. She was going to meet Susan by the cricket pitch so Winston could have a run around with Midnight — and by his excited barking, he'd just spotted his sister.

Sure enough, up ahead was Susan with Midnight at her heels. Susan never used a lead with her dog because the sweet-natured mutt was so obedient.

'You need to learn to be more like your sister,' she told Winston, as he strained at the leash, desperate to be set free. 'Hello, Susan.'

Audrey bent down and unclipped Winston's lead and the dogs barked hello at each other and then belted off across the cricket pitch.

'I wasn't sure if you'd make it today,' Audrey said to Susan. 'Isn't it today that Nancy's family are visiting.'

Susan groaned. 'Don't,' she said. 'It's literally all I've heard about all week. Nancy's frantic. She's cleaned the surgery about five times. Her cottage is immaculate. She's so nervous.'

'Aww, I can see why she's desperate to impress them though,' Audrey said. 'She just wants her father to see she's doing a good job.'

'Yes, well I don't see how me cleaning the lav three times will help with that,' Susan said with a roll of her eyes. But she sounded like she didn't really mind.

Audrey laughed. 'The surgery's doing well now, isn't it? I reckon her dad will be blown away.'

'We're so busy, Nancy's upped Cathy's hours,' Susan said. 'I'm helping as much as I can, but I've got exams coming up so I can't do lots.'

'Still hoping to go to university?' said Audrey. The idea of spending hours poring over books horrified her, but Susan seemed to thrive on it.

Susan nodded. 'If it wasn't for Nancy I'd not have a clue how to do it, but she's really helping.'

Audrey grinned. 'She's a good one, is Nancy.'

336

'I hope her parents are nice to her.'

'Are you going to meet them later?' Nancy had invited all her friends to meet the Tate family in the village.

'I am,' Susan said. 'Are you?'

Audrey nodded. 'Yes, Ned and I are going along. I'm interested to see what her father's like. She seems almost scared of him.'

Audrey thought of her own father, who infuriated her — often — but never scared her and wondered what it would be like to feel that way.

Susan looked sad. 'I was scared of my father sometimes,' she said. 'But it doesn't mean I don't wish he was here with me now.'

'Oh goodness,' Audrey felt bad for chattering about families when Susan had none to speak of. 'I'm sorry.'

'Don't be,' Susan said simply. 'I like talking about them.' Midnight dropped a stick at Susan's feet and she picked it up and threw it, watching the dog charge after it. 'Is that Betty over there?'

Audrey squinted into the sun. Sure enough, there was Betty, sitting on the steps of the cricket pavilion, her arms wrapped round her knees.

'It is Betty,' she said. 'Shall we go over?'

Susan frowned. 'She doesn't look like she wants company.'

That was true. Betty looked like she had the weight of the world on her shoulders. She was hunched over and looked so unlike the usual happy, dancing Betty that Audrey had to look again to make sure it really was her.

'I wonder what's wrong.'

'She might be sad about Ernie,' Susan suggested.

Audrey made a face. Ernie's death had cast a shadow over the village, that was true, but Betty had been gloomy since before he died she thought. She wasn't sure it was just Ernie's death that was affecting their friend's mood.

'Let's go and see her,' she said. 'If she doesn't want company, we'll carry on walking.'

Together they walked across the field, the dogs scampering around them, towards Betty.

'Hello,' Audrey called. Betty looked up and gave them a small smile. 'We saw you from across the way and thought you looked a bit fed up. But if you don't want company just tell us and we'll carry on walking.'

Betty thought about it for a second, then she smiled more genuinely this time. 'Some company would be nice,' she said.

Audrey sat down next to her and Susan leaned against the stair rail, watching the dogs.

'So what's got you looking so troubled?' Audrey said.

Betty sighed. 'I got an offer to join ENSA.'

Audrey gasped. 'That's wonderful,' she said.

But Betty looked wretched. 'I'm going to turn it down.'

'Really?'

'Well I was but now . . . '

Audrey looked at Betty, who looked more miserable than she'd ever seen her.

'Tell me everything,' she said. 'I'll try to help.'

'I got the offer on the same day I found out about Ernie,' Betty said. 'I was heartbroken for my Seth. Really sad for him.'

'Us too,' said Audrey, noticing with a tiny thrill that she thought of her and Ned as one now.

'So, straightaway I thought, no, I couldn't join ENSA. Why would I? How could I go away goodness knows where, and leave Seth to mourn his best friend without me?'

Audrey nodded. 'I can understand that.'

Betty sighed. 'But Seth's absolutely fine, isn't he? I mean, he's not fine. But he's getting on with it. He says the best way to honour Ernie is by getting back to normal. Only trouble is . . . ' she paused and then with almost a wail she said: 'I don't want to get back to normal.'

Audrey had a sharp sense of recognition. Betty's feelings were very similar to how she'd felt before she joined the Land Girls.

'I know what you mean,' she said. 'How can we go back to normal now? Everything's changed.'

Betty sighed. 'During the Great War, my mum lived in Leeds. She worked in a munitions factory.'

'Tough work.'

Betty nodded. 'It was tough, but Mum loved it. She had money in her pocket, she was doing something useful, you know?'

Audrey knew exactly. She felt the same.

'And then after the war, it just all changed.'

'Went back to normal,' Audrey said.

'Mum says she didn't mind, she was just pleased to have Dad back and get wed, and have us. But sometimes I see a look in her eye and I wonder, you know?'

Audrey didn't need to say anything. Everything Betty was saying made perfect sense to her.

'Margaret's going to be a nurse,' Betty said suddenly.

'She is?' Audrey was pleased. Betty's sister was such a sweet, caring girl that nursing seemed a great job for her.

'So she'll be set, won't she? If this war ever ends, she'll still have a job. So will you.' She nodded at Audrey. 'Because farming's not going anywhere. And Susan's going to be a vet.'

She tilted her head at Susan, who wasn't listening because she was focused on the pups running round and round the cricket pitch.

'You've got a good job,' said Audrey, knowing it sounded weak.

'It's a fine job,' Betty said. 'It is. And I know I'm lucky, but it's not helping the war effort, and it's not helping me either.' She sighed. 'I want to dance, Audrey. I don't want to be a receptionist.'

'Then you should dance,' Audrey said. It seemed simple to her. 'When I first saw the posters for the Women's Land Army, it seemed impossible. How could I ever work on a farm? With one hand? I knew my parents would be horrified if I even mentioned it to them because they worry about me constantly.'

'That's because they love you,' Betty said.

'I know,' Audrey said. 'But it was still stifling.'

'Stifling,' breathed Betty. 'That's the word.'

'So I went to the recruitment office in Sussex and the man there laughed at me.'

'What a sod.'

'I don't blame him, really,' said Audrey. 'And he was nice in the end. He listened when I told him what I could do. And he sent me for a medical with a doctor he knew was sympathetic. And I came here.'

'And talked Jacob into letting you have a chance too,' said Betty. 'You don't let anything stand in your way, do you?'

Audrey screwed up her nose. 'I wanted to be a Land Girl so badly, and it was definitely the right decision. I love it, Betty. And I'm so proud to be part of the war effort, helping feed the nation. Jacob says we're fighting a war in the fields and I think he's right. I'm a soldier.'

Betty looked a bit taken aback by Audrey's passionate speech, but Audrey pressed on regardless.

'If you want to join ENSA, you should. You're a beautiful dancer, you'd be a great asset to them and you'd have the knowledge that you are helping us fight this blasted war.'

There was a pause and then Betty raised an eyebrow. 'You're wasted as a Land Girl,' she said archly. 'You should be making speeches like Mr Churchill.'

Audrey giggled. 'So what do you reckon?'

Betty bit her lip. 'I reckon I could wait for Seth forever,' she said. 'Once upon a time I wanted to be Mrs Armstrong but now I'm not sure. If I thought he loved me the way I love him, then perhaps there would be something worth waiting for. But if he was going to realise life's too short to mess about, then surely he'd have done it by now. Now Ernie's gone?'

Audrey felt sorry for her friend. She took her hand.

'You might be right,' she said.

'If I thought Seth and I could build a life together, then I'd be desperate to stay,' Betty said. 'But what sort of life would it be? Him in the Woolie every night playing silly beggars with his friends and me at home, bored out of my mind?'

Audrey jiggled on the stair, excited. 'So you're going?' she said. 'You're going to join ENSA, and be a dancer? Oh, Betty. I think this is such a wonderful idea. You'll love it.'

But Betty was shaking her head. 'No,' she wailed. 'No I'm not. Because I'm stupid.'

Audrey was bewildered. 'But you just said . . . '

'I know what I said. I want to join ENSA but I can't. Because I threw the stupid call-up papers in the bin.'

'Oh, Betty,' breathed Audrey.

'I know!'

Audrey wasn't sure what to say. Could Betty somehow contact ENSA and ask for duplicate papers? She wasn't sure how it worked. But then Susan, who was crouched down on the grass, playing with Midnight, looked up.

'You threw them in the bin,' she said. 'And Nancy took them out again.'

Betty sat up, poker straight. 'What?'

'When you threw them in the bin, Nancy took them out,' Susan said patiently. 'She said sometimes people didn't know what was best for themselves, like when you sent the *Courier* to her dad. She said it was just in case.'

Betty stood up. 'Where are they?' she said. 'Where are the call-up papers?'

Susan grinned. 'They're at the surgery.'

Without another word, Betty took off, running across the field towards the village.

Audrey watched her go, laughing to herself.

'Shall we follow?' she said to Susan.

'Definitely.'

Audrey whistled for Winston, and with the dogs jumping along beside them, she and Susan dashed round the edge of the cricket pitch to find out what Betty was going to do.

33

Nancy was brimming with pride. Her parents had arrived first thing that morning, coming off the bus from Hotten with her brother Nigel, his wife Maureen and their little boy, Frank. Nancy's nerves were so frayed before the visit, that she had woken up several times in the night worrying about what her father would think of the surgery, of her cottage, of everything she'd done. But as soon as she'd seen her family, her worries had all but disappeared. Her mother had swept her into a hug and squeezed her tight and told her how much she'd missed her. Her father had given her a nod and an uncharacteristically broad smile, and even Nigel had given her an affectionate thump on her arm. Little Frank — who had grown a lot since Nancy last saw him — was sweetly pleased to see her, showing her the wooden truck he'd brought along to distract him on the long journey.

She'd taken them to her cottage first, amused by how they filled the tiny lounge. Her mother said all the right things. She even admired the crocheted throw Nancy had draped over the back of the couch to hide the stains, though Nancy had spotted her surreptitiously running her finger along the mantlepiece to check for dust. Not that there was any dust to find; Nancy had cleaned the whole place from top to bottom.

Now they were heading to the surgery and

Nancy's nerves were back. This was so important to her, she was trembling. She could barely open the door because her hands were so shaky but she managed to get the key in the lock and led everyone inside.

'Well, well,' said her father, Francis, looking around. 'Well, well.'

Nancy felt sick. She knew it was pathetic to be so desperate for his approval but the pain of being passed over to take on the family practice was still raw, and she wanted to show him what she could do.

'Oh Francis, look at the drugs cabinet,' said Maureen, much to Nancy's surprise. Her sister-in-law didn't talk much. 'That's the one I think we should get. We need more space.'

Nancy blinked as her father headed over to the drugs cabinet beside Betty's desk. 'Ah yes, I see what you mean. It's useful to have that extra space.'

He and Maureen bent over the cabinet and Nancy turned to her brother Nigel, in surprise.

'Is Mo working with Dad?'

Nigel grinned. 'She's the practice manager,' he said. 'She's got a real business head on her shoulders.'

'So you don't do anything at all at the vets?' Nancy bit down the resentment she felt. Her father had signed over his practice to Nigel hoping to retire but it seemed he was still working at the surgery and Nigel wasn't involved at all.

'I had planned to take on the business side of things, but we got a big contract at the haulage

firm and I couldn't manage it all,' Nigel
explained. 'We're shifting a lot of shingle from
the coast to airfields . . . '

But Nancy wasn't interested in haulage, she
wanted to know about the vets. 'So Mo took
over?'

'She and Dad get on rather well,' Nigel said.
Nancy could tell he was on the defensive — he'd
obviously had to explain their set-up more than
once. 'And she wasn't suited to being at home
with Frank all the time. Not now he's at school.
She does all the paperwork and Dad sees the
animals. It's taken the pressure off him a bit and
stopped him nagging me to take over.'

Despite herself, Nancy was impressed with
her sister-in-law. 'Mo, would you like to see the
books?' she asked. 'Betty's been a marvel when it
comes to sorting out my invoicing. And Dad,
would you like to see the treatment room?'

'I'll take Frank outside and let him run
around,' Nancy's mother said. 'He's getting a bit
restless.'

'Don't you want to see the animals, Frank?'
Nancy asked. 'We've got some baby rabbits.
They're called kittens.'

'I want to play with my truck,' he said.

Nigel gave Nancy a sheepish smile. 'He's a chip
off the old block, I'm afraid.' He and Nancy's
mother shepherded the little boy outside.

'Come through,' Nancy said to her father.

She showed him into the gleaming treatment
area. He admired the way she'd set out the table,
and had a look at the rabbits, who were snuggled
up with their mother and looking so sweet that

Nancy couldn't bear to think that they were destined for the pot. While he was looking, Nancy told him the tale of Audrey haring it down the hill from Emmerdale Farm to fetch her to save a cow who wasn't even hers.

'She was so frightened the War Ag would come and fine them for losing livestock that she didn't stop to check the tag,' Nancy told him.

'She did the right thing.'

'She's marvellous. She says people have always underestimated her.'

Francis nodded, then he turned to his daughter. 'I'm afraid I've rather underestimated you,' he said.

Nancy wanted to say: 'Yes, you really have.' But instead she made a face. 'Not your fault,' she mumbled.

'It was my fault,' Francis said. 'I was so fixated on having my son take over my business — Tate and Son — I didn't think that the best person for the job might have been my daughter.'

'Tate and Daughter,' said Nancy.

'Exactly.' Francis paused, searching for the right words. 'I made a mistake,' he said. 'And I'm very sorry. I want you to know that if you're interested in coming back to Scarborough, when the war's over and your Mr Walters is back in situ, we can make you and Nigel business partners in the surgery.'

'Tate and Brother,' Nancy said. Her father chuckled.

'Now that does have a certain ring to it.' He came over to her and looped his arm through hers. 'What do you say?'

Nancy looked round the room and then at her father and smiled. 'Can I think about it?' she said.

He nodded. 'Of course.'

They grinned at one another and then he looked at the rabbits. 'So, tell me about rabbits. I'm seeing a lot of them at home.'

Nancy groaned. 'They're everywhere,' she said. 'They don't need a lot of looking after really, but this doe was found in Mrs Carter's garden nibbling on her spring cabbages. She caught her and brought her to me to check her over because she was thinking she'd keep her to breed and lo and behold she was already pregnant. Mrs Carter's delighted.'

'I've never been fond of rabbit stew,' her father said, peering in at the babies. 'Because I've always been rather fond of rabbits.'

Nancy nudged her dad with affection. 'You old softie.'

The sound of the surgery door banging made them both jump.

'Is that Frank back already?' she said. But it was Betty's voice she heard, calling out to her.

'Nancy? Are you there?'

Nancy and her dad went out into the waiting area. Betty was there looking red in the face and out of breath. Her hair was askew and her usual well-put-together air was missing. Nancy frowned.

'Are you all right,' she asked. 'Has something happened?'

Still puffing and panting, Betty went to sit down at her desk and realised Maureen was there, watching her with curiosity. 'Who are you?' she asked.

Maureen stood up and stuck her hand out. 'I'm Maureen, Nancy's sister-in-law.'

Betty's face went from confusion to shock to perfect manners in three beats, making Nancy giggle to herself.

'Of course, your family are visiting,' she said to Nancy. She shook Mo's hand. 'How do you do, Maureen? I'm Elizabeth Prendagast, Nancy's receptionist. Call me Betty.'

'Hello, Betty,' Maureen said. 'I'm so impressed by your system of invoicing.'

Betty preened a bit. 'Thank you,' she said.

'This is my father, Francis,' Nancy said.

'You sent me the newspaper,' Francis said, shaking Betty's hand vigorously. 'What a clever thing to do.'

Betty beamed at him. 'I did,' she said. She glanced at Nancy. 'Actually, that's why I'm here.'

'For the *Hotten Courier?*'

'No,' said Betty, jiggling on the spot. 'For my call-up papers.'

Nancy was delighted. 'You changed your mind?'

'I did,' said Betty. She looked at Maureen and Francis. 'I got called-up to join ENSA,' she said, her words tumbling over themselves. 'But I thought I shouldn't go, because my Seth, he needs me here. And I threw the papers away. But then I thought, well, if he really loved me, he'd show it, wouldn't he? Make some grand gesture. And he hasn't. So he doesn't. Not really. Not ever. So I changed my mind.'

Francis looked completely in the dark, but remarkably, Maureen had followed Betty's

349

excitable explanation.

'But you threw the papers away?'

Betty clapped her hands. 'I did, and apparently, Nancy here dug them out of the waste paper basket without telling me.'

She looked at Nancy expectantly and Nancy grinned. 'They're in your top drawer,' she said.

Betty shrieked with excitement and threw her arms round Nancy.

Francis laughed. 'I've got absolutely no idea what's going on,' he said. 'But I believe we're all going to the local pub to meet some more of Nancy's friends. Would you like to join us? It seems we're celebrating . . . ' he paused. 'Erm, celebrating something.'

'I'd love to,' Betty said, not bothering to mention that she had already been invited, much to Nancy's delight.

'Will Seth be there,' Nancy asked. 'Does he know?'

Betty's enthusiasm dipped, just a little. 'I've not told him yet,' she admitted.

'Does he know you were thinking about it?' Maureen asked, obviously gripped by the drama.

'No,' Betty squeaked.

'It won't be a shock, though, will it? He knows you love dancing,' Nancy pointed out.

'He thinks I love Beckindale,' Betty said. 'Which I do, of course, but he can't even imagine it not being enough for me. It's never even entered his head, because he loves it here so much. He lives and breathes this countryside and he thinks I feel the same.'

She looked at Nancy. 'But I don't,' she said

honestly. 'I don't feel the same.'

Nancy took Betty's hand. 'You're doing the right thing.'

Betty nodded. 'I know that. If we were married already, or if I even thought he loved me enough to put me first, I'd stay in a heartbeat. But the countryside comes first for Seth. Then the Woolie. Then me.'

Nancy squeezed her friend's fingers. 'If he loves you enough, he'll wait,' she said. 'Maybe you can have some adventures with ENSA and Seth.'

Betty looked thoughtful. 'Maybe,' she said. But Nancy thought her head was already far away from Beckindale, on a stage in front of hundreds of soldiers, cheering her and shouting her name.

Betty danced a little polka where she stood. 'Seth's working this afternoon anyway,' she said. 'He said I won't see him until later. Gives me time to work out what to say.'

The door to the surgery flew open again and in tumbled Audrey and Susan and the two dogs, barking wildly.

'Did you get them?' Audrey said. 'Did you get the papers?'

Betty waved them triumphantly and Audrey and Susan both cheered.

'Still none the wiser,' said Francis cheerfully. 'We're going to the pub. Are you girls coming?'

'Leave the dogs in the back,' Nancy said, then changed her mind, thinking of the tiny rabbits in one of the cages. 'Actually, no. Audrey, do you want to take Winston to my cottage. He can have

351

a snooze on my couch. And Susan, you could take Midnight home?'

'Ah-ha!' said Francis, pointing at Audrey and Susan. 'I know who you are.'

'Dad, it's not an Agatha Christie novel,' Nancy said, chuckling. 'This is Audrey, who I told you about, and Susan's been helping me around the surgery because she wants to be a vet.'

'Do you?' Francis said, eyeing Susan appraisingly. 'How old are you?'

Susan looked shocked to be addressed directly but she managed to stutter, 'I'm sixteen, sir.'

He nodded. 'Good for you. I think women make marvellous vets. Marvellous.'

'Women can do all sorts now, sir,' Susan said, much to Nancy's surprise. 'My friend Ruby wants to be a professional cyclist.'

'Does she now?' said Francis. 'Well I never.'

Susan grinned at him and then at Nancy, and Nancy smiled back, pleased as punch with her father's reaction to everything.

'Well in that case, I think we definitely need to celebrate,' Betty said. She took Maureen's arm. Maureen looked alarmed at first and then relaxed. She obviously thought Betty was quite something. Which, of course, she was.

Following Betty's lead, Nancy took Audrey's arm.

'Shall we go?'

34

It may have only been mid-afternoon, but there was a real party atmosphere in the pub. Nancy's dad was holding court, telling a group of rapt farmers hilarious stories from his years as a vet. Nancy's brother was in the corner, speaking very seriously to Adam Braithwaite, a builder who lived just outside the village, and drawing diagrams on a piece of paper. Betty knew Adam well because he was friendly with her father, and she knew he had an eye for a deal. She thought there would be a hand shake and some sort of partnership between the men before the afternoon was out. Little Frank had worn himself out, charging round the village so he was asleep on one of the chairs still clutching his toy truck, and Maureen was chatting to Lily Proudfoot.

Larry had done some sandwiches, and the ale was flowing, and it was the most fun Betty had had for ages. She realised, looking round at her friends, that she wasn't the only one who was feeling weary. There was an air of sadness that had descended on the village since Ernie's death and it hadn't ever really lifted and people seemed exhausted. Everyone was thinner than they had been, because rationing was getting tighter and tighter and Betty — like everyone else — couldn't believe the war had gone on so long and was showing no sign of ending any time soon.

But this afternoon, everyone was having fun. A

chance to relax after a long, hard winter and let off some steam. In fact, thought Betty, there was only one thing missing.

'Shall we get some music on?' she said. 'Is Mikey here? He can play the piano.'

Mikey, a lad who'd been a few years ahead of Betty at school and now had a farm over Hotten way, stood up looking pleased. 'Thought you'd never ask,' he said.

Betty smiled. 'Let's push some tables back, then people can have a dance,' she said.

'Give over, Betty, it's barely lunchtime,' called someone but Betty was undeterred. She and Nancy pushed some of the pub tables to the side and cleared a space, Mikey struck a chord and Betty took to the floor, giggling merrily. She felt an enormous release of pressure, as though she'd been dragging round a heavy weight and now she'd let it go. She twirled and spun to Mikey's music, and then pulled Nancy and Audrey up with her and, laughing, the women all danced together.

Eventually, and with a great deal of reluctance, Nancy's parents stood up.

'I'm afraid we'll have to go if we're to be back in Leeds before the blackout,' said her mother. They were staying overnight in Leeds before travelling to Scarborough the next day. Nancy threw her arms around her mother.

'Come back soon,' she said. 'It's been so wonderful having you here.'

There was a flurry of goodbyes and kisses and Francis paying everyone's bill much to Larry's delight, Nigel shaking hands with Adam just as

Betty had predicted, and then hoisting a sleepy Frank on to his shoulder, and Maureen asking if she could use Betty's invoicing methods. Then Nancy took her family out of the pub to take them to the bus stop.

Betty sat down with a sigh, next to Lily Proudfoot.

'You seem much happier,' Lily said.

'I'm going,' Betty told her. 'I'm going to join ENSA.'

Lily clapped her hands. 'Oh Betty, what a wonderful thing to do. The sheer joy of doing something you love and knowing you're doing your bit for the war, just can't be beaten.' She looked wistful for a second, then smiled. 'Mind you,' she said. 'We're all doing our bit really, aren't we?'

'We're all doing more than a bit.' Betty thought of families split up, sweethearts divided, parents going hungry so their children had extra, everyone mourning someone, like Susan and her family, the Sugdens and their Edward, or Seth and Ernie.

'That's true,' Lily said. 'Oh, you'll be wonderful on stage, Betty. Just look at how you got everyone dancing just now. You're such a natural entertainer. Isn't she, Audrey?'

Audrey, sitting on Ned's knee nearby, turned to them, her pretty face flushed with the exertion of dancing. 'She certainly is,' she said. 'I reckon folk will be joining up just to watch you dance, Betty.'

Betty beamed at them all. She was sad to be going, but she knew it was the right decision.

Her handbag was on the seat next to her. She opened it up and pulled out the papers, showing them to Lily.

'It's all thanks to Nancy. She saved the call-up papers when I threw them away.'

'She's a very clever woman.'

'She really is.'

Betty looked up as the pub door opened.

'Oh here she comes now. That was quick. The bus must have been early.'

But the bus wasn't early because it wasn't Nancy who came through the door, but Betty's mother and father, and Margaret. Her father had an odd expression on his face, sort of expectant and proud, while her mother was wearing a little hat she'd cut down from an old trilby of her dad's and trimmed with ribbon. Margaret looked sulky and cross. Betty was confused. Her parents had been chuffed when Margaret announced she was going to be a nurse, and Margaret herself had been on cloud nine since she got accepted. Why was she looking so annoyed now?

'Betty,' her dad said. 'There's someone here to see you.'

Betty screwed up her face. Who would come to see her?

Her dad stepped to one side and behind him was Seth. Her Seth. He was wearing his best jacket and he'd had his hair cut.

The pub fell silent as he walked towards her, looking nervous, and suddenly Betty understood why he was here, why her parents were being so odd, and why Margaret looked sulky.

Oh no, she thought. Not now. Not here. No.

But Seth, rather awkwardly, stopped right in front of her and with a sweet, crooked smile that made her heart lurch, he took her hand.

'Betty Prendagast,' he said. 'We've been knocking about together for a few years now.'

'Romantic,' muttered Lily. Seth shot her a fierce look.

'I've always known you were the one for me, but I have to be honest, I just took it for granted. Like spring following winter, or the leaves falling in autumn. But I took Ernie for granted too, and now he's gone.' His voice cracked a little, and he took a deep breath. 'And now he's gone, I realise I don't want to risk losing you too.'

'Oh Seth,' breathed Betty. Six months ago she'd have been thrilled with this scenario. She'd have been jumping up and down screaming 'yes!' before Seth had even finished speaking. But now everything seemed different.

And yet, there was her Seth, in front of her, saying the words she'd wanted to hear for so long. Just a couple of hours ago, she'd been longing for him to make a grand gesture, to show her he was serious about her — that he wanted to commit to her — and now he was doing it. She would stay, she'd told the others, if she thought Seth cared enough. And now here he was, proving that he really did care enough. She felt tears well in her eyes and wiped them away quickly. In front of her, Seth was watching her intently, hope written all over his face.

'Betty,' Seth said. 'I love you.'

'I love you too,' said Betty honestly, wondering if that was enough. With a jolt she realised she was still clutching her ENSA call-up papers behind her back. She reached behind her, holding them out to Lily and was relieved when they were taken from her grasp.

Clumsily, Seth got down on one knee.

'Get up!' Betty wanted to shout. 'Get up!' But she didn't. She pressed her lips together and tried to smile.

'Betty Prendagast,' Seth said. 'Elizabeth.'

The watching crowd of pub customers all chuckled and Seth tutted.

'You've broken my flow now,' he complained.

'Get on with it,' shouted one of the men sitting at the bar and Seth grinned as the customers all cheered again. 'Shut up,' he said. He started again: 'Elizabeth Prendagast, I love you and I want to make it official. Will you marry me?'

The pub customers all went wild, cheering and clapping. But Seth was still looking at Betty. She gave him a weak smile.

'Seth,' she began, but she didn't have the words to say what she wanted to say.

'Betty,' he said. 'Will you? Will you marry me?'

Epilogue

APRIL 1943

Annie Pearson stood nervously at the door of Emmerdale Farm. She never used to knock; she always walked straight into the kitchen as though she was one of the family. But it had been so long since she'd been there and things felt different without Edward there.

She raised her hand to the heavy door-knocker and rapped. Immediately she heard barking from inside and Maggie's voice saying: 'Calm down, Winston. Calm down.'

Winston? thought Annie. That must be the puppy Jacob had told her about in one of his letters. He'd kept her up to date with all the goings on at the farm and in the village. He'd even sent her a copy of the *Hotten Courier* a while ago with a glorious photograph of Betty Prendagast on the front page and a dramatic account of how she and Annie's friend, Lily Proudfoot, had rescued a young girl from the floods. Annie was rather hoping to meet Audrey, the Land Girl that had been working at Emmerdale Farm and who had also been involved in the rescue, along with the new vet — a woman of all things. It all sounded very exciting and Annie was half sorry she'd missed it. Mind you, she loved being a Wren. She was working in communications and though it was sometimes monotonous and always exhausting, she was enjoying every minute. She felt part of something. Something bigger than herself.

She straightened up as she heard Maggie unlocking the door.

'Annie!' Maggie said with genuine delight and Annie found herself bundled into a tight hug while a small black and white dog bounced around her feet. 'What a wonderful surprise. I didn't know you were coming.'

'I didn't know myself,' Annie said, bending down to stroke the excitable little mutt. 'I just got given four days of leave, suddenly.'

She knew why, of course, vaguely. People of her rank didn't get to know the details but she knew something was happening and there was a large operation being planned by the RAF. The top brass clearly thought whatever it was would mean the Wrens would be busier than ever so they'd all been told to take leave now, because who knew when they'd next have a chance.

'It's lovely to see you,' Maggie said. 'You look so well.'

'So do you.' Annie looked at her face carefully, searching for signs of fatigue. 'Are you recovered?'

'I'm getting there.' Maggie nodded. 'Jacob's been such a treasure looking after me, and so has Audrey.'

'Your Land Girl?'

'That's her.'

'She sounds like a real character.'

Maggie smiled indulgently. 'She is.'

For the first time, Annie took in what Maggie

was wearing. Instead of her usual mucky farming garb, or an apron if she was cooking, Maggie was clad in a pretty red-checked dress and she'd done her hair nicely.

'Are you going somewhere? You look lovely.'

Maggie gave her a twirl, laughing. 'This dress is made from a grain sack, would you believe? They've started making them in pretty patterns.'

'Clever,' said Annie approvingly.

'Itchy,' said Maggie, wriggling. Annie chuckled and Maggie carried on: 'We're off down to the village hall. There's a bit of a party going on. Why don't you come along? Everyone would love to see you.'

'Really?' Annie was pleased but found she was a bit nervous about walking into a room full of old faces — and new. She'd half hoped to just see Jacob on his own, not have to chat to him over the noise of a party.

'Of course. Jacob's down there already. He's helping Larry take over some barrels of ale. But Audrey's here. And Ned. We'll all walk down together. Come and say hello to Joseph, too. He'll be so pleased to see you.'

Feeling slightly overwhelmed, Annie let Maggie bustle her into the kitchen, where Joe was indeed thrilled to see her.

'Looking good,' he said.

Annie kissed his good cheek. 'You too, Joe,' she said.

'This is Audrey,' Maggie said. Annie looked up to see a pretty young woman standing in the kitchen doorway. She too was wearing a grain-sack dress, though hers was blue and her

361

short hair was styled neatly.

'Are you Annie?' Audrey said. 'Oh my goodness, I've wanted to meet you for ages.' She rushed to Annie and gave her a hug.

'Likewise,' Annie said, as Audrey let her go. 'I've heard a lot about you.'

'You remember Ned?' Audrey said, gesturing to the attractive man standing behind her.

'Little Ned Barlow.' Annie gave him a kiss on his cheek and he grinned at her.

'Sarah's going to be chuffed to bits to see you,' he said.

Annie nodded.

'And me her,' she said. She didn't ask about Elizabeth, Ned's other sister. She didn't care if she was still stepping out with Oliver Skilbeck or not. That was all in the past, as far as Annie was concerned.

'Shall we get off then?' Maggie said.

They said goodbye to Joseph and walked down to the village together. Ned and Audrey were very sweet together, holding hands as they strolled along.

'Who'd have thought Ned Barlow would be so romantic,' Annie said in a quiet voice to Maggie.

'He's head over heels for our Audrey,' she said. 'He says he's saving up so they can get a farm of their own when the war's over.'

Annie smiled sadly. That had been her and Edward's dream once upon a time. As if sensing her mood, Maggie looped her arm through Annie's. 'Jacob's not going to believe that you're here,' she said. 'He'll be thrilled.'

'I'm looking forward to seeing him,' Annie said

honestly. It surprised her, to be honest, that she was telling the truth. Jacob's letters had been annoying at first. She still felt a lot of anger towards him for making sure it had been Edward who went to war. To begin with his letters had been apologetic, and then he'd stopped saying sorry and just started telling her about Beckindale and what was going on. He'd written about the farm, and their inspections by the man from the War Ag, and what they were doing to make sure they got a good grading. He'd talked about how difficult it was to harvest the flax, and about Bella's puppies, and all sorts. And gradually Annie had realised she was looking forward to his letters. And she'd started writing back.

Now, she thought, she and Jacob were building a friendship of sorts. And she was looking forward to seeing him, in a way.

As they approached the village hall, Annie saw Lily Proudfoot up ahead, holding the tiny hand of a toddler, who was waddling along unsteadily. Delighted, she rushed towards them.

'Lily,' she said. 'And Hope! Oh my goodness, how big she's got.'

The little girl stared up at her with wide eyes and then, clearly having decided Annie was worthy of her attention, gave her a huge, toothy grin.

'She looks just like you,' she said to Lily.

Lily gave Annie a similar, though less toothy, smile. 'Thank goodness.'

The women hugged. 'I didn't know you were coming,' Lily said. 'But what good timing. You've met Audrey I see.'

'I have,' Annie said with a smile. 'She's sweet.'

Lily made a face. 'Don't be fooled; she's fierce as anything when she wants to be.'

Annie wasn't convinced but she nodded. 'If you say so.'

'And you need to meet Nancy,' Lily continued. 'She's marvellous. We all adore her now.'

'Now?'

'She was a bit scary to begin with, but she's a sweetheart. Oh I'm so thrilled you're here. You go ahead to the party. I'm just going to get Hope settled and then I'll come along.'

The women embraced again and Annie scurried over to where Maggie, Audrey and Ned were waiting patiently.

'I don't know what the party's for,' Annie said suddenly as they approached the village hall and the sound of music drifted out. 'What are we celebrating?'

'We're celebrating an engagement,' Maggie said. 'Betty Prendagast and Seth Armstrong have finally made it official.'

'Oh how lovely,' said Annie, pleased for the young couple. She chuckled. 'I was worried that me waltzing in, after so long away, wearing my uniform, would steal the limelight but if I know Betty, she won't let that happen.'

Audrey giggled. 'You've got that right.'

Together they all walked into the hall. There was a long table with a buffet laid out to one side. It was sparse, compared to the buffets Annie remembered from before the war, but it was still a good spread. Larry and Jed were in the corner, behind a makeshift bar, serving glasses of dark ale. Mikey Webb was playing the piano with gusto, Stan Dobbs was sawing away on his fiddle and making the most wonderful sound considering he was just a little lad, and there was Betty, pretty as a picture, dancing with Stan's sister, young Ruby Dobbs — looking much taller and nearly grown-up — and another young woman who Annie thought must be Susan Roberts.

Seth, the groom-to-be, wasn't on the dance-floor with his fiancée. Instead he was sitting at a table, laughing raucously with old Harry and some of the lads from the estate. As Annie watched she saw Betty pause in her dancing and look over at Seth. Just for a second, her expression darkened as she saw him drain his glass and hold it out for Larry to refill. And then Ruby tugged Betty's hand and the bride-to-be threw her head back, and gave the young girl a dazzling, film-star smile.

'Come on, everyone,' Betty called. 'Come and dance. It's a celebration.'

She span off across the floor, and Annie wondered if she really was as happy as she seemed to be.

'Annie Pearson,' said a voice behind her and she turned to see Jacob Sugden, smiling shyly.

'Jacob.'

'I couldn't believe it when Ma said you'd turned up.'

Annie looked over and saw Maggie standing chatting to Nina Dingle, Lily's stepmother. Maggie raised a glass and Annie smiled. Then she turned to Jacob.

'I'm pleased to see you,' she said.

'Really?' Jacob looked doubtful.

'Really.' Annie looked around and saw two chairs in a quiet corner. She took Jacob's hand and pulled him over, away from the dancers and Betty's wild twirling.

'I wanted to say something to you.'

Jacob looked alarmed.

'It's not bad,' she said. 'I just wanted to say . . . ' She took a breath. 'I forgive you.'

Jacob stared at her and to Annie's surprise, she saw tears in his eyes.

'You do?'

She nodded. 'I've met a lot of sailors while I've been in the Wrens,' she said. 'Sailors, and soldiers and airmen. And I know that nothing would have stopped them signing up. And I know Edward would have gone, whatever you did that day.'

Jacob opened his mouth to speak and Annie stopped him. 'I forgive you,' she said again.

There was a pause and Jacob swallowed. 'Can I say something too?' he said. He didn't wait for Annie to reply. He simply spoke, his words tumbling over each other in his eagerness to get them out. 'I know that I did wrong when I fiddled with those straws. And that's something I'm going to have to live with every day of my life. But Audrey said I had to forgive myself before you'd forgive me . . . '

'She said that?' Annie was impressed.

Jacob nodded. 'I had to forgive myself first. And it took me a while, but I did it. And seems Audrey was right, because now you've forgiven me too.'

Annie took his hand and squeezed it gently. 'I'm still grieving,' she said. 'I still miss Edward all the time. But I think maybe we could be friends. What do you think?'

Jacob looked delighted. 'I'd like that very much.'

Betty twirled past them, noticing Annie for the first time.

'Annie Pearson,' she said, her cheeks flushed with the effort of dancing. 'How lovely to see you. Come and dance!'

Annie stood up and held her hand out to Jacob. 'Shall we?' she said.

With a smile, Jacob got to his feet, put his hand in Annie's and together they went to dance.

Acknowledgements

As a life-long soapie and enormous *Emmerdale* fan, writing this book has been a dream for me. I need to say huge thanks to my agent, Felicity Trew, and to Caroline Sheldon, for giving me the opportunity to write the story. Also, thanks to everyone at Trapeze, especially my editor, Katie Brown, for her help. And to Alasdair at ITV, who has shared his amazing knowledge of *Emmerdale* and patiently answered all my questions about the history of the show.

Watching the soaps has taught me so much about plotting, character, drama, and writing the perfect cliff-hanger, so of course the biggest thanks of all should go to *Emmerdale*.

Credits

Trapeze would like to thank everyone at Orion who worked on the publication of *Hope Comes to Emmerdale*.

Editorial
Katie Brown
Sarah Fortune
Charlie Panayiotou
Jane Hughes
Alice Davis

Copy-editor
Laura Gerrard

Proofreader
Karen Ball

Audio
Paul Stark
Amber Bates

Marketing
Amy Davies

Finance
Jennifer Muchan
Jasdip Nandra
Afeera Ahmed
Rabale Mustafa

Contracts
Anne Goddard
Paul Bulos
Jake Alderson

Design
Loulou Clark
Lucie Stericker
Rachael Lancaster
Joanna Ridley
Nick May
Clare Sivell
Helen Ewing

Publicity
Kate Moreton
Ellie Kyrke-Smith
Ben Goddard
Georgina Cutler
Barbara Ronan
Andrew Hally
Dominic Smith
Maggy Park
Linda McGregor

Elizabeth Beaumont
Sue Baker
Victor Falola

Production
Claire Keep
Fiona McIntosh

Sales
Jen Wilson
Laura Fletcher
Esther Waters
Rachael Hum

Rights
Susan Howe
Richard King
Krystyna Kujawinska
Jessica Purdue
Louise Henderson

Operations
Jo Jacobs
Sharon Willis
Lucy Brem
Lisa Pryde